Felicity's War

Jean Fullerton is the author of twenty historical novels and a memoir, *A Child of the East End*. She is a qualified District and Queen's nurse who has spent most of her working life in the East End of London, first as a Sister in charge of a team, and then as a District Nurse tutor. She is also a qualified teacher and spent twelve years lecturing on community nursing studies at a London university. She now writes full time.

Find out more at www.jeanfullerton.com

Felicity's War

JEAN FULLERTON

CORVUS

First published in paperback in Great Britain in 2024 by Corvus, an imprint of Atlantic Books Ltd.

10 9 8 7 6 5 4 3 2 1

A CIP catalogue record for this book is available from the British Library.

Paperback ISBN: 978 1 83895 761 2
E-book ISBN: 978 1 83895 762 9

Printed in Great Britain.

Corvus
An imprint of Atlantic Books Ltd
Ormond House
26–27 Boswell Street
London
WC1N 3JZ

www.atlantic-books.co.uk

Printed and bound by CPI Group (UK) Ltd, Croydon, CR0 4YY

MIX
Paper | Supporting responsible forestry
FSC
www.fsc.org   FSC® C013604

To my three daughters: Janet, Fiona and Amy

Chapter one

AS GILES TURNED his burgundy-coloured Morris Eight into Wilton Road, Felicity Carmichael leaned forward and gathered up her handbag and umbrella from the footwell.

'You know, you really don't have to drop me at the station, Giles,' she said, as they trundled along the road. 'Victoria's only just over a twenty-minute walk from the flat.'

'I know, darling,' said Giles, briefly taking his eyes off the road to smile at her, 'but with so much rubble in the street I don't want you to twist your ankle or something along the way.'

He was right. After the Luftwaffe's six-hour visit the night before, you could barely see the tarmac outside their flat on St George's Drive for the chunks of brickwork, glass and personal possessions strewn across the road. Although the all-clear had sounded four hours ago, the ARP heavy rescue and Red Cross volunteers were still busy: digging out basements and bandaging heads respectively.

It was just after seven thirty in the morning on the first Tuesday in February 1941 and Felicity, or Fliss as

1

she preferred to be called, was sitting in the front seat of her fiancé's car.

'Plus,' continued Giles, pausing to let a line of school children carrying their satchels and gas masks cross the road, 'the North London Women's Co-operative Conference is very important, so I want to make sure my best reporter is there to get a scoop before the *Workers' Life* or the *Daily Worker*.'

Fliss smiled. She didn't need Giles to remind her that the conference was important. And it was for that reason Fliss had forgone her usual slacks and box-shoulder jacket and instead picked her navy suit and cream blouse out of the wardrobe that morning.

Despite the hard frost covering the rooftops of the Edwardian terraces on either side of the road, she felt a little warm glow in her chest at Giles's unexpected praise.

Suave and eloquent, Giles Cuthbert Naylor was halfway to his thirty-first birthday. With a lean physique, high broad forehead and straight aquiline nose, he was handsome in a rather cool and collected way. However, although he always said his height was five feet eleven, in truth, he was just over five nine and a half. As Fliss was only two inches shorter, out of consideration, since they'd become a couple, she wore low-heeled shoes. Having been sent down from Oxford after the university's Communist Society fought a pitched battle with the university's British Union of Fascists, Giles was a hero of the Socialist League.

Much to the disgust of her mother, Fliss had joined the Socialist League herself while at a Luton secretarial college, and she knew of Giles Naylor by repute before she actually met him.

After working for two years as a junior reporter at the *Bedfordshire Times and Independent*, reporting on WI meetings and village fetes – certainly not activities in the vanguard of the socialist revolution – Fliss had answered an advertisement for a reporter on the *Workers' Clarion*. Having got the job – and again, much to her mother's irritation – she had moved to London. She'd only been working at the *Clarion* for a few months when Giles joined as the senior editor.

As the last school child stepped onto the pavement, Giles let go of the clutch and pressed his foot down on the accelerator. But as the sandstone edifices of Victoria station came into view, Fliss yawned.

'Tired?' he asked.

Fliss nodded. 'Well, it was after midnight before the gang left.'

He raised his eyebrows. 'Was it? I can't say I noticed.'

The gang were a motley bunch of intellectuals and academics Giles had allied himself with, all of whom – like him – were fervently committed to the establishment of a socialist state. Exactly how this was to be achieved was something they had yet to agree on. After thrashing out the finer points of socialist revolutionary doctrine while consuming a dozen bottles of pale ale and several portions of fish and chips from the fish bar on Vauxhall Bridge Road, they had finally said their goodbyes at half past midnight.

Unfortunately, as usual, they'd left the empty bottles and screwed-up greasy newspaper behind, and it had taken Fliss another half-hour to clear away the mess before falling into bed beside Giles, who had started snoring as soon as his head hit the pillow.

Pulling up alongside the station, Giles yanked on the brake then turned in his seat to face her.

'Well, here we are,' he said, resting his right hand lightly on the steering wheel. 'Are you all set?'

'I think so,' Fliss replied, opening her handbag to check her notepad and pen yet again.

'I don't want you to be nervous, Fliss,' he said, his grey-green eyes looking earnestly at her, 'but the cream of the Labour Party's intelligentsia will be on the platform today, including one of Labour's big hitters Jennie Lee, which I'm sure you girls in the audience will be thrilled about, although I wouldn't hold your breath for any cake recipes or knitting tips: by all accounts she's a bit of a bluestocking. Even so, the Party's Central Committee sent her as the main speaker, so you will really have to get down everything she says.'

Fliss raised an eyebrow. 'Who came top in the Pitman shorthand class?'

He laughed. 'I'm sorry. It's just—'

'I know,' Fliss cut in, placing her hand on his tweed sleeve. 'The Fleet Street press will be there, and you want to make sure a small newspaper like the *Clarion* doesn't get squeezed out.'

He laughed. 'You know me so well.'

4

'I should think so, after four years,' she replied.

Strictly speaking, Giles wasn't her fiancé. And not because he didn't love her. Because he did. Just as much as she loved him. But Giles believed that marriage was an institution imposed on workers as part of the capitalist system, so wouldn't subscribe to it out of principle.

Anyway, what did it matter that she didn't have a ring on her finger or a piece of paper? She and Giles were as married as any man and woman in the land.

'So don't worry, I'll be sure to get every speech and answer to a question down, word for word,' Fliss promised. 'And I'll do my very best to bag one of the platform speakers for an in-depth interview.'

Giles winked. 'Just wriggle past a couple of the old fogeys from the National Executive Council and flutter your eyelashes. I'm sure you'll have them eating out of the palm of your hand.'

Annoyance niggled in Fliss's chest. 'I would hope, Giles, that they would be willing to talk to me about their vision of a democratic socialist society because I'm a serious journalist.'

'Of course they will, sweetheart,' Giles replied, giving her an adoring look. 'But would it hurt to use your feminine wiles to persuade them?'

Frowning slightly, Fliss didn't reply.

'Come on, Fliss, don't be a sourpuss.' Giles's lean face formed itself into a scolded-puppy expression.

Fliss studied him for a moment.

5

'So, are you going into the office today?' she asked, forcing her irritation aside and putting on a smile.

He nodded. 'I've got a pile of reports to read from the central committee. Not to mention sorting out the next edition.'

'Well, the conference doesn't finish until six,' said Fliss, 'so I can't see me getting back to the flat much before seven thirty at the earliest. I hope you don't mind a late supper.'

'I'll tell you what,' said Giles, 'why don't we eat out? To celebrate your scoop interview.'

'You're putting the cart in front of the horse, aren't you?' laughed Prue. 'I haven't got one yet.'

'Well, I have every faith that you will, my darling.' He took her hand, raising it to his lips. 'Every faith.'

They exchanged fond looks then, turning, Fliss grabbed the passenger-door handle.

'Oh, before you go, I don't suppose you've got a couple of bob I could have?' Giles asked as she opened the door.

Fliss looked over her shoulder.

'Just for a bit of petrol,' he added, his scolded-puppy face returning. 'I'm running on fumes.'

Fliss glanced at the fuel dial. Sure enough, its needle was hovering below E.

'I wouldn't ask,' he continued, 'but with articles and reports piling up on my desk, I won't have time to get to the bank until this afternoon.'

Letting go of the handle, Fliss unclipped her handbag, took out her purse and opened it.

'You're a darling,' he said, as he lifted the solitary brown ten-shilling note from her purse.

Tucking it in his inside breast pocket, Giles slid his hand along the back of her seat and drew her into an embrace.

'What would I do without you?' he said, looking deeply into her eyes, then pressing his lips onto hers.

'I ought to go,' she said reluctantly as their kiss ended.

'Yes, you should,' he agreed, giving her a smouldering look. 'Before I forget all about the North London Co-Operative Women's Conference and the mountain of paperwork on my desk and drive straight back to the flat so we can spend the rest of the day in bed.'

Fliss's heart did a little double step. Then, remembering how she'd spent days persuading Giles that she could carry out such a big assignment, she disengaged herself from his arms.

Grasping the handle again, she opened the door, chilling the car's interior in an instant.

'I'll see you this evening,' she said, swinging her legs out of the car.

Giles blew her a kiss and Fliss slammed the door.

She stood on the frost-whitened pavement and watched the Morris Eight pull away from the kerb and join the traffic heading up Buckingham Palace Road.

Turning towards the station, where sandbags were stacked to the lead canopy to protect the Southern Railway's office windows, Fliss joined the crowds of suited office employees and khaki-uniformed army

7

personal crunching through icy puddles as they streamed through the entrance.

'So finally, Miss Lee, at the next election, whenever that is, are you hoping to see more women as MPs?' Fliss asked the dark-haired women with rather pronounced eyebrows standing before her.

It was just after one o'clock. Having swiftly downed a fish-paste sandwich with curling corners from the buffet, plus a lukewarm cup of tea, Fliss was now standing in the refectory of The North London Collegiate School. Surrounding her were the other hundred and fifty conference attendees and a cacophony of women's voices.

'I cannae deny that there is a sore lack of female representation on the green benches of Parliament,' the one-time parliamentary member for North Lanarkshire replied. 'But people should vote for policies, not the sex of the candidate. However, as we have seen in the Soviet Union – where women take their place alongside men in all parts of society – only true socialism will allow women to be fully equal in all aspect of political and social life. Now, if you'd be kind enough to excuse me …'

'Of course,' said Fliss, closing her notebook. 'You must have hundreds of people wanting to speak to you.'

Giving her an enigmatic smile, the Independent Labour Party's leading light turned and walked away.

'Who's the cat that's got the cream, then?'

Fliss turned and found her friend and fellow Westminster Labour Party member, Ruth Mellows, standing behind her with two mugs of tea.

Standing six inches shorter than Fliss at five foot one and five years older, Ruth was a second-generation Irish redhead with a liberal sprinkling of snowflake-sized freckles all over her face.

'Giles will be impressed,' Ruth went on, looking quite impressed herself as she offered Fliss one of the mugs.

Tucking her notepad and pen into her handbag, Fliss took the hot drink.

'Yes, I am feeling a little pleased with myself,' she replied. 'Hopefully an interview with such a well-known Labour Party figure will boost the *Workers' Clarion* sales.'

'And stop this government banning the *Workers' Clarion* like they did the *Daily Worker* in January,' added Ruth.

'I don't think we're in danger of being closed,' said Fliss. 'After all, the *Clarion* follows the official Socialist League and Labour Party line in supporting the National Government.'

'Even so,' Ruth took a sip of tea, 'we have to be vigilant against the capitalist system protecting itself by suppressing workers.'

There was a sudden movement in the crowd, who had all started towards the refectory entrance.

'Looks like they're getting ready to begin the afternoon session.' Fliss swallowed a large mouthful of tea. 'We'd better take our seats.'

'I've got to spend a penny,' said Ruth, handing her mug to Fliss. 'Can you take my drink for me?'

Her friend hurried off and Fliss joined the throng of women making their way back into the main hall. She took her seat at the end of a row and put her handbag on the chair beside her.

The afternoon speakers began to file on to the stage as the final few members of the audience took their seats, Ruth among them.

'You'd think they would have found a venue with more than three blooming ladies' toilets, wouldn't you?' she whispered, as Fliss swung her knees aside to let her past.

Mrs Gilmore, the full-bosomed, grey-haired London-wide chairwomen for the Women's Co-operative Society took her place at the podium and the low murmur of voices subsided.

'Welcome back, ladies,' she said, casting her close-set eyes over the assembled room. 'This afternoon it is my great delight—'

The main doors at the back of the hall burst open and heavy boots echoed around the high ceiling. Every woman in the hall turned to see what the commotion was and found half a dozen police officers in helmets and two army officers with their caps tucked under their arms marching down the central aisle. The police officers stationed themselves, evenly spaced, at the end of the rows while the officers climbed onto the stage.

'What is the meaning of this?' snapped Mrs Gilmore,

a mottled flush creeping up her double chin as she glared at the two officers who halted alongside her.

'I'm afraid, ladies, you will have to vacate the premises immediately,' said the taller officer with greying hair and a pencil moustache.

'We will not, Officer,' spluttered the outraged chairwoman. 'We're holding a legitimate public meeting, and your attempt to disband that is an infringement of our democratic rights and a suppression of free speech.' Her nostrils flared like a winded horse as she drew in a deep breath. 'You may not agree with our politics but—'

'If I could just stop you there, madam,' cut in the moustachioed officer, holding up his hand. 'I don't care one jot what your politics are and neither does the thousand-ton unexploded German bomb that has tunnelled its way under the office block next door, which might be ticking down its last few minutes before sending the whole bally lot of you to Kingdom—'

There was a scrape of chairs as the audience, including Fliss, rose as one.

'So would you mind making your way out in an orderly fashion?' continued the officer, shouting over the squeal of voices and shifting furniture.

Hooking her handbag over her arm, Fliss, with Ruth a step or two behind her, hurried towards the main entrance at the rear of the hall.

'I suppose I ought to head back to work,' said Ruth with a sign of resignation as they arrived on the other side of the rope cordon, its triangular yellow flags fluttering in the chilly breeze. 'There's no point losing half a day's money. What about you?'

'I'm not sure,' said Fliss, thankful she had bagged the scoop Giles wanted for the *Clarion* before the Luftwaffe interfered. 'To be honest, we had half the Pimlico Independent Labour Party around last night, so I could do with a spare couple of hours to tidy the flat. I know Giles is up to his eyes at the office, so perhaps I'll ring him and see what he wants me to do.'

'Will I see you at the Crown on Saturday?'

'I expect so,' said Fliss, without any real enthusiasm.

The Crown was, in fact, the Crown Tavern in Clerkenwell, where it is reputed that Lenin and Stalin first met. It was also where many of their London followers met each weekend to plan the revolution while downing half their body weight in pale ale. As women were outnumbered some four to one at these radical gatherings, Fliss often found herself studying the nicotine-stained wallpaper while sipping her G&T.

Hugging Ruth briefly, Fliss waved her off and headed back towards Edgware station. Spotting a telephone box on the other side of the road, she crossed over and pulled open the door, the usual smell of ammonia and tobacco wafting over her as she stepped in. Resting her bag on the shelf, Fliss rummaged in her purse for a few coppers then picked up the black Bakelite receiver and placed it to her ear. There was a pause then a click at the other end.

'Operator. What number do you require?'

'Bloomsbury three four seven, please,' Fliss replied.

There was another pause and the operator spoke again. 'Putting you through.'

The pips sounded at the other end and Fliss pressed two thruppenny bits into the slot next to the A button.

'*Workers' Clarion*,' barked the gruff voice of Jim, the *Clarion*'s trade union reporter.

Fliss frowned. 'Jim?'

'Oh, it's you, Fliss,' he replied. 'Sorry, but the damn phone hasn't stopped all afternoon.'

'Isn't Gwen there?'

'Naw,' Jim replied. 'Got a headache before lunch and Giles sent her 'ome.'

'Poor Gwen,' said Fliss, an image of the newspaper's curvy blonde receptionist flashing briefly into her mind. 'Can I speak to Giles?'

''Fraid not,' Jim replied. 'He got a telephone call an hour ago about some strike or something and dashed out to cover it. Can I help?'

'Not really,' Fliss said, and explained about the conference's sudden end.

'Well, there's nothing to do here,' said Jim. 'You might as well call it a day and go home.'

'Perhaps I will,' Fliss replied. 'I'll see you tomorrow.'

Returning the receiver to its cradle, Fliss pressed the B button and one of the thruppenny bits rolled out of the slot beneath. Pocketing the unused coin, she pushed open the booth door and stepped out.

Having made the twenty-five-minute walk from Victoria station, Fliss turned into Warwick Square and its elegantly proportioned Edwardian townhouses just after three thirty.

When she'd moved down to London from rural Bedfordshire some four years ago, spending the odd quiet hour reading in the arboreal oasis of the central park had helped Fliss adjust to life away from fields and woodland. But now the park, like everywhere else, had been given over to the war effort. The neat shrubs and colourful flowerbeds had been dug up, and now sprouted spring cabbage and the first feathery leaves of carrots.

Passing the white wooden shed that was the Warden's Post, Fliss turned into St George's Drive and kept walking until she reached the last-but-one house where she and Giles occupied the top-floor flat.

Climbing the three steps to the front door, Fliss pushed it open, dislodging a few flakes of its peeling green paint as she stepped inside.

The grand Edwardian family house's hallway was now the ground-floor lobby for the six flats that the four-storey house had been divided into.

Grasping the handrail, Fliss made her way upstairs to her flat – which was in the old servants' quarters. Stopping in front of the door, she dived into her bag, pulled out the key and let herself in.

The flat was small, not much more than two main rooms and a bathroom. The kitchen, if you could call it that, had a butler sink, with a cold tap, a sloping draining board on one side and an ancient stove on the other.

As she closed the door behind her, surprise widened Fliss's tired eyes. Instead of the plates and glasses from the previous night being piled high in the sink, as they had been when she left that morning, they were now stacked in the bright-yellow dresser next to the stove. In addition, the four kitchen chairs had been returned to their rightful places and were tucked around the kitchen table.

Casting her gaze across to the lounge area, she noticed that the two lime-green armchairs had been set straight and the cushions on the tan-coloured leather chesterfield had been plumped and set at angles.

Confused, Fliss stared at the tidy living area for a moment.

Then she heard a noise coming from behind the closed bedroom door.

Frowning, she walked across the Turkish rug – it had been swept, she noticed – and, opening the door, was confronted by a pair of undulating bare buttocks with a pair of feet with painted toenails wrapped around them.

Fliss stared incredulously for a second or two, then found her voice. 'Giles!'

A woman screamed, and Giles jumped onto his knees with his hands covering his privates. Gwen, who had clearly got over her headache, squirmed beside him, clutching the sheets over her still-heaving chest.

Red-faced and sweating, Giles stared wordlessly at Fliss for a moment, before he raised his right hand. 'Now, Fliss, this is not what it looks like.'

Chapter two

W**ITH HIS BREATH** visible in the freezing February
air, Detective Inspector Timothy Wallace studied number
forty-three Malmsbury Road in Bow from beneath the
brim of his fedora.

'Do you think they'll be out soon?' asked Alex Lennox,
Tim's detective sergeant, who was standing just behind
him.

Alex, who at twenty-six was four years Tim's junior and
an inch or two shorter, was dark-haired and green-eyed,
with the physique of an athlete. Whereas Tim had run the
streets of East London as a barefoot child, Alex was the
son of a country schoolmaster at a boys' school in Leyton
Buzzard, and had never left Buckinghamshire until joining
the Metropolitan Police Force a day after his twenty-first
birthday. However, after a brief spell pounding the beat
in Kilburn and passing his sergeant's exam, he'd been
transferred to Wapping CID. Although he'd tried to sign
up to fight a few days after war broke out, the medical
officer discovered he had a very slight curvature in his neck
and returned him to his post in Wapping. Intelligent and
intuitive, Alex was shaping up nicely as a detective, so the
army's loss was the Met's gain, as far as Tim was concerned.

'Depends on what they find,' Tim replied, without taking his eyes from the four-storey terraced house across the street.

It was close to eight o'clock in the evening, and he, Alex and Constable Bellman were standing in the airy – the below-pavement area that would once have been the servants' entrance – opposite the house.

'I wish they'd blooming well 'urry up,' grumbled Eric Bellman. 'My plates of meat are like blocks of ice.'

Eric, a squarely built chap with thinning blond hair, was a war reserve constable. At forty-three he was too old to be called up, but had opted to swap his desk in the rates department of Poplar Town Hall for something more exciting and more lucrative – by two pounds and five shillings a week.

Thanks to the thousand-ton bomb that had landed on the street beyond in the previous night's air raid, the house in question had square black holes instead of windows, through which tattered curtains flapped. It had fared better than some of the hundred-and-fifty-year-old houses further along, which had collapsed in on themselves like a pack of cards. Like so many East Enders, the families of Malmsbury Road had returned after a night in an air raid shelter that morning to find their homes destroyed and their possessions blown into the street. However, because of the danger of collapse, until the rescue team had finished checking the walls and floors, the families hadn't yet been allowed to return. It was for that reason that Tim and Alex, along with a small contingent of uniformed constables, had been standing in the airy at number thirty-eight for the best part of three-quarters of an hour.

'Suppose we ought to be grateful the air raid siren ain't gone off yet,' Eric continued, 'as the fog on the riv—'

Tim's raised hand stopped him mid-word as a light flickered through the empty door frame. He gave a low whistle through his teeth, which was answered by another from his right.

A couple of moments went by then the bulky figure of Chalky White, heavy rescue leader, lumbered out with five men close behind.

Straightening up to his full six foot one, Tim glanced across the low wall to find Constable Ted Tyler, a regular like himself, and constables Lambton and Rowland standing ready in the airy of number forty, next door.

He and Ted exchanged nods and then all six officers started up the stone stairs.

'All right, Chalky,' Tim called, shining his muted torch on the cobbles as he strolled across.

The burly boss of Green Team gave a hard laugh. 'Wallace. Bit chilly for an evening stroll, isn't it?'

'Inspector Wallace, if you don't mind,' Tim replied, coming to a halt just in front of him. 'And we're out because we've been receiving reports of looting.'

In the dim light from the police torches, an innocent look spread across Chalky's heavy features. 'Have you?'

'We have,' Tim replied. 'Often just after you and your lads have been in.'

A belligerent expression replaced Chalky's ingenuous one in an instant. 'I hope you're not—'

'Search 'em, boys,' snapped Tim, and the officers standing behind him surged forward.

As each of the men under his command tackled one of the heavy rescue team, Tim held out his hand. 'Give it over, Chalky,' he said, indicating the heavy canvas tool bag in his hand.

Adjusting his grip on the handle, Chalky's face screwed into a hateful glare.

'Now!' barked Tim.

Chalky hesitated for a moment longer, then shoved the bag at him. Tim placed it on the pavement between them, pulled it open and shone his torch on the contents.

The beam of Tim's torch highlighted a carriage clock, cutlery and a mother-of-pearl dressing-table set on top of the usual collection of tools.

He looked up. 'Empty your pockets and drop it into the bag.'

Chalky glared at him for a moment then, shoving his hands into the deep pockets of his navy overall, pulled out a string of pearls, two rings, a wallet and a watch on a chain.

'What you got, lads?' asked Tim, his hard gaze fixed on the man in front of him.

'A couple of purses and some jewellery,' Alex replied, after frisking one of the team.

'A canteen of cutlery and some old-fashioned silver photo frames,' Ted called across, holding up a faded sepia photograph of an elderly couple.

The other officers listed knick-knacks, more jewellery and watches, as well as a pair of leather gloves, a pack of baby's towelling nappies and a fur stole.

'You bunch of bastards,' Tim said, casting his eyes over the six members of the heavy rescue squad who were now held fast by his officers. 'If it's not enough that people have their homes blown to bits by the Luftwaffe every night, they have to come home to find that scum like you have rifled through their belongings and helped yourselves. Cuff 'em, boys.'

There was a rattle of chains as the officers snapped their handcuffs on the prisoners. As Tim reached in to retrieve his handcuffs from his trench-coat pocket, the heavy rescue team leader bunched up his shoulders and curled his hands into hammer-like fists.

Tim grinned. 'Please, Chalky, make me happy and resist arrest.'

'Right,' said Tim, shoving Chalky through the battleship-grey metal door into number four cell to join the rest of his crew. 'I hope you get a bit of sleep so you're all bright-eyed and bushy-tailed when you step into the Thames Magistrate's Court's dock tomorrow morning. Although I wouldn't worry too much if you don't,' he continued, 'because you won't be there very long. Thanks to the Emergency Powers Act, looting is now a capital offence. The presiding beak will be sending you to the Crown Court so fast your boots won't touch the ground.'

'Piss off,' snarled Chalky.

Giving him the friendliest of smiles, Tim slammed the door shut and turned the key. Handing it to the night-duty officer assigned to guard the cells, he trotted up the couple of concrete steps and along the central corridor back into the police station's front office.

As with all police stations, this space was the hub of activity. But now, at almost ten o'clock, and with the night duty already out on their beats, there were only a couple of officers sitting at their desks finishing off reports before clocking off, although the smell of male sweat and fags lingered.

Charlie Webb, who was a few years short of hanging up his helmet and truncheon for good, was a lean, balding individual whose square shoulders made it look as if he'd left the coat hanger in his uniform jacket. He was standing at a chest-height desk with a leather-bound record book on it as he completed the final details of the arrests.

Taking a long drag on his half-smoked cigarette, he looked up as Tim entered.

'You're a bit lost, aren't you, Wallace?' Giving Tim a jaundice look, Webb nodded towards the main door. 'Wapping nick is that way.'

'Me and the boys have been following White and his crew for a couple of weeks and it just so happens that we caught them on your patch,' Tim replied.

'Officers, even bloody CID ones, stuck to their own areas when I was on the beat,' Webb sighed, flicking ash into the already overloaded Bakelite ashtray on the desk.

'Well, there is a war on,' said Tim.

'So they tell me. Is that the last of 'em?'

'That it is,' he replied.

'Good riddance to them, I say,' Webb replied. 'If I'd caught them, they wouldn't be looking so pretty.'

'I catch wrong'uns; I don't act like them,' Tim said, his mouth lifting in a sideways smile. 'Although I did offer White the chance to resist arrest. Have the rest of the team been signed off?'

Webb nodded. 'About twenty minutes ago. Your DS said he'd be in first thing to get the witness statements ready for court.' The station sergeant's thin lips lifted in a sardonic smile. 'I see you've got 'im properly trained.'

Tim smiled and crossing to the coat stand in the corner he took down his trench coat. He shrugged it on over his charcoal-grey suit then, running his fingers through his dark-brown hair, he unhooked his fedora.

'Be seeing you, Sarge,' he said, tugging the brim slightly down over his left eye as he headed for the back door of the station.

'Not if I see you first,' Webb called after him. 'And find villains to nick on your own patch in future.'

Tim laughed and raised his hand in acknowledgement.

Passing half a dozen empty offices along the rear corridor, Tim pushed open the green door at the end and stepped out into the backyard. The tangy smell of manure and hay from the Mounted Branch horses in the stables opposite drifted into his nostrils as he headed for the double gates.

The temperature had dropped several degrees in the hour and a half he'd been in the station, and the thick cloud that had blanketed the area had disappeared, leaving a clear moonlit sky. Bad news: even now, dozens of Luftwaffe pilots were probably taxiing their Messerschmitts and Dorniers along the captured runways in northern France.

Resigned to another night on a truckle bed in the section house's bomb shelter basement rather than his comfortable room upstairs, Tim had only walked a couple of steps when a Black Maria parked across the road tooted.

'Where you heading, Inspector?' asked the officer, leaning out of the passenger window.

'Tenter Street,' Tim replied.

'I can give you a lift to Stepney station,' came the reply.

'You're a pal,' said Tim.

'Hop in.'

Going to the back of the vehicle, Tim opened one of the van's rear doors and climbed in. Sitting himself on one of the side benches, he planted his boots wide to steady himself and the van pulled away from the kerb.

As they trundled westwards, past St Clements Hospital and People's Palace, Tim and his fellow officers exchanged a couple of amusing stories and complained about the lack of equipment. Within ten minutes, they were pulling up just before Stepney Green underground station in Mile End Road.

Clambering to the rear of the van, Tim unlocked the back door and jumped down. 'Thanks, mates.'

'Any time,' the driver called over his shoulder.

Slamming the van door, he banged on the side and it sped away, turning left into Globe Road.

H Division's section house was situated in Tenter Street, behind Leman Street police station, just a stone's throw from the Tower of London and a couple of miles' walk along Mile End Road; however, after waiting for an ARP lorry to roll past, Tim crossed the road to take a shortcut.

Switching on his torch, he walked south down Whitehorse Lane, past St Winifred's sprawling rectory and into Stepney High Street, just as the clock on the ancient church of the same name struck ten thirty. But as he strode past the graveyard, he noticed the lone figure of a woman swaying back and forth as she sat on one of the headstones.

Tim frowned. Apart from the obvious dangers of having bombs dropped on you from a great height every night, young women, particularly if they were slightly the worse for wear, were now in peril of becoming victims of two crimes that had almost trebled since the start of the blackout eighteen months ago: sexual assault and rape. Hoping the young woman in the graveyard wasn't such a victim, Tim stepped over the low wall surrounding the burial ground and made his way over to where she was sitting.

'Excuse me, miss,' he said, noting she had a suitcase on the floor next to her and a bottle of half-drunk gin in her hand. 'Can I be of any assistance?'

She glanced up at him.

'No thank you,' she replied, the hint of a rural accent in her voice.

'Then why are you sitting in a churchyard?' he asked.

She took a swig from the bottle. 'I'm having a rest.'

'What, perched on a tomb in the middle of the night?'

'Well, firstly ...' She bent her arm and looked at her wristwatch. 'It's ... well, the light's not very good so I don't know the time exactly, but I think it would be safe to say it is *not* the middle of the night. And secondly,' she looked up at him, 'who are you anyway?'

'Detective Inspector Wallace,' Tim replied, taking his warrant card from his pocket and shining his torch on it.

She raised her eyebrows as she peered at it and seemed to unbalance for a moment, swaying dangerously to the right.

'So you are,' she said. 'An instrument of the capitalist state to repress the proletariat.'

'If you like,' said Tim. 'But right now I'm just a bloke who's trying to help you stay safe.'

'Well, Mr Policeman,' she slurred, 'although I'm not an expert in such matters, as far as I can remember there is no law against sitting in a graveyard at any time of the day.'

Tim took a steady breath. 'No, there isn't. But it's dangerous.'

'I can take care of myself,' she snapped back.

Tim's gaze ran over her willowy frame, and he gave a hard laugh. 'Against a drunken fifteen-stone docker? I doubt it. What's your name, miss?'

'Mith F–f … Fl … sss … ty Car – car … M … Miss Flissssy.'

Tim sighed. 'Look, miss, you've clearly had one too many and my concern is that sitting in a dark, isolated churchyard all alone could bring you to harm, and I wouldn't want you to be hurt.'

Her head snapped around and Tim found himself staring into a pair of very large, very brown and very angry eyes.

Gripping the bottle, she sprang to her feet and glared at him.

'You men are all the same,' she said, swaying slightly. 'You pretend you care about us and then jump into bed with the first blonde trollop …'

Tim gazed at her in the hazy torch beam for a moment then her face crumpled.

'How could he?' she sobbed, tears pouring down her face. 'And with—'

The wail of an air raid siren fixed on the memorial hall roof swallowed her words.

Tim studied her as she sobbed helplessly in front of him for a moment, then he pulled his folded handkerchief from his jacket pocket and offered it to her. 'It's clean.'

'Tha … tha … thank y–you,' she shivered.

Tearing open the buttons of his overcoat, he shrugged it off.

'There, there, miss,' he said, wrapping it around her shaking shoulders, catching a faint hint of perfume as he did. 'Whoever he is he's not worth it.'

'No, he's not,' she squeaked. 'The pig.'

She raised her head and gave him a little tipsy smile. 'Your coat is warm.'

Running his gaze over her high-cheek-boned, oval face and slightly unfocused brown eyes, Tim realised he still had his arm around her.

He also realised that her eyes were level with his chin so he only needed to dip his head slightly to press his lips onto hers.

Feeling a bit of a pig himself, Tim let her go.

'Now, miss,' he said, pulling down the front of his jacket then picking up her suitcase, 'the bombers will be here in a short while, so let's get you to safety. Come with me. And I'll take that,' he added, extracting the bottle of Gordon's from her hand.

Taking her elbow, Tim guided her towards the front door of the church. Swamped in his coat, the young woman took a couple of steps then wobbled off her heels. His arm went around her again to steady her.

With her leaning heavily on him for support, they made their way to the entrance of St Winifred's church and joined the stragglers going into its shelter in the crypt.

Although in the middle of one of the most deprived and dilapidated areas of London, the interior of St Winifred's was very much as you'd find in any village church. A wide central aisle flanked by solid rows of pews led to the chancel, which had a Lady chapel on one side and the vestry and an enormous multi-piped organ on the other. There were memorials to the parish's past rich and famous along with military plaques and ragged and threadbare regimental flags hanging above.

To be honest, after seeing his mother praying daily for deliverance from the hell of her marriage, Tim was pretty much done with the Almighty, but even he could appreciate the beauty and tranquility of Stepney's ancient parish church.

'Your missis not well or something, mate?' asked the elderly ARP warden who was ushering people in.

'She's not my wife,' Tim replied.

The woman slumped against him raised her head. 'I c-certainly am not,' she slurred. 'Cause marriage sss a institu ... instiuu tun impo–oo on workers assss.'

Her head slumped against his shoulder again.

'I'm a copper at Wapping nick,' Tim explained, adjusting his hold on her. 'I've just found this young lady sitting on one of the gravestones, so I thought you might know her?'

'She looks familiar.' The warden frowned. 'I 'ope as how she ain't one of those Cable Street floozies looking for trade up this way.'

Tim glanced at the drunken young woman's expensive polished shoes.

'She's not. But she's certainly had a skinful.' He held up the bottle of gin. 'I think she's been unlucky in love.'

'Haven't we all?' chuckled the warden. 'Take her down to the crypt and I'm sure one of the WVS girls will find her a bunk where she can sleep it off.'

Gripping the woman's shoulders again, Tim guided her past the first-aider preparing for the night ahead in the Lady chapel and headed towards the arched door in front of the chancel. After waiting for a mother with her baby to descend, Tim ducked his head and – scraping the crown of his hat against the stonework as he entered and holding her suitcase and gin bottle in the other hand – guided the young woman down the worn narrow steps.

The crypt was roughly the same size as the ancient building above and lit by a string of lights along the ceiling. Now, as it was almost eleven, the lights were being turned off and many of those sheltering were tucked up in the bunk beds at the far end of the cellar. In one of the alcoves, a couple of matrons in bottle-green WVS uniforms were tidying away. Not everyone had turned in for the night, though: a small cluster of women were sitting on deckchairs by a hurricane light, knitting. They looked around as Tim and his drunken companion lumbered in. Horror flashed across one of the knitter's faces and thrusting aside her needles, she jumped up and dashed towards them.

'Fliss!'

The woman slumped against Tim slowly raised her head. 'Oh, Prue.'

Slipping out of Tim's supportive arm, and letting his coat slip to the floor, she staggered forward and wrapped her arms about the auburn-haired young woman.

'I take it you know her,' said Tim, putting the suitcase on the floor.

'Yes, she's my sister,' the knitter replied. 'Where did you find her?'

'Sitting on one of the gravestones outside. With this ...' He handed her the gin bottle.

'You were right, Prue,' said Fliss, looking blearily at her sister. 'Giles sss ... a pig and I h-hate him.'

She slumped against Prue, who staggered under her sister's weight. Tim stepped forward and took up the strain.

'I'm DI Wallace from Wapping nick,' he said, feeling it necessary to introduce himself to the young woman whose sister was currently draped over him. 'Is there somewhere we could lie her down?' he asked, as Fliss transferred her arms from her sister's neck to his, pressing her soft breasts rather pleasingly into his chest.

Prue nodded. 'Over here.'

They started off but after a couple of steps Fliss's legs gave way. Catching her as she fell, Tim held her in his arms and her head flopped into his shoulder. With a couple of strands of her hair caught on his evening bristles, Tim stepped over his coat on the floor and followed her sister to the rear of the shelter. Gently laying the young women on one of the bottom bunks, he turned her on her side, so her head was hanging over the edge.

Tim straightened up and took his pocketbook from his inside pocket. 'She was unable to give her name—'

'I'm not surprised,' cut in Prue, glancing down at her unconscious sister.

'So would you oblige?' He dabbed the end of his pencil on his tongue. 'Is she miss or mrs?'

'Miss,' she replied. 'Carmichael. Felicity Hermione Evadne. Seven St George's Drive, Pimlico.'

'Date of birth?' Tim asked as he scribbled down the address.

'Thirtieth June, nineteen-fifteen.'

Tim looked up. 'And you are?'

'Mrs Quinn. Prudence.' She raised an eyebrow. 'I hope you're not going to ask me my date of birth, Inspector.'

Tim grinned. 'I wouldn't be that cheeky.' He returned his pocketbook to its place. 'Now I know your sister is in safe hands I'll be on my way.'

He scooped his crumpled trench coat off the floor.

'There might still be a cup in the pot,' Prue said, nodding towards the two WVS women at the refreshments table.

'That's very kind,' Tim replied, as he shrugged it on, 'but I've been on duty since six this morning, so all I'm in need of now is my bed.' He touched the front of his fedora. 'Goodnight, Mrs Quinn.'

'Goodnight, Officer,' she replied. 'And thank you for looking after her.'

'Don't mention it; just doing my duty as an "instrument of the capitalist state",' said Tim, raising an eyebrow and the corresponding corner of his mouth.

Prue pulled a face. 'I'm afraid my sister is rather outspoken.'

'So I discovered.' He glanced at the young woman, her auburn hair in disarray snoring softly. 'She's going to know about it in the morning.'

Prue raised her eyebrow again. 'That's putting it mildly.' She looked fondly at her sister and sighed. 'I suppose that's what love can drive you to.'

Tim touched the brim of his hat again. 'Which is why I studiously avoid it.'

Chapter three

'MORNING, HARRY,' said Kenny Williams, the Colonial & Orient shipping company's clerk, as he stopped in front of the dock worker.

'Morning,' Harry Gunn replied, then took a long drag on his roll-up.

It was Wednesday, and as he had been every working day for half his thirty years, Harry was standing in London Dock. The *Maid of Gibraltar*, a 5,500-ton steam merchant cargo ship, was anchored beside him in Shadwell New Basin.

It was so early in the morning the first streaks of winter sunlight had yet to make their appearance in the eastern sky. In fact, it was so early that the blackout was still in force and would be for another two hours until eight o'clock.

It was freezing, too, which was to be expected just five weeks after the New Year. There were even clumps of soot-dusted snow from last week's downfall sitting on the dockside office roofs. And the grey water of the Thames, thirty feet below where they were standing, was as cold and forbidding as the jaws of Hades. Despite this, Harry was dressed in his usual worn cord trousers, collarless shirt and shapeless donkey jacket – and that would soon be off once he started humping hundredweight sacks about in the hold.

'The Luftwaffe made a bit of a mess of the place last night, don't you think?' continued the company's eagle-eyed tally man, gesturing towards the dozen firemen who were still hosing down a warehouse. 'It's Logan and McKay's, isn't it?'

Running his gaze over the gutted building on the other side of the quay, Harry nodded.

Kenny frowned. 'What you waiting around for?'

Spotting Ernie Milligan, the Fairchild & Son Stevedore Company's representative, marching across the unloading area, Harry grinned. 'Him.'

Kenny glanced behind him. 'I'll leave you to it then, Harry.'

He left to take up his position on deck by the open hatch ready to count and make a note of what was unloaded for the import company.

'Milligan looks a mite put out, don't he?' said Ben, who had just strolled over to join them.

Ben was not only the number-one man in Harry's team but also his younger brother. He had the same red hue in his hair and tendency to grow freckles in the sun. He hadn't yet reached Harry's five foot ten, but after two years on the docks he was certainly building muscle.

In fact, all of the eight-strong gang of men loitering around Harry were Gunn family members, either by birth or by marriage.

Harry sniggered at the red-faced hiring clerk slipping and sliding across the concrete waterfront.

'What do you think you're playing at, Gunn?' Ernie shouted, waving his short arms as he approached. 'The crane operator and the tally man are ready, so why are you and your team standing around like a bunch of bloody lemons?'

Peeling himself off the cast-iron bollard he'd been leaning on for the past twenty minutes, Harry pulled himself up to his full height. 'The sacks are wonky. Aren't they, boys?'

The men close by muttered their agreement.

Ernie frowned. 'Wonky? What d'you mean "wonky"?'

'I mean it's going to take a bit more jiggery-pokery to get 'em out of the hold than a quid a ton,' Harry replied.

In the muted light shining up from the *Maid of Gibraltar*'s number-three hold, Ernie's fleshy jowls started to quiver. 'But that's what we agreed.'

'We did,' Harry agreed. 'But before I realised that the price set by capitalist scum exploited the working man.'

Ernie ran his fingers through his thinning hair. 'But that flour needs unloading before the rats get in. If it spoils, I'll have some Ministry of Food fellas down here asking why.'

Harry held the hiring governor's furious glare. 'A guinea a ton.'

'That's blackmail!'

'A guinea a ton,' repeated Harry. 'Or, as shop steward of the Transport and General Workers' Union, I'll convene a members' meeting.'

'You can't,' snapped Ernie. 'Strikes are illegal.'

'I ain't calling a strike, Milligan,' Harry replied. 'But as the dockworkers' shop steward, I will convene a union meeting as I'm entitled to do and I'll be sending word to our members in London and St Katherine Docks, too. Of course, they'll have to down tools but—'

'All right, all right, a guinea a ton it is,' cut in Ernie. 'But I want it all out by knocking-off time so the shore team can get in and clean.'

Harry took another lungful of nicotine down then, pinching it out, he stowed the roll-up behind his right ear.

'Right, lads,' he said, rubbing his hands together, 'you 'eard what Ernie said, so lets get on wiv it.'

The men sprang into action and clambered on board the ship.

'You pull a stunt like this again, Gunn,' snarled Ernie, 'and I'll—'

'You'll what?' cut in Harry. 'Ignore us standing outside the gates at morning call?' He bared his teeth and loomed over the diminutive clerk. 'I wouldn't do that if you know what's good for you.'

Ernie, fleshy jowls quivering, glared up at him for a moment then turned and marched back across the unloading area.

'I 'ope as 'ow you ain't gone and upset little Ernie,' said Micky, Ernie's ginger-haired, freckle-faced cousin, as he strolled past with a tarpaulin cargo sling draped over his shoulder.

Harry looked around.

'Don't I always?' he said, grinning. 'And, Micky, do me a favour. When you trot off to the bog, have a quick squint in the L&M.' He nodded towards the smouldering warehouse on the other side of the water. 'I saw Dicky Robbins' crew moving tea chests in there on Tuesday and our national brew being in short supply, it'll be worth our while to rescue a crate or two.'

Chapter four

DESPERATELY TRYING not to move her head off the upright, Fliss raised the mug of black coffee to her lips and took a sip.

Holding the hot, sweet liquid in her mouth until the yawning feeling in her stomach subsided, she swallowed it down.

'How are you feeling, Fliss?'

Slowly lifting her head, she looked up at her sister Prue, who was straightening the bed linen on the top bunk.

Fliss gave her a wan smile. 'Not so bad.'

That, of course, was a complete lie because truthfully she didn't believe anyone could feel this ghastly and still be this side of the grave.

'What's the time?' she asked.

'Just before seven,' her sister replied. 'The all-clear sounded an hour ago.'

'Did it?'

Prue gave her an exasperate look. 'Can't you remember anything?'

'I remember walking in on that louse Giles.' With the raw pain in her chest tightening, Fliss told her sister about discovering Giles in bed with the receptionist from the *Workers' Clarion*.

Prue frowned. 'The toerag. Then what happened?'

'We argued.'

'Argued!' her sister shrieked. 'I would have broken a vase or something over his head.'

Fliss gave her a sideways look.

Prue laughed. 'You didn't hit him, did you?'

'I punched him in the mouth,' Fliss replied, remembering the satisfaction as her fist busted Giles's bottom lip. 'After which, I packed my suitcase and left. I wandered up to Victoria station and caught a train home.'

'So, when did you acquire this?' Prue held up the bottle of Gordon's gin.

Staring at the green glass flickering in the low lighting of the overhead bulbs, fragmented images of the previous day passed across Fliss's pounding brain. 'In the pub opposite Stepney station, I think. I needed a bit of Dutch courage before I pitched up at the rectory.'

Prue gave her a deeply sympathetic look, as well she might.

'So you don't remember how you got here?'

Fliss swallowed another mouthful of coffee. 'No, it's a complete blank.'

'Well, according to the police officer who found you, you were sitting on one of the gravestones in the churchyard,' Prue explained. 'Unsurprisingly, as you were completely sozzled, you couldn't tell him your name but luckily, as you were obviously incapable of looking after yourself and the air raid siren had just gone off, he brought you here. And when I say brought you, Fliss, I mean carried you, because you were, as they say around these parts, legless. What are you going to do now?'

'Go and tell Mother that I've come home to do a piece on something for the paper,' said Fliss.

'About what?'

'I don't know; the docks or something,' said Fliss, as the lamps went on overhead and light sliced through her eyes. 'I just need a week or two to figure out what to do next.'

'Why don't you just tell her the truth?'

An image of her mother's tight-lipped face loomed into Fliss's mind. She shook her head then bitterly wished she hadn't.

'I can't,' she replied. 'I just can't face her. Not like—'

A wave of nausea rose up. Grabbing the bucket alongside her bunk, Fliss threw herself on her knees and retched up what was left in her hollow stomach.

With a ragged tooth saw grinding slowly through her brain, Fliss leaned on the side of pail.

'I'd come with you,' said Prue as she rubbed her back gently, 'but …'

Raising her head, Fliss forced a smile. 'It's all right, Sis. Anyhow, I'd better make myself look respectable before I pitch up at the rectory.'

Prue nodded. 'There's a couple of washing cubicles in the side crypt behind the stairs. I'll get your washbag.'

As her sister opened her case, which had been stowed under the bed, and rummaged around in the contents, Fliss summoned all her strength and stood up.

'You know,' said Prue as she handed Fliss her washbag, 'it's a pity you can't remember your knight in shining armour, because,' an oddly starry-eyed expression spread across her pretty face, 'he really was quite a dish. Had a bit of the Errol Flynn about him but without the moustache.'

Fliss gave a dry, mirthless laugh. 'Well, it wouldn't matter to me if he was actually Errol Flynn in a doublet and hose because, Prue, from now on I'm off men completely.'

With the blood thundering in her ears, Fliss waited for the rag and bone man's horse and wagon to trundle past then adjusted her grip on her suitcase and crossed Whitehorse Lane.

Stopping in front of two Portland-stone pillars that had once had an ornate wrought-iron trellis gate between them that was now most likely part of a spitfire or battleship, Fliss studied her parents' home, St Winifred's Rectory.

Although the vast majority of houses in this part of London were squat, two-up two-down terraced houses or tightly packed tenements, the manse where her father, the Reverend Hugh Carmichael, and her mother, Marjorie, had moved to almost ten months ago was more like a dwelling for the lord of the manor rather than a parish priest.

Of course, the homes provided to the clergy by the established Church of the land, though often draughty and short of modern amenities such as hot running water and a stove built in the current century, could never have been described as poky. But with the baronial-style casement windows protected now with criss-crossed tape, five bedrooms, three reception rooms, a study, a music room, kitchen and cellar, St Winifred's Rectory rivalled most bishops' palaces. There were even a couple of mature apple trees thrusting their bare winter branches above the side wall.

Of course, in times past, along with the clergy's family, this would have been the workplace for a bevy of servants who would have been housed in quarters behind the row of dormer windows under the rafters.

Fliss studied the solid front door for a moment, then with the bustling exhaust-choked street behind her, she entered the rectory's enclosed garden and walked up the path.

Taking a long deep breath, Fliss grasped the enamel knob beside the door and pulled. The bell at the other end of the hall rang faintly and as the sound faded the bolt on the other side of the door slid back. The door opened and Dolly Lavender stood on the coconut mat behind it.

As always, the rectory's middle-aged, broad-in-the-beam housekeeper wore a flowery wraparound apron over her mud-coloured gown, the sleeves of which were rolled back to reveal brawny forearms. As she was just about to start the housework, her greying brown hair was tided away under a colourful scarf. She also had her mid-morning roll-up tucked behind her ear.

She looked at Fliss for a moment then opened the door wider.

'Sorry, Miss Felicity,' she said. 'It took a minute for me brain to catch up with me peepers. Come in out of the cold.'

Smiling at the housekeeper, Fliss stepped into the vast hallway. She caught the faint smell of fried bacon.

'I hope I haven't dragged you away from anything,' she said, as her stomach rolled uncomfortably.

'Only washing up the breakfast things.' The housekeeper's gaze flickered on to Fliss's suitcase. 'Your ma didn't mention you were coming to stay.'

'I didn't tell her,' Fliss replied. 'It was last minute; you know, chasing a story.'

The old housekeeper's wrinkled face lifted in an indulgent smile. 'Chasing a story! You modern girls. In my day the only thing a young woman chased was a wedding ring.'

Despite the memory of Giles's false promises clawing at Fliss's chest, she forced a smile. 'Are my parents in?'

'Your dad's over at the church, but your mother's in the small parlour,' Mrs Lavender replied. 'Do you want me to bring you a cuppa?'

'That would be lovely,' Fliss said. 'But only if it's not too much trouble.'

'No trouble at all,' said Mrs Lavender. 'You go through, and I'll fetch you one.'

She turned and headed for the kitchen at the back of the house.

The rectory hall was wide enough to park her father's Austin Six motor car. The broad staircase to the floor above was on the right. When they'd arrived the year before, the polished treads had been covered in dull green carpet held in place by rods, but somehow since her last visit at Christmas, despite the rationing and shortages, this had been replaced with a regal navy.

The décor had changed too, from brick-red emulsion halfway up the walls with cream above to a pale green throughout, on which a selection of her mother's pastoral and country-life watercolours, inherited from a long-dead relative, were displayed. Even the doors on either side of the hallway and the one at the far end that led though to the kitchen and scullery had had a fresh coat of white paint applied.

Careful to keep her head upright, Fliss put her suitcase on the floor beside the mahogany table that held her grandmother's substantial majolica vase. She took off her jacket and hat and hung them on the stand.

Fliss turned towards the hall mirror to check her hair, only to find that dabbing her cheeks with rouge, mascaraing her lashes and adding her wild-cherry lipstick meant that the reflection looking back at her bore more than a striking resemblance to a fairground Aunt Sally.

Turning, she headed towards the small rear parlour. Fliss grasped the brass door handle, took another deep breath, and walked in.

A century ago, this room would have been the place where the lady of the house would have chosen each week's menu with the cook and listened to the housekeeper give a weekly run-down of the household. Now, however, with a pair of saggy chintz sofas facing each other in front of the fireplace and a solid teak wireless in the corner, it served as a family lounge, leaving the larger front parlour for more formal occasions.

In contrast to the chilly hall, thanks to the small fire burning in the grate, the room was comfortably warm. Marjorie was sitting at her spindle-legged Regency lady's desk in front of the French windows, pouring over what looked like an account ledger.

'I thought I told you, Mrs Lavender, I didn't want to be disturbed,' she said, without looking up.

'Good morning, Mother,' said Fliss.

Marjorie's head snapped around and her eyes stretched wide in surprise.

With tightly permed brown hair halfway on its transition to steely grey and uncomfortably direct hazel eyes, Fliss's mother was what the women's magazines politely described as 'full-bodied'.

Dressed in her everyday parish wear of a Harris Tweed skirt, a coffee-coloured twinset and a modest string of pearl around her plump neck, she stared open-mouthed for a moment before she found her voice.

'Felicity! What are you doing here?'

'I've come home for a few days,' Fliss replied as a

streak of sunlight through the French doors set her head throbbing again.

Marjorie's deep-set eyes scrutinised Fliss's face. 'You look absolutely awful.'

'I had a rough night,' Fliss replied.

'Didn't we all?' said her mother. 'Six hours the raid lasted last night. Six hours! I tell you, after five months of bombing, everyone is at the end of their tether. If it goes on much longer, the whole country will be nervous wrecks.'

'I think that's the point, Mother.'

'Well, it's barbaric.' Marjorie's substantial eyebrows pulled together. 'That ghastly communist layabout Giles isn't with you, is he?'

'No,' Fliss replied. 'It's just me.'

'Well, then it's lovely,' she said, standing and crossing the space between them. 'But I wish you'd told me you were coming.'

'It was last minute.' Marjorie turned her head and Fliss gave her a quick peck on her downy cheek. 'For work.'

'Work?'

'Yes, I'm writing an article for the newspaper,' Fliss replied, her stomach rebelling again at her mother's lily of the valley perfume.

Her mother rolled her eyes. 'Newspaper! Is that what you call it? Traitorous communist rag would be nearer the mark.'

'I'm doing a piece about the docks,' continued Fliss, unable for once to summon up the strength to argue the finer points of socialism.

Her mother's pale lips lifted slightly at the corners. 'Well, whatever the reason it's lovely to have you home for a little while.' She glanced at the carriage clock on the mantelshelf. 'Now I'm sorry, Felicity, but I have a flower guild meeting in half an—'

'That's all right, Mother,' Fliss cut in, sending a small prayer skywards for giving her an excuse to escape. 'I've got to unpack.'

Her mother smiled. 'I'll see you at luncheon; I think Mrs Lavender is presenting us with stewed tripe, greens and potato.'

'Until later,' Fliss replied, willing her stomach to remain where it was.

Leaving her mother to return to her parish tasks, Fliss left the room and nearly collided with Mrs Lavender holding a mug of tea in her hand.

'Sorry for taking so long, Miss Fliss,' said the housekeeper. 'But my son just popped in to drop off some bits for me pantry. Nothing dodgy, you understand – I wouldn't want you to think that – it was just a tin or two of salmon, that all. Here's your tea.'

She thrust the mug at Fliss.

Amazed that anyone in London had even seen a tin of salmon let alone bought one, Fliss took the mug.

'Thank you, Mrs L. I'll drink it upstairs while I'm unpacking my things.'

With the soles of her slipper slapping on the black-and-white tiles of the hallway floor, the housekeeper hurried back to the kitchen.

After retrieving her suitcase and holding her hot drink in the other hand, Fliss made her way upstairs. Crossing the upstairs landing, she all but staggered into the bedroom she and her sister had shared overlooking the rectory garden.

Kicking off her shoes, she dropped her case on the floor and placed the mug on the mantelshelf before she collapsed on to her bed. Laying spread-eagle on the rose-pink candlewick counterpane, she tried to focus on the frosted-glass lampshade above her in an attempt to stop the flowery wallpaper spinning around.

She lay there for a moment then sprang up, clamped her hand over her mouth and dashed to the bedroom door. Tearing it open she reeled across to the toilet and threw herself on her knees. Gripping the porcelain bowl, she hung her head over it a split second before she retched.

With a thousand hammers pummelling her brain and the last few fluid ounces left in her stomach floating on the water below, Fliss groaned and slumped into a miserable heap on the lino floor.

A gently hand rubbed her back.

Fliss looked up and managed to focus on a pair of very dark eyes looking anxiously at her.

'Come,' said a woman's voice softly. 'Let me help.'

Propped up on her bed with her gaze fixed on the frosty cherry tree branches outside her window, Fliss took long, slow breaths.

There was a faint knock on the door before it opened, and Hester walked in carrying a glass of opaque liquid in one hand and a jug of the same in the other.

Austrian-born Hester Kratz – or more correctly Dr Hester Kratz, paediatrician – worked at the Jewish Hospital, which was a short walk from the rectory.

Hester had been halfway through her training at the American Hospital in Paris when the Belgian army surrendered in the previous May, and she had walked the hundred-plus miles to Honfleur carrying her life in a small suitcase.

She was a couple of years older than Fliss's twenty-five years, with raven hair, cheekbones that would make a catwalk model green with envy and a well-defined jawline. Unlike the modern fashion for flowery fabrics, frills and pin-tucks, Hester favoured tailored suits and understated outfits. Today this was a six-panelled navy skirt, a cream blouse with a Peter Pan collar and modest lace-up, low-heeled shoes.

Hester had arrived last July, not long after the three refugee families who had been housed in the servants' quarter at the top of the house. However, Prue, who had organised their arrival, had allocated Hester Fliss's bedroom across the hall.

'How are you feeling?' she asked, closing the door gently with her foot.

'Like I've got a steam hammer going in my head,' Fliss replied.

'I am not surprised.' Hester's full mouth lifted at the corner. 'Scotch or brandy?'

'Gin,' Fliss replied. 'Best part of a bottle, I think.'

'I would strongly recommend you drink this,' Hester said, as she offered Fliss the glass of cloudy liquid. 'It is barley water, with Epsom salt plus a spoonful of sugar. It will help restore you.'

Fliss took the drink from her. 'Thank you.'

'Have you taken anything?' Hester asked.

'A couple of aspirins about an hour ago,' Fliss reply.

Hester delved into her skirt pocket and pulled out a small bottle which she set on Fliss's dressing table.

'Here are some more, but I would advise you not to take any more until at least midday,' said Hester. 'And make sure you drink plenty; that will help to … resolve your present predicament.'

'Thank you,' said Fliss. 'And I'm sorry if I've made you late for work.'

'You have not,' Hester replied. 'I am not on duty until eleven thirty, but actually I do have to go as I have to run through our research notes with Professor Kleinman.'

'Well, thank you again for helping me out,' said Fliss. 'I really appreciate it.'

Hester waved her words away. 'Do not speak of it. Just remember to drink plenty and try to eat some lunch later.'

'I will,' said Fliss.

Hester glanced at Fliss's suitcase. 'Leave unpacking and rest for an hour or so and I am sure you will be much recovered.' Her eyebrow rose. 'Doctor's orders.'

Despite the ragged toothed saw sliding back and forth through her brain, Fliss forced a smile. 'Thank you again.'

Hester walked across the Turkish patterned rug to the door, but as she reached for the handle she turned back.

'I am thinking your present state is due to some man who has betrayed you.'

Tears pinched the corners of Fliss's eyes. Unable to speak, she gave the smallest of nods.

A sympathetic expression stole over Hester's striking features. 'Believe me, Felicity, I know exactly how you feel.'

Chapter five

'How we doing, Ben?' asked Harry, stacking a box of Mazawattee tea on top of another that had just been loaded into the back of the van.

'Another half-dozen boxes with tins of fruit and we'll be done,' said his brother, the whites of his eyes bright in the reflected light from the searchlights streaking across the sky.

It was the early hours of Thursday and Harry and Frankie Deacon, their brother-in-law, had been humping crates of tea for the past two hours.

Frankie was married to Harry's oldest sister Martha. The Deacon family, all twelve of them, had lived across the street from the Gunns for as long as Harry could remember. Two years older than Harry, he and Martha had been childhood sweethearts. With tight curly black hair and skin the colour of milky coffee, his family had clearly been touched by the tar brush somewhere up the family tree. With hands like shovels, Frankie was solid in all senses and one of the leading men in Harry's gang.

Sammy Button was on the first floor of the Logan & McKay warehouse that Harry had sent Micky to investigate on Wednesday morning.

With a shot of unruly blond hair and blue eyes, Sammy was Frankie's cousin, although you'd be hard-pressed to know it. Just short of his twenty-fifth birthday, Sammy had tried a bit of shop work when he left school, which didn't last long – mainly because he kept getting his hand caught in the till. As a favour to Sammy's long-suffering mother Polly, Frankie had spoken up for him to Harry, who took him on the team. A stroke of luck, as it turned out, because there wasn't a lock yet invented that Sammy couldn't pick.

The air raid siren had gone off just as the sun was setting at around nine, and after the first wave of enemy aircraft had done their job, knowing the ARP and police would be busy, Harry and his crew had set out.

Part of the roof had caved in, but the warehouse itself looked safe enough – although Harry had advised his team, who were all built like brick shit-houses, to avoid standing together on the creaky floorboards on the upper levels in case they ended up sprawled on the ground floor with their legs broken.

Making sure the box he'd just put down was stable, Harry turned to see Tommy Lavender emerge from the warehouse with his arms full, just as a red flare from a bomb a little way off shot flames and sparks skywards.

Tommy Zeppelin Lavender – thus called because while carrying him his mother had been caught in a Zeppelin raid and gave birth to him soon after – was a wiry chap with sharp features. His profession could best be described as a bit of this and that; he wasn't one of Harry's regular team but a solid bloke if needed. As cousin Ernie's van was on its way to Romford with tubs of molasses they'd half-inched two nights before, Harry had offered Tommy a couple of blue five-pound notes to swift their newly acquired merchandise away.

'It's getting a bit lively out there, Harry,' said Tommy, placing a box of Sunny Smile dried fruit on top of three others on the metal van floor.

Harry gazed through the shattered panes of the warehouse window towards Limehouse, where one of the barrage balloons anchored above the Royal Docks had just ignited in a ball of orange and red flames.

He watched it spiral down onto the Royal Air Force balloon crew manning the cable below, then took the roll-up from behind his ear and relit it.

'I think that's just about the lot,' said Freddie the lad, a big-boned youth with an oddly angelic-looking face who was Harry's nephew, as he loaded a smaller box. 'And we,' he indicated his older brother Punchy, just behind him and balancing an identical box on his left shoulder, 'just found these tucked at the back. Eight-ounce tins of Nescafé.'

'Sweet,' said Harry, giving the two brothers an approving look. 'We should be able to flog them for three bob a pop. Load them up and then let's get going.'

Having added their boxes to the crates and boxes already in the back of the lorry, Freddie and Punchy clambered in and Harry pulled the tailgate down and secured it. He then ambled around to the passenger side of the lorry's cab to join the other men. Tommy was already in the driver's seat, but as Harry opened the cab's door Ben grabbed his arm.

'Who the bloody hell is that?' he asked, indicating a figure silhouetted against the burning skyline and walking through the main gates at the other end of the warehouse yard.

'Bugger,' spat Sammy, poking his head over the top of the front passenger seat. 'Another couple of yards and he'll see us.'

'What should we do, Harry?' asked Tommy, gripping the steering wheel with both hands.

In the red glow from the flaming sky, Harry studied the figure making his way across the open space towards the warehouse offices on the ground floor. He took a long drag from his cigarette then flicked it on to the floor.

'You get off and stow the gear,' he said, crushing the butt under his size-ten boot. 'I'll care of our unexpected visitor.'

'What do you think, Guv?' Alex asked as Tim studied the middle-aged man's body that lay in a mangled heap among the rubble.

It was a chilly Thursday morning and two days after they'd arrested Chalky White's crew, who, as Tim had predicted, had been sent for trail at the Crown Court and were now remanded in custody pending their appearance in three weeks.

He and Alex had arrived in the office at eight to a pile of crimes that had happened over night; top of the pile was the discovery of a man's body.

Which was why he and Alex were now standing among the wreckage of what had been the Devonshire Arms in Bow Common Lane. The sun had just crested the slate roofs of the terraced houses opposite but was still behind a thick column of black smoke from the burning factories along the Limehouse Cut running nearby towards the River Lee two miles away.

The all-clear had only sounded an hour ago, so the air was laden with spent munitions, broken brick dust and woodsmoke, which caught in your throat as you inhaled.

Like so many times before after a cloudless night, the dwellings and industry on both sides of the Thames had taken a pounding from the squadrons of Dorniers and Messerschmitts that had visited them for the fourth time in as many nights. So Tim and his sergeant weren't alone: across from them, in front of the shell of the old Mariners' Mission Hall, were parked two heavy rescue vehicles, their ten-man crews painstakingly removing bricks and masonry. However, as the line of bodies covered with tarpaulin on the kerb nearby testified, the likelihood of finding survivors under the devastation was fast receding.

'You've found him, then!'

Tim turned to see Sergeant Charlie Latimer lumbering across the debris of the adjoining houses.

Built like a barrel and sporting an impressive set of sideburns beneath the strap of his helmet, and wearing his hip-length cape over his uniform, Charlie looked as if he'd just walked out of a Victorian issue of the *Police Gazette*. He was an old-style copper who knew every villain on his patch and where there was pot of tea brewing day or night.

Have completed his full twenty-five years, as both a constable and a sergeant keeping the king's peace on the streets of East London, by rights Latimer should have been pulling pints in a county pub somewhere or taking a daily stroll along the seafront at Clacton. However, like many who had joined the Met having survived the previous war with Germany, he'd opted to stay on to take up the slack after hundreds of his younger colleagues signed up to fight.

'Yes, thanks for calling me, Charlie,' Tim replied as the Limehouse nick's sergeant joined them.

'Well, I 'ad to seeing as how, thanks to Sergeant Reilly signing up and that silly arse West breaking both legs by falling into a bomb crater, you two are the only CID still standing,' Latimer chuckled.

'How many dead so far?' asked Alex.

'Twenty-six,' Charlie replied. 'Most like this poor sod when it collapsed on them. No doubt there'll be a dozen more before the lads from the heavy are done. All the others they dug out had the usual glass cuts to their clothes and cordite burns on their face and hands, but this chap,' he nodded towards the corpse between them, 'well, he just didn't look kosher.'

'Any idea who he is?' asked Tim.

'According to his ID card he's a Reginald Albert Wiggins, general manager at the Logan & McKay warehouse that sits along the western moorings in London Dock,' the long-serving sergeant replied.

Alex frowned. 'Wasn't there a report on your desk about the Logan and McKay being cleaned out last night, Guv?'

Chewing his bottom lip, Tim nodded.

After a moment, Charlie touched the peak of his helmet. 'I'll leave you to it then, Inspector.'

Looking up, Tim gave him a brief smile. 'Thank you, Sergeant.'

The elderly sergeant turned and wandered back to where a couple of the heavy rescue fellas were carefully carrying another body away from the rubble.

'So, Guv, what do you think?' Alex asked.

'Well, at first glance it looks as if Mr Reginald Albert Wiggins copped it in last night's raid,' Tim replied. 'However, I don't buy it.'

'Why not? That dent on his head looks pretty convincing.'

'Perhaps,' Tim replied, hunkering down to look more closely at the blood and hair mattered in the indentation in the scull. 'But why has he got a busted lower lip and a missing front tooth? And look at the position he's in.'

Frowning slightly, Alex cast his eyes over the body in front of them. 'I don't—'

From his crouched position, Tim looked up at his subordinate. 'Imagine you're about to have a couple of

58

hundredweight of brickwork land on your noggin, what position would you get yourself into?'

Alex considered the question for a moment. 'I suppose I'd automatically curl up and cover my head.'

'Exactly, but this chap looks as if he's just been thrown on the floor, and compared to the other casualties recovered by heave rescue, his clothing – especially at the front – is surprisingly free of dust. However,' Tim continued, straightening up again, 'what I really find suspicious about this death is the fact that the morning after the Logan and McKay warehouse is looted the general manager is found dead in the rubble of a pub three miles away.'

'It could be just a coincidence?' his sergeant replied. Tim raised an eyebrow. 'What are the odds?'

Two fresh-faced auxiliary ambulance lads in white doctor-like overalls who were holding a rolled-up stretcher were hovering close by.

'It's all right, we're done here,' said Tim, beckoning them over.

He and Alex moved aside to give them space.

Climbing carefully over the uneven surface, the ambulance men covered Wiggins with a sheet of khaki canvas.

Tim and his sergeant took off their hats and looked on in silence as the first-aiders loaded the body onto the unfurled stretcher and carried the deceased ware-houseman away.

'What now, Guv?' asked Alex.

'Well,' Tim replied, pulling his collar a little tighter around his ears, 'while you're breaking the sad news to Mrs Wiggins and seeing if she can throw any light on what her husband was doing last night, I'm going to have a little word with a friend.'

An hour later, after cadging a lift to London Hospital from one of the undertakers taking some of the recovered bodies to the mortuary, Tim headed due south until he finally reached Old Gravel Lane. The dog-leg lane ran from the Highway down to the river and like nearly every other street and lane in Wapping was lined on either side by tall Victorian warehouses. However, as he reached the cobbled thoroughfare of Wapping High Street, Tim was confronted with the aftermath of damage inflicted on the Victorian warehouses from the Luftwaffe's visit the previous night. Acknowledging the fire and rescue crews still working among the rubble, he continued on towards the grey stone walls of the Tower until he spotted the person he was seeking.

After ensuring he wasn't stepping out in front of a three-ton lorry, Tim crossed the road and strolled over.

'Morning, Wally, how's tricks?' he asked, as he reached the street sweeper shovelling up detritus gathered around a drain in Wapping Lane.

Tipping the foul-smelling waste into his cart, Wally looked up. 'Not so bad. And yourself?'

Wally Green had been sweeping the streets of Wapping for a dozen year. Although only a few years older than Tim, thanks to a twisted spine he barely reached the inspector's shoulder. However, while his back might be warped his eyes and ears worked perfectly.

'Busy enough.' Delving in his pocket, Tim pulled out a packet of ten Player's Navy Cut. 'Fag?'

Although he was one of the few officers at Wapping nick who didn't smoke, Tim still found it worth his while to carry a packet.

'Ta,' Wally replied, taking one and lighting it. From under his low eyebrows his eyes flickered towards the column of black smoke spiralling skyward. 'I hear Logan and McKay warehouse was cleared out last night.'

'Clean as a whistle, according to the night-duty sergeant's report,' Tim said. 'Heard anything about it?'

'Can't say I have, Inspector,' Wally replied, forming his irregular featured into an angelic expression.

'Pity,' said Tim.

'But you know me, Inspector Wallace. I keep me shell-likes open,' Wally assured him.

'I'm glad to hear it,' said Tim. 'Especially as at the very time his warehouse was being stripped bare, Logan and McKay's manager seems to have got his head stoved in and dumped on what remains of the Devonshire Arms in Bow Common Lane.' The street cleaner's pale complexion blanched further. 'Some would call that a coincidence, Wally,' Tim continued, holding the other man's watery gaze. 'But I don't believe in coincidences.'

'We … well, now, Inspector Wallace,' said the street sweeper, blinking rapidly. 'Although I ain't 'eard no actual name, you understand, someone did spot Tommy Lavender's van hereabouts last night.'

'Did they? ' said Tim.

Wally's head nodded like a rag doll in a toddler's hands.

'What time was that?' asked Tim.

'They didn't say but it must have been after midnight cause they were just walking 'ome from the shelter after the all-clear sounded.'

'Thanks, Wally. Keep 'em,' he added, as the street sweeper went to hand the cigarettes back. 'One good turn deserves another. Let us know if you get wind of anything else.' Wally touched the peak of his saggy cap and, stowing his shovel and broom on the side hooks of his cart, grasped the handle and started off down the street.

'Oh, and tell Dora at the WVS canteen outside the library that I'll stand you a cuppa,' Tim called after him.

The street cleaner raised his hand in acknowledgement and continued on his way.

Tim watched him disappear into the murk. Then, tucking his scarf around his neck, and with the fog swirling around his long legs, he headed off in the opposite direction.

Chapter six

As FLISS STACKED the last of the breakfast dishes on the rectory kitchen draining board, the kitchen door opened and Hester Kratz walked in dragging her feet.

Fliss glanced up at the clock on the wall showing almost nine o'clock on Saturday morning. 'Goodness, have you only just finished your night shift?'

Hester nodded. 'Half an hour ago. An incendiary bomb landed on the tramlines at Gardiner's Corner and warped them, so Dr Fleishman had to walk from Shoreditch.'

Fliss gave her a sympathetic look. 'Bad night?'

Placing her Gladstone bag on one of the kitchen chairs, the Jewish Hospital's head paediatrician gave her a wan smile.

Actually, Hester didn't need to confirm it as the truth was written in weariness across her strikingly handsome face. And, to be honest, when would it ever be a good night having to care for children injured by high explosives?

'Sit down and I'll make you a cuppa,' said Fliss, feeling more than a little ashamed for focusing on her own misery when there was so much more worthy heartbreak with every new dawn.

Crossing to the stove, she relit the gas under the squat kettle. 'It might take a moment or two,' she said, as the smallest of flames spluttered into life. 'It looks like the gas company have us on half rations again.'

'That's fine,' Hester replied, as Fliss spooned tea into the pot. 'At least you have some here. The gas mains to the hospital has been broken for four days, so the kitchens are having to cook all the children's food on camping stoves. But never mind me. You look as if you've been up all night, too.'

'It's the air raid last night,' Fliss said, pouring milk into two cups.

Hester gave her a sceptical look but didn't comment.

Actually, the Luftwaffe's visit the night before had been over by one in the morning, but while those sheltering in St Winifred's crypt slept undisturbed, Fliss had stared up at the wooden slats of her sister's bunk, one moment fighting back tears and the next boiling with fury as she replayed the scene of Giles in bed with Gwen in her head. The kettle's whistle cut through her thoughts and brought her back to the here and now.

She had just put the strainer onto the first mug when Ingrid Haas's head appeared around the kitchen door.

As the Germans swept across Europe the year before, causing many to flee to England in fear for their lives, Fliss's sister Prue had volunteered to house Jewish refugees in the three empty rooms that had been the rectory's servants' quarters. The resettlement officers aimed not to split up families wherever possible, so Prue had offered to accommodate three. One family, the Leitners, had left after Christmas to live with relatives in Golders Green, but the other two – along with Hester – remained.

Ingrid Haas, a fine-boned Nordic woman with ice-blue eyes, had adapted well to her new surroundings; her two children, Nicolas and Freda, had already dashed out of the house earlier to beat the school bell.

'I know you've been up all night, Hester,' Ingrid said, looking apologetically at the weary doctor, 'but little Peter has had a fever since just after midnight. And I know there have been a few cases of *kinkhoest* – I mean the whooping cough – locally … Johanna is wondering, if it is not too much trouble—'

'It is no trouble at all,' said Hester, rising to her feet and picking up her bag.

'I'll bring your tea up,' said Fliss as her friend followed Ingrid out of the room.

Ten minutes later, when the kettle had finally returned to the boil, Fliss went upstairs. Rather than going to Hester's room at the end of the hallway, she continued up the narrow uncarpeted flight of stairs that led up into the rectory's eaves.

With the floorboards creaking and a cup of steaming tea in her hand, she made her way along to the far end room where the Bakker family lived.

Knocking lightly on the door, Fliss walked in to see Hester bending over a toddler's cot with seventeen-year-old Johanna Bakker standing on the other side, looking anxiously at her eighteen-month-old brother Peter.

This time last year, Johanna Bakker had been preparing for her end-of-year exams in her family home. However, as the might of the German army advanced towards the small Dutch town she'd lived in all her life, she had packed a few belongings and escaped. Carrying her baby brother Peter on her back and holding her ten-year-old sister Eva's by the hand, she'd trudged thirty miles along bomb-damaged roads and across fields to the coast, where mercifully the Red Cross had lugged the children onto one of the boats ferrying refugees across the Channel.

She'd been little more than skin and bone when she arrived at the rectory. And although she no longer looked half-starved and had resumed her studies at Toynbee Hall, she was in effect now acting as mother to her two siblings.

Hester moved the flat side of the stethoscope around Peter's chest a few more time then straightened up.

'Well, Johanna,' she said, smiling across at the young woman, 'I am very pleased to tell you that Peter is not suffering from whooping cough but a slight upper respiratory infection. It's very common in children of his age. Helps them build up resistance.'

'Thank goodness,' said Johanna, visibly relieved.

Hester slipped her stethoscope back into her heavy brown leather case. 'You just need to give him half an aspirin every six hours and plenty of fluids and he will be running around as usual before too long.'

Johanna's attention shifted from the flushed-looking toddler who was sitting himself upright in the cot to Fliss.

'I am sorry to ask, Miss Carmichael, but I will have to let my tutor know I will not be able to attend my tutorial this afternoon to care for Peter, so could I use the telephone, please?'

'You can, Johanna, but it seems a shame for you to miss your extra lesson, especially this close to your exams,' said Fliss. 'I'm not planning to go anywhere this afternoon; I don't mind looking after Peter.'

If she were being honest, the sum of Fliss's knowledge about babies would fit on the back of an envelope, but as Peter would only be in her care for a few hours she was sure she would manage just fine.

Looking down uncertainly at her brother, Johanna bit her lower lip.

'Honestly, I don't mind,' said Fliss, plastering a confident expression on her face.

'And Fliss can call me if she is at all worried,' added Hester.

The young woman's uncertain gaze shifted from Fliss to Hester and then back again.

'As long as it is not too much trouble, Miss Carmichael,' Johanna said.

Fliss smiled. 'Not at all,' she replied, silently praying her good deed wouldn't involve a nappy. 'And please, call me Fliss.'

'While I try to track down the elusive Mr Lavender,' said Tim, his breath visible in the morning chill, 'I want you to take a report from the manager at the West Indies and Empire Company then come back to the nick and get out all the notes we have so far on the Logan and McKay's case – I want to go over it again,' said Tim.

'Right you are, Guv,' said Alex.

It was just after eleven thirty and they were standing outside the solid Victorian red-brick and stone building that was Wapping police station two days after Tim's interesting conversation with Wally Green.

The gut-wrenching stench from the river testified to it being high tide, which meant that the quayside of every dock along the Thames from St Katherine's to Tilbury would be crammed with moored ships.

The two men parted company, Alex heading west towards the Tower of London, while Tim set off in the opposite direction up Gravel Lane until he reached Commercial Road.

Like Wapping High Street, the Highway running west to east was crowded with lorries loaded with goods collected from the docks, along with ARP and Army lorries passing in either direction. Women, carrying shopping bags or pushing prams, queued outside the shops in their ceaseless attempts to put something in front of their husband when he came home at the end of a long day.

Waiting until an eastbound tram to Poplar had passed, Tim crossed to the other side of the busy highway then turned north, reaching his destination, St Winifred's Rectory, some twenty minutes later.

Strolling between the sturdy Portland stone pillars, Tim headed down the path to the black-painted front door. He pulled on the doorbell and somewhere in the house a bell tinkled.

Casting his gaze over the enormous house and the high garden walls either side, he waited for a moment or two then the lock rattled, and the door opened.

It took Tim's brain a moment or two to catch up with his eyes, because standing on the threshold was the young woman who he'd first encountered perched on a gravestone clutching a half-empty bottle of gin. She was wearing a pair of loose-fitting black slacks and a rather fetching bright red polka-dot blouse with a white collar and cuffs.

However, this time, instead of her brown eyes being red-rimmed and unfocused, they looked at him with surprising frankness and not one spark of recognition.

She smiled and a bolt of something Tim couldn't identify shot through him.

'Good morning,' she said, as Tim continued to stare at her. 'What can I do for you? If it's the Rector you're after then I'm afraid he's out at the moment.'

Tim got a grip of himself. 'Good morning. I'm DI Wallace and I'd like to speak to Mrs Lavender. I believe she's the rector's housekeeper, Miss …?'

'Carmichael. I'm the rector's daughter. It's not bad news, is it?' she asked.

'No, it's not,' Tim replied.

'Thank goodness.' She sighed. 'I'm afraid Mrs Lavender is out shopping so perhaps you could come back ano—'

'Would you mind if I came in and waited?' Tim cut in.

She hesitated a moment. 'Of course not. My mother has a meeting in the lounge, so you'll have to come through to the kitchen.'

She stood aside and Tim walked in.

Shutting the door, she headed for the back of the house. Taking off his hat and gloves, he held them close and followed her, noting in passing that her trousers drew attention to her long legs.

The room she led him into straddled the back of the house overlooking the garden and was as large as his room in the police section house behind Leman Street police station.

Beneath the window was a double-sized porcelain butler's sink with a draining board on either side. Under one was a round, cream-coloured electric washing tub with a washboard leaning against it. At the far end was a purpose-built kitchen dresser with fancy-looking crockery and glasses stacked on it along with white-and-blue-striped jars, each labelled with its contents: sugar, tea, flour or oats. In the centre of the room was an enormous scrubbed-pine table that would have comfortably sat ten adults but had six chairs tucked under it.

'Would you like a cup of tea while you wait, Inspector?' Fliss asked, turning to face him.

'That's very kind of you, miss,' Tim replied, finding himself face to face with the young woman he'd last seen dead drunk and sprawled on a lower bunk bed.

To be honest, he was unexpectedly pleased to see her again, not least because her dark eyes and the feel of her in his arms had drifted back into his mind more than once since their encounter in St Winifred's crypt.

Placing his hat on the end of the table, he pulled out one of the chairs.

'I feel like I've met you before,' he said, sitting down.

Miss Carmichael's fine brows drew together. 'No, I don't think so.'

'Funny,' he replied, as the image of her slumped on that gravestone flashed across his mind once more. 'I could have sworn I know you from somewhere.'

'I shouldn't think so,' she said, looking blankly at him as she crossed the room to fetch the kettle from the six-ring stove.

Tim smiled. 'That's the trouble with being a copper, you're trained to remember faces.' He crossed his legs. 'Something smells nice.'

Actually, it didn't because it was a faint smell of burning rather than anything appetising that lingered in the air.

'It's the cake I've just taken out of the oven,' she replied, indicating the slab of solid-looking something on the wire cooling rack on the windowsill. 'It's for the children's tea. We have two refugee families living in the rectory. We did have nine in total at one time, but Mrs Leitner and her children left a few weeks ago.'

'That's very generous of you,' he replied.

'It was my sister Prue's idea really,' she said. 'The rectory's huge so she offered a home to three refugee families. You can have a slice if you like,' she indicated the brown brick recently liberated from the oven. 'Although I wouldn't advise it.'

Tim's eyebrows rose. 'Wouldn't you?'

'Not unless you're ravenously hungry,' Fliss replied, 'because I'm not much of a cook but I'm not at all bothered because I reject the patriarchal assumption that a woman's role in society is a domestic one.'

Turning to the stove, she lit the gas under the kettle.

Staring at her auburn hair as it flowed over her shoulders as she spooned in tea into the pot, a smile lifted one corner of Tim's mouth.

In his experience, most young women held great store by their cooking skills and were more than eager to convince you of them. Obviously, Miss Carmichael wasn't one of them.

He decided to avoid the thorny subject of the place of women in society and move onto safer small talk.

'How long have you and your family lived in the rectory?' Tim asked, trying not to become distracted by her long legs and slim figure as she reached up for the cups.

'Only since last May when my dad was appointed rector of St Winifred's,' she replied. 'But I'm just visiting my parents for a few days.'

'Why don't you join me?' he said. He found himself surprisingly intrigued by her unconventional attitude.

'Actually,' she said, after a moment's hesitation, 'I've been typing for an hour so I could do with a break.' She took down another mug and poured milk from a white jug into both of them.

They studied each other for a moment then she turned back and poured their tea. Tim cast his eye around the room and alighted on four items he'd not seen for at least six or seven month: oranges in a bowl on the windowsill, and then, more interestingly, a tin of Nescafé on the dresser.

'So what is it you want to talk to our housekeeper about?' Fliss asked, setting a mug in front of him.

'Just following up on inquires.' He glanced at the cake. 'Is it a sponge cake?'

'No, fruit. Unbelievably, Mrs Lavender managed to get hold of a packet of Sunny Smiles dried fruit yesterday,' she said.

Tim looked suitably impressed.

'I know, according to my mother she's an absolute treasure when it comes to searching out bargains in the market,' Fliss added, taking the seat opposite him.

Picking up his tea, Tim blew across the top. 'So, were you typing up your father's sermon for tomorrow?'

'No, I wasn't,' she replied. 'I was writing up the interview I did last week with Jennie Lee, the former-Labour Party MP.'

'You work for a newspaper?'

'Yes, I do, as a journalist. And I don't write about knitting or cooking either; I'm a political reporter.' She raised an eyebrow. 'It might come as a bit of a shock to you, Inspector, but women are no longer just wives and mothers but actually work outside the home.'

'I'm well aware of that, Miss Carmichael,' he replied, holding her challenging gaze, 'as we have a dozen or so policewomen on patrol in H Division. Also, I hear women no longer grow faint at the sight of piano legs and can actually add up several numbers in their heads without having a touch of the vapours.'

To Tim's satisfaction, two red patches appeared on Fliss's cheeks as fury flashed in her rather lovely eyes.

'What newspaper do you work on?' he asked.

'The *Workers' Clarion*,' she replied, 'which champions the cause of the workers of this country and the introduction of a truly socialist society. Although I don't suppose you, an instrument of the capitalist state, would read or have even *heard* of the *Clarion*.'

'You mean The Socialist League publication that has its offices in Bloomsbury and comes out every Thursday,' he replied, enjoying the barely suppressed irritation that flashed across Fliss's face.

Smiling coolly at her, Tim took a mouthful of tea, while Fliss opened her mouth to speak – no doubt to inform him that come the revolution he'd be one of the first rounded up and sent to a gulag. But the rectory's back door swinging open forestalled her, and Dolly Lavender walked in carrying a shopping bag in each hand.

Although she was the only reason he was sitting in the rectory's cosy kitchen, cradling a warm cup of tea opposite the strikingly attractive Miss Carmichael, Dolly's appearance was inexplicably annoying.

She spotted Tim sitting at the table and stopped dead. 'Inspector Wallace!'

Tim gave her a friendly smile. 'Hello, Dolly, how's tricks?'

'What are you doing here?' she asked.

'Waiting for you,' he replied, bestowing a friendly smile on her while pinning her with a penetrating stare.

Dolly dumped the bags at the far end of the kitchen table then turned to face him again. 'Me!'

'Don't worry, Mrs L.' Fliss stood up and planted herself squarely in front of the rectory's housekeeper, extended her arms, somewhat over dramatically, as if protecting her from Tim. 'You've done nothing wrong, and you don't have to answer any of the inspector's questions.'

Ignoring her challenging stance, Tim finished the last mouthful of tea his tea and stood up. 'Well, Dolly, it's not you I'm after exactly but your Tommy. In fact, I've been looking for him for the past two days.'

Anxiety flashed across the housekeeper's face. 'Tommy! Wot you want 'im for?'

'Just a chat.'

''E ain't done nuffink,' Dolly replied.

'I never said he had,' Tim countered. 'I've been around to his blonde in Shadwell and the widow who owns the tobacconist's at the back of Dock Street and neither of them can tell me where he is, so I'm wondering if you can?'

Dolly shrugged. 'Search me. You know wot my Tommy's like. 'Ere, there and everywhere. I only know where 'e is when he pitches up down home.'

'Are you sure you've no idea where I might find him?' Tim persisted, as the housekeeper's right eyelid started to flicker.

'I think Mrs Lavender has just answered your question, Inspector,' Fliss cut in, her eyes boring into him. 'So I'll thank you not to try to oppress this hard-working woman any further.'

Raising a cynical eyebrow, Tim held her forceful gaze for a moment then turned his attention back to the old woman beside her.

Dolly gave him a toothy grin. 'But if 'e turns up, Inspector, I'll be sure to tell him that you're looking for 'im.'

Tim glanced at the housekeeper's bulging shopping bags. 'You've had a successful trip to the shops.'

'Just a few midweek bits, that's all,' Dolly replied. 'You 'ave to grab 'em when you sees 'em nowadays.'

Tim picked up his hat. 'And you've struck it lucky, I see.' She looked puzzled. 'A tin of Nescafé.'

He indicated the eight-ounce tub of coffee on the dresser and Dolly's puzzled expression vanished.

'Mrs Lavender has told you all she knows, Inspector,' said Miss Carmichael. 'So I'll show you out.'

Tim followed her as she retraced her steps to the front door and opened it.

'Show me off the premises, don't you mean?' he said, stepping through it.

'Your words not mine.' She gave him the sweetest of

smiles. 'But I won't stand idly by while a working-class sister is grilled by an establishment enforcer, so goodbye, Inspector.'

Feeling his hackles and several choice words rising up, Tim matched her unfriendly expression and raised his hat.

'Miss Carmichael.'

Repositioning his hat, Tim turned sharply on his steel-tipped heels and marched down the rectory's front steps, but as he reached the path he turned back.

'By the way, Miss Carmichael,' she looked up at him, 'I don't know if it's escaped your notice, but working-class women don't live in huge houses with half an acre of garden around them. Nor do they have a housekeeper who shops for and prepares their meals.'

Fliss gasped as her captivating eyes flew open and her jaw dropped.

'Unlike those who have such advantages,' Tim continued, letting his irritation at her patronising attitude show in his eyes, 'they have never *just* been wives and mothers but have had to work at menial jobs to keep a roof over their families' heads and put food on the table.'

Having had the satisfaction of wiping the judgemental smile off Fliss's face, Tim touched the brim of his fedora with his fingertips again then marched down the path. This time he didn't turn back.

Chapter seven

'THERE YOU ARE, Fliss,' said Prue, placing a metal tray with two cups and two plates with a slice of cake on the circular wrought-iron table. 'That will warm you up.'

'Thank you,' said Fliss, picking up the cup nearest to her and wrapping her gloved hands around it.

She certainly hoped it would chase away the chill, because even though it was the middle of the afternoon and the sun was shining weakly, the temperature couldn't have been much more than forty degrees.

It was Sunday, five days since she'd arrived home, and Prue had persuaded her to catch a train the four stops on the District Line for a stroll along the river and to gaze at the grey walls of the Tower of London. Indeed, gaze at the walls was all they could do as, like every other building in the capital, the eight-hundred-year-old fortress had been given over to the war effort. Inside the forbidding stone walls, the ancient citadel had reverted to one of its earlier roles: that of a prison; a number of unnamed prisoners were currently being held there for treason against the realm.

Having enjoyed their walk, the sisters had managed to nab one of the last free tables clustered around the

WVS mobile canteen parked on the cobbled area known as Tower Hill on the west side of the medieval castle. High above their heads in the bright-blue winter sky and tugging at its tether was a silver-grey barrage balloon christened Bill by the locals.

In spite of a couple of columns of black smoke spiralling skywards after the previous night's air raid, those out for a Sunday-afternoon stroll did their best to remain jolly.

Of course, men's Sunday suits and women's best outfits had been replaced by the khaki and navy uniforms of the Home Guard and air raid wardens respectively. There was even the odd flash of light blue as airmen stationed in airfields close to London took a well-earned afternoon's leave.

However, there were a few like Fliss and her sister who'd decided to dress up a bit. In Prue's case this was a square-shouldered overcoat that covered her wine-coloured woollen dress, while Fliss wore slacks and a jumper under her three-quarter-length camel-coloured duffel coat. Of course, wearing trousers on a Sunday had earned her a censorious look from her mother when she'd arrived for breakfast.

'They only had carrot cake,' said Prue, as she tucked her coat under herself and sat down.

'That's all right, I suppose we should be thankful it's not potato cake as spuds seem to be in everything else,' Fliss replied. 'Mrs Lavender served up potato scones for afternoon tea the other day, much to Mother's annoyance.'

'I bet. So?' said Prue, looking at her sister.

'So what?' Fliss asked.

Prue rolled her eyes. 'Have you heard from Giles?'

The raw pain of her feckless so-called fiancé's betrayal gnawed at Fliss again.

'No, I haven't,' she replied. 'He's probably too busy poking Gwen.'

Prue's eyes flew open. 'Fliss!'

'Well, that's what I caught him doing red-handed – or should I say bare-arsed? And I'm just so ...' Taking a deep breath, she pressed her lips together.

'Upset?'

'No, blasted well angry!' Fliss replied, as the pain of Giles's betrayal twisted tighter. 'And mostly with myself for being so blooming stupid?'

Prue took a sip of tea. 'Have you told Mother yet?'

'Not yet,' Fliss replied. 'It's bad enough having her constantly lecturing me about how God has ordained our station in life so therefore socialism is flouting His will, without giving her the opportunity to remind me that she'd warned me not to associate with a bunch of ne'er-do-wells like Giles and his kind.'

'At least she hasn't banned you from the rectory,' said Prue.

Fliss gave her sister a sympathetic look.

Their mother had always harboured the dream that one of her daughters would follow in her footsteps and become a clergyman's wife. However, when it became abundantly clear after Fliss staged a protest in the school chapel in support of the General Strike at eleven that it wasn't likely to be her, Marjorie had pinned her hopes on her younger daughter.

And when she met David Harmsworth, St Winifred's curate, when they arrived last May it looked as if her long-held ambition was about to be realised. That was before railway engineer Jack Quinn stepped into Prue's life and stole her heart.

For her daughter to marry an ordinary working man would have been bad enough for Marjorie to swallow, but when she found out that Jack was a divorcee she nearly had an apoplectic fit. The upshot was that she told Prue that if she married Jack she would never be allowed over the threshold of the rectory again, which was why Prue was now sporting a wedding ring and living with her sister-in-law, Rosie Stapleton.

'Honestly, once I have a job—'

'What do you mean "once I have a job"?' cut in Prue.

'Well, I can't very well stay at the *Clarion*, can I? Not after ...' The scene in the flat's bedroom loomed into Fliss's mind and tears pinched the corner of her eyes. 'Anyway, I sent Giles my resignation on Friday so it should be sitting on his desk when he gets in on Monday morning, and when I do find a new job I might delve into my savings and find a room somewhere local.'

'Well, good luck with that, Fliss,' said Prue. 'With half the housing stock east of the City flattened or damaged, rent prices have gone through the roof – that's if you can even find anywhere.'

'Well, I'll cross that bridge when I come to it,' Fliss

replied. 'For now I've made a start by applying for a job at the *East London Chronicle*. I've heard nothing so far, but I'm hopeful. If not I'll try my luck at the *Hackney Gazétte* or even the *Stratford Standard* just to tide me over until I can land a post at one of the dailies in Fleet Street.' She gave Prue a plucky smile. 'Who knows, I might even try my hand at war reporting.'

'But don't you need some sort of army experience for that?' said Prue.

'Well, I've been crossing swords with Mother for the past ten years, so surely that's enough battle experience to face any foe,' Fliss replied. 'In the meantime, I might pitch a story about the men working day and night to keep shops fully stocked to the *Mirror* or *Herald* or perhaps the *Picture Post*, just to get my foot in the door. They usually pay a couple of quid for stuff like that. I've also spoken to Hester about an article on her work and research in the hospital. You know, "A doctor rescued from the clutches of Nazi evil contributing to the War effort". What do you think?'

'Sounds like the perfect antidote to the reports coming out about the North African campaign,' Prue replied, raising her cup to her lips again. 'I'm glad Rob's still in Scotland and not part of the assault on Benghazi.'

Rob was, in fact, Captain Robert Carmichael, their older brother, who was stationed somewhere in Scotland with the King's Own Infantry, ready to repulse the enemy should they try to invade across the North Sea from Norway.

'And it's because of all the grim news about that and the blooming U-boats that the press are crying out for good-news stories to put in their papers,' continued Fliss. 'One thing that will help to sell it is that Hester is very good looking – editors always want a pretty face on the page. And who knows? If it gets accepted, I might even pitch one about your bomb shelter under St Winifred's. "Ancient parish stood up to Cromwell and now does the same to Hitler",' she added, sweeping her hand in an arch to indicate the banner headline.

'Perhaps the nationals would be interested in "Rectory's daughter quizzed by CID",' said Prue, sweeping her hand across in a similar fashion.

Fliss's eyes stretched wide with surprise. 'Who told you?'

'For goodness' sake,' laughed Prue. 'At least three people when I was shopping in the Waste Market yesterday afternoon.'

'And how did they know as he wasn't in uniform?' said Fliss.

Prue raised an eyebrow. 'I think it's fair to say that members of the local constabulary are well known to the people around here.' Lifting her cup, Prue blew across the top. 'Especially if they are CID.'

'Well, if you must know he was actually after Mrs Lavender,' Fliss explained. 'Apparently he wants to have a word with her son Tommy.'

'I imagine half the police force in East London would like to have a word with Tommy Lavender. Who was he?'

'A DI Wallace,' said Fliss. 'From Wapping. Do you know him?'

Prue shook her head. 'Can't say I do. What was he like?'

'Actually, he was rather handsome,' said Fliss, an image of Inspector Wallace's angular face and astute brown eyes flashing across her mind. 'But you know the old saying: "Handsome is as handsome does".'

Prue looked puzzled.

'Well firstly, he practically barged his way in,' said Fliss, ignoring the twinge of guilt at the exaggeration. 'Then he made a sarcastic remark about women fainting at the sight of piano legs after I pointed out that we were now breaking free from the shackles of domesticity, and he practically called dear Mrs Lavender a liar when she said she didn't know where her son was. And on top of that he had the nerve to imply that because I was brought up in a rectory, I had no idea about the real lives of working-class women, which is completely untrue.'

A smile tugged at the corner of her sister's lips.

'All right,' Fliss continued, 'I admit he may not be completely wrong, but it's not my fault I grew up in a vicarage twice the size of the average house, is it? Or that we have a daily help, hot running water and a refrigerator? But once I woke up to the injustices of the class system, haven't I worked tirelessly to right that wrong?'

'Yes, you have, Fliss,' Prue agreed.

'And aren't I particularly passionate about improving women's lives, such as better family planning and maternity service?'

'For as long as I can remember,' Prue replied, raising her cup to her lips.

DI Wallace's cynical expression rose up again in Fliss's mind and her brows drew together.

'So what right did this state lackey have to lecture me about what working-class women do and don't do?' asked Fliss.

'None at all, Fliss,' said Prue. 'And I'm sure you'll tell him so when you next see him.'

'I certainly will,' snapped Fliss. 'Although to be honest if I don't see him again this side of eternity it will be too soon.'

Running through exactly what she might say to DI Wallace if she ever had the misfortune to run into him again, she buried her nose in her cup.

'Looks like we're in for some entertainment, Fliss.'

Fliss turned to see a small crowd gathering on the other side of the cobbled space. 'What's happening?'

'This area of Tower Hill is the East End's version of Hyde Park's Speakers' Corner, so it could be anything from an acrobat to a street preacher,' Prue replied. 'The last time I was here it was an escape artist who wrapped himself in chains. Although judging from the banner that's just gone up, it looks as if it's one of your friends this afternoon.'

Fliss followed her sister's gaze and saw a Labour Party banner fluttering in the winter breeze.

'If you've finished your tea, Fliss, we could go and see what they have to say,' Prue suggested, placing her empty cup back on the tray.

Returning their crockery to the WVS mobile canteen, the two sisters made their way across to the crowd. They came to a halt as the young chap standing on a stout box was getting into his political stride. Although he was smartly dressed in a Home Guard uniform, Fliss couldn't help but think that a school uniform would have been more in keeping with his fresh-faced looks.

The Stepney and Wapping Branch of the Labour Party banner behind the youthful political orator was being held upright by a couple of men, with a few others standing alongside.

'So, my brothers and sisters,' said the young Home Guardsman, gazing around at his audience, 'unlike previous conflict, this war against Hitler and his Nazi regime – as well as being fought on battlefields on far distant shores – is being fought in every home in this land.'

'Well said,' shouted Fliss, clapping loudly.

After a second or two those around her joined in.

'A Member of Parliament in the making, I shouldn't wonder,' whispered Prue, joining in with the applause.

Fliss nodded.

'And it looks like he has the branch committee behind him, too,' Prue added, indicating the group of men standing alongside the banner holders.

Fliss's attention shifted from the budding politician to his supporters. Although they were all wearing the same worn cord trousers, donkey jackets and leather caps, one in particular caught Fliss's eye. Hardly surprising, really, as he stood half a head taller than his companions and the bright winter sun had turned his curly rust-coloured hair to burnished bronze.

'This is the people's war,' continued the speaker as the ovation subsided. 'And it should be the people's peace, and only the Labour Party can guarantee it will be. Start now and join Labour's fight so we can be—'

'The Labour Party!' shouted a man on the other side of the crowd. 'You politicians are only in it to line your own pockets.'

'That's not true,' the young man shouted back, a hot flush colouring his beardless cheeks. 'My father is the Member of Parliament for Manchester—'

'Well then, that's wot I was saying,' interrupted the heckler. 'His old man's doing nicely on the old gravy train and so now 'is nipper wants to jump on board.'

A couple of people clapped, but they were drowned out by murmurs of 'belt up', 'pipe down' and 'put a sock in it'.

'It's a free country, ain't it? So I can say wot I like,' shouted the troublemaker.

Fliss frowned. 'Under the Labour Party the workers will be properly rewarded for their toil, not like the Tories, who prop up the industrialists and aristocrats who exploit and oppress the workers,' she shouted.

The agitator, a stout, unshaven man wearing a shapeless overcoat, turned his beady eyes on Fliss. 'And you can shut your gob an' all, you toffee-nosed tart.'

'Now, sir,' shouted the young man on the soapbox,

'I'd ask you not to address the young lady in such a—'

'And you,' the agitator jabbed his grubby finger at Fliss, 'should get back in the kitchen where you belong, cos I don't need no bloody la-di-da bint to learn me.'

Prue tugged at her sleeve. 'Don't argue with him, Fliss.'

'Well, it seems you do,' Fliss snapped back, mentally rolling up her sleeves and preparing to do battle. 'Weren't the working people of this country promised "a Land fit for Heroes" after the last war? And what did you get? Years of mass unemployment, hunger marches, and you still have to scrap a few coppers together before calling a doctor.'

Many of those standing around Fliss murmured their agreement and there was a ripple of applause.

'So if you don't want history to repeat itself then make sure you stop the Conservatives putting the yoke back on our necks again by voting Labour,' Fliss shouted, pulling herself up to her full five-foot seven. 'Now if you don't mind, we'd like to listen to the young man on the rostrum not some old misery like you. So clear off.'

'Bill,' said Harry under his breath as the Labour Party's new golden boy started speaking again, 'could you and Micky go and have a quick word with our gobby comrade.'

Bill Roland, who was standing behind him, murmured his assent, then he and the man alongside him moved away.

As they sidled through the crowd to deal with the heckler, Harry's attention returned to the young woman who'd taken him to task.

He'd noticed her, of course, when she and her friend first stopped at the edge of the crowd. Truthfully, it was hard not to. It wasn't only that she had a face straight off a fashion magazine, but she was at least four inches taller than the other women gathered around. To be fair, he'd also noticed the giggly blonde who had threaded her way through to the front and was more his usual type.

However, when she stepped forward and gave the oaf troublemaker a good telling-off, he'd taken a closer look. It was clear as soon as she opened her mouth that she wasn't from anywhere around here, and although he couldn't place it, she definitely had a soft and rather pleasant county accent. What really surprised him was that despite obviously being a posh totty, she'd actually managed to get her tiny brain around socialism.

As the earnest lad dressed in Home Guard uniform continued to set out his vision of a Labour Party land of milk and honey, the dark-haired looker had nodded agreement and clapped enthusiastically.

After his final rallying call for those listening to join the Labour Party and be soldiers in the fight to build a workers' paradise, the fresh-faced speaker thanked his audience then stepped down from his soapbox.

Leaving his fellow Party members to tidy away the banner and hand pamphlets out to the dispersing audience, Harry strolled across to where the young woman and her friend were standing.

'Good afternoon, ladies,' he said, smiling at them briefly before focusing on the taller of the two. 'Hope you don't think as how I'm out of order, but I admired the way you stood up to that chap in the crowd.'

'Thank you,' Fliss replied, giving him the sort of frank look he wouldn't have expected of a skirt, even a posh one. 'But I've argued down bigger and better than him before.'

Harry's eyebrows rose.

She laughed. 'You should have heard me tell the Liberal Party chap his fortune at the open rally in Birmingham's Bullring last year.' She thrust out her woolly gloved hand. 'Felicity Carmichael, Fliss. And this is my sister, Mrs Quinn,' she added, indicating the auburn-haired women with the rounder face standing next to her.

'Harry Gunn,' he said, taking her hand in a firm grip. 'So you approve of our speaker, then?'

'He certainly knew his stuff,' she replied. 'Who is he?'

'Some chap called Anthony Wedgwood Benn,' Harry replied, pleased that she was just as tasty-looking close up. 'His old man was a liberal MP somewhere, but don't let his name fool you; he's pure red flag. And once he gets a bit more experience under his belt, he'll do just fine. The top brass of the Party has high hopes for him standing as an MP at the next election, whenever—'

'Oi, oi, Harry,' shouted one of the men who had been holding the banner. 'Shake a leg!'

'We ought to get going too,' said Prue. 'Nice to meet you, Mr Gunn.'

'You too, ladies.' Looking at Fliss, Harry's mouth widened into more than just a purely friendly smile. 'And I hope I run into you again soon, Miss Carmichael.'

A car hooter blasted.

Raising his hand in acknowledgement, Harry turned and strolled over to where the lorry stood idling at the kerb. Making his way around to the front passenger door, Harry jumped in.

Fred Matlock, who had a mop of unruly straw-coloured hair and a squint in his right eye, was sitting behind the wheel.

'I might have guessed,' he said, as Harry settled in his seat. 'Trust you to be chatting up totty while we do all the work.'

'With her country accent and the fact that the clobber on her back probably cost more than a docker's weekly wage, I don't think Miss Felicity Carmichael would take kindly to being described as totty, ' Harry grinned, ' but I wouldn't say no.'

As the bullets pinged off Will Hay's suit of armour, those around Tim roared with laughter. He just managed an amused smile.

The film was coming to its somewhat predicable end, and Tim – who was sitting in the ninepenny seats in the Ritz Cinema, St Stephen's Road – reckoned it must be close to nine thirty. As its rather grand facade and entrance hall testified, this was one of the oldest cinemas in the area and was still referred to by some of the neighbourhood's senior residents as the Old Ford Picture Palace. Built at a time when films were in their infancy, the interior of the cinema emulated a music hall theatre, with plaster cherubs high on the walls and floral garlands draped beneath. The seats, too, were fashioned in the same way and less than comfortable for someone of Tim's height and breadth.

One of the actors on the screen staged an exaggerated pratfall up the stairs and the audience roared again.

Leaning back in his seat, Tim glanced at his companion for the evening's entertainment, Angela McEvoy. Although in the flickering reflection of the silver screen she looked colourless, she was in fact a strawberry blonde with hazel eyes and a turned-up nose. She was, as always, prettily dressed, with a flowery frock beneath her dusky pink coat, topped off by a little raspberry-coloured hat.

They'd met when he and a small detachment had raided the offices of a uniform factory in Spitalfields to arrest the owner for claiming war-work wage subsidies for non-existent workers. Angela had been one of the typists working in the accounts department and had given them access to the ledgers in the company safe.

That was just before Christmas and they had been walking out, air raids and his shifts permitting, once or twice a week ever since.

A blast of jolly trumpets signalled that the film had

finally come to an end and the titles rolled. The lights went up as the audience got to their feet, causing the dull thud of dozens of seats flipping back into place to fill the space. Tim stood up and after gathering her handbag together, Angela did the same. They then picked their way over the discarded sweet wrappers, cigarette butts and occasional apple cores to the end of the row.

Ignoring the opening bars of the National Anthem blaring out from the speakers high on the walls, Tim followed Angela towards the aisle where they joined the stream of people making their way out.

Within moments they were through the auditorium doors and out into the foyer. Angela joined the stream of women headed for the Ladies and emerged a few minutes later as Tim was putting on his coat. Taking his pencil torch from his pocket, they emerged from the warmth of the cinema into the damp February evening.

Angela took his arm as Tim pointed the narrow beam of light onto the pavement, joining the dozens of other couples heading home past the boarded-up shops in Roman Road.

'That was good fun, wasn't it?' Angela said, as they made their way along the street.

'It was.'

She laughed. 'You're a terrible liar.'

Tim certainly was. However, it could have been worse. After all, he might have ended up having to sit through a musical or one of those dreadful Old Mother Riley films instead.

He forced a smile. 'Well, the truth is I'm not a big Will Hay fan, but I'm obviously in the minority.'

She squeezed his arm. 'Well, next time you can choose what we see.'

'Or we could hop on the tram to Stratford and go dancing at the Regal,' Tim replied, hoping that for once she might agree.

Even in the dark of the blackout he could see her frown. 'I'd love too but you know how Mum and Dad worry if there's an air raid and I'm too far from home.'

Angela was an only child of rather over-protective parents, which was why they always stayed this side of the River Lee when they went out. A small bubble of annoyance started in Tim's chest, but he cut it short. Given what his own father had been like, he couldn't very well criticise a man for caring too much about his child.

They turned into Dane Place then wove their way around the various turnings and streets lined with two-up two-down workmen's cottages constructed in the last century. Although Bow was some four miles from the Luftwaffe's main target in this part of the capital, the London and Royal docks, it was just a stone's throw from the industrial area on either side of the River Lee and Stratford's shunting yards beyond. Therefore, like every other street you walked down, the smell of charred beams filled the air and piles of rubble punctuated the neat rows of houses where someone's home once stood.

However, as they passed beneath the London and

North Eastern railway arch into Coburn Road, Tim laughed.

'What?' asked Angela.

'Oh, nothing really,' he replied. 'I was down here a week or so back on duty.'

'What, were you arresting some fiendish German spies or some blood-thirsty murderer?' she asked, squeezing his arm playfully.

'Nothing so exciting, I'm afraid,' Tim replied, as from nowhere an image of Fliss Carmichael materialised in his mind. 'Although, my stroll home afterwards was eventful. I happened to be walking home on Stepney High Street when I spotted ...' He told Angela about meeting Miss Carmichael in St Winifred's churchyard as they made their way along the street.

'Drunk!' she said, when he'd finished.

'Very,' chuckled Tim.

In the gloom, Angela's lips tightened. 'How deplorable.'

'Well, to be fair, she *was* very upset,' said Tim, remembering Fliss perched on a gravestone swinging a bottle of gin around.

'Even so,' Angela continued, 'getting drunk in a public place is hardly very ladylike, is it?'

'Well, from what I've seen of Miss Carmichael I think she would take that as a compliment,' Tim replied.

Angela looked at him sharply. 'You've met her again?'

'Yes, by pure coincidence ...' Tim told her about his visit to the rectory.

'What a thing to say.' Angela squeezed his arm and

looked adoringly up at him. 'I don't blame you for being annoyed.'

'Annoyed! I was furious,' said Tim, as Miss Carmichael's words stung him afresh. 'It was her high-handed assumption that I wouldn't have heard of the precious little rabble-rousing rag she worked on that riled me.'

Angela tutted as they turned into Norman Grove, where she lived.

Lapsing into silence, as he'd done for the past week, Tim replayed the scene in the rectory's kitchen between himself and the opinionated Miss Carmichael.

'Here we are,' said Angela, cutting through his thoughts, as his imagination had moved him past arguing with the undeniably attractive revolutionary and onto something much more ... conjoined.

He looked around to find he was standing in front of the three-storey house where Angela lived.

Tim turned to face her. 'Sorry, I was miles away.'

'I could tell,' she replied.

Clearing his mind, Tim took Angela in his arms. 'Will I see you next week?'

Placing her hands on his chest, she smiled up at him. 'If you want to.'

Dipping his head, he kissed her lightly on the lips. 'Does that answer your question?' In the faint light from his torch, she smiled her assent. 'I'll telephone.'

'Make sure you do.' Standing on tiptoes, she kissed him briefly then slipped out of his arms and trotted up the half-dozen steps to the smartly painted front door. Halfway up, she stopped and turned around.

'This Miss Carmichael ... Is she pretty?'

'Pretty!' Tim forced a light laugh. 'I suppose she is, but not like you are.'

Beaming, Angela trotted back down and gave him a quick peck on the cheek, then ran up the stairs again and entered the house.

In the almost impenetrable blackout Tim stared after her then, as it seemed to with annoying regularity, the image of Fliss Carmichael, with her bold brown eyes, sculptured cheekbones and mobile mouth, floated back into his mind. No, Fliss Carmichael wasn't pretty at all. She was strikingly beautiful.

Chapter eight

STUDYING THE LINE of text she'd just typed, Fliss took the pencil from behind her ear and used the rubber end to brush gently through the word 'large'.

It was just after ten thirty on Friday, and almost two weeks since she'd arrived back at the rectory.

She was sitting at her typewriter under the window in the back parlour finishing off an article about the Shadwell branch of the WVS and their newly acquired mobile canteen donated by the America Red Cross.

Well, when she said her typewriter, it was really her father's from the rectory study. It was a Royal and so old that Noah must have typed the passengers list for the ark on it. As her father wrote everything by hand, it had been moved from his desk to the basement, where it had been gathering dust ever since.

However, after giving it a thorough clean, squirting sewing-machine oil over the moving parts and replacing the ribbon, it was more than adequate, even if the strikers occasionally jammed together.

Gripping the pencil between her teeth, Fliss repositioned the carriage and typed 'huge' over the smudge.

The door opened and her mother, still in her brown tweed coat and brown felt weekday hat, walked in.

'I'm back.'

'So I see,' Fliss replied, slotting the pencil back behind her ear. 'Did your Mothers' Union meeting go well?'

Marjorie sighed. 'As well as can be expected,' she said, pulling off her gloves. 'But honestly, I don't know why the members have to bring their babies and toddlers with them.'

'I suspect the clue is in the name, isn't it, Mother?'

Marjorie gave her a cool look. 'Don't be tiresome, Felicity; you know exactly what I mean. How am I supposed to conduct business if I can hardly hear myself speak? Did anyone telephone for me while I was out?'

'Not that I know of,' Fliss replied.

'Good,' said Marjorie. 'I want to get a letter to dear Robert in the afternoon post so let's hope it stays that way, at least until lunch. I'll be across the hallway in the main lounge if there's an absolute emergency; otherwise, I am *not* here.'

She left the room and Fliss returned to her task, but she'd only typed two lines when the doorbell rang.

Fliss's lips lifted slightly at the corners. You learn very early on when you live in a vicarage or rectory that every day – and often well into the evening – it is like Piccadilly Circus, with people 'just popping in' to quickly and often not so quickly ask the vicar something.

She heard Mrs Lavender's footsteps padding across the hall's floor tiles, followed by the sound of the front door opening and a male voice. Thinking no more of it, Fliss's attention returned to the scribbled shorthand jottings on her notepad. However, as she placed her fingers onto the keys the door opened, and Mrs Lavender lumbered in.

'This gentleman wants to see you,' she announced.

Despite her never wanting to lay eyes on him again, for one ridiculous moment Fliss wondered if it might be Inspector Wallace, but then Giles strode into the room.

Slowly rising to her feet, Fliss stared dumbly across at him.

Instead of his hair skimming his collar it had been neatly trimmed. He was cleanly shaven, too, and wearing his rarely seen suit and tie. But what made Fliss's eyes stretch wide with surprised was the fact he was carrying a bunch of half a dozen red roses.

He stood motionless for a moment then thrust out the flowers. 'Happy Valentine's Day, sweetheart.'

She didn't move.

He took a half-step forward and offered her the flowers. 'I'm really sorry, Fliss, and I hope that this small token goes some way to make amends.'

Images of Giles and Gwen loomed in her mind, causing the bitter hurt of their betrayal, which was slowly fading, to surge through her again.

She studied his peace offering for a moment then took the flowers from him.

Relief loosened her so-called fiancé's slender shoulders and he smiled. 'Thank goodness. I know when you—'

Silencing him with a glacial look, Fliss marched to the fireplace and dumped the flowers in the wastepaper bin.

'What the hell are you doing?' he shouted. 'They cost me bloody five bob.'

'Well, you should have saved your money or given them to Gwen, shouldn't you?' Fliss yelled back, the pain of that afternoon ripping at her heart afresh.

He racked his fingers through his light-brown hair. 'Look, I said I was sorry, didn't I?'

'That's all right then, is it, Giles?' Fliss yelled. 'You pitch up here after a couple of weeks and—'

'I would have come sooner but I thought I'd give you time to get over … you know,' he cut in.

'Screwing the office receptionist?'

He didn't reply.

'I'm sure you are sorry,' she yelled. 'Sorry you were caught, that is. And I doubt it was the first time either, was it?'

His gaze shifted slightly, giving her the answer. Fliss clenched her fists and dug her nails into her palms to keep the tears that burned in her eyes at bay.

'I didn't know what I was doing, Fliss?' he continued.

'That wasn't the impression I got from the door,' Fliss shouted.

'Gwen means nothing to me, Fliss. In fact, I'll sack her just to prove it,' he continued. 'I love you, Fliss, and doesn't everything we have together mean any—'

Fliss's ear-piercing scream cut across his words as the grief and fury since that afternoon burst up in her.

The door opened and her mother walked in.

'What on earth is—' She spotted Giles. 'Mr Naylor.'

Giles sighed with relief. 'Mrs Carmichael, thank goodness. Fliss is a bit upset because, well, frankly I've been a bit of a fool.'

'Putting two completely different shoes on is being a bit of a fool, Giles,' snapped Fliss. 'Sleeping with the secretary behind my back is being a complete bastard.'

Horror stretched Marjorie's face. 'Felicity!'

'No, Mrs Carmichael,' he said. 'Fli … Felicity is right: I've been an utter cad. But I wasn't thinking straight and, well, not to put too fine a point on it, the young lady in question has been giving me the eye since she started at the office. The truth is I gave in to temptation.'

Shifting his attention back to Fliss, Giles's lean features transformed into his scolded-puppy expression. 'I'm begging you, my darling; please forgive me.'

He held out his hand. Fliss studied the long, slim fingers for a moment then her gaze returned to his face.

Crossing the space between them she looked him in the eyes for a moment, then, balling her right, first, smashed him in the mouth.

'You sneaked another woman into our flat and then humped her in *our* bed!' she screamed, oblivious of the pain across her knuckles as Giles recoiled from the blow. 'I'll never, ever forgive you. And in case you didn't get the letter I sent you last week, here's my resignation from the *Workers' Clarion* again,' she yelled, punching him a second time. 'Now get out!'

Giles dragged a handkerchief from his jacket pocket then placed it over his swollen lip and bleeding nose. Giving Fliss and her mother a shamefaced look, he skulked from the room.

'And I never want to see you again, ever,' Fliss screamed as the door closed behind him.

She stared at it for a moment then, with her shattered heart laying in a hundred pieces at her feet, she looked beseechingly at her white-faced mother.

Marjorie stared back at her for a long moment then clutched her hands dramatically to her bosom. '*Our* bed, Felicity?'

'I have to remark, my dear,' said the Reverend Hugh Carmichael, as he plunged his spoon into the pudding and custard in his bowl, 'that Mrs Lavender is a real treasure when it comes to searching out something a little special for lunch. That gammon is as good as anything I've ever tasted, and where on earth did she find the plums for this sweet?'

'Indeed, my dear, even if her dusting skills leave a lot to be desired,' his wife replied, which was the longest sentence she'd spoken in Fliss's hearing since Giles left an hour ago.

In fact, as the front door banged shut, Marjorie had swept out of the room.

Fliss had listened as her mother stormed upstairs before running up to her bedroom and throwing herself on the bed. With her head pounding, Fliss had stared blindly up at the gold satin lampshade until she heard her father return to the rectory some twenty minutes later.

It was now just after half past one and although she felt more like vomiting than eating, Fliss was sitting at the dining-room table opposite her mother, with her father in his usual seat at the top of the table.

Like much of the house, the room where the family took their meals had off-white paintwork and tired flowery wallpaper, but it had been brightened up somewhat by the many gilt-framed paintings of country and hunting scenes that were d'Apremont family heirlooms.

The large Hepplewhite sideboard, dresser and eighteen-seater table that dominated the room had also come down through the d'Apremont family. Although you wouldn't usually find such lavish fixtures in a clergy home, the majority of their furniture – along with the generous annuity that supplemented Fliss's father's modest stipend – were courtesy of Marjorie's wealthy maiden aunt who had lived on the family's vast estate in Lincolnshire.

'Did I tell you that Mr Harvey found a box of Victorian choral scores in the vestry?' Hugh asked.

'How exciting,' Marjorie replied, sounding anything but as she scooped what she called a lady's portion – half a spoonful – of her dessert.

'I intend to ask Mr Granger if perhaps we could use one or two of them during the Easter service.' Hugh scooped up a spoonful of pudding and custard. 'As it says in Psalm thirty-three, verse nine, "Praise the Lord with harp and an instrument of ten strings", or in our case St Winifred's forty-four pipe organ.' Her father's attention shifted to Fliss.

'You're very quiet today, Felicity,' he said, looking at her with concern.

She forced a smile. 'Am I?'

'Well yes, because you're usually chatting away about something or other,' he replied. 'Are you having trouble with your article about the docks?'

Fliss shook her head. 'No, no, it's just quite a lot of information.'

Resting his spoon in the empty bowl, he stretched across and placed his delicate hand over hers.

'Good,' he said, giving it a squeeze. 'Because it means you'll be with us for a while yet. But you've hurt your hand,' he said, noticing the raw skin where Fliss's knuckles had connected with Giles's front teeth.

'She shut it in a door,' said his wife.

Hugh's white-grey eyebrows drew together.

'You look a little peaky, too, my love, doesn't she, Mother?' Marjorie didn't reply. 'And you've hardly eaten a thing,' he continued, glancing at the bowl of untouched plum pudding and custard in front of her. 'Are you ailing?'

Fliss forced a smile. 'Just a little tired, that's all.'

'Ah, yes, this nightly bombing is taking its toll,' he replied. 'I did hope by now our government would have done something to stop all this fighting, and as it says

105

in Isaiah chapter two, verse four, "They shall beat their swords into—"'

'Aren't you meeting the archdeacon at the church at two o'clock, Hugh?' cut in Marjorie.

Fliss's father looked across at the grandfather clock in the corner and alarm flashed across his finely boned face.

'Indeed I am,' he replied, tearing the linen napkin from his dog collar. 'And thank you for reminding me, my dear. I do not want to be late, as he may have news of a new curate for St Winifred's.'

'I pray it is so,' Marjorie replied.

Rising to his feet, Hugh headed towards the door and left the room.

As the door clicked shut, Marjorie placed her spoon into her pudding bowl and looked across at Fliss.

'You do know that no man will marry you now, don't you, Felicity?' she said, fixing her daughter with a fierce stare. 'Not now you've been deflowered.'

'For goodness' sake, Mother.' Fliss gave a mirthless laugh. 'I'm not a medieval maiden who's been ravished.'

Fear flashed across Marjorie's face. 'You're not with child?'

'No, Mother, I am not with child, as you so quaintly put it.'

Placing her hand on her chest, her mother looked gratefully skywards.

'And I'm so grateful, in my hour of pain and need, to be comforted by such a kind, loving mother. What a solace it is to me to rest my head on your tender bosom.'

'Don't be tiresome, Felicity,' her mother snapped. 'This has nothing to do with love, it's to do with God's law and the Church's teaching on chastity and marriage. A bride's purity is a gift for her husband on their wedding night.'

Before she could stop herself, Fliss rolled her eyes.

'Oh yes, of course, I'm sure a woman saving herself for her husband is laughed at by your vagrant anarchists and communist friends,' her mother countered. 'But let me tell you this, Felicity Carmichael, no man, whoever he is, will ever want to marry soiled goods.'

From nowhere the image of Inspector Wallace flitted through Fliss's mind before evaporating.

'So now you know I've been living with—'

'Living in sin, Felicity,' her mother cut in. 'That's what it's called. The operative word being *sin*!'

'Well, Mother, now you've discovered I've been *living in sin* with Giles, are you going to throw me out like you did Prue?' Fliss asked in the same sharp tone.

'She chose to leave,' her mother replied.

'Yes, after you told her that if she married Jack Quinn she would never be allowed into the rectory again,' said Fliss. 'A very Christian attitude, I must say.'

'For goodness sake, Felicity!' snapped her mother. 'Your sister turned her back on a secure life as a clergyman's wife to marry a railway engineer.'

'Who she loves,' said Fliss.

Marjorie gave her an exasperated look. 'On top of which,' she continued, 'once she refused David's offer of marriage his honour compelled him to leave – he had

107

no choice but to find another church, leaving your father without a curate.' Her mouth pulled into a hard line. 'And no. I am not throwing you out, as you put it, Felicity. There's been enough gossip generated by your sister's actions without adding more.'

'Thank you,' said Fliss as some of the tension of the past couple of hours faded. 'I'll ring Ben at the *Clarion* and ask him if he wouldn't mid bringing the rest of my things from the flat over.' Fliss placed her napkin on the table and stood up. 'Now, if you'll excuse me, I've got an article to finish before I go to see Prue.'

As a white-painted horsebox with a red cross on the side denoting its war-time function whizzed down Stepney Way, Fliss turned left into the cobbled thoroughfare of Arbour Terrace. Like nearly every other street in the parish, it was lined on both sides with three-up and three-down terraced houses, with front doors that opened straight onto a narrow pavement.

Careful not to step in the newly scrubbed half-circles outside the houses, which seemed to be a feature peculiar to the area, Fliss continued along the side street towards her sister's house, the last but one on the right.

Once there, instead of knocking on the front door she slipped down the dank passageway between the house and its neighbour. Lifting the latch on the back gate, Fliss walked into the handkerchief-size yard, passing the women's bike resting under the kitchen window and the wringer stowed by the wall, and crossed to the back door.

Fliss pushed it open and stepped inside, a meaty smell from the oven filling the air. The kitchen was small but spotlessly clean, with a scrubbed table with four chairs tucked in around it and a highchair next to it. In the corner next to the dresser was an old-style deep-bodied pram in which Ellen Stapleton, Prue's five-month-old niece, was having her afternoon nap.

'Hello?' she said.

'In here,' Prue called through from the room beyond.

Fliss hooked her three-quarter-length coat onto one of the nails hammered into the back door then went through to the parlour.

The family's main room was just as spotless as the kitchen, from its cream-coloured antimacassars on the back of the sofa and chairs to the tiles around the cast-iron hearth. A box of toys was tucked in the corner and family photos lined the mantelshelf.

Prue, sitting on one of the fireside chairs, coals glowing in the hearth and cup of tea in hand, smiled as Fliss walked in.

'Goodness, I thought you'd got lost,' said Prue, putting down her drink on the coffee table next to her and picking up the teapot.

'Yes, sorry I'm late; there was a queue in the post office,' Fliss replied.

'There always is on a Friday, with army wives collecting their weekly allowance. Never mind, you're here now,' her sister said, as she poured Fliss's tea.

'No Rosie?' asked Fliss.

Handing Fliss a brightly coloured mug with a 'Jolly Southend' running around it, Prue shook her head. 'She's gone down to help Sister Martha with the Bring and Take clothing afternoon in the church hall. She's dug out a few of the clothes the boys have outgrown with her in the hope of replacing them. And I've got an afternoon with Ellen.'

'Who is, I can reliably report, still in the land of nod,' said Fliss. 'I see you've got a card from Jack.' She nodded towards the Valentine card with a heart and a bunch of forget-me-nots on the mantelshelf. 'At least I hope it's from Jack.'

Prue laughed. 'Yes, it's from Jack. It arrived in the morning post, which is quite a surprise considering how hit and miss the post has been. And I got a letter from Rob, too, saying he's coming home on leave soon.'

'Yes,' said Fliss, taking a biscuit from the plate on the tea tray, 'a letter from him arrived yesterday and Mother has talked about little else since.'

'I can't wait to see him,' said Prue. 'Do you think Lydia will descend on us too?'

'I should jolly well hope so,' said Fliss, settling herself in the chair opposite her sister. 'She is Rob's fiancée, after all'. She took a sip of tea. 'Let's just pray she only stays for a day or two.'

'Amen,' said Prue. 'Those trousers look very smart.'

Fliss sighed. 'That's not how Mother described them. Although now, unfortunately, she's found a much better

110

subject to berate me about.' She took a deep breath. 'Giles came to the rectory this morning.'

Prue's eyes stretched wide with astonishment. 'He's got a nerve, considering you left almost two weeks ago.'

'Apparently he wanted to come sooner,' Fliss replied, 'but thought it was best to let me "get over" it.'

Fliss told her about Giles's visit.

Her sister gave her a sympathetic look. 'So, Mother now knows about you and Giles living together …'

'"In sin, Felicity. That's what it's called,"' she said, mimicking her mother's landed gentry tones.

Prue grimaced. 'Oh dear.'

'"You do know that no man will marry you now, don't you, Felicity?"' Fliss continued in her mother's strident tone. '"Not now you've been deflowered." She said I was soiled goods.'

Her sister winced. 'I'm guessing Dad knows nothing of this.'

'No and I've been warned not to say a word as apparently "the shock would kill him". And it's so hypocritical. Mother knew Rob was more than just friendly with that farmer's daughter out Kimbolton way, but she didn't label him of being "soiled goods".'

'It's different for men,' said Prue.

'Well, it shouldn't be,' Fliss replied. She gave her an affectionate smile. 'And I appreciate you not saying "I told you so" about what a rotter Giles was.'

'I would be very happy to have been proved wrong,' Prue replied. 'Besides, I know how you felt about Giles.

And, to be honest, if there had been no other way of being with Jack than to live in sin, I would have moved in without a second thought.'

'Yes, but your Jack's not a cheating bastard like Giles,' Fliss replied. She took a sip of tea. 'Honestly, Prue, the way Mother's gone on you'd think I'd murdered someone rather than just, well, being stupid enough to trust a complete liar like Giles. All his rubbish about marriage being a way that a patriarchal society controls women and how capitalist marriage was a way of transferring property and power was just his way of having his blooming cake and eating it.' Pain squeezed Fliss's chest again, but she forced a bright smile. 'Anyway, there's no point crying over spilt milk. What's done is done. I'm at home now, so I have to put this behind me and get on with my life.' Fliss noticed her sister hadn't touched her drink. 'And because you've been listening to me drone on you've let your tea get cold.'

Prue gave her wan smile. 'Actually, I'm finding that recently tea makes me feel a bit sick.'

'You might have a bug or something,' said Fliss, scrutinising her sister. 'Have you seen the doctor?'

Prue nodded and a happy smile spread across her face. 'And the midwife at Munroe House.'

'Oh, Prue,' said Fliss. 'I'm so, so happy for you. How far are you?'

'Just over four months, according to the midwife I saw last week,' Prue replied.

'Last week!' shrieked Fliss. 'Why didn't you tell me immediately?'

'I wanted to tell Rachel first,' Prue replied.

'What did she say?'

Prue's smile widened. 'She said, "Could I have a sister, Auntie Prue, as I've already got a brother."'

Rachel was Prue's stepdaughter who lived with her mother Alma in East Ham. Alma, too, had remarried and had given birth to a baby boy on New Year's Day.

They both laughed then Fliss pulled a face.

'I have to say, Prue, I'm a bit surprised, as you and Jack had only been married two days before he had to report for duty.'

A wistful look appeared in her sister's eyes. 'I know, but we made the most of it.'

There was a small cry from the other room.

'Oh, well,' said Prue, swallowing a mouthful of tea and putting her mug back on the tray, 'I suppose I'd better get some practice.'

She rose to her feet and walked across to the kitchen door, but as she went to step through she paused and turned to her sister.

'Ignore Mother, Fliss,' she said. 'You will meet a man who will love you regardless of what has happened and, frankly, a man who won't, isn't worth marrying.'

Chapter nine

'So as you can see, Mr Longman,' said Fliss, looking across the desk at the chief editor of the *East London Chronicle*, 'I have a great deal of experience both in reporting events such as meetings and rallies and in writing features, articles and in-depth interviews.'

'Can you type?' asked Mr Longman, as the column of ash at the end of the cigarette clamped between his teeth lost it fight with gravity, sprinkling his shirt with pale-grey dust.

The man in charge of the *Chronicle*'s newsroom was a stout individual with thinning hair, a ruddy complexion and the dress sense of Harpo Marx. He was sitting on the other side of a desk, obscured by newspaper cuttings, an over-spilling ashtray and a couple of grubby coffee cups, and clutched Fliss's application letter in his chubby hand.

It was just after one thirty in the afternoon on Thursday 20 February and she was in the *East London Chronicle*'s offices, halfway down New Road. The offices were situated on the floor above a wholesale haberdasher and accessed by a set of cast-iron stairs that ran up the side of the building.

The main space looked very much like every newsroom she'd ever been in, with a dozen desks arranged back to back, a typewriter on each and a telephone at the end of a flex dangling from the ceiling between them. There was a long bookcase against one wall containing telephone, business and street directories. Next to it were three battleship-grey filing cabinets, presumably where useful snippets of information were filed away. A handful of framed certificates and photographs were dotted around the walls. The two men hammering away on the keys had looked up briefly as she walked in but continued in their tasks as she was shown to Mr Longman's office at the far end.

Having sent her letter just over a week ago, she had received a reply the day before yesterday apologising for the delay but explaining that due to a water pipe being fractured in a bombing raid, the main sorting office in Stepney had been closed so her application had only arrived on Monday.

Fliss was very relieved, as that day's post had also contained a rejection from both *The Lady* and *The Times* for interest pieces she'd recently submitted. What bothered her more than the sting of rejection was the loss of the three pounds she would have been paid, had one of the pieces been accepted. And she needed it because her notice at the Workers' Clarion had finished last Friday, along with her monthly twenty-eight-pound sixteen shillings wage.

'I'm proficient in shorthand, too, and I never miss a deadline,' continued Fliss. 'In addition, you can see my references from my editor at the *Workers' Clarion* are excellent.'

Pulling out the sheet behind her letter, Longman's deep-set eyes skimmed over it.

'As is the one from the *Bedfordshire Times and Independent*, too,' she added.

Shuffling the papers in his hand, Longman gave that a cursory glance too then put both down and looked across at Fliss from under his ragged brow.

'Ten pound ten and six a week with another half a crown if you have to do two out- of-hours reports in one week,' he said. 'Yeah or nay?'

Fliss blinked. 'Yes, thank you, Mr Longman, I would be—'

'Good. The hours are eight a.m. until six, with three-quarters of an hour for lunch,' he cut in. 'On call one weekend a month to cover any story that comes in. All copy ready to go to the printer by midday Thursday for the Friday-night run, and you'll be on a trial period for a month.'

'I understand,' said Fliss, trying not to let the relief flooding through her show on her face.

'When can you start?' he asked.

'Er …'

'You're not working your notice, are you?' he asked.

'No … No I'm not; I can start right away,' Fliss replied.

'Monday then. Eight o'clock sharp.' He thrust a scrap of paper at her. 'Here's your first assignment: some woman who's knitted a hundred pairs of gloves or hats or something as part of the war effort. Just a couple of hundred words for the women's page, and if you find she's under thirty with a decent boat race I'll send Larry our photographer down there later. Betty!'

The door opened and the smart middle-aged woman who had been sitting at the desk outside Longman's office put her head around the door.

'Yes, Mr Longman?'

'This is Miss Carmichael. She'll be starting here on Monday, so could you give her a quick tour?'

Standing up, Fliss took the note from him and slipped it in her pocket. 'Thank you,' she said, to the top of his glistening head.

She turned to the woman standing in the doorway, who beckoned her out.

'Nice to meet you, Miss Carmichael,' she said, as she closed the editor's office door.

'You too, and it's Fliss,' she said.

'And I'm Betty, as you no doubt gathered,' Betty said. 'I'm Sid's – that is, Mr Longman's – secretary and general dogsbody. Now follow me and I'll show you where you'll be sitting.'

Half an hour later, having been shown her desk and introduced to other two reporters, Fliss bade Betty farewell and made her way out of the door and down the metal stairs back to the street.

With her mind trying to find some interesting question about knitting for her first assignment, she stepped off the bottom rung but caught the heel of her left shoe in the grid. However, with her balance already forward in anticipation of her next step, Fliss hopped a couple of times then, just as she was about to land sprawled across the pavement, strong arms caught her and set her back on her feet.

Placing her hands on her rescuer's firm chest and with his arms still around her, Fliss looked up into a pair of warm brown eyes, as a hint of cologne tickled her nose. She had a moment of déjà vu then she came back to the here and now.

'Inspector Wallace,' she said.

A smile lifted one corner of his well-formed mouth. Letting her go, he bent down and retrieved her captured shoe.

'Miss Carmichael,' he said, handing it to her.

'Thank you.' She dropped the shoe on to the floor and slipped her foot into it.

Instead of the charcoal single-breasted suit and worn overcoat he'd been wearing when he called at the rectory, the tall and undeniably handsome officer of the law was rather snazzily dressed in a crisp white shirt under a navy suit and tie and a camel-coloured gabardine trench coat. His brown fedora was set at a rakish angle on his head.

'My pleasure,' he replied. 'Lucky I was passing. I'm on my way to Whitechapel station if you're going that way?'

'Er, yes I am,' Fliss replied, annoyingly flustered by his iron-like embrace.

Actually, she had planned to walk the twenty minutes back to the rectory, but she didn't want to seem churlish. Also, she intended to get her reporter's teeth into something much meatier than the women's column, so despite him clearly being a class traitor, it would pay her to have a friendly detective in her back pocket.

'So, have you been selling a story to the *Chronicle*?' he asked as they fell into step beside each other.

'No, actually. I've just been offered a post as one of their reporters,' Fliss replied, noticing in passing that although he'd shaved earlier, his five o'clock shadow was already visible.

'You've given up working for the *Workers' Clarion*, then?'

'Yes. The editor and I had creative differences.' Fliss's throat tightened a little as an image of Giles flashed through her mind. 'And Mr Longman offered me the job on the spot.'

'Congratulations,' said Inspector Wallace.

'Thank you,' she replied, oddly pleased at his endorsement.

'So you're leaving the cut and thrust of political argument and socialist discord to report council salvage drives, Boy Scouts' Bob a Job week and WVS knitting patterns,' he went on, a guileless expression on his angular face.

Irritation niggled at Fliss's chest, but remembering she was supposed to be keeping DI Wallace sweet, she bit her tongue and smiled as they crossed the road.

'It must be nice for your mother to have you at home again,' he said as they turned into Whitechapel Road.

'Oh, yes, my mother's thrilled to pieces,' said Fliss.

Inspector Wallace gave her a questioning look.

'Let's just say we don't exactly see eye to eye on a few things,' Fliss explained. 'Have you any brothers or sisters?'

Pain flitted briefly across his face. 'I had a younger brother, but he died.'

'I'm sorry,' said Fliss.

They lapsed into silence as they reached the edge of the kerb. With goods lorries, ARP trucks and rescue services vehicles whizzing back and forth, Inspector Wallace took Fliss's elbow gently as they crossed between the traffic in front of the London Hospital.

It was an antiquated courtesy and something Giles would have sneered at, but …

As they passed between a couple of market stalls, Fliss spoke again.

'I suppose you're on your way to investigate something or another,' she said.

'Actually, it's my day off,' he replied.

'I wondered why you were all dolled up,' Fliss said. 'Are you off to see a special someone, perhaps?'

'I am,' he replied with a private smile. 'Someone very special.'

Ridiculously, Fliss felt a little tug of disappointment, but she brushed it aside.

Of course, looking like that he was bound to have a special someone, and it was nothing to her anyway.

'And here we are,' he said, his deep voice cutting though her thoughts. 'Whitechapel station.'

'So we are,' said Fliss, giving him a bright smile.

They walked into the station and going down the half a dozen steps to the foyer Inspector Wallace turned to her.

'I'm heading to Liverpool Street, and I guess you are going the other way to Stepney Green.'

Fliss nodded.

Putting his hand in his pocket, Inspector Wallace went up to the ticket booth.

'One to Stepney Green,' he said, sliding over a couple of coppers and receiving a green ticket in return.

'There we are, Miss Carmichael, a tuppenny one,' he said, offering it to her.

'I'm not one of those women who needs a man to do everything for her, you know: I can buy my own ticket, Inspector,' she said, surprisingly aware that her fingers slid across his as she took it.

'I'm sure you can – and do a great many other things, no doubt – but I'm afraid I'm a bit old-fashioned.' He smiled and gestured towards the stairs leading down to the platforms. 'After you.'

Fliss headed towards the barrier, acutely aware of the inspector's tall figure half a step behind her. She showed her ticket to the inspector while the CID officer did the same with his warrant card and they passed through and stopped.

'Lovely to meet you again, Miss Carmichael,' he said.

Fliss smiled. 'You too.'

He tipped his hat then headed off towards the westbound platform but after a couple of steps he turned back to Fliss.

'Oh, I'm just wondering,' he said, a small frown creasing his brow, 'I don't suppose you've seen Tommy Lavender since I enquired about him at the rectory, have you?'

Fliss laughed. 'I thought you said it was your day off, Inspector?'

He gave a rumbling chuckle. 'But always on duty.'

'Well no, I haven't,' she replied. 'I'm sure his mother must have told him you wanted to speak to him so I'm surprised you've not yet caught up with him.'

He gave her a wry smile. 'I'm not.'

'I'll certainly remind him if I see him around but honestly, Inspector,' said Fliss, 'whatever you're after him for you're barking up the wrong tree because he and his mother are respectable people.'

Inspector Wallace gave her a mocking look. 'Aren't we all, Miss Carmichael?'

Tipping his hat again he strolled off towards the platform.

Having walked twenty minutes uphill in an early spring squall from Brentwood station, clutching a small bunch of flowers, Tim finally reached the towering wrought-iron gates of Warley Hospital. Whereas the rest of the country had been stripped of their ornate ironwork to make guns, tanks and aeroplanes, for safety's sake, a few places such as Warley were granted an exemption.

The main block of the hospital was housed in a Victorian mock-Gothic building made of red brick. However, the grandeur the architect had hoped to achieve was totally undermined by the grubby criss-cross-taped windows and the badly painted main doors.

Avoiding the newly formed puddles, Tim headed up the gravel driveway. With early daffodils bobbing in the spring breeze and the smell of wet in the air you, could almost forget there was a war on. Until you spotted the barrage balloons in the distance guarding Tilbury Docks and the oil refineries on Canvey Island, that is, or the half-dozen white London ambulances offloading the walking wounded who had been evacuated from central London hospitals into the north wing under the Ministry of Health's Emergency Hospital Service plan.

Taking the steps two at the time, Tim pushed open one of the heavy doors.

The redhead sitting at the reception desk in front of a brass plaque commemorating the founding members of Essex County Lunatic Asylum looked up as he walked in and grabbed the telephone. Tim strode past her and through the half-glazed door leading to the south wing.

If the reception area was chilly then the main passageway was positively glacial, complete with whistling winds and a smell reminiscent of the antelope house in London Zoo. A handful of men and women shuffled back and forth along the corridor; others leaned against the walls, staring blankly ahead. One woman had wedged herself up against a drainpipe and was twirling her hair, another lay silently crying on an abandoned hospital trolley.

With his footsteps echoing on the majolica tiles, Tim headed for Victoria Ward at the end of the corridor. Pressing the bell button beside the door, he waited for a couple of moments until the lock on the other side rattled and the door was opened by a middle-aged woman in a non-too-clean white overall.

Tim smiled. 'Good afternoon, Mrs Baxter.'

'Inspector Wallace,' she said, her pale eyes blinking rapidly behind gold-rimmed glasses. 'We weren't expecting you?'

They never were because he never told the ward staff when he was coming.

Tim walked onto the ward.

'Afternoon, Inspector,' called the sister as he passed her office on the right.

Tim acknowledged her with a short nod and then, holding his breath as he passed the sluice on his left, he headed for the recreation room at the far end which looked out over the gardens, where early cabbages and carrot tops sprouted in what had once been landscaped lawns – the hospital's part of the war effort.

He passed a selection of armchairs from which wizened old women swaddled in crocheted blankets stared blankly out at the tall curtainless windows, one or two cradling bald China dolls, and headed towards the wingback chair on wheels on the far side by the radiator.

As he gazed down at the lined face, shrunken cheeks and wispy white hair of the woman curled up in it, the wound on his heart that would never heal ached afresh.

If only he'd caught the tram instead of walking home; if only he hadn't offered to help the new apprentice or …

His lips twisted in a bitter smile. If only. Life was full of if onlys …

Tim stood motionless for a moment and then, perhaps aware of his presence, the frail woman in the chair turned her head and looked at him.

A pair of dark-brown eyes so like his own stared blankly up at him for a moment then what he hoped was recognition kindled a spark.

Pulling across a nearby straight chair, Tim sat beside her and took her bony, birdlike hand in his large one.

He smiled. 'Hello, Mum.'

Chapter ten

'SO, MRS APPLETON, have you always been a great one for knitting?' asked Fliss, her pen poised over her notebook.

'Oh, yes, ducks,' replied the motherly woman sitting opposite her, the length of knitting on her needles growing by inches as she spoke. 'My dear old mother taught me when I was knee high to a sparrow. And it's Florrie. Mrs Appleton makes me sound like me muver-in-law.'

It was Friday at the end of her first week as a reporter on the *East London Chronicle* and she was sitting in the cosy parlour of the first-floor, three-bedroom flat in Cressy Buildings where Florrie Appleton and her children lived.

By rights, she should have visited Florrie a few days before but when she walked into the office on her first day at the *Chronicle*, she learned that the East London Children's Hospital had had its nurses' home destroyed by a high-explosive bomb the night before. The locals had rallied around to find beds for the displaced nurses, and Mr Longman had sent her down there with strict instructions that she get the story ready for Thursday to go in this week's edition. Having spent all Monday afternoon and Tuesday visiting the good Samaritans of

Shadwell and Wednesday typing it up, she'd only got around to contacting Mrs Appleton via the telephone in the public house opposite on Thursday afternoon.

The phantom knitter of Stepney herself was a middle-aged woman of just over five foot in height and probably two-thirds of that in the beam. Although the area of the flat where Florrie and her husband Bill had raised four children was no bigger than the rectory's front and back lounges, the place was immaculately clean. It was also dotted with examples of its occupant's skill, with knitted antimacassars, cushion covers and placemats under photo frames and ornaments.

'Honestly, I've never known our mum without a pair of knitting needles in her 'and,' chipped in Maggie Smith, Florrie's eldest daughter, who lived across the landing with her three little ones. 'Mum used to knit us jumpers with double yarn in winter to keep us warm and then unwind 'em and reknit them as cardigans for the summer. I reckon every jumper was unravelled and made into summink else at least four times before it ended up in the rag bag and used for cleaning. Do you knit, Miss Carmichael?'

'I can manage a scarf, but nothing more involved than that, I'm afraid,' said Fliss, remembering her struggle with wool and needles as a youngster. 'So how many balaclavas have you made for our brave boys in the navy, Mrs Appl— Florrie?'

'Well now, to be honest, I can't really remember,' said Florrie. 'I started making them when our Kenny got called up and found himself on *HMS Unicorn* patrolling the Atlantic. I did a couple for 'im then a few of 'is mates wanted them and, well,' she raised her fair eyebrows and sighed, 'it sort of went from there.'

'We reckon it's about two hundred all in all, don't we, Mum?' said Maggie.

'I suppose,' her mother replied. 'But it don't seem something to make a song and dance about.'

'Well, I think my editor wants a story about what ordinary women are doing for the war effort while their menfolk are away fighting,' said Fliss.

Maggie rolled her eyes. 'I'll tell 'im what we're doing. Trying to find a blooming shop that isn't jacking up their prices.'

'You mean racketeering?' said Fliss.

'Daylight robbery is what I calls it,' said Florrie.

'And the market stalls are the worst,' added Maggie. 'They know there's nuffink in the shops, so they get 'old of stuff and sell it for twice the price. Seven pence for a tin of pilchard they were asking last week down Watney Street. Almost double what the government say they ought to be. And I'll tell you something else, Miss Carmichael, because of the cost of everything, some mothers with half a dozen mouths to feed and only half their 'usband's army pay to do it with are forced into selling their rations.'

'That's terrible,' said Fliss.

'I know,' said Maggie. 'I could tell you of at least half a dozen families practically living on spuds and turnips.'

'Have you reported it to the Food Inspector?' asked Fliss.

Maggie rolled her eyes again. 'We 'ave; 'undreds of time. They say they're going to look into it, but nothing happens. I ask you, what else can we do?'

Fliss closed her notebook with a snap. 'I'll tell you what we can do. We can join together and protest.'

'Ah, there we are, my dear,' said Fliss's father, as she walked into the rectory dining room. 'I said our Felicity would be along presently.'

With a willowy frame, thinning grey hair and light-blue eyes behind the thick lenses of his horn-rimmed spectacles, Fliss's father was what sprang into most people's minds when someone mentions a member of the clergy. Unlike his wife, who looked as if she could arm wrestle a docker, the Reverend Hugh Carmichael looked as if he would have to move around in a shower to get wet.

As always, when about his parish business, he was wearing a loose-fitting two-piece grey suit over his black clerical shirt, a stiff all-encompassing dog collar fixed with a stud at the back.

Looking up from her bowl of beef stew, Marjorie gave her daughter a sour look. 'You know dinner is at six, Felicity.'

It was, in fact, by the grandfather clock in the corner of the room, just four minutes past, but for the sake of familial peace Fliss decided not to point that out.

'Yes, I do, Mother,' she replied, hurrying across the room to the table.

'And how was your first week as the newest reporter at the *East London* er ...'Her father looked perplexed.

'*Chronicle*, Dad,' said Fliss. 'Very good. Mr Longman, the editor, is a bit gruff, but Betty and the two reporters seem friendly enough, plus I got paid today, which was very nice.'

It was. And very much needed, especially as she had depleted her post office saving account since arriving home, which would have to be replaced in time to pay her income tax in a few months.

Well, perhaps 'home' wasn't the correct word for this house, as this was the first time Fliss had spent more than a handful of nights in St Winifred's Rectory. Truthfully, like army children, clergymen's offspring were ecclesiastical nomads moving from vicarage to parsonage to rectory as their father's calling dictated. However, unlike many she'd lived in during her childhood at least the house her parents were now residing in was in London not in some rural backwater.

'And the reason I was slightly late this evening was because I had to finish an article,' she added.

'Anything exciting?' asked her father, cutting through a lump of meat with his knife.

'Not really, just knitting,' she replied, taking the seat opposite her mother.

'A very worthwhile housewifely pursuit,' said Marjorie, who had never held a pair of knitting needles in her life.

'But I did hear about something very interesting, which I'm going to follow up,' continued Fliss. 'Racketeering.'

'Shoddy business,' said her father. 'I believe our dear bishop himself condemned the practice as unchristian. And as it says in the Gospel of St Mark, "What profit is it to a man if he gains the whole world, and loses—"'

'Indeed, my dear,' interrupted his wife, mopping up a smear of gravy with the chunk of potato on her fork. 'And of course, to some extent St Mark was right, but when something people want is in short supply the cost of it rises. It's called business and it's what this country is built on.'

Fliss gave her mother a hard look. 'No, this country is built on the sweat and toil of millions of working people who have been exploited by self-enriching capitalists for the past three centuries,' she countered.

Marjorie rolled her eyes. 'Really, Felicity, do we have to suffer your half-baked socialist nonsense at every meal?'

'You do when you trot out the same old establishment rubbish, Mother,' Fliss replied, jabbing her fork at a morsel of beef.

Her father gave her a stern look and opened his mouth to remind her of the fifth commandment, no doubt, but her mother jumped in first.

'I would have thought, Felicity, after recent events with Giles, you would have come to your senses about all this utopian Bolshevik poppycock.'

The pain of Giles's betrayal threatened to rise up, but Fliss cut it short and matched her mother's chilly stare.

'Giles?' said her father, looking up from his plate. 'What about Giles?'

'If you remember, Dad, I told you two weeks ago that we'd parted company,' said Fliss.

'Ah, yes, now you mention it I do recall such a conversation.' Resting his knife on his plate, her father reached across and placed his slender hand over hers. 'As it says in chapter seven of Paul's first Epistle to the Corinthians, "If the unbeliever departs, let him—"'

'Well, thankfully he has departed, Hugh,' interrupted his wife again. 'I just wish the ridiculous communist notions our daughter has in her head had gone with him.'

'Well, whatever you dress it up as, charging people more for something than the Price of Goods Act says they should be sold at or selling rationed food to the highest bidder is immoral,' said Fliss. 'And I mean to do something about it.'

Marjorie looked up sharply. 'Do? Do what?'

Fliss smiled across at her mother. 'What ordinary people always do when they are being oppressed: protest.'

The dining-room door opened and Mrs Lavender, swathed in her wraparound apron, shuffled in.

'Mrs Haas is just sorting her children out in the kitchen, so is it all right if I pop off to the shelter, Mrs Carmichael?' she announced.

'Of course, Mrs Lavender, Felicity can do the dishes,' said Marjorie in her best vicar's-wife voice. 'And thank you, the stew was delicious.'

'I'm glad to hear it,' the housekeeper replied. 'I'll bid you all a very good night, then.'

'Good night, Mrs Lavender,' her mother replied as Dolly shuffled out. 'We all seem to have finished, so would you mind serving the pudding, Felicity?'

Laying her cutlery on her empty plate, Fliss rose to her feet. 'Sorry, Mother, I'm afraid I'm going to skip dessert as I have to leave just after a quarter past seven.'

'Surely you don't have to go to the shelter just yet,' said her mother. 'After all, the air raid siren hasn't even gone off yet. And what about the dishes?'

'Oh, I'm not going to St Winifred's shelter,' said Fliss, as she stepped out from the table. 'I'm going to an East London Labour Party meeting.' She gave her mother the sweetest of smiles. 'And as for the dishes, come the revolution, Mother, we'll all be doing our own dishes so you might as well get some practice.'

Chapter eleven

'SO IN CONCLUSION, comrades,' bellowed the stout man, gripping the edge of the mahogany lectern on the stage, 'although the war with the evils of Nazism forces us to collaborate with our class enemy the Tories, be assured that your Labour MPs are still working arduously to bring about a socialist Britain. Thank you very much.'

'Roll on the revolution,' shouted the man sitting along the row from Fliss.

Taking a crumpled white handkerchief from his jacket pocket, the guest speaker from Party headquarters mopped his glistening forehead, as a tall man in an ARP uniform stepped forward and shook his hand.

The thirty to forty people in the audience applauded and Fliss joined in.

She was sitting in the hall of the Working Lads' Institute, a solid red-brick Victorian building which she guessed had probably been built seventy or so years before. It was opposite the London Hospital and right next to Whitechapel railway station, where she'd said goodbye to the undeniably good-looking but completely insufferable Inspector Wallace.

To be honest, she'd heard better speakers, which was

a pity because as the Party official droned on about the many welfare changes Labour members of the National Government had forced their Conservative counterparts to adopt, Fliss's mind annoyingly returned to her recent encounter with the CID officer. Not so much what he said as the way his well-shaped mouth moved as he said it and his eyes sparkled. It was all very distracting when she was supposed to be supporting a comrade engaged in the struggle.

'Thank you, brothers and sisters, for giving Mr Mills such a warm East London welcome,' said the branch's chairman, his gaze running over his assembled comrades. 'Now, as always, refreshments are being served at the back of the hall. And please take a look at the new literature hot off the presses that our guest speaker has kindly brought with him tonight.'

'We meet again, Miss Carmichael.'

Fliss looked up and after a second or two the penny dropped. 'Mr Gunn,' she said, rising to her feet.

'Harry, please,' he replied, his big-boned face lifting in a friendly smile. 'It's nice to see you again, especially as I was hoping you might join us for one of our gatherings.'

To be honest, since she'd met him a few weeks before she hadn't given him a second thought, but now, with him standing before her, Fliss remembered that she'd been heartened to meet someone at last who recognised her as a kindred spirit in the class struggle. Unlike that cynical, insufferable oppressor of ordinary workers, Inspector Wallace.

135

'And you'll probably be seeing me each month now as I've moved back with my parents at the rectory,' she said, noting how the harsh strip light overhead cast deep shadows across his face.

He looked surprised. 'The rectory?'

'Yes, St Winifred's in Stepney Green; my father's the rector there,' she explained.

He studied her for a couple of seconds then a broad smile spread across his slightly freckled face. 'Let me buy you a cuppa, Miss Carmichael.'

'That would be lovely,' Fliss replied, smiling back. 'And it's Fliss.'

She sidestepped along to the end of the row.

'After you,' he said, indicating for her to go in front of him.

Fliss headed towards the back of the hall where a couple of women were pouring teas from a massive enamel teapot.

Strolling to the front of the queue, Harry smiled at the middle-aged woman with grizzled grey hair and an expression on her face like a haddock.

'I've got some committee business to attend to in a minute, so can I take a couple?' he asked, picking up a cup and saucer in each of his large hands without waiting for a reply.

He guided Fliss towards one of the cast-iron upright pillars that supported the ceiling.

'Can you hold this a mo'?' he asked, giving her his cup and taking a packet of Senior Service from his top pocket.

'So, are you the chairman or an official of the branch?' Fliss asked, shaking her head as he offered her one.

Lighting a cigarette, he returned the packet to his pocket.

'Naw, Gordon Potter over there is the bloke in charge.' He nodded at the ARP warden who had been on the stage as he took his cup back. 'I just muck in when I'm needed at branch. Besides, as the convener for the Transport and General Workers' Union in London Dock, I'm too busy keeping an eye on the bosses. But I make it my duty to make new members feel welcome, Miss Carmichael.'

'Well, I'm not exactly a new recruit, Harry,' she said. 'I've been a Party member for over six years and on the committee of the Pimlico branch. In fact, I was one of those who stormed into the Savoy's basement last September with Councillor Piratin to demand the Government open the underground so ordinary people can use them to shelter.'

Blowing a stream of smoke skywards from the side of his mouth, Harry looked impressed. 'Did you?'

'Yes, I did,' she said, giving him a prideful look. 'And nearly got arrested for assaulting a police officer, too.'

'Good for you. With something heavy, I hope,' Harry replied.

'Well, actually I didn't touch him, he fell backwards over a chair as I went towards him with a bottle in my hand,' admitted Fliss. 'So the station sergeant at Bow Street police station let me off with a caution.'

Harry laughed. 'So, apart from storming posh hotels, threatening the establishment lackeys with bottles and tackling hecklers, what else do you do?'

'I'm a newspaper reporter,' Fliss replied. 'I did work for …'

As they sipped their tea, she gave him a quick summary of her time on the *Bedfordshire Times* and then her work on the *Workers' Clarion*, naturally omitting any mention of Giles.

'And this Monday I started work as a reporter on the *East London Chronicle*,' Fliss concluded.

He raised an eyebrow. 'Parish meetings and bouncing babies at the *Chronicle* is a bit of a change from radical politics and waving the red flag in the face of the Tories on the *Workers' Clarion*.'

'It is, but don't you worry,' Fliss replied, 'I'll be keeping my eyes and ears open for anything I can write up with a socialist slant.'

'Good for you,' he said. 'It's about time women took their rightful place in the workforce like they do in the Soviet Union.'

Fliss stood a little taller.

'Thank you, Harry. I wish there were more men who has such an enlightened view on the matter,' she said, as the sharp exchange between herself and Inspector Wallace at the rectory sprang into her mind yet again.

'Although, perhaps most women would have a bit of a struggle stepping into my work boots as a docker's team leader in London Dock,' said Harry, smoke escaping from his mouth as he spoke. 'As I doubt you could hump a hundredweight of sugar out of a ship's hold.' He flexed his bicep. 'Feel that?'

'Well, I … I …'

'Go on,' he urged, moving nearer.

Reluctantly, and feeling very uncomfortable at the forced intimacy, Fliss placed her hand on his upper arm.

'Like a rock, ain't it?' he said as she gave his flexed muscle the smallest of squeezes.

'Well, yes,' she replied, catching a whiff of armpit.

'You know how I've got that?' he asked.

'Unloading ships, I imagine,' said Fliss.

'I've been in the docks man and boy for almost sixteen years, humping cargo from the bowels of ships from all four corners of the Empire,' Harry replied. 'And I doubt there's a woman alive who could do that?'

'Perhaps not,' conceded Fliss, 'but I can tackle another evil of capitalism on our very streets: profiteering.'

Interest sparked in Harry's eyes. 'Profiteering?'

'Yes,' Fliss replied. 'It seems to be rife.'

Brushing against her, Harry reached across and tapped ash into an ashtray balanced on a chair. 'I thought the Ministry of Food keep a tight grip on food supply and prices.'

'Well, not tight enough, it seems.' Feeling increasingly awkward at his closeness, Fliss inched back half a step. 'Plus, my sources believe that much of what's being sold under the counter is at vastly inflated prices.'

'That's exploitation pure and simple,' said Harry, his large face screwed tight in fury.

'I know,' said Fliss. 'And what's more, I suspect most of it has been stolen.'

Harry took a long drag on his cigarette. 'Where from?'

'I don't know exactly,' Fliss admitted, 'but I'm determined to get to the bottom of this exploitation and bust it wide open with an exposé, plus ...' She explained about the protest she was planning to organise. 'Women united and taking direct action.'

A smile spread across Harry's face. 'Well, I know my old mum, God rest 'er, worked her fingers to the bone and died young after a lifetime slaving for the bloody bourgeoisie. So if there's anything I can do to help our hard-working wives and mothers, let me—'

The screech of the air raid siren on the post office sorting depot opposite cut off Harry's words.

Mr Potter jumped back onto the stage.

'Right, everyone, I think that signals the end of our meeting,' he shouted over the whine of the siren. 'So please file out in an orderly fashion and there's a shelter in the basement if anyone is too far away from their regular one.'

Fliss knocked back the last of her tea. 'I'd better get going before they arrive. Nice to talk to you, Harry.'

Hurrying over and setting her cup on the refreshments table, Fliss made her way down the side of the hall to retrieve her coat from the back of her chair.

Harry caught up with her as she joined the queue of people filing out.

'This way's quicker.' His hand went to the small of her

back and he guided her through the crowd.

However, as they inched their way forward towards the door his hand slid down onto her bottom for a couple of seconds before returning to her waist.

Frowning, she glanced up, but with an expression of intense concentration on his face, Harry's eyes were fixed to the door in front.

Chiding herself for overreacting to what was obviously an accident, Fliss continued towards the hall's exit.

'Well,' she said, stepped away from him as they reached the street, 'I'd better get myself to St Winifred's. You?'

'I don't bother. I reckon if it's got my name on it then so be it,' he replied. 'I've a lorry over there and I'd offer you a lift but I've a bit of Union business to attend to so—'

'That's all right. I understand,' said Fliss.

'See you at a branch meeting?'

Fliss nodded.

Harry studied her for a moment then, taking his leather cap from his back pocket, he flipped it on his head and strolled away.

As a line of bombs crashed onto Surrey Docks a mile across the Thames, flaring skywards in quick succession, Harry Gunn looked at his watch.

'Wot's the time now?' asked his brother Ben, clutching the steering wheel of the grey three-ton Bedford truck they were sitting in.

'Ten minutes after the last time you asked me,' Harry replied, as a round of shells from the ack-ack guns in Southwark Park punctuated the darkness above.

It was, in fact, a quarter past two in the morning and about four hours since he strolled out of the Labour Party branch meeting. Having met up with Ben and the rest of the team in the Old Rose on the Highway, they'd had a few jars in the pub's basement, then in the lull between the second and third wave of enemy aircraft they'd loaded up and set off.

They'd been parked in the shadows between the Iberian warehouse and Minories and Blackwall offices opposite the Trinidad & Tobago warehouse for the last twenty minutes.

'All right, all right, you don't have to bite my blooming 'ead off,' Ben replied, giving him the same wounded look as when Harry pulled the arm off his teddy when they were nippers. 'Just cos you didn't get anywhere with that posh bit at tonight's meeting.'

'Who said I didn't?' Harry replied.

'Well, the way I saw it she trotted off 'ome on 'er tod and left you standing.'

'Only cos I had to meet you ugly bunch, otherwise,' Harry replied, remembering the pleasing touch of Fliss's rear in his hand when he'd sneaked a quick feel, 'I would have wooed her with my natural charm.'

Frankie, their brother-in-law, snorted from his seat in the back. 'Natural charm? Miss What's-'er-name is well out of your league.'

'It's Miss Carmichael to you riff-raff.' Harry took a long drag on his cigarette. 'And as me and Miss Carmichael are signed up members of the Labour Party, our class differences don't matter.'

'You don't actually believe all that socialist codswallop, do you, Harry?' asked Sammy, sitting beside his cousin in the rear.

'Course 'e bloody don't,' sniggered Ben. 'It just 'elps him to get 'is end away with a bit of posh totty now and again.'

In the mute light of the cab interior, a self-satisfied expression crept across Harry's face. 'What can I say, chaps? Upper-crust girlies go mad for a bit of rough.'

The men around him sniggered.

Taking another long drag on his cigarette, Harry's eyes and focus returned to the warehouse on the other side of the road.

Unlike the two buildings looming on either side of him, the tobacco warehouse had lost one of its corners and the best part of its south wall during the previous night's air raid when a firebomb had landed on it. The fire brigade had managed to extinguish the fire that tore through the upper floors, which now had charred roof timbers jutting skywards, but as far as Harry could tell from the quick gander he'd had that morning when he took a break from unloading, the bottom floors were largely unscathed and were now secured by a temporary barrier.

'You don't think some nosy ARP wallah's seen us sitting here and called the coppers?' Ben asked, the tip of his roll-up glowing red in the dim light of the lorry's interior. 'Cos if they have then—'

'For gawd's sake,' snapped Frankie, leaning forward over the front seat. 'Old Wilf Farmer who's on tonight is solid, so put a sock in it.'

'Yeah,' added Sammy, grinning and revealing a set of uneven teeth. 'And Harry's bunged him a nicker already to keep 'im that way.'

A bomb landing a few streets away set the vehicle rattling and a fire engine bell rang out as it shot along the Highway.

'And I wish they'd shut that buggering thing off,' Sammy added, as the air raid siren wailed. 'We know there's a bloody air raid.'

'Rozzers,' snapped Harry, as he spotted a police van further down the road.

Frankie and Sammy disappeared behind the partition and Harry and Ben slunk low in their seats until the Black Maria had passed.

As he straightened up he spotted a flicker of light from between the corrugated iron sheets of the Trinidad & Tobago warehouse opposite.

He cuffed Ben's arm. 'Let's go.'

His brother turned on the engine, but without switching on the lights he inched the truck across the road as one of the metal sheets was moved to the side. Once they'd entered, the sheet closed swiftly behind them.

Ben turned off the engine and Harry jumped down from off the cab.

'I thought we said ten to one, Wilf,' he said as the elderly watchman lumbered towards him.

'Sorry, mate,' Wilf replied, wheezing slightly as he came to a halt. 'There were a couple of coppers hanging about earlier and I 'ad to make sure they'd slung their hook.'

A bomb found its target somewhere to the east of them, sending hot waves of cordite-laden air pulsing over them.

'Have the assessors been in?' Harry shouted as the noise subsided.

'Fraid so,' Wilf replied hesitantly.

Harry's mouth pulled into a hard line, but after contemplating the old man for a moment he pulled his leather gloves from the back of his cord trousers.

'All right, lads,' he said, 'get cracking. We ain't got all night.'

Ben, Frankie and Sammy headed towards the warehouse and Harry followed them through the space where the two loading bay doors had been.

Passing Frankie carrying a large box with Benson & Hedges printed on the side and with stench of burning wood filling his nose, Harry entered the gloomy interior.

The fire had left just bare timbers of the floor above and one corner of the warehouse was now rubble, allowing the fires raging along the Thames to blanket the interior with a red glow. However, more important than the condition of the Victorian warehouse was the fact that the cartons stacked high on the ground floor were largely untouched by bomb damage.

'Punters are sick of war cigarettes, so just take the branded ones,' Harry said, grasping a box of Silk Cut and throwing it at Frankie, who had just walked back in. 'We'll get two bob a touch for a pack of twenty.'

Half an hour later, after all four of them had heaved dozens of cartons of cigarettes into the back of the waiting lorry, Harry raised his hand.

'That'll do,' he said, taking a grubby handkerchief from his pocket and wiping his brow.

'But there's a couple of crates of King Edwards over the other side,' said Ben, pointing to the far end of the storeroom.

'Yeah, and 'ow many blokes do you see around here with a fat cigar in their gob?' asked Harry. 'The coppers might be thick as a brick but d'you think they'd not notice some costermonger puffing away like Churchill as he weighed up half a pound of spuds?'

Ben nodded and, looking more than a little crestfallen, he ambled over to join his brother.

'Look, lad,' Harry said, 'with this type of job, it's in, out and away. Don't half-inch anything bigger or more specialised unless you've got a buyer lined up or you won't be able to shift it for love nor money. General rule of thumb: if you can't turn it round quick for cash it'll get you studying cell walls at His Majesty's pleasure.'

Ben nodded.

Harry punched him playfully on the arm. 'Now bugger off.'

His brother shot after the other two and Harry strolled

over to the crates of cigars. Punching a hole in the top, he fished out a box of King Edwards then followed his crew back outside.

Frankie and Sammy were just tying down the canvas flap at the back while Ben was standing nearby.

'A little reward,' he said, slinging the box of cigars at his brother as he made his way over to the elderly nightwatchman. 'And bring us a couple of bits of rope.'

'See you next Friday as usual, Harry?' said Wilf as Harry stopped in front of him.

Harry nodded. 'About the police.'

'Don't worry, Harry. If the cops ask, I'll say I was asleep or something.' His watery gaze shifted across to Ben coming towards them carrying a length of rope. 'Oh, yeah, make it like you overpowered me. But not out 'ere or I'll freeze to death.'

The old man shuffled towards his guard's hut on the far side of the improvised corrugated-iron gates. Harry followed, his brother half a step behind.

It was warm inside the hut thanks to the squat paraffin stove in the far corner, and it had the usual collection of mugs on an upturned box next to the kettle on the beaten-earth floor.

'All right, lads,' said Wilf, sitting on an archaic wooden dining chair and putting his arms behind his back.

In the dim light from the stove's flickering flame, Harry's eyes darted across at his brother.

Ben went around the back of the old man and started to tie his hands.

'Not too tight, lad,' said Wilf, as Ben looped the rope. 'I've got terrible arthritis in my wrists.'

'Got to make it look kosher, Wilf,' Ben replied, pulling the cord tight.

Hunkering down, he lashed the watchman's ankles to the chair legs then straightened up and stepped back.

Harry regarded the old man for a moment then took a step forward. Drawing back his fist, he smashed it into the side of watchman's face. Wilf gasped as the chair rocked back on two legs. Ben caught it and set it upright.

Harry contemplated the old man's busted lip and bleeding nose as he wheezed to catch his breath. Struggling to remain conscious, Wilf opened one swelling eye and looked beseechingly for a moment before Harry's hammer-like fist smashed into his jaw again. The chair rocked back again but this time Ben let it fall and the now unconscious watchman hit the deck.

Stepping over the old man's bound legs, Ben came to stand next to him.

'As you said, Ben,' Harry said as they studied their handiwork, 'got to make it look kosher.'

'Your mother was telling us at the Wednesday Together Tea how well you're getting on at the *East London Chronicle*, Miss Carmichael,' said the churchwarden's wife, smiling up at Fliss from beneath the brim of her Sunday hat.

'I am, Mrs Crowther,' Fliss replied, giving her father's parishioner her butter-wouldn't-melt clergyman's-daughter smile, as she held her drink poised.

'Well, I'm sure all the reporter chaps at the *Chronicle* are very pleased to have such a pretty young thing to type up their stories,' the older woman replied.

'My sister isn't a typist, Mrs Crowther,' said Prue, who was standing beside her. 'She is one of the paper's reporters.'

It was somewhere close to eleven and Prue and Fliss, along with the rest of St Winifred's congregation, were milling around in the church hall, balancing cups of tea.

Although Stepney's medieval church had escaped the worst of the Victorian fashion for modernisation, a large parish room had been built adjacent to it, which was where Fliss was now standing. Through the serving hatch, the good ladies of the parish, in their best hats, were serving second cups and gathering in the dirty crockery.

Some of the older folk were resting their weary bones on the chairs dotted around the end of the hall, but the rest were standing and huddled in small groups.

Surprise registered on the church matron's face. 'How very modern. It makes one wonder what girls will do next.'

'Well,' said Fliss, giving her an ingenuous look, 'as the women of the Air Transport Auxiliary are flying aircraft, who knows?'

There was a pause, then Mrs Crowther gave them both a polite smile. 'Well, I must get on.' And she hurried away.

'Honestly,' said Fliss, watching her go, 'you'd think it was 1841 instead of 1941.'

Her sister laughed but then her gaze flickered past Fliss briefly and she pulled a face. 'Drat, Mother's on her way over.'

Fliss turned to see her mother, in her customary tweed suit, lace-up shoes and with a face like a gargoyle that had caught it's claw in a door, homing in on them.

'Good morning, Mother,' said Prue, as she stopped beside them. 'And how are you and Dad?'

'Good morning, Prudence. Your father and I are tolerably well,' Marjorie replied, pointedly not looking at her younger daughter.

'It was a lovely service, Mother,' said Fliss.

'Don't lovely service me, my girl,' Marjorie snapped, the feathers adorning her hat shuddering a little as she spoke. 'I suppose it's you who put that communist poster up on the church hall noticeboard.'

'It certainly was,' said Fliss. 'And it's not a communist poster, it's a Labour Party one.'

'And who, may I ask, gave you permission to put up such trash?' her mother snapped back.

'Mr Webb, the church warden,' Fliss replied. 'I believe he is in charge of the hall and he also happens to be the Labour councillor for the St Winifred ward. He gave me permission to have the meeting here on Thursday, too. And if you're thinking of taking the poster down, Mother, I'll just replace it with the larger one I have rolled up under my bed.'

'Well, I'm sure holding a meeting must be contravening some sort of rule under the Emergency Powers Act,' Marjorie countered.

'I've checked and it's not,' Fliss replied. 'But even if it were I'd still be rallying the women of the area to protest against the criminal racketeering that's going on.'

'And get yourself arrested in the process, no doubt,' Marjorie replied.

Fliss and Prue exchanged looks, which thankfully their mother didn't see.

'Anyway,' Marjorie continued, 'if you ask me, all this moaning about rationing and prices is un-British. After all, our great Empire was built on trade.'

'I think you mean exploitation,' countered Fliss. 'Which is exactly what racketeering is. I have heard that ...' She recounted her conversation with Mrs Appleton regarding poor people selling their rations and children being fed on potatoes.

'Well then, Felicity, if things are as bad as you say,' her mother said when she'd finished, 'tell me this, how is it that Mrs Lavender, who shops in the same shops as everyone else in the area, has absolutely no trouble obtaining everything she requires to put three meals on the table each day and run the rectory?'

'Because Tommy Lavender is her son,' Prue replied.

Their mother looked baffled.

'They say he's in the supply and demand business,' Prue added. 'You demand it and he supplies it.'

The penny dropped.

'Are you suggesting that Mrs Lavender is getting the rectory provisions on the black market?' Marjorie snapped, glaring at her younger daughter.

'I'm suggesting that you might like to consider how it is that despite there often only being offal in the butchers, you always seem to have a roast joint on Sunday,' Prue replied.

Her mother's jaw dropped open but as she was about to speak, something at the end of the hall distracted her.

'Who on earth is that?'

Fliss turned and, much to her irritation before she could stop it, her heart did a little double step as her eyes ran over the tall figure, fedora in hand, standing in the hall doorway.

'Detective Inspector Wallace from Wapping police station,' she replied.

He was dressed, as always, in a suit and tie but, as the weather had turned slightly warmer over the past week, without his trench coat. She also noticed that several of the young women in the room were also looking his way with more than passing interest.

'How do you know him?' asked her mother, cutting across Fliss's thoughts. Marjorie clutched the string of pearls resting on her pillow-like bosom. 'Please do not tell me that you have had a run-in with the police—'

'No, I haven't, Mother,' Fliss cut in. 'He called at the rectory a few days after I arrived home to ask Mrs Lavender the whereabouts of her son.'

'What a coincidence. We were just talking about him, weren't we, Mother?' said Prue, not even trying to hide her amusement.

'Don't be tiresome, Prudence,' her mother snapped, shooting her a furious look.

Strolling up to the church matrons serving behind the hatch, DI Wallace put his hand in his trouser pocket and, having passed over a few coppers, got a cup of tea in return. He had a couple of words with one of them then, cup in hand, his dark eyes skimmed over St Winifred's parishioners until they meet Fliss's. A flicker of something passed across his angular face then he started towards them.

Feeling ridiculously flustered, Fliss watched him approach.

'Good morning, ladies,' he said, smiling at them. 'I'm DI Wallace from Wapping police station.'

'Nice to meet you again,' said Prue.

'And you, Mrs Quinn.'

Fliss gave her sister a puzzled look and Prue responded with an amused twinkle in her eye.

'What can we do for you, Inspector?' their mother asked, giving him her vicar's-wife smile.

As the officer's attention shifted to their mother, Fliss gave her sister a questioning look and Prue grinned.

'As Miss Carmichael might have told you, I called at the rectory a while back looking for Tommy Lavender.' The detective took a sip of tea. 'And as your daughter was at pains to explain that Tommy was a hard-working young man from a respectable church-going family, I thought I'd pop by to see if I could catch up with him after he'd made his peace with God at the communion rail.'

Out of the corner of her eye Fliss saw Prue whip out a handkerchief and pretend to blow her nose.

'I am afraid Mr Lavender didn't attend the Eucharist service this morning,' Marjorie said, bestowing a benevolent smile on him. 'Could I ask why you are seeking him?'

'A few things really,' he replied. 'But mainly about information I've received appertaining to black-market goods.'

A purple flush coloured Marjorie's double chin as she struggled to maintain her pleasant expression.

'Well, Inspector,' she continued, a slight quiver in her voice, 'should I see Mr Lavender I will be sure to tell him you're looking for him. Now, if you'll excuse me, I have parish duties to attend to.'

The officer matched her agreeable expression with one of his own. 'Of course. Thank you for your time, Mrs Carmichael.'

Marjorie dashed away as if Beelzebub and all his demons were at her heels.

The detective turned his attention back to Fliss. 'And how are you getting on at the *East London Chronicle*?'

'Very well, thank you,' said Fliss. 'DI Wallace and I ran into each other as I came out of the newspaper offices after my interview,' she explained to her sister.

'Oh, you two seem to be running into each other quite a lot, then,' said Prue.

'I don't think twice qualifies as a lot, Prue,' Fliss replied.

The increasingly irritating spark of amusement glinted in her sister's eyes again, but she didn't comment so Fliss turned her attention back the tall officer.

'And did you have a nice afternoon visiting your special someone?' she asked.

'I certainly did,' he replied, his dark eyes looking into hers.

Images of him, hat and jacket off, gazing down at someone else flashed through Fliss's mind.

They stood looking at each other for a moment, then he cleared his throat.

'Well, I should be off.' He finished off the last of his drink and placed his empty cup back in the saucer.

'Goodbye, Inspector,' said Prue. 'And Sunday Eucharist starts at nine thirty if you'd care to join us any time?'

He smiled and Fliss's heart did another little double step. 'Thank you for the invitation, Mrs Quinn, I'll remember that.' His attention shifted back to Fliss. 'I hope to see you again, Miss Carmichael.'

With that he walked back across the hall, Fliss's eyes glued to him all the way.

Prue started giggling and Fliss spun around.

'Would you mind letting me in on this joke that's had you at the point of bursting since DI Wallace walked in the hall?' she said.

'You don't remember, do you?' her sister laughed.

Fliss frowned. 'Remember what?'

'You know that night when you were found sitting on a gravestone swigging gin by a passing stranger and brought down to the shelter,' Prue began.

'Vaguely,' Fliss replied.

'Well, that passing stranger was none other than DI Wallace,' Prue finished.

Fliss looked at her sister in astonishment. 'When you said a policeman I assumed you meant a uniformed office and certainly not him!'

'Well, it was, and very gallant he was too, laying you gently face down on the bunk bed so you wouldn't choke if you vomited.'

'He never said.'

'What gentleman would?' Prue replied. 'And you want to be thankful it was him, because another man might have taken advantage of a pretty young girl too drunk to know what she was doing.'

As a series of half-formed images of that evening tumbled over in her mind, Fliss's gaze returned to the hall door that DI Wallace had just disappeared through. Then they were crowded out by a very different memory – that of a deep voice, a warm coat and a strong pair of arms around her.

Chapter twelve

'SO LET ME GET this straight, Mr Farmer,' said Tim, glancing down at his notebook. 'You say some chap called you to the gate about two o'clock and said his mate was injured, but when you opened the gate a gang of men forced their way in?'

''at's right, Officer,' said the old man through his swollen mouth.

'If it 'urts too much, Dad, just nod,' said Lily Watson, who was sitting next to her father on the two-seat sofa.

It was just after nine on Monday morning and Tim was sitting on one of the fireside chairs in the poky but spotlessly clean front room of number thirty-two Anthony Street, where Wilf lived with his daughter.

He was there interviewing Wilfred Farmer, an elderly nightwatchman at the Trinidad & Tobago warehouse who had spent the weekend in the London Hospital, having been tied up and beaten during a robbery at the warehouse in the early hours of Saturday morning.

'But you say you can't remember how many there were?' said Tim.

Wilf shook his head.

'And you didn't recognise any of them?'

The watchman shook his head again.

'Perhaps you'd like to come to Wapping station in a few days and take a look through our mugshots,' Tim suggested.

Wilf's bruised face lifted in a regretful lopsided smile. 'It was dark, so I can't say I got a good look at them. I'd only be wasting your time, Officer.'

Struggling to contain his exasperation, Tim persisted. 'And you didn't hear them say any names?'

'I might have 'eard one or two at the time but they've gone now,' Wilf replied. 'Must be the knock on the head.'

Tim sighed. 'So just to recap, you were sitting in your hut minding your own business when someone knocked on the gate and asked for help. You opened it and a number of men rushed in but you don't know how many or who they were and you can't remember any names.'

'That's about the sum of it, Officer,' mumbled Wilf. 'Rushed in before I could stop 'em and tied me up.'

'I don't know why you keep on at him, Inspector; Dad's told you all he knows,' snapped Lily. 'And you can see the state 'e's in.'

'I can, Mrs Watson. But what I can't understand is why, if this gang overpowered your dad and tied him up before he could do anything to stop them, they then decided to beat him until his face resembled chopped liver. Unless, of course, it was to make your father's account of the events look convincing.'

Watching them closely, Tim let the silence sit between them.

Wilf's left eye, that hadn't been closed by a vicious blow, shifted under Tim's scrutiny and Lily lowered her gaze and fiddled with a crease in her apron.

'Well,' Lily said finally, standing up, 'if that's all, I ought to get on.'

Picking up the empty teacups, she hurried out of the room.

Closing his notebook, Tim stowed it back in the inside pocket of his suit and rose to his feet.

'Well, thank you, Mr Farmer,' he said, picking up his hat. 'If you think of anything else, you know where I am. And I wish you a speedy recovery.'

'Thank you, Inspector, I will,' said Wilf, visibly relieved that Tim had finished his questions.

Leaving the old man in the chair making a roll-up, Tim strolled out into the narrow hallway then turned towards the scullery where Lily was standing at the sink.

'Thank you for the tea,' he said, stopping in the doorway.

'Any time, Inspector,' she replied, giving Tim a friendly smile. 'And I'm sorry Dad couldn't be more help, but 'e's an old man and his faculties aren't what they used to be.'

'But mine are still sharp,' Tim replied. 'And I'll tell you straight: after a beating like that you're lucky your dad's sitting in your front room and not lying on a slab in the morgue.' Putting on his hat he tugged it down slightly over his left eye. 'Good day, Mrs Watson, and I'll see myself out.'

*

'Morning, all,' Fliss said brightly, as she strode through the main door of the *Chronicle*'s office, putting her dripping umbrella into the holder under the coat rack.

'And felicitation of the merry morning to you too, my dear girl,' called George, from his desk by the window.

It was Monday and a week since she'd joined the staff at the *East London Chronicle*.

'Afternoon, don't you mean?' said Norman Ogdon, glancing at the office clock showing five to ten.

Lanky, with a constant crop of juvenile spots and a mop of light-brown hair that grew in several directions, sixteen-year-old Norman was the newspaper's junior reporter. Wearing a grey suit that looked as if it belonged to a man two sizes bigger and with a Windsor knot almost as big as his very pronounced Adam's apple, Norman, a lifelong West Ham fan, always volunteered to report on the local sports fixtures, from the local boys' and amateur football leagues to snooker tournaments and inter-club boxing matches.

Actually, to be truthful, Norman wasn't wrong about the time as it was almost time for the office's mid-morning cuppa.

'I've been working.' Plonking her satchel on the table, Fliss took out her reporter's pad and smiled across at him. 'You might want to try it someday.'

Unbuttoning her jacket, Fliss draped it over the back of her chair to dry and sat down. Pulling the cover off her typewriter, she opened her notebook.

Humming 'You are my Sunshine' to herself, Fliss

started loading two sheets with a carbon between into the carriage.

'Goodness, you're very chipper today, Fliss,' said Betty.

Actually, she did feel rather jolly, despite a twenty-minute walk in the pouring rain.

The unexpected appearance of DI Wallace the day before in the church hall meant that when she reached the metal stairway to the office the memory of falling into his strong arms sprang back into her mind and had lightened her mood in an instant.

'Perhaps Felicity is in love. If I might take a small liberty with our great Bard, "Love comforteth like sunshine" *despite* the rain,' said George Templeton, his waistcoat buttons straining to remain in their allotted holes as he leaned back on his office chair.

The image of DI Wallace's rather unsettling dark gaze started to form in Fliss's mind again but she cut it short and looked across at George, the *Chronicle*'s self-appointed arts and culture correspondent.

George, as he was at pains to tell Fliss the moment she arrived, had at one time been the chief theatre correspondent for the *Tatler* until he and the editor had 'artistic differences'. However, judging by his florid complexion after lunch each day and the hipflask he slid from his pocket when he thought he was unobserved, Fliss judged George's falling-out with his previous boss was of a liquid rather than creative nature.

'Anything in?' she asked, as she strolled across to the office tea bar and relit the primus stove gas under the kettle.

'Apart from the couple of dozen people killed in last night's bombing raid that the Ministry of Information says we can't report on,' said Sid Longman, coming out of his office with his morning coffee, 'not really.'

'Someone phoned first thing to say a couple of auxiliary firemen from the Bethnal Green station rescued a cat from beneath the rubble,' said Betty, looking at the dog-eared office message book.

'Whoo, hold the front page,' Norman sneered, his top lip curled over his prominent front teeth.

'A family near Roman Road had a lucky escape when their Anderson shelter had a direct hit,' continued Betty, as Fliss poured a teaspoonful of liquid Camp coffee into a mug.

'How so?' asked Sid.

'According to this,' Betty continued, reading down the page, 'they were travelling back from visiting family in Wickford when the army requisitioned the train they were on and spent the night freezing on Romford station instead of tucked up in their shelter. And the Bow Road branch of the Chamber of Commerce will be presenting a new canteen van to the Mile End Women's Voluntary Service next Thursday at Popular Town Hall.'

Taking a sip of his drink, Sid looked across at his newest recruit. 'That sounds like two for you, Fliss. You know: the feminine point of view, and all that.'

Fliss forced a smile. She had already been allocated to report on the nurses at Monroe House, who had set up a maternity clinic in the Tilbury Shelter.

'And finally,' said Betty, reaching the bottom of the page, 'there's a report that some poor woman who'd gone into labour on her way to the shelter gave birth in a doorway with the help of a passing policeman.'

A vision of DI Wallace's strong, dexterous fingers holding her elbow lightly darted into Fliss's mind.

'Another one for you I think, Fliss,' said her editor, his voice cutting across her wandering thoughts.

'Anything else?' Fliss asked, ignoring the odd feeling in her chest.

Betty shook her head. 'That's about it for—'

The black telephone on her desk sprang into life and she picked it up. 'Good morning, *East London Chronicle*. How can I assist you?' Tucking the receiver into her neck, she took a pencil from the pot in front of her and sat down. 'Where did you say this happened?' she asked, turning over a page in the message book. 'And when?' She scribbled down the reply then frowned. 'Poor chap. That's terrible. Yes, I'm sure our editor will send someone to report on the incident straight away and thank you for letting us know.' She put down the receiver and looked up. 'Thieves broke into the Trinidad and Tobago warehouse on Friday night and took dozens of boxes of cigarettes.'

Norman whistled through his widely spaced front teeth. 'That's a lot of fags.'

'The nightwatchman, a Mr Farmer, was badly beaten,' continued Betty. 'And Wapping CID are investigating.'

'Well then, that's something for Friday's front page,'

said Sid, clearly heartened by war-related news they could go to print for once. 'Who—'

'I'll go,' said Fliss, jumping to her feet.

'My dear girl,' laughed George, 'the docks are no place for a lady.'

'Cos you might ladder your stockings,' smirked Norman.

'Well, that's all right then, isn't it?' said Fliss, closing her notebook and returning it to her bag. 'Because firstly, Norman, in case you hadn't noticed, I'm wearing trousers and secondly, George,' picking up her satchel from the back of her chair, Fliss slung it over her shoulder, 'I'm not a lady. I'm a reporter.'

'Good morning,' said Fliss, putting on her friendliest smile. 'I wonder if you could direct me to the Trinidad and Tobago warehouse.'

The man overseeing the comings and goings on number four gate of London Dock, an unshaven individual in his early sixties wearing a threadbare jacket, looked her up and down.

'And who are you when you're at 'ome?' he replied, the roll-up stuck to his lower lip bobbing up and down as he spoke.

'Miss Carmichael from the *East London Chronicle*,' Fliss replied, taking her newly issued press badge from her pocket and flashing it at him. 'And you are?'

'Tilman,' he replied. 'Mr, to you.'

'I just want to have a quick—'

A six-ton Foden lorry stacked high with crates and splashing dirty rainwater left by the early shower roared past her towards the main road, drowning out her words.

'As I said,' coughed Fliss as the acid sting of the diesel exhaust caught in the back of her throat, 'I just was a quick word with Mr Levy the manager.'

'Is 'e expecting you?' the security guard asked.

'Not as such, but—'

'Well, I can't just let anyone wander about the docks, you know,' Tilman replied.

'But if you point me towards the Trinidad and Tobago warehouse I won't be wandering, will I?' Fliss replied, struggling to keep her frustration in check. 'Please.'

His thin lips pulled into a straight line and he shook his head. 'I'll be the one who gets it in the neck if you fall in the drink or get your brains knocked out by a swinging hook or summink. And, 'ow do I know you ain't no German spy?'

Fliss gave an exasperated sigh. 'Do I look like a spy?'

'That's what that floozy Mata Hari said when they nabbed 'er during our last run-in with the Boche,' the gateman replied. 'And even if you're not a secret agent for the Nazis, I tell you it's more than my job's worth to let anyone who fancies it wander about the docks.' The dock's elderly sentinel's hostile expression remained. 'Now if you don't mind, miss,' he waved her back, 'some of us have a job to do.'

Unhooking a battered clipboard from a hook in his watchman's hut, he stepped into the path of a low-loading lorry chugging towards the entrance and raised his hand.

Somehow managing to maintain her pleasant expression, Fliss waited until he'd seen the driver's paperwork.

'Well, can you tell me anything about Friday night's robbery, Mr Tilman?' she asked

'Like wot?' Tilman asked.

'Do you know how the thieves got in?' asked Fliss.

'I'm not at liberty to say, miss,' Tilman sniffed.

'I understand a quantity of cigarettes was taken. Is that right?' asked Fliss.

The gateman crossed his arms. 'It's not my place to tell you.'

'Well, what about the nightwatchman?' asked Fliss, barely suppressing her growing annoyance. 'I understand he was badly beaten by the gang.'

'That 'e was.' Tilman's mulish expression softened a fraction.

'Do you know if he's all right?'

'Barely,' replied a deep voice behind her.

Turning, Fliss found DI Wallace standing just behind her.

He was dressed in his usual off-the-peg three-piece grey suit, white shirt, a Windsor knot at his throat, and slightly damp trench coat.

Although it shouldn't – him being an establishment lackey and all that – her heart did a little double step.

Gazing down at her from beneath the rakish angle of his fedora brim, his eyes changed somehow then that mildly unsettling smile of his spread across his face. 'Miss Carmichael. Why am I not surprised?'

Despite Fliss Carmichael being the most opinionated, stubborn and infuriating woman Tim had met in a very long time, she was also an extremely attractive one. Therefore, he shouldn't have been at all surprised when without any reference to his head, his heart quickened like a callow youth's when he spotted her quizzing Ernie Tilman.

Today she was dressed in a pair of tailored bottle-green trousers with a chocolate-brown three-quarter-length jacket and Robin-Hood-style felt hat of the same colour topping off her workaday ensemble.

Ernie Tilman stood to attention. 'Detective Wallace. Sir.'

'Morning, Ernie,' Tim replied, glancing briefly at him.

'I know as 'ow you don't take kindly to the press sniffing around, so I ain't told her nuffink,' the gateman added.

Tim nodded.

'In fact, Inspector Wallace,' Ernie laughed, 'she only wanted to go wandering about by 'erself, if you can Adam and Eve such a thing.'

Tim certainly could.

'Do you know how the nightwatchman is?' asked Fliss, a note of sympathy in her voice.

'I've just come from Wilf Farmer's house and all I can say is that whoever gave him such a hammering was lucky they didn't kill him,' Tim replied, touched by her obvious concern.

'That ain't proper,' muttered Ernie. 'Ain't proper at all, not to an old boy like Wilf.'

'No, it wasn't,' Tim replied, shifting his attention from Miss Carmichael to the gateman. 'I don't suppose you have any idea who that might be, do you, Ernie?'

Panic flitted across Ernie's haggard face. 'Wot me?'

Fixing him with a piercing stare, Tim nodded.

With some effort, Ernie managed to hold his eye.

'No, Inspector, sir.' He forced a light laugh. 'I ain't got a blessed clue wot buggers did it.'

He was lying and they both knew it.

'Actually, Inspector Wallace,' said Fliss, 'as you're here, perhaps I could ask you a few questions about the break-in?'

Tim's attention returned to the *Chronicle*'s newest reporter and her rather lovely eyes.

Of course, finding the press, albeit just the local one, at the scene of a crime he was still investigating would usually have annoyed him no end, but …

'I'll tell you what, Miss Carmichael, why don't you accompany me as I head over to the Trinidad and Tobago,' he said, more than a little surprised at himself for suggesting it.

She looked astonished for a brief moment then smiled. 'Thank you, Inspector, that would be very helpful.'

Leaving Ernie to return to his duties on number four gate, and keeping close to the warehouses to avoid the stevedore teams unloading the dozen or so ships moored up along the north side of London Basin, Tim led Fliss to the far end of the dock.

'Here we are,' he said, stopping by the rope with fluttering red bunting strung along in front of the damaged warehouse.

Unhooking her satchel from her shoulder, Fliss pulled out a well-worn notepad and pen.

'Goodness, the thieves didn't have to work all that hard to get in, did they?' she said, scribbling down a few notes as she spoke.

'No, they had a field day, courtesy of the Luftwaffe,' he replied.

'Can I go in?'

Tim shook his head. 'It's too dangerous. The roof's charred beams look as if they are ready to fall any moment and I don't know how that south wall is still standing,' he added, as they gazed at the yawning hole in the brickwork where the storehouse's solid gates had been.

Fliss scribbled down a few more notes then wandered along the rope barrier.

'How many cigarettes did they take?' she asked, gazing up at the warehouse's blackened beams that stretched like fingers toward the clouds scurrying across the sky.

'About four dozen boxes, as near as the manager can work out, although it's difficult to be precise due to the bomb damage,' Tim replied.

'Anything else?' she asked, as Tim studied her aristo-cratic profile.

'A box of King of Edwards cigars.'

Fliss frowned. 'Just one? Isn't that a little odd?'

'Not really,' he replied, as he followed her along to the end of the barrier. 'It's easy enough to flog cigarettes to tobacconists and in pubs, but fat cigars aren't something most people around here can afford. They probably took them for—'

A shrill two-tone whistle cut between them.

'Mind your backs,' bellowed a porter as he barrelled towards them.

Without thinking, Tim hooked his arm around Fliss's waist and pulled her against him. She gasped and her hands flew to his chest as the barrow, piled high with crates, whizzed past them.

Fliss looked up and her brown eyes locked with his. They changed in some way that caused him to tighten his embrace.

Enjoying the feeling of her in his arms, and with her lips only inches from his, the desire to kiss her rose up in Tim.

As if she knew his thoughts, Fliss's lips parted slightly, the air around them stilled and they stared into each other's eyes.

'Oi, oi, Fliss.'

Breaking from Tim's gaze, she looked around.

So did Tim, to see Harry Gunn, dressed in shabby cords, collarless shirt, worn donkey jacket and a leather cap, striding towards them with a broad smile fixed to his square face.

Reluctantly, Tim released Fliss from his embrace and stepped back.

'Harry,' she said, smiling up at him as he stopped in front of them.

'But wot are you up to down here?' His grey-green eyes shifted onto Tim. 'And with our very own Detective Inspector Wallace.'

'Morning, Harry,' said Tim flatly, holding the other man's mildly hostile stare.

'I 'ope you're not arresting Miss Carmichael,' Harry continued, 'because the East London branch of the Labour Party wouldn't take kindly to a lackey of the ruling classes harassing a comrade.'

Tim raised an eyebrow in reply.

Fliss laughed. 'Don't worry, Harry, DI Wallace isn't harassing me.'

'I'm glad to 'ear it,' he replied. 'Although I can't say as 'ow I blame 'im getting you in a clinch, because you look quite the sight for sore eyes today, don't she, Stretch?'

Although he wouldn't argue with one word, Tim did not reply.

And not just because he wouldn't play Harry's game; hearing Fliss's name on Harry Gunn's lips was unexpectedly causing anger to rise in his chest.

Fliss looked from Harry to Tim and back again. 'Stretch?'

'That's wot we called 'im at school on account of 'im being a long streak of pi—' He grinned. 'Very tall.'

'So you two know each other, then?' Fliss said.

'Used to,' said Tim.

'Yeah, before we went our separate ways, as you might say,' Harry added.

Tim matched the other man's belligerent look for a moment then Harry switched his attention to Fliss.

'So what are you doing with Wapping's answer to Sherlock Holmes then?' he asked.

'Inspector Wallace is helping me with my story,' Fliss replied, seemingly unaware of the swirling tension between the two men.

Harry looked puzzled. 'Story?'

'I'm doing a piece for this week's *Chronicle* on the robbery at the Trinidad and Tobago warehouse the other night,' Fliss replied.

'That's a turn-up for the books, isn't it, Wallace? I didn't think you were keen on the press poking about on crime scenes.' A hint of a sneer curled Harry's top lip. 'But perhaps even the long arm of the law can be swayed by a pretty face.'

'Heard about the break-in, have you, Harry?' asked Tim, refusing to rise to the bait and regarding the docker dispassionately.

'Course,' said Harry. 'Who hasn't?'

'And about the elderly nightwatchman who was badly beaten by the gang,' added Fliss.

A horrified expression settled on Harry's hard-bitten

face. 'I did. Poor old Wilf.'

'Yes, poor old Wilf, Harry,' echoed Tim. 'When I visited him an hour ago, his face resembled three-day-old liver.'

'It's despicable,' chipped in Fliss.

'It is,' agreed Harry, shaking his head dolefully. 'Who would do such a thing to an old man?'

'That's what I'd like to know, but whoever it *was*,' continued Tim, looking Harry square in the eye, 'they're lucky I'm after them for burglary and grievous bodily harm and not murder.'

The two men stood eyeballing each other frostily for a long moment then Harry grinned.

'Well, the *Maid of Belfast* won't unload itself.' His attention shifted to Fliss. 'I'll see you at the next ELLP branch meeting?'

She nodded and a tendril of hair escaped from beneath her hat, nestling against her cheek. 'You certainly will.'

Touching the peak of his cap, Harry headed towards the dilapidated ship at the far end of the quayside, but he'd only taken a couple of steps when he turned again.

'By the way, Detective Inspector Wallace,' he called back, 'send my regards to your old muver – I can never remember if it's the nut-hutch at Claybury or Warley where she's locked up.'

Suppressing the urge to cross the distance between them and smash his fist into Harry's smirking face, Tim watched the other man go for a moment then, taking a deep breath, he turned to Fliss, who stood beside him wide-eyed with astonishment.

'Right, Miss Carmichael,' he said, smiling pleasantly at her, 'is there anything else you want to know about the burglary?'

Chapter thirteen

WITH THE DRONE of enemy aircraft getting ever louder as the third wave that night headed towards East London, Harry turned the lorry into the cobbled alleyway next to the Bull's Head in St Katherine's Way and turned off the engine.

The Bull's Head was situated next to Harrison Wharf and so near to the river you could smell it. It stood at the end of a tightly packed row of terraced shops in one of the few ancient streets that once surrounded St Katherine's church and convent. The present structure was probably built a hundred and fifty years ago, but Harry would put a pound to a penny that there had been an ale house or tavern on that spot for five hundred years or more.

As the searchlight in the Tower's moat raked the sky above, the smell of sulphur and cordite hanging in the air, he pushed open the salon door and strolled in.

With wooden floorboards, half a dozen booths fixed against the walls and rough-hewn tables and chairs, The Bull's Head was very much like any other riverside pub. Before the start of hostilities, there had been a long-forgotten brewery's name painted on the bevelled windows, but the glass had been blown in before

Christmas. There were boards across the windows now instead of glass.

But the regulars didn't complain. With its dartboard at the far end, piano in the corner and sticky floors, the Bull's Head was a working man's pub where dockers, stevedores and labourers could savour a well-earned pint at the end of the day.

As you'd expect in the middle of an air raid, the bar was empty. However, Tubby Bell, the publican, wasn't one to let the Luftwaffe interfere with business and so he'd made contingency plans. Sliding in behind the counter, Harry pushed open the door to the right of the bar and descended the stone steps.

The cellar below, with its crude stone pillars and roughly plastered walls, showed the Bull's Head had a history going back into the last century. There was even a rumour of a secret passage leading from the public house to the river that the Thames pirates had used for smuggling; but if it existed, it had never been found.

Now, though, the low-ceilinged vault was packed with drinkers who had decided that if they had to spend all night below ground, they might as well do it somewhere with booze and company. Last orders at ten thirty had been half an hour ago but with bombs dropping all around them, the police had more to worry about than the licensing laws. Tubby had set up an improvised bar out of an old door balanced on a couple of barrels, behind which he and Maureen, the Bull's Head's long-serving barmaid, were pouring pints. Gloria, a well-endowed redhead in her early forties, was wiping the counter with a rag that looked suspiciously like a pair of dirty underpants.

A bomb landed somewhere close by, and the strip lighting overhead danced about for a bit, flashing shadows around the space. The drinkers seemed unperturbed, just putting their hands over their drinks to stop the grit and plaster from the ceiling falling in.

As the aftershock subsided, Harry glanced around and spotted his brother Ben with Frankie and Sammy at the back of the crowded cellar.

'Oi, oi, the wanderer returns,' shouted Georgie, Harry's twenty-six-year-old brother, who was leaning on the bar.

He was the same height as Harry, give or take a fag paper, but was dark like their mum Kitty, whose family had pitched up half-starved from Ireland three-quarters of a century ago.

Georgie wasn't part of Harry's active crew, so to speak; his job was more what you'd describe as the family's wholesaler. He knew every pub landlord, night club proprietor and corner shop owner from the Aldgate Pump to Barking Creek, and, more importantly, what they were keen to acquire, no questions asked.

He had a well-deserved reputation as a ladies' man. There were at least three or four kiddies Harry knew of with his brother's pointed chin and wonky nose.

As usual Georgie had homed in on an available bit of skirt to try his luck. In this case it was the slender Mildred Bell, Tubby's blonde daughter, who was giving a hand behind the makeshift bar.

Weaving through the drinkers, Harry made his way over to join his middle brother.

'Get Harry his usual, will you, luv?' said Georgie, as somewhere high above them the rat-tat-tat of the ack-ack guns on Tower Green filtered down.

'Where's the old man?' Harry asked as his pint arrived.

'Over there.' His brother nodded towards the far corner, where their father sat with Boxy Poole, one of the fences they used to shift stuff.

Harry took a sip and looked at his brother.

'Just a word of advice,' he said. 'You're wasting your time with Mildred, Georgie. That one's going to keep her knees together until she's got a ring on her finger. Believe me, I know cos I've tried.'

Leaving his brother with that thought and slurping the head off his pint, Harry wandered across and stopped in front of the small beer-stained table his father was sitting at.

With grizzled grey-ginger hair and a face etched with deep lines from a lifetime of humping cargo in and out of ships in all weather, Joe Gunn looked a decade older than his fifty-two years. But looks can be deceiving, as Harry had seen him best a man half his age in a fight more than once. Although he and Harry's mother Kitty had been together for thirty-five years, Joe had never actually got around to marrying her.

He was sharp, too; had he been born with a silver spoon in his mouth instead of left on the workhouse steps wrapped in a rag, he would have made his fortune in

India or in the African colonies; instead, he'd built up his own empire here in the docks.

Looking at his barrel-chested, hammer-fisted father dressed in his working clothes, Harry always felt he was seeing himself twenty years down the road.

The cellar shook again as another bomb found its riverside target. Joe, white bristles visible in the overhead lighting, looked up and acknowledged Harry with a nod before turning back to Boxy.

'So, seventy thirty then, Boxy?' Joe asked.

Looking less than happy, Boxy chewed his gums.

'Or I'll find someone else,' Harry's father added nonchalantly.

The black-market middleman hesitated for a couple of seconds then spat on his right palm and offered his hand. Joe did the same and the two men shook.

Boxy threw back the last of his pint and stood up. 'I'll have the readies in a couple of days.'

'Just give me a nod,' Joe replied. 'Nice doing business with you.'

Boxy nodded at Harry and made his way to the door.

Putting his drink on the table, Harry took the box of Senior Service from his pocket.

'That's the last of your fags away and for a nice bit of wedge, too,' his father said as Harry sat in the chair the fence had just vacated. 'Anything new in the offing?'

Lighting his cigarette, Harry shook his head. 'The Caledonian warehouse copped it last night but by the time the firemen had put out the blaze there was nothing much left.'

'Pity,' said Joe as the cellar shuddered again.

Throwing the packet of cigarettes on the table Harry gave his father a crooked smile. 'Yeah, you'd think the krauts would have more consideration.'

His father gave a gruff laugh and lifted his glass to his lips.

'But don't worry.' Harry took a long draw on his cigarette, enjoying the tingle of nicotine in his lungs. 'I'm mulling over a few possibilities.'

'Evening.'

When Harry looked around he found Tommy Lavender standing there.

A few years younger and several stone lighter than Harry, Tommy Lavender was blond with sharp grey eyes. He always put himself down as a casual porter at Spitalfields' market on official forms, but had his fingers in a great number of pies. Be it a wireless, a pram, a new mattress or a tea set fit for royalty, if you wanted it Tommy Lavender could find it for you.

'Can I buy you another, Mr Gunn? Harry?' he asked.

'Me and Dad are good,' Harry replied, flicking ash onto the floor.

'But get yourself one, Tommy, and put it on my slate,' added Joe, picking up his son's cigarettes.

'That's very kind of you, Mr Gunn.'

Tommy went to the bar and returned a few moments later with a pint of frothy ale.

'Take a seat, Tommy,' Joe said, snorting smoke from his broken nose as he spoke.

Tommy pulled up a chair and Joe offered him a score to shift the twenty boxes of cigarettes currently stored under a railway arch in Chapmen Street in Soapy Annie's secondhand clothes yard.

'Just give me a nod, Mr Gunn,' said Tommy.

'Where will I find you?' asked Harry.

Officially Tommy was registered at the town hall as living with his mother Dolly in Maroon Street, but with lady friends dotted all over East London you never knew where he was hanging his hat on any particular day.

Tommy swallowed a mouthful of beer. 'With Rita just off Globe Road, but you can leave word in the Duke of Norfolk as she works there. But keep it quiet.'

'Wot, has one of your lady love's 'usbands come 'ome on leave?' laughed Harry.

Tommy shook his head and, gulping down another swig of his drink, leaned forward.

'Truth is, that rozzer Wallace from Wapping nick's looking for me,' he said in a low voice.

Joe frowned. 'Wot for?'

Tommy shrugged. 'Search me. 'E told my muver he was following up an inquiry, but I'm laying low until some other bugger tells him what 'e wants to know.'

Harry and his father exchanged looks.

'Naw, don't worry, Mr Gunn,' said Tommy, seeing the prospect of twenty quid in his back pocket in jeopardy. 'I'm still good for your job.'

Harry's father studied him for a moment then blew a

stream of smoke from the side of his mouth. 'The Duke of Norfolk it is.'

Tommy let out a long breath. 'Thank you, Mr Gunn.'

Grasping his pint firmly, he stood up and went to join the rest of the drinkers in the main part of the cellar.

Joe Gunn studied him from beneath his shaggy ginger eyebrows for a long moment then dropped his cigarette butt on the rough clay floor.

'I sent Ben round to bung Lily Watson another tenner this afternoon,' he said.

'That's good of you,' said Harry, blowing smoke into the thick cloud of the same floating above him.

'The old boy's still not right, you know.'

'I 'ad to make it so the cops bought 'is story,' said Harry.

'Except they didn't,' said Joe. 'Because the same Inspector Wallace who's looking for Tommy went to see Wilf and saw right through 'is story and more or less told Lily as much.'

Harry sneered. 'Wallace!'

'I'd pay him more mind than that if you've got any sense,' his father replied. ''E ain't one of those cops who don't know their arse from their elbow. 'E grew up the 'ard way in these streets, so 'e knows the way things are.'

A self-assured expression spread across Harry's hard-boned face. 'Don't worry.' He took a large mouthful of bitter. 'Me and Wallace have cross swords before, so if he starts sniffing around too much I'll deal with 'im.'

Chapter fourteen

CHECKING IN THE hall mirror that her lipstick hadn't smudged, Fliss was just about to slip her arm into her light-blue plastic mac when the front door opened.

Her father, dressed in his black cassock, dog collar and overcoat, walked in, bringing a gust of wind and rain with him.

'Good morning, my dear,' he said, as he deposited his umbrella in the stand. 'You're off to work early this morning.'

'I've a long piece on the WVS to finish,' Fliss replied, carefully positioning the transparent hood over her black felt hat.

'Sounds like you've got a busy day,' continued Hugh, as he hung up his coat. 'I hope you've had a proper breakfast.'

Fliss smiled but didn't reply.

She hadn't had breakfast because she'd left the shelter before Olive and her team from the Women's Voluntary Service team had set up their morning canteen and at her mother's instructions, Mrs Lavender never served breakfast before eight, but it didn't matter as there was a Jewish baker just down from the *Chronicle*'s office that

sold freshly made bagels. Once she'd polished that off –
that and had a couple of cups of coffee – she'd be ready
for anything.

The air raid sirens had gone off just after six the
evening before, heralding the imminent arrival of the
Luftwaffe, who had blitzed the area with wave after wave
of bombers until the all-clear sounded at dawn.

Although it had been the unremitting explosions
that had caused most people's broken nights, Fliss had
woken when a high explosive nearby rocked the church
crypt then spent the rest of the night staring up at Prue's
bunk bed overhead. When she'd first returned home,
her sleepless hours had been spent arguing with Giles
in her head. However, the man who intruded into her
thoughts most often at this hour was the very annoying
but undeniably attractive DI Wallace.

And it wasn't bad enough that the blasted man
invaded her dreams; annoyingly during the day she
found herself wondering if DI Wallace's special someone
was a blonde or a brunette and why his mother was in a
mental institute.

Pulling herself together, Fliss returned her attention to
her father. 'Were there many at morning prayers?'

'The usual number,' he replied, 'which was heartening,
considering the dreadful night we all suffered last night.
Several times your mother and I thought we were about
to meet the Almighty.' Hugh shook his head dolefully.
'But praise be, we were spared.'

'We were,' said Fliss, putting on a plucky smile. 'And

now I have to get to work or I'll have Mr Longman after me.' Crossing the hallway, she stretched up and planted a quick kiss on her father's cheek. 'I'll see you later.'

Picking up her satchel, she hurried to the front door and left the rectory.

Despite the earlier rain, the acrid smell of cordite, spent armaments and burned wood still hung heavy in the spring air. Walking through the rectory's gateposts, Fliss turned right and headed towards the High Street, noting that columns of thick black smoke were still darkening the morning sky over London and Limehouse docks to the south.

Thankfully, the buildings in the High Street and Ben Jonson Road still seemed to be standing, albeit with the glass from their windows lying shattered on the pavement. As always, even though it was only after seven thirty, the shopkeepers were already taking down their shutters, checking for any damage and sweeping up stray shrapnel, dislodged plaster and glass. They weren't the only ones out and about: Stepney's main street was alive with ARP personal. At the far end, the local warden had set up an information desk and there was already a line of people queuing to check the overnight casualty lists. There was also a group of weary-looking auxiliary firemen lounging around their appliances, while a couple of local women served them each a well-deserved cuppa.

Passing St Winifred's on her left, Fliss stood back as an ambulance threw dirty water on to the pavement, then crossed the road into Stepney Way. She was greeted with the all too familiar sight after a night of heavy bombing: a stream of heavy-eyed, rain-sodden women, with children on their hips, pushing prams, all heading towards the council relief centre in the Ocean Street School.

Giving them a sympathetic look as she passed, Fliss carried on. However, as Arbour Square police station came into view, she spotted a couple of familiar figures, both with rain dripping off their coats, coming towards her. One was pushing a pram with a small boy perched on top and an older child walking alongside clutching the handle. The other had her coat unbuttoned to accommodate her growing stomach.

Fliss quickened her pace.

'Not you too, Prue?' she gasped as she reached the forlorn little party.

With tears brimming in her eyes, her sister nodded. 'There was a direct hit on Edie Miller's house three doors away and it brought the whole terrace down.'

'Was anyone hurt?'

'The heavy rescue chaps are still digging for the Andersons at number twelve,' said Prue, her voice faltering with shock and emotion. 'But there's not much hope as their house is just a pile of rubble now. Thankfully, most of the street were in one shelter or another last night.'

'Everything's gone,' added Rosie, tears streaming down her cheeks. 'All our clothes, Mick's fishing gear, the boys' toys, my mum's special China … Everything.'

Prue put her arms around her sister-in-law. 'It's all right, Rosie. They'll sort us out at the relief centre.'

Fliss frowned. 'No they won't,' she said, stripping off her see-through rain mac and placing it over her sister's soggy shoulders. 'Because you're all coming to the rectory.'

'You poor luvs,' said Mrs Lavender, her wrinkled face a picture of sympathy as she regarded the bedraggled party dripping rainwater onto the black-and-white hall tiles. 'You boys run into the kitchen, and I might be able to find you both a biscuit or two to put a smile back on those angel faces of yours.'

Needing no further urging, nine-year-old Michael and six-year-old Russell, grey school socks gathering around their ankles, dashed towards the back of the house.

'Thank you, Mrs Lavender,' said Rosie, shifting baby Ellen onto the other hip.

The housekeeper's expression softened further.

'She's such a little poppet,' she said, offering the baby a gnarled finger to grab. 'And she looks just like your mum.'

'I know,' whispered Rosie, as tears welled up in her eyes again.

'You come with me too, ducks, cos it looks as if you're in need of a hot sweet cuppa,' added the housekeeper.

She trotted off down the hall towards the kitchen. Rosie followed, however, as she passed Fliss and Prue, she gave them an uncertain look. 'Are you sure your mother won't mind, Fliss?'

Fliss forced a light laugh. 'Of course not. Now you go and get warm while Prue and I have a quick chat with her.'

Balancing her daughter on her hip, Rosie headed for the housekeeper's domain.

On hearing the door click shut, Prue turned to Fliss and burst into tears.

Taking her sister in her arms, Fliss held her close while Prue sobbed for a full minute or more on her shoulder.

'It's all gone. Ev-everything …' she said, raising her tear-stained face.

'But you're still here and so is your baby, as well as Rosie and children,' Fliss replied, taking her fresh handkerchief from her sleeve and handing it to her. 'And that's all that matters right now, isn't it?'

Giving her a plucky little smile, Prue nodded then frowned. 'Mother won't like it.'

'Well, she'll have to lump it then, won't she?' Fliss replied.

They both turned in the direction of the small parlour that overlooked the garden. Fliss knocked once, then, grasping the brass handle, she opened the door.

Their mother, wearing a tweed skirt and a camel-coloured twinset, was sitting at the antique bureau her grandmother had given her as a wedding present in front of the French window. Pen in hand, she was bent over a leather-bound record book with several tradesmen's receipts beside it.

'I'm sorry to interrupt you, Mother,' said Fliss,

stopping on the rug that covered the parquet floor. 'But something's happened.'

'Well,' Marjorie said, putting down her pen, 'I hope it is important, Felicity, because—'

She turned and through the lenses of her reading glasses her pale-grey eyes fixed on Prue.

'What the—'

'Arbour Terrace suffered a direct hit last night so Prue, Rosie and her children have been bombed out,' cut in Fliss. 'Now Mrs Leitner and her children have gone, there's a spare room upstairs for the Stapletons and Prue can come in with me.'

'Can she?' said Marjorie crossly.

Fliss regarded her mother levelly. 'Yes, she can.'

'And I'm supposed to agree, am I? Just like that?' said Marjorie.

'Yes, because Prue is your daughter,' said Fliss.

'It's a pity she didn't remember that when she decided to transgress God's holy law and marry a divorcee.'

'What I did, Mother, was marry the man I love,' Prue replied, glaring at her mother. 'But don't worry, I know when I'm not welcome. So if it's all right with you, I'll let Rosie and the boys finish with Mrs Lavender and then we'll head off to the relief centre.'

Placing a restraining hand on her sister's arm, Fliss glared across her mother. 'Either Prue, Rosie and the children move in or—'

'Or what, Fliss?' Her mother gave a hard laugh. 'You'll leave too? That would be no great loss, since in the last

189

month you've spent all your time doing goodness knows what for this upstart Labour Party of yours and absolutely nothing around the parish.'

'In case it's escaped your notice, Mother, I have a full-time job.'

'Well brought-up young ladies never had jobs when I was your age,' Marjorie replied.

'No, but they've invented aeroplanes since then.' Mother and daughter exchanged frosty looks then Fliss smiled. 'However, I do have a job and you might be interested to know I'm supposed to be writing an article about the way the Boy Scouts and Girl Guides are helping us fight Hitler for this week's edition. However, I could as easily write a story about an unnamed rector's wife who turned away her youngest daughter who is pregnant—'

'Pregnant!' interrupted Marjorie, her eyes flying open.

'Yes, almost five months,' said Prue, looking incredulously at their mother. 'Surely you noticed.'

Over her spectacles Marjorie eyes flickered over Prue's slightly swollen stomach. 'I just thought you'd eaten too much of that ghastly pie and mash the locals guzzle.'

'And,' continued Fliss as her mother's attention returned to her, 'what do you think St Winifred's Mothers' Union and Flower Guild would make of that when they read it over their toast and marmalade on Saturday?'

Marjorie's hard gaze wavered. 'You wouldn't dare!'

Fliss folded her arms. 'Try me!'

With the familiar flush of annoyance creeping up Marjorie's several chins, her lips pulled together.

'Very well,' she said grudgingly after a couple of moments. 'I suppose it's my Christian duty, but it doesn't mean I have changed my mind one jot about your marriage, Prudence.'

'I didn't for one moment think you had,' said Prue. 'But thank you anyway for letting me, Rosie and the children stay.'

Giving them an infuriated look, Marjorie huffed by way of reply then turned back to her task.

'Come on, Prue,' said Fliss, slipping her arm through her sister's, 'I'll ring the office and let them know I'll be late in then I'll give you and Rosie a hand settling in.

'Oh, and by the by,' Fliss gave her mother a sweet smile, 'I'll tell Mrs Lavender that Prue, Rosie and the children will be having their meals with us in the dining room with the rest of the family.'

Chapter fifteen

'JUST TEN MINUTES and we'll be opening the doors to the multitudes,' said Mavis Pringle, the East London Labour Party's secretary.

'Good,' said Fliss as she put a programme on the last chair in the back row. 'Let's hope we have a good turn-out.'

It was Wednesday 19 March and just past seven in the evening. Fliss was one of the handful of volunteers helping the committee members of the Stepney and Whitechapel Branch of the Labour Party to prepare Myrtle Street School Hall for a public meeting.

'I hear Ernest Bevin himself might be coming,' said Mavis, her pale-blue eyes lighting up with excitement behind her spectacle's bulky lenses.

A machinist by trade, Mavis had joined the Party as a mere slip of a girl some forty years before. Grey-haired and wide of beam after giving birth to six strapping boys, she had a propensity for wearing the most ill-matched combination. Tonight was no exception as she'd teamed a tartan kilt with a flowery blouse and a multicoloured horizontal-striped cardigan.

'It would be a bit of a coup for the branch if he did,' she added.

Although she thought it unlikely that the Minister of Labour and National Service would attend, Fliss refrained from saying as much.

'I ought to just go and make sure Mr and Mrs Tully have everything they need; they're in charge of our information point this evening,' said Mavis. 'I'll see you later.'

She hurried off toward Ivy and John Tully, the middle-aged couple manning the refectory table covered with Labour Party pamphlets and books.

Taking another pile of programmes, Fliss made her way along the next row of chairs but after dropping a leaflet on a couple of seats, her mind wandered back to the topic she'd been mulling over for the last few weeks: Harry Gunn's words about DI Wallace's mother. Was she in a mental institution and if she was, then why? He said he had a brother who died, so did his mother have something to do with it? And what about his father? Is he dead and if not, where is he now? The reporter in Fliss couldn't help thinking it must be quite a story.

'Do you think we're ready to open the doors?' asked Reg Moore, branch membership secretary, cutting into her musings.

'Pretty much,' said Fliss. 'Any sign of our guest speakers?'

Pressing his lips together, Reg shook his head. 'But I hope they get here soon. We start in ten minutes and Pete Ellis has just gone to let people—'

The door opened as the members of the public poured in.

'Looks like we're going to have a good crowd,' said George Summers, one of the committee members, raising his voice over the sound of chatter and scraping chairs. 'We'd better go and find ourselves a seat. Shall I save you one, Fliss?'

She shook her head. 'I said I'd give a hand with the book stall, so I've nabbed myself a seat at the back.'

Fliss watched the crowds shuffle in and find seats.

'Thank goodness,' said Reg, with a heavy sigh of relief. 'Our speakers have arrived.'

Fliss turned and her heart lurched. Standing in the doorway behind the milling crowds, stood three men. Two she knew vaguely as the London Area Party treasurer and the prospective Labour candidate for Leytonstone and Wanstead; unfortunately the third she knew only too well.

Wearing a sombre dark-grey suit and a superior expression on his face, there stood Giles low-life bastard Naylor.

Taking off their hats, they all shook hands with Reg, who then led the three of them down the side of the hall towards the stage. However, they'd only taken half a dozen steps when Giles glanced across and spotted Fliss.

He caught Reg's arm and quickly spoke to him before breaking way from the platform party and, as an icy-feeling drained through Fliss, hurrying over to where she was standing.

'Fliss,' he said, as he reached her.

Despite her hammering heart, she gave him a glacial look. 'Miss Carmichael, if you don't mind.' Fliss glanced behind him. 'No Gwen tonight.'

He frowned. 'Look, about Gwen—'

'Sorry to interrupt,' said Dora Abraham, the branch's national rep, 'but Mr Potter is about to open the meeting, so they need you on the stage, Mr Naylor.'

'You'd better go,' said Fliss flatly.

Looking beseechingly at her, he hesitated.

'Mr Naylor,' Dora repeated, with just a hint of panic in her tone.

He pressed his lips together then, much to Fliss's relief, he followed Dora to the stage, where he took the vacant seat beside the chairman.

As the room quietened in anticipation, Fliss slipped into the back row. However, as Gordon Potter rose to his feet the hall door swung open again. Fliss automatically glanced around, and her heart started hammering all over again.

With the collar of his trench coat turned up and the brim of his fedora at its usually rakish angle, DI Wallace stood by the door. Removing his hat, his dark eyes surveyed the room for a second then fell on her. Their gazes locked for a long moment then, after glancing around, the inspector made his way across to the other side of the hall from Fliss and took a seat.

Crossing her legs for the umpteenth time in the past hour, Fliss forced her attention back to the speaker, who was just about coming to the end of his allocated half-hour.

In his mid-forties and dressed in an old tweed suit, the evening's main guest had a thick Welsh accent, which

Fliss could barely understand. This didn't really matter because she spent half her time trying to ignore Giles and the other half dragging her eyes from DI Wallace. Giles, on the other hand, spent the whole meeting staring across at her with that scolded-puppy expression. This irritated Fliss no end, but oddly not half as much as the fact that DI Wallace hadn't glanced her way once.

Finally, Mr Bevan rounded up the Party's arguments for a new system of universal health care and the branch chairman stood up and led the applause. Leaving her seat, Fliss went to join the elderly couple on the information table.

'How's it going?' she asked in a low voice as a man sitting in the audience in front of her asked a question about unemployment benefit.

'Not so bad,' Ivy replied in the same low tone. 'Actually, could you mind the shop while we get a cuppa before the rush?'

'Of course,' Fliss replied.

Ivy and John headed off to the refreshments table.

Straightening up a couple of the piles of leaflets, Fliss's eyes strayed back to DI Wallace. He was sitting with his long legs crossed and his arm outstretched across the back of the empty chair next to him. Her gaze rested on his well-formed hand and dexterous fingers, which set off an odd sensation and conjured up several unexpected yet rather pleasant thoughts in her head.

A burst of applause brought her mind back from its wandering as the meeting came to an end. Seats scraped as the audience stood up and headed for the refreshments at the back of the room. A few committee members had joined those on the stage as they milled around congratulating themselves, but after giving them a cursory glance, Fliss's eyes returned to DI Wallace, who was chatting to a couple of young chaps who had been sitting near to him.

'Fliss.' She turned and found Giles standing beside the trestle table.

Giving him a chilly look, her eyes flicked over him. For almost as long as she'd known him Giles had sought to play down his privileged background by donning the universal uniform of the working man: canvas trousers, flannel shirt, baggy jumper beneath his dune-coloured corduroy jacket. Tonight, however, as he was mixing with members of the Party's ruling council, he'd forgone his usual efforts to look like a factory worker or labourer and slipped back into his public school and university-educated persona, and was wearing a suit and tie.

Looking at him standing there not an arm's length from her, Fliss wondered, not for the first time, how she could have been so stupid; how could she not have seen him for the arrogant, lying bastard he really was?

'I can't tell you how happy I am to see you,' he said, smiling warmly at her.

'Well, the feeling is certainly not mutual,' she replied, handing a pamphlet to a couple of youthful Home Guards men.

'You're looking very pretty tonight as always,' said Giles, looking beseechingly at her.

Giving him a caustic look, Fliss turned her back to him and handed a pamphlet to a young woman in buff-coloured dungarees and a scarf turban.

She noticed DI Wallace had made his way to the refreshments table and was chatting to a young woman with fair hair and very red, very smiley lips. She was looking up at him with a wide-eyed wonder – as well she might, thought Fliss, somewhat peeved by the blonde's flirtation, as there was no denying that the CID officer was looking very handsome tonight.

Shoving aside an odd niggle of irritation, Fliss turned her attention to a middle-aged couple flipping through the leaflets. 'Did you enjoy the meeting?'

'I'd vote for that Welsh bloke,' said the women, in a forest-green Women's Voluntary Service uniform.

'Politicians! They're all the blooming same,' scoffed the man in rough working clothes standing beside her. 'Liars, the lot of them. I mean, see a doctor for nuffink! I should cocoa.'

'But it'll be different when we have a Labour government. Here,' Fliss thrust a leaflet at him. 'At least have a read and see what we plan to do about housing and health.'

Sneering at the pamphlet Fliss was holding, he stomped off towards the door.

'Thanks, luv,' said his wife, taking it from Fliss. 'Don't mind my Stan. 'E was in the last run-in with the Boche and ain't been the same since.'

She set off after her husband as other people gathered around the table.

'Look, Fliss,' said Giles, stepping into her eyeline, 'if you'd just—'

'Please take one, they're free,' Fliss said, ignoring him and smiling at a couple of young men in National Fire Service uniforms who were browsing the publications on the table.

Giles frowned. 'Fliss ...' But before he could say any more he was cornered by an earnest-looking young man wearing a circular red badge with the words 'Labour Party and Liberty' on it.

'Everything all right?' asked Ivy, as she and her husband returned, cup in hand, to their posts at the information table.

'Yes, thank you,' she replied. 'I'll think I'll go and get myself a cuppa.'

Stepping out of from behind the table, Fliss headed across to the refreshments, noticing in passing that the blonde talking to DI Wallace was still batting her overly made-up eyes at him and giggling.

The thought that he might be one of those men who prefer blondes to brunettes was just forming in her mind when someone grabbed her arm.

Pulling it free, her head snapped around. 'Giles?'

'This has gone on long enough, Fliss,' he said, as she glared at him.

'I agree. So push off.' She turned and took a step, but he grabbed her arm again.

She tried to tug it loose again, but his grip held firm.

'You're hurting me. Let go,' said Fliss, as his fingers tightened on her upper arm.

His frown deepened. 'I will when you stop behaving hysterically.'

'Excuse me, Miss Carmichael,' said a deep voice behind her. 'Is this man bothering you?'

Tim's sole reason for attending the political meeting was to let Harry Gunn know that he had him in his sights for the Trinidad & Tobago warehouse job, among other things. However, despite his quarry being nowhere to be seen, when he walked in and saw Fliss Carmichael sitting in the audience, an unexpected feeling of something he couldn't quite name swelled in his chest.

This was irritating on two levels. Firstly, because, despite her assuming that all police officers were raging Tories, he actually agreed with many of the post-war welfare reforms the Labour Party were proposing so was interested in what the speaker had to say. And secondly because Fliss Carmichael already took up more of his waking hours and, arousingly, his sleeping hours than he liked.

He'd purposely decided not to take one of the empty seats alongside her, but despite the eloquence of the speakers he found his mind constantly drifting across to where she was sitting. Although he'd been tempted to make a beeline for her when the proceedings ended, he held back. However, when the man she was clearly trying to get away from grabbed her, fury sent Tim striding across the hall in an instant and now the look of relief in her eyes set Tim's senses reeling.

The chap let her go.

Tim shifted his attention to Fliss, who was rubbing her arm. 'Are you hurt?'

'Nothing that won't mend,' she replied, giving her assailant a hard look.

'Now look here,' said the fellow, looking haughtily down his nose at Tim. 'Miss Carmichael and I are having a private conversation so I'd be obliged if you would—'

'Conversation?' Tim replied, matching the other man's hostile stare. 'Looked to me like you were assaulting her. Who are you, anyway?'

Pulling down the front of his tailored jacket, Giles drew himself up to his full height.

'Giles Naylor, editor of the *Workers' Clarion*, chairman of the Pimlico branch of the Labour Party and member of the Party's central committee,' he said, regarding Tim with a rather imperious expression for an avowed socialist.

So this was the bastard who'd betrayed Fliss and for whom, in her hurt and pain, she had downed half a bottle of gin. Thoughts of what might have befallen her in the graveyard that night loomed up in Tim's mind, and he clenched his fists.

'And I don't see what business it is of yours,' added Naylor, maintaining his haughty expression, 'but if you must know, Miss Carmichael and I were engaged until we had a bit of a misunderstanding recently and—'

'Ha, *misunderstanding*.' Fliss crossed her arms and glared at him. 'Being discovered in bed with your secretary is hardly a misunderstanding.'

Naylor gave her an exasperated look. 'Look, Fliss, darling, I—'

She raised her hand. 'I don't want to hear it, Giles.'

'But, Fliss—'

'You heard Miss Carmichael,' cut in Tim, stepping closer to her.

'How dare you?' spluttered Naylor. 'Who the hell are you, anyway?'

'This is Detective Inspector Wallace,' chipped in Fliss, giving her erstwhile fiancé a somewhat smug look.

Naylor blanched and his gaze wavered. 'You … you're a police officer?'

'I am,' Tim replied. 'But even if I wasn't, I wouldn't stand by and let a woman be manhandled or bullied.'

Naylor stood biting his lip, looking suddenly uncertain.

'Very well,' he said after a moment or two. 'But really, Fliss, given your upbringing, I'd thought you of all people would be a little more forgiving.'

Fliss considered her unfaithful ex-fiancé for a moment and hope flared in Naylor's eyes.

'Do me a favour, Giles,' she said.

'Anything, darling,' he replied, giving her a doe-eyed look. 'Anything at all. Just name it.'

'Well then: push off,' Fliss replied. 'And don't ever bother me again.'

An angry expression replaced Giles's doting one in an instant. His gaze darted from Fliss to Tim and back again, and anger enflamed his cheeks as he struggled to control his annoyance. For a moment Tim thought – no, *hoped* – he would argue, but instead the man spun on his heels and stomped off.

They both watched him for a moment then Fliss rubbed her arm again.

'Did he hurt you?' Tim asked again as he turned to face her.

'A bit,' she replied.

Frowning, Tim looked across the top of her head to where Giles was now talking to a couple of young women.

Feeling a gentle touch, he gazed down at Fliss's small hand on his forearm, then into her dark-brown eyes.

'As I said, it's nothing that won't heal. But thank you for stepping in and ...' She gave him a bashful look. 'Well, thank you for rescuing me in St Winifred's graveyard last month, too.'

Tim raised an eyebrow. 'I didn't think you remembered.'

'I don't,' Fliss replied. 'My sister told me. It was the day ...'

'You found out about Giles,' Tim said.

She nodded, then gave him what could only be described as a flirtatious look. 'Because I don't want you to think I make a habit of downing half a bottle of gin.'

'I'm pleased to hear it,' he replied, responding with a look of his own.

'But I did pay for it,' she continued, 'as I had one hell of a hangover the next morning.'

Tim laughed. 'I bet.'

'And we all know what that's like,' she said.

'Actually, I don't drink,' he replied.

She gave him the same astonished look he'd seen a hundred times before when he'd told people he was teetotal.

'My father was a drinker,' Tim replied. 'Actually, he wasn't just a drinker. He was a drunk,' he added without thinking. 'That's why I don't drink and because …'

Fliss gave him a curious look. 'Because?'

Childhood memories of pressing his hands over his ears to block out the raised voices and crashing furniture flitted through Tim's mind.

'It's a long story—'

The air raid siren on top of the building screamed out its warning and everyone in the school hall started to file out.

Putting on his hat, Tim positioned himself behind Fliss to prevent her being jostled in the crush and they made their way out onto the street.

'St Winifred's is just five minutes away, so why don't you join me there?' shouted Fliss, over the wail of the siren. 'I'm sure we can squeeze you in.'

'Thanks for the offer,' he shouted back, 'but I ought to get back to the nick to see what's what. Let me see you safely to the shelter first,' he added.

'No, honestly,' she shouted. 'It's just five minutes—'

'It's no trouble,' he persisted, mindful of the reports detailing the assault and rape of women that were sitting on his desk.

Giving him a slightly exasperated look, she set off towards the church. Tim fell into step beside her and as she'd predicted, within five minutes they were standing between St Winifred's stone gateposts.

'Well, here we are,' she yelled, as people walked either side of them towards the safety of the church.

'Indeed,' Tim yelled back. 'Nice to meet you again, Miss Carmichael.'

She nodded. 'And thank you again, DI Wallace.'

'All part of my job. Rescuing damsels in distress, Miss Carmichael,' he replied, his gaze holding hers.

'Perhaps one day I'll return the favour, DI Wallace.'

She stared up at him for a long moment then turned and headed for the church doors.

Although the low hum of squadrons of approaching aircraft was growing lounder overhead, Tim watched her until she entered the safety of the church. As he did, he pondered how, despite having never mentioned his father to another living soul, it had seemed quite natural to tell Fliss. In fact, had the air raid not interrupted them, he knew he would have told Fliss Carmichael everything about the alcohol-fuelled nightmare of his childhood.

Chapter sixteen

Reading to the bottom of the sheet, Fliss slipped it behind the next page and read the last couple of paragraphs of the two-page essay. Then she looked up at the sixteen-year-old girl sitting opposite her.

'It's very good, Johanna,' she said. 'I've only had to correct a couple of grammatical mistakes, and I'm sure you'll get top marks.'

Johanna's narrow shoulders sagged with relief. 'Thank goodness. I so want to get a merit in my English.'

It was a little after five fifteen in the afternoon on the last Friday in March, over a week since the Labour Party meeting. Fliss was sitting with Johanna in the back parlour, which was smaller than the main parlour on the other side of the hall.

Although when they first moved into the rectory, her parents had used this room as their main sitting room, the arrival of the refugee families had seen it slowly become their communal room – as was evident by the toy box beside the sofa with bricks and tinplate cars piled in it, the rag dolls propped up on the easy chairs and the copies of *Boy's Own* and *Beano* lying on the coffee table.

The room also overlooked the garden, which had similarly been transformed after the bishop, much to Marjorie's annoyance, sent a directive urging the clergy to sign up for the government's Dig for Victory campaign and a dozen men from the parish arrived with spades and hoes.

The summerhouse against the rectory's far wall had been signed up for war service too, and was now home to a dozen battery hens whose produce would provide the children's supper that day. While waiting for their scrambled egg on toast, Johanna's sister Eva and Nicolas and Freda Haas were sitting cross-legged in front of the huge cabinet-built Bush radio at the far end of the parlour listening to *Children's Hour*.

Fliss glanced over the young girl's essay again. 'Well, Johanna, I'd be very surprised if you didn't earn a distinction. Is there any news yet about the scholarship for college?'

Johanna shook her head. 'Mr King said it's early days yet and he would contact the Queen Wilhelmina Educational Fund again after Easter. What are you working on?' She pointed to the sheet of paper rolled around the carriage of Fliss's typewriter.

'I'm writing a piece about the thefts from the docks,' Fliss replied, handing the assignment back to her. 'It doesn't have to be in until Tuesday, but I want to finish it before my brother arrives on Monday.'

'You must be excited to see him,' said Johanna, as her own eighteen-month-old brother, who'd been playing with his bricks on the hearth rug, waddled over to join them.

'I am. It's been almost nine months since his last leave,' Fliss replied, as Johanna set the toddler on her lap.

She was indeed looking forward to Rob's visit, but not as much as her mother, who was behaving as though she was expecting the Messiah returning from the Golden City rather than her eldest offspring visiting from his army barracks in Inverness.

As the closing couple of bars of the *Children's Hour* signature tune floated across the room, the doorbell rang.

There was a pause as Mrs Lavender made her way through the house to open the door, followed by the sound of a man's voice. For one ridiculous moment the thought that it might be DI Wallace flashed through Fliss's mind, until the door opened and someone else entirely strode in.

'Rob!' she yelled, jumping to her feet and throwing herself into her brother's embrace.

'Hello, Fliss,' he said softly, his arms encircling her.

Resting her face against the khaki barathea of his captain's uniform, tears pressed at the back of Fliss's eyes.

After a moment he released her, and they smiled at each other.

With long limbs, finely sculptured features and a firm chin, Rob, like her, favoured their mother's aristocratic d'Apremont lineage. However, the spark of wit and humour in his light-blue eyes showed there wasn't a haughty bone in her brother's athletic body.

'This is such a surprise,' she said.

'A nice one, I hope.' He grinned.

'Of course, you great loon,' said Fliss, slapping his upper arm lightly. 'But we weren't expecting you until Monday.'

'Well, I managed to scrounge a lift to Edinburgh so I caught the train south a few days early,' he replied. 'Where is everyone?'

'Mother and Dad are at a clergy dinner at the bishop's house in West Ham,' said Fliss.

'Lucky them,' said Rob.

'Not really,' laughed Fliss. 'It's Lent, so they'll be fortunate if they have anything other than bubble and sque—'

The door opened again.

'Rob!' shouted Prue, as she crossed the space between them and launched herself into his arms.

He hugged her for a moment then held her away from him and looked puzzled.

'What are you—'

'Doing here?' she cut in. 'We got bombed out and …' She told him briefly about meeting Fliss on her way to the relief centre and the subsequent conversation with their mother.

'I should think so, too,' he said when she'd finished.

'I did write and tell you,' said Fliss.

'I'm sure you did,' said Rob. 'But our camp is so remote it takes a while for anything to reach us, including the post. It'll no doubt be waiting for me when I get back. And anyway, it's an extra surprise. And we'll have another one to look forward to when Master or Miss Quinn arrive?'

'You've got a bit of a wait, I'm afraid. Three months, in fact. However,' Prue slipped her arm through her brother's, 'you'll be pleased to hear we've got a neck of lamb hotpot simmering away in the oven and if I peel a few extra potatoes and shell a few more peas we can enjoy dinner together. In the meantime, let me make you a nice cuppa.'

'So, Rob,' said Fliss, as he took a sip of his tea, 'although Mr Longman is forever sending me out to cover so-called women's stories, I'm determined to get my teeth into something meatier.'

'I'm sure you will,' Rob replied, giving his sister a weary smile.

Although every bone in his body ached from having his six-foot-one frame cramped in a succession of overcrowded carriages on his two-day train journey home from Inverness, after sitting for the past half-hour listening to his sisters talking to him about domestic rather than military happenings, a sense of peace stole over Rob Carmichael.

The three siblings were enjoying a cup of tea and a slice of Madeira cake at the long pine table in the kitchen at the back of the house. Rob let his gaze wander out onto the garden at the back of the house. Since he was last home in the summer, it had undergone a transformation from an oasis of rural tranquillity into a smallholding complete with rows of potato fronds and runner bean poles. He wondered what his mother made of it all.

Actually, although he would never mention it to anyone, Rob had felt slightly relieved that his mother wasn't there when he arrived, as she did have a tendency to fuss over him as if he were ten, rather than thirty.

'Well, you seem to have landed on your feet, Fliss,' Rob said. 'And I'm sorry about you and Giles.'

Actually, Rob wasn't sorry because he had identified Giles as an absolute bastard of the first order the minute he'd laid eyes on the man.

Fliss forced a smile. 'Thank you, Rob. It's nice to have someone be understanding.'

'Mother?'

She nodded.

'Just ignore her,' Rob replied.

'That's what I told her,' said Prue, who was sitting next to Rob.

'It's not so easy when you have to sit opposite her at the dining-room table twice a day,' Fliss replied. 'Although it's a lot easier now Prue's here.'

'Yes, we can share her disapproval between us,' said Prue, giving her sister a fond look.

'How is Jack?' Rob asked, taking a sip of tea.

'Still off in the wilds somewhere,' Prue replied, longing for her absent husband clear in her voice. 'He writes when he can, but from what I can understand he is out on manoeuvres in remote areas for days, sometime weeks, so I might get a letter a day for a week or two then nothing for a month. I sometimes wish he could tell me what he's doing, but maybe I'm better off not knowing.'

She was probably right. Although Rob couldn't be absolutely certain, from what he'd gleaned from Jack when he'd last seen him he'd say that his brother-in-law was probably attached to a company preparing for some behind-enemy-lines operation somewhere.

'Still, at least we don't have to suffer Mother's reproachful looks all night too, because as soon as the air raid siren sounds we decamp to St Winifred's crypt, don't we, Prue?' said Fliss.

He didn't blame them. Although his parents had set up a very comfortable shelter for themselves in the rectory's wine cellar, he wouldn't relish several hours of his father's foghorn snoring or witnessing the spectre of his mother in curlers and night cream smeared over her face.

'Is Lydia coming to see you?' asked Fliss.

'She's going to try to get back to London,' he said. 'But now that she's been taken on by the film division of the Ministry of Information, alongside her catwalk work at the House of Beaumont, she hardly has a moment to herself.'

'The film division?' Fliss looked impressed. 'What's she been in?'

'Oh, you know, this and that,' he replied airily.

Actually, he had no idea what his fiancée had been up to, but she was obviously very busy as he hadn't received a letter from her for almost three weeks, despite having sent her two, including the one telling her when he would be home on leave.

Suppressing the niggle of annoyance in his chest, Rob broke eye contact with his sister and bit into his cake.

'Delicious,' he said, pulling a blissful expression. 'Did you make it?'

Fliss raised an eyebrow. 'What do you think? It's Prue's.'

Rob laughed and was just about to take another mouthful when he heard the rectory's front door open. There was a pause then the sound of high heels clip-clopping towards the kitchen over the black-and-white floor tiles before a slender young woman with braided black hair pinned like a halo across her head appeared at the kitchen door.

She was wearing an unadorned dark-green suit with a cream blouse, a silver Star of David resting on the bow at her neck, and carrying a tan briefcase.

Rob stared at her for a moment then remembered his manners.

'Dr Kratz,' he said, rising to his feet.

'Captain Carmichael,' she replied, giving him a polite smile. 'How nice it is to see you.'

'And you,' he replied, looking into her very large, very dark-brown and very confident eyes.

'Are you home on leave?'

'Yes, I arrived about an hour ago,' he replied, noting in passing that her German accent was less noticeable that when he'd first met her last August.

Her expression softened. 'And are you well?'

'Very well, thank you.' His smile widened. 'All the better for being home again.'

'I imagine you would be,' she replied. 'But I am interrupting. Please excuse me, I—'

'Not at all, Hester,' cut in Fliss. 'You look like you could do with a cuppa.'

'And a slice of Madeira, too,' added Prue.

Hester hesitated for a moment then, placing her briefcase on one kitchen chair, she pulled out another.

'That is for sure.' She sighed as she sat down. 'As long as I am not getting in the way.'

'Of course not,' said Rob before either of his sisters could reply.

'Anyway, I'm sure Rob is sick to the back teeth of me telling him about my job and anti-racketeering campaign,' said Fliss.

'Just as Fliss has had enough of me telling her about the how tedious and dull army life is in the wilds of the Grampian Mountains with just the grouse and the odd red deer to keep you company,' Rob added.

He and Fliss exchanged affectionate looks then Fliss turned her attention back to Hester.

'Bad day?' asked Prue, as she stood up to get another mug.

'No more than usual,' Hester replied. 'Just a casualty full of asthmatic children gasping for breath because of the smoke from last night's bombing raid.'

'I thought most of the children had been evacuated

from London,' said Rob as Prue poured another cup of tea.

'They were,' Pre explained, tucking a wedge of cake on the side of the saucer. 'But some of the children were treated little better than animals and cheap labour by the people who were supposed to be caring for them, so their mothers fetched them back.'

'I wanted to write an article about it but no doubt the Ministry of Information's censors would block it as being bad for morale,' said Fliss.

'That's why the authorities have reopened many of the schools and the children's wards in all the hospitals are overflowing with youngsters injured either by the nightly bombing directly or from playing on the destroyed buildings it leaves in its wake.' Hester raised an eyebrow. 'To be honest, Captain Carmichael, we would welcome a couple of days of dull tedium in East London.'

'Are you finished for the day, then?' asked Fliss.

Hester shook her head. A tendril of hair escaped to graze her cheek, replacing her crisp, professional persona with a softer one in an instant.

'I've got an evening clinic at the East London Children's Hospital,' she explained. 'Actually, I have a pile of notes to write up, so if you would all excuse me, I'll take my tea through to the parlour so I can make a start on them.'

'Of course,' said Fliss.

Hester stood up and so did Rob.

'Lovely to see you again, Dr Kratz.'

'You too, Captain Carmichael,' she replied.

'Rob, please,' he laughed. 'Captain Carmichael makes me think I'm back on the parade ground.'

She smiled. 'Then I'll ask you call me Hester in return.'

His light-blue eyes gazed into her dark-brown ones for a moment then, picking up her tea in one hand and her briefcase in the other, she gave the three siblings a brief smile and walked out of the kitchen, taking something Rob couldn't quite identify with her.

Chapter seventeen

'THAT'S RIGHT, EDDY, keep your arms tight in so you deliver the punch from your body, ' said Tim, as Eddy Kenton jabbed his right boxing glove at the impact paddle on Tim's hand.

It was just after six thirty, and as always at this time on a Friday evening when not on duty, Tim was at St Mungo's Boys' Boxing Club.

He was in the main ring, putting a few of the bigger boys through their paces. The younger lads were learning their footwork on the mats with Micky Littlewood, who had started in the club ten years ago as a rowdy six-year-old and was now a rising star on the East London junior lightweight circuit.

On the other side of the room, beating seven bells out of the punchbags, were a couple of the up-and-coming lads who were preparing for local contests; others were using the weights and benches.

The boxing club had been a permanent fixture in Wapping for almost fifty years, founded by Father Michael, who had devoted his life to the poor souls in one of the most impoverished parts of England's capital.

The club was situated in the larger of the two halls within the building, and as the lads of the area lunged and grunted through their session, the smaller hall was hosting the local Brownie pack's meeting. Their singing around the toadstool and badge work was a gentle contrast to the smell of fresh sweat and chalk dust on this side of the building.

Just shy of his eleventh birthday and with the physique of a pipe cleaner, Tim's sparring partner Eddy was one of eight children who lived in two upstairs rooms in one of the old workmen's cottages on the Chapman Estate behind Watney Street Market. Eddy's father had left the scene some while before, and his mother spent her days on her knees scrubbing City offices in order to keep a roof over her family's head and food on the table – a family life Tim knew only too well.

Unlike Tim, who wore a singlet, boxing shorts and soft leather boots, Eddy – in common with most of the boys – was dressed in a worn-out grey vest, his school shorts and a pair of plimsolls, while the gloves he sported had been donated by the one of the charities that supported the club's work.

'Right now, lads,' Tim said, running his gaze over the three other boys of Eddy's age who were hanging on the ropes watching, 'the secret is to keep an eye on your opponent's centre of gravity and as soon as it shifts you can land them one, in the direction they're going, see.' Tim moved his training glove to within a couple of inches of the young boy's left cheek. 'And knock them off balance.' He patted his padded gloves together. 'Right, now you try it.'

Crouching down, Eddy held up his hands ready and then following Tim's instructions punched from his body. Tim fended him off a couple of times then purposely shifted his weight so he was balancing on his right leg. Eddy jumped forward and landed a blow on his left.

'That's the ticket,' said Tim, stepping sideways.

Grinning, Eddy threw a couple more.

'Good, good,' said Tim, as he deflected them. 'But don't get carried away.' Thrusting out his left hand, Tim tapped Teddy lightly on his cheek. 'And keep up your guard.'

'I will, Mr Wallace,' said Eddy.

'All right, lads,' bellowed Father Aiden, who was supervising the hanging speed ball on the other side of the hall. 'It's almost seven, so time to start packing up.'

With shoulders like a bull and fists like hammers, you'd be forgiven for thinking the latest man of the cloth to run the boxing club was an underworld enforcer rather than a Catholic priest. He'd taken up the challenge of keeping the wild and mouthy boys running barefoot over the cobbles away from delinquency and petty crime some twenty years before, something Tim was personally truly thankful for.

'Off you go, lads,' said Tim, ruffling Eddy's unruly straw-coloured hair. 'Off to the shelters with you else your mammies will be worrying, and I'll see you next week.'

The boys scurried off to get changed and Tim swung himself over the top of the ropes, landing lightly on his feet.

Picking up his towel from the bench next to the ring, he flipped it over his shoulder and strolled across to join Father Aiden, who was packing away the hand-held dumbbells and medicine ball.

'Thanks as always, Tim,' said the priest.

'Don't mention it,' he replied. 'I'd rather meet them here than have to collar them later for pinching sweets off a shop counter or apples from a stall.'

Father Aiden studied him from beneath his bushy grey eyebrows. 'You have a natural way with the lads.'

Tim gave a hard laugh. 'Well, that's hardly surprising, is it, Father?'

The priest's sharp grey-blue eyes scrutinised Tim. 'How is your mother?'

'Much the same when I saw her the day before yesterday,' Tim replied, the memory of his hour and a half visit sitting holding his mother's hand in the mental hospital flickered through his mind.

'Any change?' the priest asked.

Tim shook his head. 'And how can there be? You know yourself that the neurologist said her brain was injured beyond repair.'

'That may be,' said Father Aiden, 'but I wouldn't give up on a miracle.'

'Is there any news about a place in St Joseph's Convent?' asked Tim.

'Not yet,' the priest replied.

'Perhaps I'll pay them another visit,' said Tim. 'You know, to keep Mum fresh in their minds, because the sooner I can move her out of that place the better.'

'You're a good son,' said Father Aiden.

'I try to be.' A wry smile lifted one corner of Tim's mouth.

'And you'll be a good father too, one day. Of course, you'll have to find yourself a wife first,' added the priest.

The image of infuriately opinionated Miss Carmichael at the Labour Party meeting the week before loomed into his mind. Shoving aside the memory of her hand on his forearm and the trace of her perfume in his nose, Tim forced a nonchalant laugh.

'Perhaps,' he said, 'but just now all I'm intent on doing is getting a shower.' And he raised his arm slightly and sniffed his armpit.

Waiting until a freight train had passed by to avoid the possibility of pigeon droppings, Tim left the fading sunlight of a rather lovely March evening and passed under the dank and fetid railway arch carrying the Liverpool Street to Stratford main line. Turning right, then immediately left into St Stephen's Road, he glanced at his watch.

Ten past eight. Blast!

Picking up his pace, Tim strode up the road toward the Essex Arms, outside of which were a handful of children sitting on the kerb while their parents enjoyed a pint or two at the bar. Remembering how many times he'd done the same, Tim gave them a cheery smile then pushed on the door's brass plate and marched into the public bar.

The Essex Arms was very much like any other East End pub: faded Regency-stripe flock wallpaper, scuffed floorboards littered with ash and crushed cigarette butts. There was also a piano up against the far wall and a pitted dartboard fixed to the back wall next to the toilets.

The Essex's customers were a mix of shop, factory and clerical workers, as well as a few stallholders from Roman Road Market around the corner and the odd driver and conductor from Bow bus garage a few streets away. However, despite the variety of professions of those enjoying an end-of-day drink, the visage before Tim was almost universally navy or khaki: navy for the volunteer ARP wardens and auxiliary fire service and the khaki of the part-time Home Guard. Before Chamberlain's fateful broadcast two and half years ago the only women in the bar would have been there with their husbands, but now there were a fair number of women standing together while sipping their G&Ts or vodka and orange.

Squeezing his way through the drinkers, Tim headed for the quiet area to the right of the horseshoe-shaped bar. There were small groups of elderly women and a couple of wizened old men playing dominos at the half-dozen tables. Striding past them, Tim made his way to the table in the corner where Angela, wearing a light-blue dress and matching jacket, sat. She looked up as he approached.

'I've been sitting here by myself for ten minutes,' she said as he reached her.

'I know and I'm sorry,' he said, giving her an apologetic smile. 'I had to pop into Arbour Square police station on my way here.'

'You had to do that last week.'

Taking off his trench coat, Tim draped it over an empty chair. 'I know, but I'm afraid some things have to be dealt with immediately. It's the nature of police work.'

'I suppose so,' she replied petulantly. 'But people think a woman alone in a pub is looking to be picked up.'

'I'm sure no one would think that of you, Angela, an—'

'Even so,' she cut in, 'a gentleman doesn't keep a lady waiting.'

'I'm sorry.'

Looking sideways at him from under her lashes, she thrust out her lower lip. 'All right, I'll forgive you this time.'

'What are you drinking?' he asked, indicating her almost empty glass in the table. 'Whisky and ginger,' she replied.

Wishing she would at least try to understand that police work was not a regular nine-to-five job, Tim went to the bar.

Seeing him waiting to be served, the barman, a rotund individual with a crooked nose, flipped his grubby tea towel over his shoulder and ambled over.

'What's your poison, mate?' he asked, ash from the top if his cigarette dotting his waistcoat as he spoke.

'A Bell's and ginger and an orange juice,' Tim replied.

The landlord went off to fulfil Tim's order, returning a few minutes later carrying two glasses.

'Half a crown,' he said, setting them on the towelling mat with Mackeson printed on it.

Rummaging in his pocket, Tim handed over the appropriate coins then carried the drinks over to where Angela was sitting.

He placed her glass in front of her. 'For m'lady.'

'Thank you, kind sir,' she replied, fluttering her eyelashes and smiling demurely at him.

Moving a chair nearer to her, Tim sat down and picked up his orange juice.

'I'm still baffled as to why you don't you drink,' she said, as he took a sip from her glass.

'It's a long story.'

'So you always say,' she continued. 'But you must be the only man I've ever meet, apart from that potty religious chap who lives around the corner in Norman's Grove, who doesn't have a pint now and—'

'How are things at Brown and Co?' he cut in, not wishing to explain his long-standing personal aversion to alcohol. 'Has Miss Looker sorted out the new typist yet?'

'Well, funny you should ask because only today …' Leaving the topic of his abstinence aside, Angela started telling him about the previous week's typing-pool gossip and drama. However, after a few moments Tim's mind drifted away from who said what about whom in the canteen and back to his encounter with Miss Carmichael at the Labour Party meeting the week before. Well, more precisely to her dark, intelligent eyes.

'I'm right, aren't I?' said Angela, cutting across his thoughts.

Tim dragged himself back to the here and now. 'Sorry I—'

The pub door swung open, and Tim blinked with surprise as the very woman he'd just been thinking about walked into the bar.

With her auburn hair swept back under a snazzy little hat, Fliss Carmichael was wearing a fitted waist-length forest-green jacket over a cream-coloured jumper and slim-fitting black slacks. There was a large kitbag slung over her shoulder, and she was holding a wodge of leaflets in her hand.

She wasn't alone: another young woman with curly blonde hair, wearing dungarees and a dark blouson-style jacket, entered the pub a step behind her. The two women exchanged a few words then Fliss's companion headed off to the other side of the bar.

'About Mary, I mean?' Angela went on, from what seemed to be a long way away.

Tearing his gaze from Fliss, Tim forced himself to concentrate on the woman sitting beside him.

'I'm sure you are,' he said, hoping that he wasn't agreeing to attend one of her work colleague's engagement party or something.

'I mean, I'm sure it's the same in your police station,' continued Angela, as Tim watched Fliss out of the corner of his eye. 'Those who've been with the company longest get to pick their holiday week first.'

Sensing his lack of attention, Angela glanced around and looked puzzled. 'I thought the Salvation Army women wore bonnets.'

'I don't think they're selling copies of *The War Cry*,' said Tim, as Fliss gave a leaflet to a couple of drinkers propping up the bar.

'Well, if they're doing a collection for a spitfire or something they're out of luck because we have a jar for our spare change at work,' Angela went on, as Tim's gaze slipped down to Fliss's rounded rear and back up to her sculptured profile.

Handing a flyer over the bar to the friendly-faced barmaid, Fliss turned.

Her eyes skimmed the room for a moment then they collided with Tim's.

Surprise flickered briefly across her face before she spotted Angela beside him and what could only be described as an impish smile lifted one corner of her mouth.

With her gaze fixed on him, she sashayed towards them, stopping on the other side of the table.

'DI Wallace,' she said, amusement dancing in her eyes. 'Fancy meeting you here.'

'I could say the same, Miss Carmichael,' he replied, as the memory of her falling into his arms flashed across his mind for the umpteenth time. 'I'm just having a quiet drink. What about you?'

'Spreading the word, as always,' she replied.

Angela gave Tim a smug look. 'See, Tim. I said the ladies were with the Salvation Army.'

Fliss's gaze shifted from Tim to his date.

'This is Miss Carmichael, Angela,' Tim said.

Angela gave Fliss the sweetest smile and offered her hand. 'Charmed, I'm sure.'

'Nice to meet you,' said Fliss, shaking hands briefly. 'And I'm with the Workers' Army not the Sally Army. The Labour Party,' she added, seeing Tim's companion's baffled expression. 'You know, the political party that is fighting against the exploitation of the ordinary working people of this country.'

'My father votes Conservative,' said Angela, 'so Mummy and I do the same. Men are so much better at understanding these things than us women.'

Amusement lifted Fliss's memorising lips. 'Really?'

'Oh, yes.' She looked adoringly up at Tim and sighed. 'I think their brains are so much better at complicated things like politics than ours.'

Fliss gave a hard laugh. 'Well, if we all had that attitude, we'd still be worrying about showing our ankles and dressing in whalebone corsets. Anyway, I have another half a dozen pubs to visit before we're done, Luftwaffe permitting, so as much as I'd like to debate the point of the political issues of the day with you, Miss …?'

'McAvoy,' said Angela frostily, as the image of Fliss Carmichael laced into a Victorian corset ran around in Tim's head.

'Miss McAvoy, but I'd better get on.' Fliss's attention shifted to Tim. 'Nice to meet you again, Inspector.'

'You too,' said Tim, feeling himself falling into her striking brown eyes.

Placing a leaflet in front of Angela, Fliss smiled. 'I'll leave you a leaflet, but if it's too complicated for you to understand, Miss McEvoy, give it to your father.'

Looking at Tim with barely concealed mirth, Fliss joined the crowd at the bar.

Tim watched her go for a moment then turned his attention back to Angela.

'Do you want another drink, sweetheart?' he asked, picking up his own.

'So *that's* Miss Carmichael, is it?' she said.

'Er, yes.'

'Well, Miss Carmichael has a lot to say for herself, hasn't she?' said Angela, her eyes narrowing as she watched Fliss chatting to a couple of air raid wardens by the bar.

'She has strong convictions, if that's what you mean,' said Tim.

Angela's attention returned to Tim. 'You sound as if you've got a soft spot for her.'

Tim forced a light laugh. 'Don't be daft. I just admire anyone who is willing to stand up for what they believe in. And although I don't agree with everything the Labour Party are campaigning for, I for one would like to see better housing and fairer wages for ordinary people.'

'Well, I think all this welfare state business is nonsense,' Angela replied.

'And why's that, Angela?' Tim asked, resisting the temptation of looking at Fliss.

'Because it is.' Her lower lip jutted out again. 'And I thought you asked me out for a nice quiet drink, Tim, not to argue about politics.'

Tim sighed. 'You're right. Let's drink our drinks and talk about something else.'

He swallowed a mouthful of orange juice while Angela sipped her Scotch and ginger.

'Also, Tim,' said Angela, shooting a hateful look across the bar at Fliss, 'I thought you said she wasn't pretty.'

'Well, I—'

'Not that her looks will do her any good,' Angela continued, still eyeing Fliss disapprovingly. 'Men don't want a wife who will argue about politics with them. They want one who will provide them with a comfortable home, look after their children and have a meal on the table ready for them each night. After all, the way to a man's heart is through his stomach, isn't it?'

Tim's gaze returned to Fliss and fixed on her rich auburn hair bouncing on her shoulders, and he didn't reply. He couldn't because, to be honest, whoever first said that didn't know anything very much about men.

'I really wish you'd telephoned to say that you were arriving early, Robert,' said Marjorie, looking earnestly at her son as he tucked into his bacon and eggs.

229

It was just after eight and the Carmichael family were having breakfast in the dining room.

Fliss, Prue, Rosie and the children had arrived back from the shelter three-quarters of an hour before. An igloo without a doorway would have been warmer than the reception their mother had given Prue as she came in, so she had eaten a quick breakfast and was now upstairs, helping Rosie get the boys ready for their Saturday-morning boys' club at the church.

Fliss had taken a quick soak in the regulation six inches of bath water and donned her casual navy slacks and Fair Isle jumper before coming down for breakfast just as Mrs Lavender waddled through from the kitchen pushing the serving trolley loaded with a second helping of the hot elements of the family's first meal of the day plus fresh tea and toast.

'I managed to cadge a lift at the last minute,' Rob replied, as he sawed through a slice of streaky bacon. 'And even then, with so many railway lines bomb damaged and the army requisitioning trains for troop movements at the drop of a hat, I didn't want to telephone and say I was on my way because it would only have worried you if I hadn't arrived, Mother.'

Pausing in the buttering of her toast, Marjorie turned and gazed at Rob, her solid features lifted in a simpering smile. 'Aren't we blessed, Father, with the most considerate of sons?'

With his teacup halfway to his lips, her husband paused and nodded. 'As it says in Psalm one hundred and

230

twenty-seven, verse three, "Lo, children are a heritage, that is to say, a gift from the Lord".'

'Except, of course, if they happen to marry for love or believe in social justice,' said Fliss.

'Your sister married a man far beneath her social status, and well ...' Marjorie regarded her icily across the table. 'Look where your ridiculous socialist ideas have got you.'

Despite her mother's words jabbing at her heart, Fliss gave her the sweetest smile. 'Would you mind passing the jam?'

Her mother slid the Crown Derby jam pot across the table.

'Thank you,' said Fliss, maintaining her syrupy expression as she took a triangle of toast from the antique silver rack sitting between them.

There was a long silence then Fliss's father cleared his throat. 'Well, Robert, I don't know if you've heard yet, but the parish had some very good news this week, didn't it, Mother?'

His wife's face lit up. 'Indeed we have, Robert, as Father Daniel Molyneux, St Winifred's new curate, is coming to join us in two weeks, on Easter Saturday.'

'That's good news,' said Rob.

'It is, and we're lucky to get him,' added Marjorie. 'Not many newly ordained priests are keen to take up posts in major cities, especially London.'

'He was one of the top in his theological classes,' said Hugh. 'And he comes highly recommended by Cannon

Braithwaite, the dean of Durham College where he trained, and by our own Bishop George.'

'What's he like?' asked Robert, scooping up a portion of egg yolk on his fork.

'Well, thanks to the government's tedious restrictions on travel, we haven't actually met him, but he's a Molyneux!' said Marjorie.

Fliss looked blankly at her mother.

'For goodness' sake, Felicity, why must you be so tiresome?' Marjorie looked exasperated. 'Surely you remember Sir Rufus Molyneux who owns half of Warwickshire. We met him at the Bishop of Bedford's garden party a few years ago.'

'Sorry, I'm afraid I don't,' said Fliss.

'Anyway,' continued her mother, turning her attention back to her first born, who was pouring himself another cup of tea, 'the Molyneux always send a son into the Church, and Sir Rufus's father was a Daniel, so St Winifred's new curate must be one of the current viscount's five sons. I'd say securing him was quite an achievement for your father, who, thanks to your sister, has had to single-handily shoulder the work of the parish for the past six months.'

'No one made Father David leave,' said Fliss.

'Well, he couldn't very well stay, could he?' snapped her mother. 'Not after your sister turned down his marriage proposal to marry a grubby railway engineer.'

'I don't know, Mother, Jack Quinn seems like a decent enough bloke.' Rob took a mouthful of tea. 'And Prue is certainly very happy being Mrs Quinn.'

'Not in the eyes of the Church,' Marjorie replied. 'Because he has a first wife who is still very much alive and the Church doesn't recognise divorce, does it, Hugh?'

Fliss's father nodded. 'In Matthew chapter nineteen, verse nine, Our Lord himself said, "Whosoever shall put away his wife, and shall marry another, committeth adultery".'

'But I know lots of people who are divorced and tie the knot again or get hitched to someone who has been married before,' said Rob.

'Perhaps you do, Robert,' Marjorie replied. 'But I doubt if any of them have a father who is a clergyman in the Church of England. And I don't think you, Felicity, are in any position to lecture anyone about Christian values, are you?' She fixed Fliss with a granite-like stare.

Her words hit Fliss like a blow.

'Well,' said Rob, spotting tears gathering in his sister's eyes, 'I'd hate to be married to someone I didn't love, which is why I'm so lucky to have met Lydia.'

'How is the dear girl?' asked Hugh.

'Very well and very busy, Dad, especially now ...'

As Rob recounted his fiancée's growing success in the House of Beaumont and on the silver screen with the Ministry of Information's film division, Fliss stared blindly at the half-eaten slice of toast on her breakfast plate. Taking the napkin from her lap, she placed it on the table.

'I'm sorry,' she said, forcing a smile on her face as she rose to her feet, 'but I've just seen the time so if you'll excuse me I have a piece to finish for work.'

Without waiting for an answer, she sidestepped out of her chair and fled from the room just as an escaping tear rolled down her right cheek.

Reaching the hallway, she paused for a moment in the cool air, then wiping her eyes she looked at herself in the hall mirror. It wasn't her mother's assertion that she was completely ruined or, for that matter, that she was no longer a virgin that caused tears to gather in her eyes and her heart to constrict, it was knowing how utterly stupid she was to have been taken in by Giles's hollow words.

Chapter eighteen

'I CAN SEE A FLURRY of hands,' said Fliss, casting her eyes over the women sitting on the rows of chairs. 'Perhaps we can hear a few words from the lady in the third row wearing the red polka-dot headscarf.'

A matronly woman wearing a fawn-coloured mac and a headful of curlers stood up. 'Maisie Williams, from Head Street around the corner. And that crook on the pitch outside the Old House at Home in Watney Street was asking two bob for a battered tin of ham from a box under his stall. It ain't right.'

It was Thursday 10 April and according to the clock on the wall over the serving hatch, it was just after three. Fliss was in St Winifred's church hall and had been there for an hour. In front of her were thirty or so housewives from all over the area, most dressed in wraparound aprons beneath their coats. There were a few hats dotted among them, but most of Fliss's audience wore brightly coloured scarf turbans.

'No it ain't.' A redhead wearing a man's duffel coat over her stout figure stood up behind Maisie.

'And it ain't just on the markets, is it, Gertie?' added a young blonde holding a sleeping baby in her arms. 'Some of the shopkeepers are bloody thieves, too. I tried to get some Carnation Milk for the baby's bottle and the woman serving behind the counter said I could 'ave it but for five bob more than the price on the tin.'

'Maureen, my dear,' said the soft voice beside Fliss, 'if you ever need anything for the baby you know you only have to knock on my door.'

Maureen's gaze shifted to the older woman sitting at the table next to Fliss. 'Fanks, Sister, but I got a tin in the 'Ome and Colonial in the end.'

The sister the young mother was referring to was not her own but Sister Martha, St Winifred's long-serving lay-nun.

As always, she was dressed in her light-grey nun's habit and a pair of stout brown lace-ups. However, the white cowl of her short veil sat far enough back to show the wispy light-grey hair beneath. With a birdlike frame, a face etched with fine lines and a pair of soft blue eyes, you could be forgiven for judging Sister Martha as just a sweet little old lady. However, you'd be wrong. Even in her short acquaintance with the elderly nun since returning home, Fliss had come to realise that Sister Martha would carry you on her back through the fires of Hell if she could help you.

'It's a bloody liberty,' chipped in a woman in a yellow and black check coat. 'There's nothing on the blooming shelves, but they tell you to come around the back after they close for the night and they might be able to help you out.'

'Yeah, at double the price, Lil,' added her thin-faced friend beside her.

'And we know that most of it's nicked or looted,' piped up a round-faced woman with curly brown hair bouncing a toddler on her knee.

There were murmurs of 'bloody liberty', 'lowlife swindlers' and 'heartless bastards'.

'Well, ladies,' said Fliss, as the muttering died away, 'I say we do what you did a few years ago when you formed a Housewives' Defence League.'

'You mean like the Tenants' Defence League we had when the ruddy landlords put the rents up?' asked someone else.

'That's right,' said Fliss.

'Show 'em we mean business!' shouted a young woman sitting at the end of one of the rows and rocking a pram.

'Make some placards and then plant ourselves outside shops that have hiked up their prices to protest,' said an older woman with grey hair.

'We can do all that and more,' said Fliss. 'But we need to gather our evidence. I therefore propose the motion that today we set up the Stepney Housewives' Defence League, the primary aim of which is to stop shopkeepers and stallholders from inflating their prices above the government's Price of Goods Act.'

A mutter of agreement went around the room.

'But we have to do this properly so that when we present the officials at the Ministry of Food with the facts and evidence, they have to take us seriously,' continued Fliss. 'I'm happy to be the chair of our organisation and Sister Martha has kindly agreed to act as our secretary, but we need a couple of you to be on the committee so we can coordinate our efforts. Any volunteers?'

'Madge Riley, East Field Street, used to organise the factory's yearly beano to Clacton, so count me in,' said a woman with auburn victory rolls on the top of her head.

Sister Martha's pen scratched across the open notebook in front of her as she recorded the volunteer's name.

'Me too,' called a strawberry-blonde in the back row, raising a hand with a cigarette between her nail-vanished fingers. 'Doris Topper, Jubilee Buildings.'

'Thank you, Doris,' said Sister Martha.

A couple more women volunteered.

'Now I propose we have our next meeting in two weeks' time,' said Fliss, when the nun had finished jotting down names. 'We were lucky to get the use of the hall today because the Red Cross, who usually run their first-aid classes here at this time, are taking part in an ARP emergency exercise. Next time I propose that the half a dozen of us helping organise the Defence League meet in the rectory. In the meantime, I want everyone to make a note of any shops or stallholders putting up prices illegally, so we have concrete evidence to take to the Ministry of Food's inspectors. And, of course, to the police.'

From nowhere an image of DI Wallace, tall and with his fedora at a rakish angle, flashed through Fliss's mind.

Cries of 'tell the rozzers' and 'grass to the cops' and

'they're a bunch of crooks an all' rose up in the hall.

'Well, if you want these crooks arrested then the police will have to told,' said Fliss, as her brain added the infuriatingly good-looking officer's smile to the mix.

Dragging her mind back from its wandering, she maintained her cool expression and waited. Although the faces in the room looked less than pleased at the mention of the police, after a moment or two the grumbles subsided.

Forcing a smile, Fliss looked out across the gathered women. 'So unless anyone has anything else they'd like to raise, I think that's the end of the inaugural meeting of the Stepney Housewives' Defence League. Thank you all for coming and help yourself to a cuppa before you go.'

There was a combined scraping of chairs as the women rose and made their way to the table at the back of the hall where Prue had just finished pouring tea into the church hall's duck-egg-blue cups and saucers.

Sister Martha stood up.

'Well done, my dear, I think that went very well indeed,' she said, her wrinkled face lifting in a kindly smile as she gathered her paperwork together. 'Now, if you'd excuse me, I want to have a quick word with Maureen Tucker before she leaves.'

The elderly nun crossed the hall to where the young mother was chatting to a pregnant woman.

'Well done, Fliss,' said Prue, as she reached her carrying two mugs. 'And you certainly deserve this.' She handed Fliss her drink. 'Sorry, there's no biscuits.'

'As long as this is wet and warm, it's all I need.' Fliss took a deep mouthful of tea.

'Fliss,' said Prue as she stirred her tea slowly, 'you have told Mother that you're going to invite members of the Stepney Housewives' Defence League to the rectory, haven't you?'

'Not as such,' Fliss replied, airily ignoring the image of her mother's disgruntled face that loomed into her head. 'But it's only a handful of women and so it will be fine. After all, racketeering is a crime.'

Amusement lifted the corner of Prue's lips. 'A handful of women and possibly your knight in shining armour, the handsome DI Wallace?'

As Fliss slotted her key in the front door, a couple of hooters in nearby factories blared out, signalling six o'clock, the end of the working day.

She slipped off her jacket and was just about to hang it on the rack when the parlour door opened.

Prue emerged and, seeing her sister, hurried over.

'Thank goodness you're back,' she said, in a low voice. 'Lydia's here.'

Fliss gave a heavy sigh. 'Oh, no.'

'Oh, yes,' continued her sister in the same hushed tone. 'She arrived just after three and is in the parlour with me and Mother having a pre-dinner sherry.'

'How long is she staying?' asked Fliss.

'Thankfully only two days, but that's long enough,' Prue replied.

'Where's Rob?'

'Up in town seeing some general or other and Rosie's escaped upstairs with the children, lucky woman, so I've been stuck with *her* and Mother for over two hours. But you're here now ...' Prue grabbed Fliss's hand and dragged her towards the front parlour door. 'So, Sis, we can suffer both of them together.'

Before Fliss could protest, Prue opened the door and propelled her though it.

'Look who's here,' she said as she shut the door behind them.

Marjorie, who was in her usual fireside chair, looked across, as did the young woman sitting in the chair opposite, with one long leg crossed over the other, Lydia Fincham.

Rob's fiancée could top Fliss's five foot seven by a good two inches and was at least a dress size ten to her twelve. With bright-blue eyes and cheekbones you could cut paper with, it was hardly surprising that Lydia was the House of Beaumont's top model and had been snapped up by the Ministry of Information film division. Also, given she took a thirty-eight D-cup brassière, it was even less surprising that her brother Rob, usually a level-headed and sensible sort of man, was completely besotted with her.

As always, Lydia was dressed as if she was about to meet royalty. Today it was a tightly fitted brick-red jacket, with a small peplum and a row of buttons down the front, over a matching pencil skirt. On her feet she wore a pair of black patent shoes with impossibly high heels. There was a small matching handbag on the floor beside her and a pillbox hat with an enormous pheasant feather stretching towards the plasterwork perched on her head.

'Felicity, darling,' said Marjorie, bestowing one of her rare maternal smiles. 'I was beginning to worry; I was expecting you home sooner.'

'I had to go back to the office to man the phones until five thirty because Betty had to take her mother somewhere,' Fliss replied. 'And then there was an unexploded bomb along Stepney Way, so I ended up having to take the long way home via Mile End Road.'

'Well, you're here now and that's all that matters,' said Marjorie. 'And look who's come to visit us. Dear Lydia.'

Forcing a friendly smile onto her face, Fliss looked across at her brother's fiancée. 'I can see and what a lovely surprise. How are you?'

'Busy,' Lydia replied, as Fliss and Prue sat on the sofa. 'War work, you know.'

Refraining from pointing out that prancing up and down a catwalk or being filmed pretending to be building bombers in a factory wasn't what most people meant by 'war work', Fliss just maintained her pleasant expression.

'And so much has changed since I saw you all last August,' continued Lydia. 'For one, Prue's married and to that train driver chap.'

'I am,' Prue replied. 'And very happily. And Jack's an engineer not a driver.'

'Isn't that the same thing?'

'Not at all,' Prue replied. 'A driver drives trains from place to place, whereas an engineer like Jack makes locomotives in the first place then repairs them when they break down.'

Lydia frowned slightly as she tried to grasp the unfathomable mystery of different railway workers, then the bright expression returned to her face.

'And you're having a baby, too,' she said, bobbing slightly on the cushion.

'I am.' Prue ran her hands over her bulging stomach. 'In about three months.'

Lydia's bright blue eyes shifted to Marjorie. 'You must be very excited to be having your first grandchild, Mrs Carmichael.'

'She is,' chipped in Prue. 'Aren't you, Mother?'

Despite the flush creeping up from her collar, Marjorie managed a tight smile. 'Thrilled.'

'And don't worry, Prue,' continued Lydia, 'I'm sure John will still love you, even if having a baby ruins your figure.'

Prue smiled calmly at her future sister-in-law. 'I'm sure Jack will.'

Lydia turned her attention to Fliss and a deeply sympathetic expression spread across her immaculately made-up face. 'Your mother tells me that you've called off your engagement to Giles.'

'Well, we weren't really—'

'Yes, she has,' cut in Marjorie, giving Fliss a hard look. 'Although to my mind, Giles Naylor was never the right man for my eldest daughter. Far too common.'

'Well, I hope you find Mr Right before you get too old,' said Lydia.

'My sister's twenty-five not forty-five, Lydia,' said Prue.

Their future sister-in-law re-crossed her legs and gave them a syrupy smile.

'Of course. There's plenty of time yet to meet someone,' she said, without a trace of conviction.

From nowhere the image of DI Wallace, looking at her from beneath his fedora brim, flashed through Fliss's mind.

The front door banged again, bringing Fliss's mind back from its wandering and making all four women look at the parlour door.

There was a pause then the door opened and Rob, dressed in his khaki captain's uniform, brass buttons twinkling in the light from the sash windows, strode into the room.

'Sorry I'm—' He stopped dead in his tracks.

'Lydia!'

She rose majestically to her feet. Placing one foot forward she posed there for a moment then threw her arms wide and swayed towards him.

Winding her arms around his neck she smiled up at him. 'Surprised, darling?'

'Very,' said Rob, as his arm slipped around her waist. 'But how—'

'Well, Rob,' said Marjorie, rising to her feet, 'I'm sure you and Lydia have a great deal to talk about, so perhaps I'll go and see what Mrs Lavender is up to. Dinner will be at seven.'

Marjorie crossed the rug to the door and left.

As Rob and Lydia stared dreamily into each other's eyes, Fliss and Prue exchanged looks then stood up.

'I ought to give Rosie a hand,' said Prue.

'And I need to freshen up after work,' added Fliss.

Neither Rob nor Lydia replied, so the two sisters followed their mother out. Just as Fliss turned to shut the door, she caught sight of the lovers, and the loneliness of her loveless, emotionless life washed over her.

However, instead of her mind showing her a memory of Giles, it conjured up the possibility of once again finding love and being entwined in the strong and passionate embrace of a man. And disturbingly, not just any man, but Detective Inspector Tim Wallace.

With his fingers laced together and his hands behind his head, Rob stared up at the fringed lampshade dangling above his bed. The all-clear had sounded about half an hour ago, but that wasn't what had woken him. Stupid, really, as this was his last night in the comfort of his own bed before … Well, before who knew what?

His parents were no doubt still tucked up in their

camp beds in their basement shelter. Despite his mother's persistence, Rob had repeatedly declined to join them. He'd told them he didn't want to intrude on their privacy, which was true but also listening to his parents snoring wasn't exactly conducive to a restful night's sleep.

His sisters and the lodgers had trooped over to the air raid shelter as soon as the sirens started up, so apart from him the rectory was empty. This had been a blessing when Lydia arrived, as it meant that after having to express their longing for each other in letters they had finally been able to let their passion reign and she had slipped into his room each night without fear of encountering anyone on the landing. Of course, by rights and the teachings he'd had drummed into him during countless sermons over the years, they should have waited until they were married but, well … they were desperately in love and who knew when they would see each other again?

The faint echo of the grandfather clock in the hallway below started to chime the hour. It stopped after four.

Rob drew in a long breath through his nose then, unlocking his fingers, he threw the covers off and swung his legs out of bed. Sliding his feet in his leather slippers, he stood up and walked across his bedroom. Grabbing his dressing gown from the hook as he passed, he opened the door. Stepping out, he glanced at the bedroom door at the far end of the landing.

Actually, to be completely truthful, he was not the only person in the rectory now because Hester Kratz, the children's doctor, didn't go to the shelter.

Although, as per blackout regulations, the heavy curtains on the staircase window were pulled tightly across, thanks to double summertime there was a faint hint of spring dawn breaking in the eastern sky above. Not bothering to switch on the landing light and avoiding the two squeaking floorboards in his path, Rob shrugged his dressing gown over his bare torso and Y-fronts and padded down the stairs.

With just the tick of the clock echoing around the rectory's spacious hallway, he turned at the bottom of the stairs and headed for the kitchen. Winding up the blackout blinds at the window, he went to the stove, checked there was water in the kettle, then lit the gas under it. Spooning tea into the pot, he set it on the dresser beside the cooker then returned to the window.

Lost in thought, he gazed out over the sprouting vegetables until suddenly he became aware of someone behind him. He turned to find Hester standing in the kitchen doorway.

She was wearing a cherry-coloured topcoat of some quality and a small, brimmed hat, and gripped a briefcase in her hand. Her extraordinarily dark-brown eyes were heavy with weariness, but something sparked in them as they flickered briefly down to Rob's chest before returning to his face.

'Hester,' he said, pulling his dressing gown across him a little more. 'I thought you were upstairs in bed.'

'I should be,' she replied, setting the briefcase on the nearest chair and flexing her hand. 'But one of our night-shift doctors was killed last night in a raid so I stayed on.'

'I'm very sorry,' said Rob. He gave her a sympathetic look then remembered why he was in the kitchen.

'I'm just making myself a cup of tea. Would you like one?'

'Thank you, yes.' Hester gave him a weary smile. 'That would be very nice.'

'Here,' he pulled out a chair, 'you take the weight off your feet while I make it.'

'Take the weight off your feet,' she repeated. 'That is another one of your English phrases I will have to remember, like "getting your skates on" and "when all is said and done".'

'Not forgetting "pulling your leg" and "beating about the bush",' added Rob, as he returned to the dresser and took down another mug.

Hester gave a low throaty laugh.

An odd feeling ran through Rob but vanished when the shrill of the whistle brought him back to the here and now.

Stirring a splash of milk into each mug, he made the tea then carried them both to the table.

'One cup of Rosie Lee,' he said, placing it before her.

'Thank you.'

She picked up her drink as Rob took the seat on the opposite side of the table.

'Sugar?' he asked, indicating the bowl sitting on the table between them.

'Not for me, thank you,' she replied.

Rob helped himself to two spoonfuls.

'Did you have a busy night?'

'The usual,' Hester replied. 'But I'm not on duty until two this afternoon so I'm looking forward to a straight eight hours' sleep.' Cradling her mug in her hands, Hester looked across the top of it at him. 'That is *my* reason for being awake at this time in the morning, Captain Carmichael, what is yours?'

Resting back on the chair, Rob forced a smile. 'Just couldn't sleep.'

'Are you worrying about going back to camp?' she asked.

Rob laughed. 'No, not at all. I'm excited, actually, to be returning to duties tomorrow. I've been stuck up in Scotland since last year, peering across the North Sea at the Germans in Norway, and now my regiment and a dozen others are being shipped out to North Africa to join the XIII Corps and drive the Italians out of Egypt,' he explained, giving her the potted version of his hour-long briefing at army headquarters in Whitehall. 'I've told Fliss and Prue, of course, but I have to say I'm not much looking forward to telling my parents, especially Mother. She tends to fuss about such things.'

One corner of Hester's full lips lifted, turning her usually serious expression into a playful one. 'I have observed this to be the case.'

'That is a very diplomatic way of putting it.' Rob matched her wry smile. 'Honestly, you'd think I was still in short trousers not a grown man.'

Hester's gaze flickered briefly onto the open front of Rob's dressing gown again then back to his face. A flash of something lit her eyes for a second and sent that odd feeling racing through him again.

'And your fiancée,' she said.

Rob frowned. 'My ...?'

'Your fiancée. Lydia?' she added, looking baffled.

'Oh, yes, Lydia, of course,' Rob said, pulling himself together. 'Sorry, my brain wandered for a moment. Yes, of course. I told her straight away. She'll miss me, naturally, but she knows how keen I am to get back in the fray. And to be honest, now she's doing film work as well as her modelling, I'm sure she'll have plenty to keep her occupied.'

'Your fiancée, she has departed.'

'Yes, Saturday morning,' Rob replied. 'She had to catch the ten-thirty at Liverpool Street and as she's hopeless at arriving anywhere on time I drove her to the station myself so she wouldn't miss her train.'

'It sounds as if she has a very glamorous job,' said Hester, taking a sip of her tea.

'It does, but I'm sure working for the Ministry of Information film division isn't as much fun as it sounds,' Rob replied. 'But she's doing her bit for the war effort, just like the rest of us.'

'Well, at least you can look forward to receiving her letters while you're away,' said Hester.

Rob forced a nonchalant smile. 'To be honest, my fiancée isn't much of a letter writer.'

Although each time they parted Lydia promised, hand on heart, that she would write every day, truthfully he was lucky if he received a letter from her every week.

'But I don't mind, honestly, and Prue and Fliss send me a letter most days so I can keep up with the home news,' he continued, seeing a trace of pity in Hester's dark eyes. 'As I said, Lydia's very busy, especially now. And it's her dream to catch the eye of a producer at somewhere like Shepperton Studios or Gainsborough Pictures,' added Rob.

'Well, she's certainly eye-catching,' Hester replied.

An image of Lydia in the emerald-green cocktail dress he liked floated into Rob's mind and a slow smile spread across his face. 'Yes, isn't she?'

An emotion flashed across Hester's face so swiftly that Rob couldn't interpret it, then an urbane smile lifted the corners of her mouth. Still holding her cup, she stood up. 'I have a full clinic this afternoon and an evening shift to cover in Casualty, so I should …'

'Of course,' said Rob, rising to his feet.

Hester's gaze flickered briefly down to the open front of his dressing gown again before returning to his face. 'I wish you all the very best for your new posting in North Africa, Captain Carmichael.'

'Thank you,' Rob replied, oddly captured by her darkest of brown eyes.

They stared at each other for another long moment then Hester smiled and turned for the door.

Hester was a brunette whereas Lydia was blonde with rolling curves as opposed to Hester's shapely but petite

251

figure. In fact, the Jewish paediatrician was the complete opposite to his fiancée in every way imaginable. However, as he stared at her as she walked out of the room, Rob found himself wondering what Hester Kratz would look like in an emerald-green cocktail dress.

Chapter nineteen

W ELL, THAT'S ANOTHER tin done,' said Fliss, squeezing the last fresh roll of gauze bandage into the twelve-by-twelve white-painted tin.

''Ow many's that?' asked Rosie, who was sitting at the other end of the drop-leaf table.

Pressing the lid down firmly, Fliss cast her eye down the stack of tins. 'A dozen.'

'Not bad for a couple of hours' work,' said Prue, who was cutting long strips of three-inch-wide gauze from the bale.

It was just after eleven thirty, on 12 April – Easter Saturday, in fact, and Fliss, Prue and Rosie were sitting together at the table rolling up bandages for the Red Cross. They were accompanied by the sound of BBC Scottish Orchestra drifting out from the cabinet-built mahogany wireless. Ingrid had taken Rosie's two boys to the park to play football with her children, while Rosie's daughter Ellen was kicking her legs on the hearth rug in front of the empty grate.

'Have you scooped any interesting stories recently, Fliss?' asked Rosie.

'Loads,' Fliss replied. 'Like my report into the men of

Italian descent that are still, after almost a year, being held at the Victoria Park internment camp and the story about the lost medical records at the London Hospital, which meant that a bomb victim had the wrong leg amputated, both of which the local Ministry of Information Office would ban immediately. I did get one last week that escaped the censor's black pens, although quite by accident,' she continued, twiddling a fresh length of gauze through her fingers. 'I drew the short straw and ended up being the reporter assigned to write up the Council's monthly building committee meeting at Stepney Town Hall.'

'Sounds like fun,' said Prue.

'Trust me,' said Fliss, with feeling, 'paint drying would be ten times more interesting, except halfway through a long report about the purchase of extra wooden props to shore up bomb-damaged houses, the council-chamber door burst open and some Home Guard chap rushed in brandishing a revolver.'

Prue and Rosie's jaws dropped.

'Oh my goodness,' said Prue, looking wide-eyed at her across the table. 'What did you do?'

'Froze like everyone else,' said Fliss. 'But I soon realised the only person in any danger was Mr Murray, Stepney's housing manager, because apparently, he was having an affair with the gun-toting chap's wife.'

'No!' said Prue and Rosie in unison.

'I didn't believe it either,' said Fliss. 'Especially as Unwin Murray makes Frankenstein's monster look like Tyrone Power.'

Prue and Rosie laughed.

'Still, I suppose every woman has a different idea about what makes a man handsome,' said Rosie, stuffing another rolled bandage into a tin.

As had become something of a habit now, at the slightest mention of men or love and, unnervingly, babies, a vision of Inspector Wallace floated across Fliss's mind.

'Did he shoot him, then?' asked Rosie, cutting into Fliss's pleasing daydream.

'No,' said Fliss, resuming her rolling. 'The police came and took him away.'

'Mrs Lavender!' screeched Marjorie's voice from the other side of the parlour door and the three women looked in that direction.

'What time are you expecting him?' asked Rosie, turning the end of a long fabric strip in her hands.

'The letter said midday,' Prue replied. 'But given how the trains are at the moment, I wouldn't be surprised if Father Daniel didn't arrive until this afternoon.'

'I hope not,' said Fliss, as her mother shrieked for the housekeeper again. 'Mother won't have any voice left by then.'

Instead of swanning down for a leisurely breakfast as she usually did when her husband returned from morning prayers at eight, Marjorie had been up since the crack of dawn, making sure everything was in order in the old coachman's quarters above the garage, which was now the curate's lodgings. Not content with checking the linen had been aired properly and the carpets had been swept to her satisfaction, she'd progressed down to the kitchen – supposedly to help Mrs Lavender prepare lunch but, in reality, to spend most of the morning getting in her way.

Packing her completed bandage alongside the one Rosie had just finished, Fliss took another length of fabric from the pile, but just as she'd rolled it in on itself a couple of times the parlour door opened.

In view of the occasion, Marjorie had dispensed with her everyday dress-and-jacket combination in favour of the light-blue suit she'd worn for Rob's passing-out at Sandhurst a few years before, plus her mother's pearls.

Through her spectacle lenses her grey eyes darted around the room then focused on the three women working on the table. She pursed her lips disapprovingly.

'I'm sure Father Daniel won't object if he finds us busy making first-aid supplies when he arrives, Mother,' said Fliss, guessing her mother's thoughts.

'And didn't you read that one wing of the family's ancient pile near Coventry has been converted into a convalescent home for wounded servicemen?' added Prue.

'In *The Lady*, yes,' Marjorie replied. 'The Molyneux have been a military family back to Cromwell's times, but my d'Apremont family can trace our lineage back to the Conqueror, so I don't want Father Daniel to think we're just middling folk.'

'I'm sure 'e won't fink that at all, Mrs Carmichael,' said Rosie, smiling across at her.

Marjorie's lips tightened. She opened her mouth to speak, but the jingling of the rectory's doorbell forestalled her.

'Sounds like Father Daniel has arrived,' said Prue.

'Indeed,' said Marjorie, glancing at the clock. 'And on time, too. That's a sure sign of breeding.'

Crossing to the sofa, she perched on the edge.

'And, Rosie,' she added, as she studied the parlour door.

'Yes, Mrs Carmichael.'

'Please try to remember your Hs when you speak.'

Placing a hand on her sister-in-law's, Prue mouthed 'ignore her' to Rosie, as Fliss rolled her eyes in sympathy.

There was a knock on the door.

'Come in,' shrilled Marjorie.

The handle rattled and the door opened.

Mrs Lavender waddled through, followed by a stocky young man wearing a casual charcoal-grey suit that had seen better days, a black shirt and a high dog collar. He was probably in his mid-thirties. He was fair-skinned and sported a squashed nose peppered with freckles and what could only be described as a mop of bright-ginger hair.

St Winifred's new curate's bright-blue eyes scanned the all-female welcoming committee for a moment until, smiling, Marjorie rose majestically from the sofa.

'Father Daniel,' she said, in her best vicar's-wife voice. 'I'm Mrs Carmichael, the rector's wife, and can I say what an absolute pleasure it is to welcome you to St Winifred's Church and Rectory.'

A smile spread across the new curate's broad face, and he offered a chubby hand. "Ow do, Mrs Carmichael?' he said, in the thickest of Brummie accents. 'And I'm not one for la-di-da airs and graces, so call me Father Danny if you like.'

'So all in all we have seven young children in the rectory,' said Fliss, as she concluded the rundown of the rectory's occupants.

'Sounds like you have a right 'ouse full, Mrs Carmichael,' said the new curate, looking at his host sitting next to him.

'We have,' Marjorie replied flatly.

Twenty minutes had passed since Father Danny, as he insisted on being called, arrived. He was now sitting in one of the chintz armchairs on the other side of the coffee table while Marjorie sat, somewhat unbendingly, in the other. Having completed the introductions and shown Father Danny the downstairs cloakroom, they had taken their seats and gone through the usual chit-chat about the weather and Father Danny's journey that morning, before moving on to those living under the rectory's roof. Well, at least Fliss, Prue and Rosie had chatted with the new curate; Marjorie had been a little more muted than usual.

'And it's all thanks to Prue, who was the first to step forward to house the refugees last May,' added Fliss, sitting at one end of the sofa alongside her sister and Rosie, who now had Ellen on her knee.

The parlour door opened and Mrs Lavender, carrying a tray loaded with cups and saucers, waddled in.

Obviously on her employer's instructions she was wearing the newest of her many wraparound aprons and for once didn't have a half-smoked roll-up behind her right ear.

'There you are,' she said, setting the china jiggling as she placed their refreshments on the low coffee table in front of them.

'Thank you, Mrs Lavender,' said Marjorie as the housekeeper reached for her rarely used silver teapot.

'That looks right grand, Mrs L,' added Father Danny, giving the housekeeper a dazzling smile.

Blushing, the elderly housekeeper bestowed a girlish smile then caught her employer's gimlet-eyed stare.

'Right you are, then,' sniffed Mrs Lavender. 'I'll go and see 'ow dinner is faring.'

Marjorie gave her a tight smile and for once didn't correct her about incorrectly naming the midday meal.

'Shall I be mother?' asked Prue, smiling as she picked up the teapot.

Everyone laughed except Marjorie, who forced a polite smile.

'Excuse me for saying, Father Daniel,' her mother began as she took her tea from Prue, 'but I was under the impression that you were connected to the Molyneux family who have several estates in Warwickshire.'

'I am,' he said, as Fliss handed him his drink, 'in a manner of speaking.'

'And what manner would that be?' asked Marjorie, a slight flush creeping up above her collar.

'Well, it's like this, Mrs Carmichael, the day I was left on the steps of the workhouse—'

Marjorie's face drained of colour. 'The workhouse!'

'Aye, Dudley workhouse up on Burton Road,' he explained, as he cradled the delicate porcelain cup in the palm of his beefy left hand. 'And as all I had around me, like, was a dirty bum clout and a ragged grey blanket, they had no idea oo I was or even if I had a name.'

'So how is it, then, that your surname is Molyneux?' asked Fliss.

Father Danny took a noisy slurp of tea and Marjorie's lips tightened further.

'Well, now that's a queer thing,' he chuckled. 'It just so 'appened that on the very same day that I pitched up as a wailing bundle of dirty linen, Sir Rufus Molyneux, who is a trustee of the workhouse, was visiting and so the matron asked him if they could name their latest foundling in 'is honour, like. He said aye they could, but as his father had recently died why not name the baby after 'im as, like, he'd been a long-standing benefactor of the workhouse, hence me being christened Daniel instead of Rufus.'

Fliss glanced at her sister and saw that like herself Prue was struggling to keep a straight face.

'It weren't easy but I survived,' Father Danny continued. 'But I will confess, Mrs Carmichael, pretty soon after I left, I had a run-in with the law and, well, not to put too fine a point of it, I found myself locked up in Winson Green.'

Caught mid-swallow, Marjorie started coughing.

'But being sent down for a two-year stretch were the making of me, I can tell you,' Father Danny went on. 'Because it were in that cold cell that Jesus 'imself came to me, just like he did to St Paul on the road to Damascus and said to me, "Danny, lad, you's to give up thou ungodly ways and go, tell the prostitutes, wrongdoers, the down-trodden and destitute of my Father's love."' He slurped another mouthful of tea then beamed across at his host. 'So, Mrs Carmichael, 'ere I be.'

Fliss and Prue exchanged amused looks.

It seemed that Father Danny's time at St Winifred's would be very different from the way their mother had envisioned it.

With the searchlights from the army battery on Tower Green criss-crossing the ink-black sky, Tim pulled down the peak of his worn leather cap and slipped into the side alley between the pawnbroker's and the wholesale fabric merchant in Star Yard.

The last time he'd glanced at his watch as he reached Aldgate bus garage it had been one thirty, so after a twenty-minute walk through Spitalfields' dilapidated streets he reckoned it was nudging two in the early hours of the Sunday after Easter.

He continued on for about twenty yards, then, grasping the wrought-iron handrail he trotted down the dozen worn stone steps into the airy.

The heavy with a broken nose dressed in a threadbare tuxedo gave Tim a nod of acknowledgement as he passed through the shabby-looking door with 'The Shangri-La' painted across it in faded black letters.

Entering a dimly lit corridor, Tim took off his headgear and, rolling it up, shoved it in his jacket pocket. Not the pocket of his usual suit, but the second-hand suit he'd bought a few years ago for such occasions, because although he was on duty if he'd been dressed in anything but rough working clothes the Shangri-La customers would have thrown back their drinks and slipped out of the side doors.

Parting the tatty bead curtain, Tim walked into the club. His understanding of Shangri-La was that it was a place full of unending happiness, a veritable heaven on earth, whereas the damp cellar he was standing in now was anything but.

It was situated in what had once been the storeroom of the trader who lived and did business above, and there was still the odd rusty iron bracket that had supported shelves jutting out of the bare brickwork. However, instead of the space beneath the four-storey Regency house being filled with the wares of a respectable tea, wine or silk merchant, it was currently a meeting place for those engaged in less reputable dealings.

When his eyes had adjusted to the muted light, Tim cast his gaze around the cigarette-smoke haze at the club's customers tucked into dark booths and huddled over tables, and a smile spread across his face.

Tim headed over to the far end of the basement.

'Hello, Tommy.' He stopped behind a familiar figure propping up the rough-hewn bar.

With his pint poised halfway to his mouth, Tim's quarry turned.

Somewhere in his mid-twenties and standing a good four or five inches shorter than Tim's six foot one, Tommy Zeppelin Lavender was a wiry individual with wayward blond hair and deep-set eyes.

'Inspector Wa-Wallace,' he said, blinking rapidly. 'W-w-wot a surprise.'

'I've been looking for you?' said Tim, maintaining his pleasant expression.

Panic flashed across Tommy's sharp face for a second then he recovered himself. 'Ha-have you?'

'I have,' said Tim. 'In fact, I've been after having a word with you for the past eight weeks.'

The Shangri-La's grubby barman shuffled over.

'In fact,' Tim said again, waving him away, 'I was beginning to think you're avoiding me, Tommy.'

Tommy forced a light laugh. 'Now why would I do that, Inspector Wallace?'

'I can think of a couple of reasons but mainly because I heard you've been seen hanging around in the Bull's Head with Harry Gunn and his crew.'

Scratching his head, Tommy pulled a thoughtful face for a moment then it was replaced by a guileless one. 'I've had a couple of drinks down there and come to think of it, Harry and his old man were in the bar, but I'd 'ardly call it 'anging around wiv 'em.'

'I'm glad to hear it,' said Tim. 'Because the whisper is they are planning something big down at the docks. Know anything about it, Tommy?'

'Me?' he asked, feigning surprise.

Holding the other man's nervous gaze, Tim regarded him coolly.

'Honest, Inspector Wallace,' Tommy added, not a dicky bird. An-and you know, I'd be the first one to tell you if I had.'

'I hope so, for your mum's sake,' said Tim.

Tommy looked puzzled.

'Under the provisions of the Emergency Powers Act,' Tim explained, 'theft of vital supplies, especially food, will have you swinging at the end of a rope, and you wouldn't want to do that to Dolly, would you?'

Even in the murky light of the club, Tommy went visibly white.

'So you keep your lug'oles open and you know where to find me,' Tim added.

'That I will, Inspector Wallace.' Tommy threw the last of his drink down his throat. 'Well, I'd better be off as I don't want to worry the little woman.'

'Which little woman is that, then?' asked Tim.

Winking, Tommy Lavender tapped the side of his nose. 'Now, Inspector Wallace, you know yourself a gentleman never tells.'

Despite himself, Tim's mouth lifted slightly at the corners.

Placing his glass on the scuffed wood of the bar, Tommy turned and sauntered across the crowded basement towards the exit.

'You sure you don't want somefink, guv?'

Tim turned to find the dishevelled barman standing behind him.

'I'll have a tonic water,' he replied after a moment.

The barman placed the glass he'd polishing on the bar next to Tommy's empty one and took a small bottle from beneath the counter.

'Sure you don't want anything in it?' he asked as he flipped off the lid on the bottle opener fixed to the bar.

'Well, a slice of lemon would go down a treat, but I doubt you have any,' Tim replied.

The barman snorted a laugh, indicating that like everyone else he probably hadn't seen a citrus fruit of any kind for the past year and a half.

Tim pulled out a handful of coins from his pocket but the barman raised his hand. 'The Old Bill's on the house.'

Tim slid a shilling across the bar towards him and after a moment's hesitation the barman picked it up.

Taking his drink, Tim turned and leaned against the bar, perusing the subterranean room again.

There were a couple of familiar faces, mostly duckers and divers and runners who took bets for illegal bookies, lookouts who alerted those selling stolen goods out of suitcases of approaching police officers and a couple of enforcers attached to the many gangs in the area. Although most of those in the club were men, there were a dozen or so women dotted among them. A few were local tarts that Tim recognised for having been pulled into the various police stations in the area for soliciting, plus the odd woman out with someone she shouldn't be.

However, as he peered through the smoke haze, his eyes alighted on a woman sitting in one of the booths and shock jolted through him. Although she had her back to him, Tim would have recognised that mass of bouncy auburn hair anywhere. Why wouldn't he? After all, how many nights had he woken with his pulse hammering, having dreamed of tangling his fingers in it and kissing its owner.

But what, in the name of all that was holy, was Fliss Carmichael doing in a dive like this? Chasing a story, no doubt, but here! But now! In the middle of the night!

Tim's gaze shifted to the heavy features of the man sitting opposite her and his blood turned to ice.

Was she stark raving mad? Clearly, yes, she was, otherwise she wouldn't be sitting in a gloomy corner having a cosy tête-à-tête with Jack Comer, the gangster who terrorised the tenements of Whitechapel and what remained of Spitalfields' Victorian rookery.

Tim surveyed the scene, chewing the inside of his cheek, but just as he was debating whether or not to rescue Fliss Carmichael from her brainless foolishness, a tall figure dressed like a mannequin in the window of a Savile Row tailor honed into view. Tim didn't recognise him but by his chiselled features and Mediterranean colouring he wondered if he was one of the Cypriot gangs operating in Islington and Tottenham.

Tim glanced around then, spotting Lenny Lomax, East London's foremost underworld villain, striding across to the table. Fliss stood up as he approached. After greeting Comer briefly, the newcomer took Fliss in his arms and kissed her.

A feeling that Tim couldn't recall having every experienced before surged up so strongly that it took his breath away. He watched as Fliss melted into this villain's arms for a few moments then she broke away and turned around.

The emotions swirling in Tim's chest vanished instantly when he realised that the woman in her lover's arms wasn't Fliss.

Wondering what on earth had come over him, Tim turned back to the bar and threw back the last of his tonic water.

'Another?' asked the barman.

'Not for me,' Tim yawned.

'You better pop off, guv, and get your head down, in case the bloody Boche come back,' said the barman, taking Tim's glass.

Tim nodded and, smiling to himself, made his way out. The bartender was right: he ought to get some sleep, because he was so tired he was beginning to imagine things.

Swatting the ever-present flies that buzzed around the fetid communal dock urinals and re-buttoning his flies as he went, Harry strolled past the dirt-encrusted enamel sink and back into the mid-morning sunlight.

It was the fourth Wednesday in April, and according to the clock above the main loading bay of Rutherford & Milton LTD's warehouse across the way, it was now somewhere close to eleven and some five hours since he and his gang were given the call to unload the *Duchess of Kentucky*.

The boys were still down in the hold, but after humping sacks of flour on to spreads – the sheets of canvas with metal awnings at each corner where the crane hooks were attached – Harry felt he'd earned a bit of a break. Of course, he hadn't left the rest of the Gunn crew sweating in the hold purely for his own benefit.

Taking his half-smoked cigarette from behind his ear, Harry relit it and headed off down the quayside.

To be honest, the U-boats must have been having a bit of a rest because both London and Shadwell Basin, where he and his team were working today, were packed to the gunnels with ships of all shapes and size. Above the heads of the workers, the static steam crane bobbed up and down, hauling everything from crates of food to timber from Canada and precious rubber from Ceylon and Burma. Between the vast ocean-going vessels, barges puttered back and forth ferrying unloaded cargo to waiting trains at Blackwall or onward into the Regent's Canal at Limehouse to be taken north to manufacturing centres in the Midlands and beyond.

'Oi, oi, Harry, you on an 'arf day, then?' called Samson McIntyre, the Baltic Trading Company's tally man, who was perched on a bollard next to a merchantman called the *Lady of Windermere*.

With grizzly grey hair and a handful of yellowing teeth, Samson, like many of the old men still eking out a living along the waterfront, had started in the docks as a boy of thirteen during the dying decades of the old Queen's reign, but after forty years of break-breaking dock work he'd been forced to take the lighter and less well-paid job of tallying the cargo as it came out of the hold.

'Naw, just stretching me legs a bit.' Harry nodded towards the ship. 'That old crate looks old enough to have taken Captain Cook to Australia.'

'I recon it could,' chuckled Samson. 'But beggars can't be choosers, can they?'

'What's it carrying?' asked Harry as the rattling winch chain brought up another pallet stacked high with boxwood crates.'

'Dried fruit,' Samson replied. 'Interested?'

Harry gave a little nod.

'A quid a crate,' said Samson.

Harry whistled through his teeth. 'That's a bit stiff, ain't it, for an old mate? I was thinking more ten bob.'

'Eighteen,' countered Samson.

Spitting on his palm, Harry offered him his hand. 'Fifteen.'

Samson eyed him for a moment then spat on his own palm and grasped Harry's hand.

'How many?' Samson asked as they shook.

'Half a dozen in the usual place and I'll send Ben when the fireworks start tonight.' Taking two green pound notes from his pocket, Harry slipped them into the old man's arthritic hand. 'On account.'

Samson touched the peak of his cap and Harry strolled on, stopping next to a large cargo ship berthed by the Imperial & Britannia's refrigerated warehouse with the name *Prince of Argentina* emblazed on its prow.

The McManus crew were working the ship and several of Rory McManus's team were trudging down the gangplank carrying frozen carcasses of lamb. Like Harry's team, the McManus team were close relatives, and all had the short forehead, deep-set eyes and brawny physique of their haggis-eating Jock ancestors.

Rory McManus was overseeing the unloading consignment, but standing alongside the lorry into which the carcasses were being loaded, clipboard in hand, was an unfamiliar figure in a light-grey suit.

Whoever he was he looked at least fifteen years older than Harry and was at least four inches shorter, and shaped like a spinning top. His pale hair was heading northwards, and he squinted at the ledger in his hand through a pair of metal-rimmed spectacles with lenses like the bottoms of milk bottles.

Inhaling the last lungful of tobacco smoke from his spent cigarette, Harry flicked it into the dock and ambled across.

'All right, Rory,' said Harry, as he came to a halt.

The gang leader turned and his bovine features lifted in what Harry took to be a smile. 'All right, Harry. 'ow's tricks?'

'Not so bad,' he replied. 'They giving you top dollar for this, I 'ope?' He indicated the cargo coming from the hold.

'I told them either they did or I was calling my shop steward,' Rory replied.

Harry grinned.

'Who's the geezer in the suit?' continued Harry as a pallet loaded with frozen beef carcasses was winched up from the ship's hold.

'Pollock, chief inspector at the Ministry of Food's offices in Cambridge Heath Road,' Rory replied.

Harry raised an eyebrow. 'Wot's he doing here?'

Rory shrugged. 'Why don't you ask 'im?'

Leaving Rory to oversee his merry band, Harry wandered across.

'Mr Pollock, isn't it?' he said, as he stopped beside the inspector, who was ticking off the frozen meat as the dockers delivered it into the back of the lorry.

The man from the ministry turned. 'I am, but I don't think I—'

'Harry Gunn. Shop steward for the Transport and General Workers' Union hereabouts. Pleased to meet you.' He offered his hand.

Pollock hesitated for a second or two then took it in a limp handshake.

Retrieving a pack of Senior Service from the pocket of his corduroys, Harry flipped open the top. 'Smoke?'

The food inspector took one and so did Harry.

'Nice to see the Ministry of Food down here making sure everything is as it should be,' Harry said, striking a match and holding it for him, 'and accounted for properly.' He took a long drag on his cigarette. 'After all, we don't want any of this ending up on the black market, do we?'

'Indeed we do not,' agreed Pollock, his fleshy face taking on an earnest expression.

'Each according to their need, that's the socialist way of doing things,' continued Harry, in his best public-meeting voice. 'And not having criminals exploiting ordinary working people for gain. After this war, when we have crushed the fascist evil, it is the proletariat not the bourgeoisie oppressors who will reap the rewards of their sacrifice.'

'Quite,' agreed the food inspector somewhat half-heartedly. 'Which is why we have a robust system.'

As one of the McManus crew, half a pig draped over his shoulder, marched past them, Pollock tapped the clipboard with his finger.

Harry gave him a querying look. 'System?'

'Yes,' said Pollock. 'Each wholesale meat merchant sends their order into the office. Once we check that, they're given a docket by the Ministry of Food authorising them to collect their allocated meat.'

'Wot about if it's not allocated or the driver gets delayed?' asked Harry.

'That's simple,' said Pollock. 'It gets stored for a few days in there,' he indicated the Imperial & Britannia's refrigerated warehouse behind them, 'until it's allocated.'

Harry opened his eyes wide in admiration. 'Cor, some right brainy bloke must have thought that one up.'

'Actually,' said Pollock, a hint of smugness curling his top lip, 'it was me who devised it, and if I say so myself – and I shouldn't – it's pretty much foolproof.'

'Wiv all the dockets and whatnot, I should say you have the right of it, Mr Pollock,' Harry went on, thinking of at least three ways off the top of his head of sidestepping the process.

Pollock basked in Harry's fabricated admiration for a moment then Pat 'the bear' McManus, Rory's son, hove into view carrying a side of beef across his ox-like shoulders.

To avoid being whacked on the side of the head by a frozen knee joint, Pollock stepped back. Harry jerked his elbow, knocking the clipboard out of the food inspector's hand and flying across the concrete of the dock.

However, among the dockets and inventories, here was also today's *Daily Herald*. It landed with the sporting section on the back page facing upwards and several of the horses running at Nottingham that afternoon were circled.

'Sorry, mate,' said Harry, stooping to pick up the clipboard, newspaper and paperwork in one grab.

He handed it back to the food inspector, who pinned everything back under the metal clip on the board.

'Well, I'd best be off,' Harry said, pinching out his cigarette and stowing it behind his ear. 'Time and tide, and all that. Nice to meet you, Mr Pollock, and,' an ingenuous smile spread across Harry's freckled face, 'I'll be seeing you.'

Chapter twenty

'RIGHT, WE'RE HERE,' said Fliss, holding her banner high in the manner of Boudicca leading her tribe to battle. 'And before we get started, I know how busy you all are, so I want to thank you for coming. As I've said before, the only way we can change things in this country is by workers standing united against capitalism.'

It was nine in the morning on Thursday 1 May, and as it was International Workers' Day, Fliss thought it the perfect day for the newly formed Stepney Housewives' Defence League to strike a blow against the capitalist system and the exploitation of hard-working wives and mothers. They were assembled on the corner of Cable Street and Watney Street, on a bright but blustery morning.

Pride swelled her chest as her gaze skimmed over the two dozen or so women gathered around her. Despite spending the night in the shelters, at dawn they'd emerged to pack their children off to school before sweeping up glass and rubble from the previous night's air raid, after which they had forgone their usual routine of housework and cooking to fight for justice. Also, half their number were pushing prams, with at least one chubby-faced infant propped up inside, the sight of which caused an odd emotion to catch in her chest.

With a few exceptions, the women were dressed in their workaday wraparound aprons and shapeless jackets, their hair tided away beneath turban headscarves. Although Fliss favoured trousers, finding them much more practical for her job, the vast majority of women in East London still regarded them as slightly racy. So, to show solidarity, Fliss had pulled out her military-cut jacket with a six-panelled skirt, which she'd bought for her interview at the *Bedfordshire Times and Independent* some six years before.

'And are we all clear which shops and stalls each team will be picketing?' said Fliss, getting quite excited at the prospect of being part of direct action against corruption.

'Me and the girls are outside Tyler's,' said Madge, her jacket opening to reveal her six-month-gone stomach as she brandished her placard.

'And we've got Abrahams,' said Doris, indicating the three women standing around her.

Maisie Williams took a last drag on her roll-up then dropped it on the pavement. 'We're giving old Pegram a headache, aren't we, Gertie?'

'Too right, Mais.' Gertie rolled her eyes. 'One and six for a block of carbolic! Bloody swindler.'

'Good,' said Fliss. 'Now are we ready, girls?'

Cries of 'we are', 'let us at 'em' and 'bloody crooks' went up.

Feeling the blood coursing through her veins, Fliss grinned. 'Then follow me.'

Raising her placard with 'The Stepney Housewives' Defence League' painted in red, like a regimental flag, Fliss led the two dozen women behind her into battle.

Watney Street ran from Commercial Road in the north to Cable Street in the south. Until just two weeks ago, the Victorian mock-Gothic church of Christ Church had stood at the top, but an incendiary bomb crashing through its lead roof had reduced it to a pile of burned-out rubble surrounded by what remained of its walls. At the bottom of the market, where the protesters were heading, stood Shadwell Station. Like markets up and down the land, Watney Street Market sold the usual fare of meat, fish and vegetables, along with hardware such as galvanised buckets and cleaning products. However, there were other items – Gefilte fish, bagels and challah bread – that Fliss had never heard of until she moved to Stepney some twelve weeks ago. In addition, the arches beneath the railway line housed a car mechanic, a second-hand clothing business and a rag and bone man's yard.

As it was Thursday the cobbled street market was lined on both sides with stalls, all of which had women with prams crowding around them. Unlike the rectory, none of the two-up two-down houses Fliss had ever visited in the area had that rarest of kitchen appliances, a refrigerator. This meant that housewives shopped every day, so be they a newlywed or a pensioner they pushed a pram to save them carrying loaded shopping bags home.

Holding her banner high, and with her heart beating in her chest, Fliss cleared her throat.

'Down with the racketeers,' she yelled over the sounds of the crowd in the market.

The women behind her took up the call while others whacked saucepan lids together to cut through the hurly-burly of the busy market.

The small procession made its way between the stalls, with women on either side clapping and cheering as they went.

'Racketeers are traitors,' bellowed Madge over Fliss's right shoulder.

'Lock 'm up,' yelled Doris from somewhere behind.

'String them up, don't you mean, luv?' yelled a woman queuing at a fish stall.

'And cut their naggers off while you're at it,' screeched another.

Dozens of female voices shouted their agreement while suggesting other more inventive and very much more painful ways of dealing with pricing sharks than just incarcerating them.

Reaching the Lord Nelson public house about a third of the way along the market, Fliss came to a halt.

'Right, girls, you know what to do,' she said, adjusting her hold on the broomstick handle she'd nailed her plywood placard to. 'And remember what I told you.'

'No 'itting the buggers with your board,' laughed Doris, tucking a stray strawberry- blonde curl behind her ear.

'Or punching 'em in the mush,' added Gertie.

'That's right,' said Fliss, looking at the two women.

'Remember, girls, this is a peaceful protest. I don't want anyone getting arrested.'

The women muttered their agreement, and the column broke up as small groups headed for their designated stations in the market.

'Come on,' said Fliss to her small posse. 'Let's take up our post.'

Fliss led them, their standards held high, towards the top of the market and stopped outside Banfield & Son's double-fronted grocery shop, which had a sizeable queue of women outside.

'If you and Iris stand that side, Nellie,' said Fliss, indicating the window displaying cheese, butter and a hock of ham, 'Maureen and I will take the other. And don't forget to stay on the pavement.'

Iris and Nellie took up their positions, and Fliss turned to her partner on the picket line. 'Let's get in place, Maureen.'

Grasping the handle, the young mother turned her pram, with her year-old daughter propped up in it.

'I'm sorry I had to bring Pattie,' she said, kicking on the pram brakes and giving her daughter a bickiepeg to chew on, 'but my mum got called in to 'ospital urgent.'

'Is she all right?' asked Fliss.

'Naw, there's nuffink wrong wiv 'er,' laughed Maureen. 'She a cleaner at the London. The District line is down at Plaistow, so the orderly on the Marie Celeste ward can't get in and they asked Mum to cover.'

'There's no need to apologise,' said Fliss. 'In fact, it

shows that not only are racketeers swindling housewives but they're taking the food out of children's mouths, too. Now, let's get started.'

Giving Iris and Nellie the nod, Fliss drew in a deep breath.

'Down with racketeering. Down with racketeering,' the four of them shouted.

After a couple of rounds of chanting, the line of women outside the grocery store joined in.

Pleased with the support, Fliss brandished her banner higher. 'Stop robbing housewives,' she shouted. 'Racketeers are crimina—'

'Oi, you!'

Fliss looked around to see a heavily built middle-aged man in a white apron and with matching cuff protectors steaming towards her.

'Yes, you?' he shouted, red-faced, jabbing a chubby finger at her. 'You calling me a criminal, are you?'

'I'm just protesting against shopkeepers who are robbing housewives by putting up their prices,' Fliss replied.

'Well, you lot can bloody well sling your hook, because you're trespassing on my property,' he said, his foul breath wafting in her face as he loomed over her.

'No we're not; your shop front finishes there.' Fliss pointed at the line of metal studs a foot away from where they were all standing.

'Even so, you can still bugger off somewhere else because my prices are fair as any you'll find around here,' he said.

'You call one and six for a tin of corned beef fair, do you, Arthur?' called one of the women in the queue.

'Or a shilling for four rashers of bacon you could sole your shoe with?' shouted someone else.

A murmur of agreement rippled down the line and Arthur's face went from red to purple, then his attention shifted to a point over Fliss's shoulder and he raised his hand.

'Officer! Over here, please.'

Fliss and Maureen turned around to see a tall police constable with a pair of ears that would have been a gift to playground bullies marching towards them.

'Oh, gawd,' said Maureen under her breath as the officer approached.

Nellie and Iris hurried over to join them, forming a united front by the time the officer reached them, even though they looked rather anxious.

'We're just peacefully protesting. That's all,' whispered Fliss.

'What seems to be the trouble, sir?' the constable asked, coming to a halt in front of the gathering.

'This lot,' said Arthur, indicating the four women. 'They're interfering with me carrying out my lawful business.'

'No we're not …' said Fliss, her eyes glancing down to the numbers on his upright collar, 'War Reserve Constable Forty-eight. Look, people are still going in and out of the shop unhindered.'

Giving her a jaundiced look, the officer glanced at

the shop doorway where a couple of women had just emerged, then his attention returned to the four women.

'Shouldn't you lot be at 'ome getting your husbands' dinner ready instead of making a ruddy nuisance of yourselves?' he sneered.

Fliss bristled. 'How dare—'

'Look, miss,' the constable continued, 'why don't you do us all a favour and push off 'ome with your pals before—'

'Are you threatening us, Constable?' cut in Fliss, glaring at him as she gripped her placard.

A slight flush started to creep up towards War Reserve Constable 48's Adam's apple, and under the peak of his cap his eyes narrowed. 'I'm telling you to clear off.'

'And I'm telling you, Constable ,that we're peacefully protesting against racketeering, which is our right under the common law of this land, so—' The officer grabbed her arm and tried to drag her away from the front of the shop. 'We're protesting about shopkeepers who exploit the hard-working people of this country by putting up their prices,' Fliss shouted, trying unsuccessfully to free her arm.

'Oi, Copper, leave 'er be,' shouted Nellie, trying to shove him away with her placard.

Maureen stepped into the constable's path, but he brushed past her.

The women who had been watching all the comings and goings while queuing for their provisions started to move forward.

'Leave 'er alone, Copper,' shouted someone in the crowd.

'Yeah, big ears, pick on someone your own size,' called someone else.

A mouldy potato sailed over the crowd and landed at the officer's feet.

'Stay back,' he warned, looking around at the shoppers gathering around him.

A lump of horse dung whirled past, hit the officer in the chest and slid down his tunic, leaving a mustard and brown smear in its wake.

Panic flashed across his face. Eyeing those around him nervously and with his hands trembling, he fumbled for the whistle in his top pocket. Dragging it out by the chain, he put it to his lips and blew.

A roar went up from the crowd as other missiles started flying through the air.

Judging her captor to be otherwise engaged, Fliss tried to pull free but the officer held on tight, and she stumbled. Attempting to stay upright, she swung out her arm and whacked him across the head with her placard, sending his flat cap skidding across the cobbles before it disappeared into the mêlée.

Under the red mark forming on his high forehead, the constable's brows drew together in an angry line.

'Right, miss,' he spat, gripping her upper arm painfully tight, 'you're bloody well nicked.'

*

'There you are, Sid,' said Tim, handing a florin across the bar.

'Cheers, Inspector,' said the Town of Ramsgate landlord, flipping his tea towel over his shoulder. 'I 'ope the pie was all right.'

'It certainly was,' said Tim.

'And ten times better than what gets dished up in the section-house canteen,' added DS Alex Lennox, who was standing next to him. 'And half the time no one's sure what it is.'

Sid Mullen, a stocky chap with a round face and a ready smile, laughed. 'Well, there is a war on, Sergeant.'

It was just past one o'clock, and after a full morning following inquiries on the streets, Tim had instructed his sergeant to meet him at the pub.

The Town of Ramsgate was situated on Wapping High Street, half a mile west of Wapping police station. It had a long and narrow bar with a small open area at the back that opened directly onto the river. An alleyway just wide enough for one to pass down ran along the side and led to Wapping Steps.

The Town must have been a drinking hole for those working on the river for centuries and although it was lunchtime there were a number of dockers who, having finished half a day's work, had clearly decided not to return to the dock gates for the afternoon call.

As Sid served an honest pint and didn't stand for black-marketeers or light-fingered dockers selling their knock-off gear in his bar, it was one of the few pubs in the area that the boys in blue from both Wapping and Leman Street nicks frequented.

Rummaging in the cash drawer below the mahogany bar, Sid pulled out a couple of pennies and offered Tim his change.

'Pop it in the fund,' he said, indicating the pickle jar half-full of coppers, with a newspaper photo of a spitfire glued on the side.

Sid left to serve another customer and Tim and Alex headed for the door.

'You know, Guv,' said Alex, as they stepped out onto the cobbled street, 'it still amazes me that you're the only governor who doesn't have his meal or drinks on the house.'

'I like to be different,' Tim replied, as they fell into step. 'And besides, the last thing you want to be as a copper is in debt to someone. Now, let's go through what you found out in Bethnal Green.'

Skirting around the labourers unloading lorries and careful not to walk beneath the laden crates being winched into the tall warehouses that ran along both sides of the street, Alex recounted what he'd gleaned from interviewing the shopkeeper arrested for selling cigarettes from the Trinidad & Tobago robbery as they walked back to Wapping police station.

'Spellman stuck to his story that the bloke who sold him the gear was someone called John Smith,' Alex said, as a horse-drawn wagon trundled by. 'But from the description that the old girl who lives opposite the corner shop gave, the bloke who supplied the cigarettes sound very much like Georgie Gunn.'

'The Gunn family's fence,' said Tim. 'Harry and his gang are obviously the ones who robbed the Trinidad and Tobago and beat that old watchman senseless; all we have to do now is prove it. I'll have another word with Wally tomorrow and see if he's heard anything in the wind. In the meantime, let's see what landed on my desk this morning.'

Built of dusky red bricks, with two rows of horizontal white stonework halfway up and on each corner, and with a coach entrance through to the station yard, from the front Wapping police station looked like many others in the Met. However, the rear, which at high tide had the Thames sloshing against its foundations, was quite different.

The birthplace of Britain's modern constabularies, Wapping police station had started life as a magistrates' court, with court officers whose sole purpose it was to stop the organised gangs of river pirates pilfering good off the ships anchored in the Pool of London – an endeavour the officers of Wapping police station had been engaged in ever since. To do this the river wardens needed a place to store and repair the station fleet of skiffs they used to patrol the river. Along with a floating jetty where the current motor-powered Thames Division patrol boats were moored, there was also a marine repair shop on the ground floor complete with a winch to lift craft from the river. Repairs to the current vessels were handled elsewhere now, but the space where this used to happen was still used by the current officers, whose watery beat stretched from leafy Teddington to muddy Dartford Creek.

Leaving the bustling riverside street behind them, Tim and Alex waited until one of the stations three Morris vans drove out then they walked through the open gates, greeting a couple of uniformed officers just about to start their afternoon patrol.

Walking through the coach arch, Tim headed up the half a dozen iron steps to the left, pushed open the door and went into the old repair shop.

This area opened directly onto the river, but as it was brass monkeys out there they had sensibly closed the concertina doors and lit the squat brazier in the fireplace.

The Thames Division officers looked up at Tim, who acknowledged them with an 'all right, lads', before the two men carried on into the back room of the main station.

This was where files, equipment and the gun cupboard were, and also the area where officers wrote up their statements and court paperwork. There were a couple of constables, half-smoked cigarette clutched between their lips, doing just that at their desks; both men acknowledged Tim and Alex with a nod.

Tim hung up his hat and ran his fingers through his hair then headed to the front office, the hub of the constant warfare between those upholding the law and those whose aim was to break it.

There were half a dozen telephones dotted around – the dull black ones linked to other police stations while the green and red ones went directly through to the ARP control centre and Scotland Yard. One wall was covered with a floor-to-ceiling blackboard with the officer assigned to each beat for the day chalked on it.

A waist-high counter faced out to the station foyer, where members of the public could report missing children and pilfered bikes or hand in lost property. Running the length of it was a long beechwood counter polished to perfection by two decades of felons being dragged over it. The area was dominated by an oversized desk piled high with police manuals, patrol logs and lost property books to name but a few.

As he reached the front office, Tim stopped dead and frowned.

'Where's Mellows?' he asked of two special constables, Mills and Hanson, who were lounging on the desk smoking. 'And what on earth is that blooming racket?'

Mills indicated the frosty glass of the charge-room door. ''E's is in there,' he replied. 'And that God-awful racket is the bunch of women Wingnut arrested about an hour and a half ago in Watney Street.'

'Women?' asked Alex.

'That's right,' chipped in Hanson. 'About twenty of them.'

'What were they doing?'

'Causing a riot, by the sound of it,' Mills said. 'According to 'im, they were marching up and down with placards protesting about racketeers.'

Alex looked puzzled. 'Well, there's no law against that, so why were they arrested?'

'Because the posh bird who was leading the protest whacked Wingnut across the bonce with her banner,' explained Mills.

Ludicrously, excitement fluttered in Tim's chest.

Hanson sniggered. 'She gave him a right good wallop, too. You should see the mark.'

'Mellows is in there now trying to sort it all out,' added Mills.

Tim glanced back at the door through which he could see the blurred outlines of movement.

Of course, he should leave the station sergeant to deal with it. After all, it was a uniform not a CID matter, and it wasn't as if he didn't have a mountain of work sitting on his desk, but …

'I tell you what, Sergeant,' Tim said to Alex, 'you go up and get cracking on the reports while I pop in and give old Mellows a hand.'

Without waiting for a reply and with his heart beating rapidly in his chest, Tim strode to the charge-room door and went inside.

Although the scene before him was one of women shouting, babies sitting in prams and toddlers hanging onto their mothers' skirts, Tim's gaze passed the utter chaos and fixed on the woman standing in front of Station Sergeant Mellows, who was perched at his slopping charge desk: Fliss Carmichael.

Joshua McCabe Mellows, built like a brick out-house, was one of the few officers in H Division who could look Tim in the eye. With a walrus moustache and a set of sideburns that sparrows could nest in, he ordered the day-to-day running of the uniformed officers like a ringmaster directed a circus performance. His booming voice had scar-faced ne'er-do-wells and new recruits quaking at the knees, but Tim had seen the gruff sergeant comfort a lost child with all the gentleness of a mother hen.

Having, as a wet-behind-the-ears young officer, witnessed Winston Churchill taking potshots at two anarchists during the Siege of Sidney Street, and despite having spent thirty-plus years chasing East End villains, like many of the older officers, he had volunteered to return to duty to support the war effort.

He was not a person to be trifled with, but then again,, stunning though she was, nor was Fliss Carmichael.

Even now under Mellows' granite gaze, Fliss stood straight as a die trading ferocious stares with him. No mean feat as Tim had seen hardened criminals whimper for their mother in the same circumstances.

However, standing alongside her with a colourful bruise across his brow was War Reserve Constable Davidson looking grim and determined.

Tim allowed himself the pleasure of studying Fliss in full fury for a moment, then he strolled across.

'Miss Felicity Carmichael,' he said, stopping just behind her. 'Why am I not at all surprised?'

Both officers in the charge room stood to attention while the women stopped their chattering and regarded Tim suspiciously.

'So, Sergeant, why is the charge room looking like

the WVS day nursery?' he asked, looking at the old-time copper who was supposed to be in control.

'Because sunny boy here,' said Mellows, giving Davidson a cynical look, 'let 'em into the charge room.'

'Are they under arrest?' Tim asked.

'Not all of them,' Mellows replied. 'Just Miss Carmichael, and I've already charged a couple of others with breach of the peace. Apparently the rest followed the 'urry-up wagon back to the nick.'

A flush crept up the war reserve constable's long neck. 'Well, I thought it best, sir, as they were making a right racket in the front office.'

Giving him a jaundiced look, Tim turned and cast his gaze over the dozen or so members of the Stepney Housewives' Defence League.

'Ladies,' he said, taking a couple of steps towards them, 'although having you in Wapping nick makes the whole place a great deal prettier … I wonder if you wouldn't mind making your way outside.'

The women muttered and looked uncertainly at each other.

'Please,' Tim added, giving them a charming smile.

The atmosphere in the charge room went from hostile to simpering in the blink of an eye and after the briefest pause the women started gathering themselves and their offspring together.

Tim returned to where Fliss was standing. 'Perhaps you'd like to see them out while Sergeant Mellows finishes up, Davidson.'

The constable nodded and started to shepherd the women out of the charge room, calling their farewells to Fliss and waving as they went.

Tim looked at Fliss. 'Were you out trying to start the revolution, Miss Carmichael?'

Fliss gave him a narrow-eyed look. 'No, Inspector Wallace, I was out trying to stop hard-working women being fleeced by crooks who charge exorbitant prices to line their own pockets.'

From nowhere a sudden urge to sweep her into his arms and kiss her came over Tim, but thankfully for his sanity and his job Constable Davidson returned.

'Right,' said Mellows, dipping his pen in the inkwell, 'can we get on with this before the blackout starts?'

Fliss straightened up and looked at the station sergeant.

The officer who arrested her stood to attention and cleared his throat. 'I was proceeding down Watney Market, sir, in a southerly direction, when my attention was drawn to ...'

As War Reserve Constable Davidson ran through the events of the past two hours, Tim availed himself of the opportunity to study the softness of Fliss's cheek, the sparkle of her eyes and her very kissable mouth.

'As a crowd was gathering, I asked the women to move along but they refused and things turned ugly, at which point the ringleader of these agitators, the young lady before you, Miss Carmichael, struck me with her placard, so I arrested her for assault on police and breach of the peace,' concluded Davidson.

'I didn't hit you on purpose,' said Fliss, cutting into Tim's very pleasant wandering. 'The banner I was holding slipped when you grabbed hold of me.'

'If you'd have moved on like I told you, I wouldn't have had to make you,' Davidson barked. 'A bunch of women shouting and screaming in the street.' He jabbed his finger at her. 'Your place is at 'ome looking after kiddies and cooking your old man's midday meal, not upsetting people going about their business. Bloody unnatural that's what—' His gaze flickered onto Tim, and he stood to attention.

'Very well,' said Mellows, as he scribbled along the bottom of the charge sheet in front of him. 'Felicity Hermione Evadne Carmichael, I'm charging you with assault on War Reserve Constable Davidson and causing a breach of the peace. Have you anything to say?'

Fliss shook her head.

Tim raised an eyebrow in surprise and she glared at him.

'You are to appear at Thames Magistrate's Court at nine a.m. on Monday, which is the fifth of May,' continued the station sergeant. 'And you've been granted bail on your own recognisance.' Turning the charge book to face her, he placed a beefy finger on the bottom of the page. 'If you would sign here.'

Fliss took the pen and scribbled her name.

Removing two sheets of navy carbon paper, Mellows tore out one of the duplicate sheets and handed it to Fliss.

'Thank you,' she said, folding up her part of the charge sheet and tucking it in her pocket.

'Please return Miss Carmichael's property,' said the station sergeant.

Reaching behind him, Constable Davidson retrieved Fliss's handbag and her placard.

'Perhaps I ought to take charge of that, Miss Carmichael,' said Tim, removing the banner from the constable's grasp. 'After all, I don't want you to poke the good sergeant's eye out – then we'd have to charge you with grievous bodily harm as well.'

Fliss's mouth pulled into a tight line, giving Tim a glimpse of the headstrong girl she must have been as a child.

'Thank you, Miss Carmichael. You're now free to go,' concluded Mellows.

'I'll see you out,' said Tim.

Hooking her handbag over her arm and with her head held high, Fliss marched to the door. Tim followed her in silence until they reached the station's entrance hall, where Fliss turned to face him.

'I suppose you're enjoying this, Inspector?' she said, her lovely hazel eyes flashing angrily at him.

'Immensely, Miss Carmichael,' he replied. 'In fact, I don't know how I kept a straight face.'

She glanced down at the fingerprint ink on her hands.

'Don't worry, that comes off after a couple of washes,' he said, shame nipping at his conscience.

Her head snapped up. 'What, with a bar of Palmolive

soap that cost double what it did three months ago?'

Goodness, that was Fliss. Sharp as a tack and no holes barred.

'We were only peacefully protesting,' she said, unaware of the emotions raging in Tim's chest.

'Perhaps,' he replied. 'And I'm not saying you're wrong about the inflated prices.'

She looked surprised and he laughed.

'Yes, class traitor and instrument of the state though I am,' he said, 'I come from these streets and I know first-hand what poverty and hardship people around here endure, which is why I spend my working day investigating black-market spivs and villains who'd sell their own grannies to a glue factory if they could make a few bob. But you can't go around hitting policemen with placards.' He handed the banner back to her and the smile he'd been holding back since he walked into the charge room broke through. 'You've given Constable Davidson quite a crackerjack bruise on his bonce.'

Fliss blinked in surprise then a smile spread across her face, too. Seeing the sparkle in her eyes, the urge to step forward and take her into his arms rose up so strongly in Tim that he struggled not to do so.

With a myriad emotions whirling in his heart and mind, Tim stared down at her, heedless of time and place.

'Fliss?'

Tim looked around to see Fliss's very pregnant sister, Mrs Quinn, waddling through the police station front door.

'What are you doing here?' asked Fliss as Prue stopped in front of them.

'Coming to see what's happened to you?' Prue replied. 'When we heard you'd been arrest—'

'We?' Panic flashed across Fliss's face. 'You mean Mother—'

'Well, she couldn't avoid knowing, could she, Fliss?' said Prue, looking pointedly at her. 'Not when Doris Topper burst into the Mothers' Union meeting an hour ago and announced it to everyone in the church hall.'

Chapter twenty-one

PLACING HER HAND on the brass plate, Fliss pushed the door open and walked in. The dozen or so men and women sitting at the long table in the Old Globe's upstairs room looked around.

'Sorry I'm late,' she said. 'But I've—'

'Here she is,' shouted Harry Gunn, who was sitting halfway down the table on the left hand side, 'our very own revolutionary!'

In contrast to the rest of the group, who were dressed in a variety of ARP uniforms plus the odd female member wearing a siren suit, Harry, as always, was dressed in his worn working cords and collarless drill shirt. Putting his roll-up back between his teeth, he rose to his feet and started clapping. The others quickly joined in.

'Well, I was just striking a blow for the hard-pressed housewives,' said Fliss.

'Yes, right across that copper's noddle, the way I heard it,' said Harry.

Everyone laughed and Fliss forced a smile. 'That was an accident, I didn't mean—'

'It's all right, luv, we're having tea in a bit, and you can catch up then,' cut in Gordon Potter. Adjusting his wire-framed spectacles, the branch chairman looked down at the papers in front of him. 'Now, comrades,' he said, 'the next item on the agenda is lobbying the council to pay female ARP wardens two pounds five shillings a week like their male counterparts.'

'Don't be daft, Gordon, the council'll never wear it,' said Larry Frazer, branch treasurer, flicking his ash into an already overloaded ashtray in the middle of the table.

'Well, they bloody well ought to,' chipped in Sadie Greenburg, her black tin hat with a white W painted on it hanging on the back of her chair. 'We can get blown to bits just as easily as the blokes.'

'That may be so,' said someone else from the far end of the table, 'but you have to consider …'

Although women not getting equal pay for the same work was one of her bug bears, as the argument went back and forth Fliss's concentration wandered. Instead of focusing on the machinations of local politics, her memory relived the moment in the charge room when she'd found DI Wallace, with an amused look in his face, standing behind her.

Annoyingly, before she could stop it, her heart did a bit of a fandango then settled back to its regular beat. It was stupid really, because after she realised the police van was heading for Wapping and not Arbour Square police station, Fliss knew there was a chance she would run into the tall and criminally handsome CID officer.

Actually, seeing him up close only highlighted the fact that he wasn't just tall but broad – well, at least his shoulders and chest were, despite his stomach being as flat as a washboard. Also, although it had only been early afternoon, his five o'clock shadow was already visible. Fliss couldn't help wondering what his cheek would feel like under her fingertips and what she would discover if she could unbutton his shirt or perhaps even—

'Right,' said Gordon Potter, looking around the table. 'I think it's time for a cuppa. Back in ten minutes, if you please. The sirens haven't gone off yet but it's a clear night, so let's crack on before the Luftwaffe turns up.'

Chairs scraped back as people stood up and Fliss did the same, wandering over to where Winnie was pouring the tea. Taking a cup and a Rich Tea biscuit, she resumed her seat and started to read through the various reports that had arrived in the post yesterday afternoon.

'You're looking a real treat tonight, Miss Carmichael.'

She looked up to see Harry balancing a cup of tea in his hand.

'Thank you and for the embarrassing greeting when I walked in,' Fliss said as he sat in the vacant chair beside her.

He grinned. 'It's the least we could do for our very own Boudicca.'

Fliss raised an eyebrow.

'So, what 'appened in the market, then?' he asked, pulling his chair a little nearer.

'It was all going according to plan until the war reserve constable arrived …' In between mouthfuls of tea, Fliss recounted what had occurred that morning.

'Bloody war reserve coppers are worse than the regulars,' Harry said when she'd finished. 'Stick 'em in a uniform and give 'em a bit of authority and they're no better than Hitler and his mob. Bullies the lot of them, oppressing the honest workers of this country.'

Fliss pressed her lips together. Of course, she'd said pretty much the same thing herself on numerous occasions, but ...

'I don't suppose your mother was too chuffed when she 'eard,' Harry added.

'Not very,' Fliss replied.

That, of course, was the understatement of the century. After giving Fliss a look as though she'd slaughtered a litter of puppies, Marjorie, muttering, 'What terrible sin am I guilty of that the Almighty would inflict me with such a daughter?', had taken herself to bed with one of her headaches.

'So, what are you charged with?' asked Harry.

'Assault on police and breach of the peace,' Fliss replied. 'I've to appear at Thames Magistrate's Court on Monday. But what was worse was the insufferable expression on DI Wallace's face.'

Harry gave her a sharp look. 'Wallace? What was 'e doing there?'

'Just happened to be passing, I imagine.' The journalist part of Fliss's brain buzzed. 'You know him well, don't you?'

Harry forced a laugh. 'Everyone knows Wallace.'

'But he grew up around here and you mentioned his mother that day in the docks,' said Fliss.

'Yeah, I did know him and his family,' said Harry. 'They lived in Shadwell Buildings on the floor below us. When we were nippers, we might have kicked the odd ball around but ...'

'But?'

Harry chewed his lip for a moment. 'Let's just say 'is old man was often on the wrong side of a police-cell door.'

Fliss couldn't hide her astonishment. 'And his mother?'

'She was a decent sort,' Harry replied. 'Always the first to help a neighbour, you know?'

'Then why is she in an instit—'

'If everyone is refreshed, shall we return to the agenda?' asked Gordon Potter, cutting across Fliss's question as he resumed his seat.

Winnie returned to take her place and Harry stood up. 'See ya after.'

He strolled around to the other side of the table and took his seat again.

With everyone back in their places, the room quietened.

'The next item on the agenda is branch membership, so you have the floor, Miss Masters.'

Betty Masters, stout ward sister at Bancroft Hospital, stood up and cleared her throat. 'Thank you, Mr Potter. She held up the membership register. 'Firstly, I'm pleased to report that our numbers continue to ...'

Although Fliss did her best to concentrate on the growing ranks of the East London branch of the Labour Party, after a few moments the image of Wallace's smile drifted back into her mind.

301

Throughout the uncomfortable twenty-minute journey in the back of a Black Maria to the police station, Fliss had told herself that she didn't care because he was nothing to her, but the moment she'd looked up into his dark-brown eyes, she knew that wasn't true. To be honest, standing just an arm's length away from him she had almost thrown her arms around him and kissed him.

Now, however, apart from wondering how it would feel to have his lips pressed on hers, there were a couple of other things she needed to know about DI Wallace. Firstly, how, if Tim's father was a criminal, did he become a police officer and secondly, why was his mother in an institution?

'So, Tim,' said Ernest McEvoy, puffing smoke rings from his pipe, 'you're with the Criminal Investigation Department.'

'I am,' Tim replied.

It was the first Sunday in May and just after four in the afternoon, and Tim was sitting on the stylish, mustard-coloured Art Deco sofa in Angela's parents' front parlour.

As this was the first time Angela had taken him home to meet her parents, she and her mother, Muriel, an older well-rounded version of her daughter, had retired to the kitchen ostensibly to make tea but, in reality, to allow her father and Tim to get to know each other.

Ernest, who had a sandy-coloured toothbrush moustache and thinning hair, was by trade a plumber but now in his early fifties, he was the Clerk of Works for Poplar Council. The comfortably furnished room they were sitting in, with the unheard of wall-to-wall Indian carpet, reflected his climb up the council's pecking order.

In fact, it was the sort of home Tim had dreamed of as a boy and now aspired to have for himself.

'So how long is it that you and Angela been walking out then?' the older man asked.

'Just over four months. Mainly to the cinema or for a meal and perhaps a drink,' Tim replied, hoping only he could hear the frustration in his voice. 'I did suggest we might go up West to the theatre or to the Regal at Stratford where I hear they have a decent band.'

Ernest's mouth pulled into a tight bud, and he shook his head. 'Her mother worries if Angela's too far from 'ome in case there's an air raid. I'm sure you understand.'

Tim forced a smile. 'Of course.'

He crossed one long leg over the other and brushed a speck of dust off his trousers. Like Ernest, he was dressed as the occasion warranted in his best suit. The very suit, in fact, he'd been wearing when Fliss Carmichael had fallen into his arm ten weeks and four days ago. The image of Fliss standing eyeball to eyeball with Mellows in the charge room three days before now floated into Tim's mind and his lips lifted slightly in the corner.

'You can't blame her,' continued Ernest, cutting across his pondering. 'Five babies we lost – two of them barely a day old – before we were blessed with our Angela. Our pride and joy, she is.'

'I can tell,' said Tim, glancing at the half a dozen photos of prettily dressed Angela at various ages lined up on the mantelshelf.

'And I'll let you into a little secret, young man.' Gripping his pipe by the bowl, he pointed the soggy end at Tim. 'Our Angela's very fond of you.'

Tim smiled. 'And I'm very fond of her, too, Mr McEvoy.'

'I'm glad to hear it. We're a respectable family and we've raised our Angela proper.'

A severe expression screwed up Ernest's heavy features. 'She's a good girl, if you know what I mean. And I'd take a dim view of any man trying to take advantage of her by playing on her affections.'

'I quite understand,' Tim replied, thinking it was a shame Reverend Carmichael hadn't said the same thing to that lowlife Giles Naylor.

The creak of the door opening brought him back to the here and now, as Angela's mother, in a frilly pinny over her smart dark-green dress, wheeled in the tea trolley, her best china rattling all the way across the carpet. Angela followed a step behind.

A tender expression spread across Ernest's round face. 'Here they are: the two loveliest ladies in the land.'

'Stop it, Father,' Muriel giggled.

'I'm but stating the plain truth, aren't I, Tim?' he added.

'The truth, the whole truth and nothing but the truth, Mr McEvoy,' Tim replied.

The McEvoy family laughed politely.

'There you are, Tim,' said Muriel, placing a bone-china cup and a plate, with a generous wedge of fruit cake, on the coffee table in front of him.

'Thank you, Mrs McEvoy,' he replied, smiling up at her.

'Now, now, what did I tell you?' she said, wagging a chubby finger at him. 'It's Muriel.'

'Mum, leave Tim alone,' said Angela, tucking her floaty candy-pink skirt under her and taking the seat next to Tim on the sofa.

Actually, she frequently wore flowery and feminine dresses, often with lace and ribbons, something he suspected Fliss Carmichael wouldn't have walked out of the front door of the rectory wearing.

'So how long have you been at Wapping?' asked Ernest, picking up his cup of tea.

'Three years,' Tim replied. 'I started pounding the beat as a copper in Rochester Row before being made up to sergeant and transferring to Brixton.'

'The leafy suburbs, eh?' said Ernest. 'Full of bankers and City types.'

'And thieves and con artists, too,' Tim replied. 'But when a vacancy came up for a detective sergeant in Hampstead I jumped at the chance. After a couple of years there I passed my inspectors' exam and transferred to Wapping.'

'It must be a tough job,' said Muriel, sitting in the fireside chair opposite her husband.

'It keeps me busy,' said Tim.

'They're a feral bunch down by the river,' said Ernest, through the pipe in his clenched teeth.

'Dad!' said Angela.

'Thieves and robbers the lot of 'em. Rob their own mother for a ha'penny rather than go out and do an honest day's graft like the rest of us.'

'So where do you come from, Tim?' asked Muriel, raising her cup to her lips.

'The Peabody Estate in Shadwell,' Tim replied, looking coolly across at them.

There was a moment of silence then Ernest took the pipe from his mouth. 'Of course, when I said that them living down by the docks were wrong'uns, I didn't mean everyone, did I, Mother?'

'No, of course you didn't, Father?' Muriel said. 'I'm sure your family were very respectable, Tim.'

Although memories of the rent man hammering on the door and of shivering in the dark because his mother didn't have a sixpence for the electric flashed through his mind, Tim smiled.

'Are your parents still alive?' asked Ernest.

Tim swallowed his mouthful of cake. 'My father died a few years back but my mum is.'

Muriel's face lit up. 'Oh, Tim, you must bring her round. We'd love to meet her.'

'Tim's mum is poorly and has been in a hospital for a long time,' said Angela.

'I'm very sorry to hear that, Tim,' said Muriel sympathetically. 'Which hospital is—'

'I see you're a bit of a collector, Mrs ... Muriel,' Tim cut in, indicating the glass display cabinet so crammed with figurines that the multitude of crinoline ladies were in danger of losing an eye from the pirouetting ballerinas.

'Oh yes, I'm afraid I am,' said Muriel. 'I have a weakness for Royal Doulton and Coalport. I had a few Meissen figures, but I went out into the garden and smashed them on the patio the moment Chamberlain finished his broadcast last year.'

'Very patriotic is Mother,' said Ernest, giving his wife an approving look.

'And she makes delicious cakes,' said Tim, pulling an appreciative face.

'Actually,' giggled Muriel, 'Angela made it specially. Didn't you, sweetheart?'

'It was a recipe in this week's *Woman's Own*,' said Angela. 'I'm glad it turned out to your liking, Tim.'

Tim smiled.

If he were being totally honest, it was a tad on the stodgy side, but he'd seen and tasted worse. The brick Fliss Carmichael had offered, for one.

'A very good cook is our Angela,' chipped in Ernest, scooping the last few crumbs off his plate. 'Make some man a wonderful wife one day.'

'Stop it, Father!' laughed Muriel.

Angela gave Tim a sideward glance from beneath her lashes.

'And she made a whole batch of fairy cakes, too, for the

kiddies she teaches in the Sunday school,' added Ernest. 'Sings in the church choir, too.'

An image of Fliss floated into Tim's mind as he imagined her teaching the children in St Winifred's Sunday school to sing 'The Red Flag' rather than 'All Thing Bright and Beautiful'.

Pushing the image aside, he cleared his throat. 'So, Muriel, Angela tells me you're a leading light at the Bow branch of the WVS.'

'Well, I wouldn't say that exactly, but I like to think I'm doing my bit. We're concentrating on boxing up socks, cigarettes and a few little treats for our boys in the navy. After that, the committee have decided to ...'

Tim listened politely while she ran through the various activities the 'girls', as Angela's mother described the matrons of the parish, were planning. 'Of course, our main problem is that some of the factories along the River Lee with government contracts are offering nurseries for their workers, so a lot of our younger members with small children are taking up paid war work.'

Ernest pulled a face. 'Women working in factories. I don't 'old with it. A woman's place is in the 'ome,' he said, repacking his pipe from his tobacco pouch.

'With so many men in the army, it's a case of needs must at the moment,' said Tim. 'And even before the war started there were lots of women working outside the home.'

'Perhaps so.' Ernest's lips pulled into a tight bud again. 'Call me old fashioned if you like, but as far as I'm concerned, it's the husband's job to support his wife. And I'm proud to say that my Muriel has never done a day's work since the day we walked down the aisle.' Giving Tim a considered look, he held his lighter across the bowl and drew on his pipe. 'I imagine that as a police inspector you earn a decent enough wage.'

'Dad,' said Angela. 'Stop giving Tim the third degree.'

Tim smiled at her, then, placing his empty cup back in the saucer, he returned his crockery to the tray on the coffee table.

'Thank you, Muriel, and you too, Ernest, for inviting me into your delightful home for tea,' he said, standing up. 'It's been lovely to meet you both, but I'd better head back to the section house.'

Ernest rose to his feet. 'It's been good to meet you, too, hasn't it, Mother?'

'Oh yes,' agreed Muriel. 'Especially after Angela has told us so much about you.' Ernest thrust out his hand. 'Take care, Son.'

'Thank you, Mr McEvoy,' Tim said, ignoring the cheerless memories that the word 'son' roused and taking the older man's hand.

Angela stood up too. 'I'll see you out.'

Giving her parents a friendly smile, Tim followed Angela out of the room and into the hallway. At the front door Angela stopped on the coconut mat and turned to face him.

'Don't take any notice of Dad,' she said, slipping her arm up his chest and around his neck. 'I know he's a bit of an old fuddy-duddy about things, but his heart's in the right place.'

Tim's arms slipped around her waist automatically.

Standing in the muted light, he looked down at the woman in his arms. He knew what was expected of them now. You went out a few times over a couple of months and then you met each other's parents after everyone knew you were walking out seriously. There followed cosy evenings listening to the wireless with the parents, family weddings, christening and anniversary celebrations. By this time the expectation on all sides was your engagement followed by a big white wedding within the year.

There was no denying Angela was pretty, respectable, well educated and brought up by her parents to be a good wife and mother. She would provide a clean home and a cooked meal on the table when he returned from work each night and he would give her financial security and children in return.

Angela would never be found drunk perched on a gravestone in the middle of the night or organise women to march for a cause or get arrested. Yet although she was everything a police inspector with aspirations could need in a wife, there was one thing missing.

She wasn't Fliss.

Angela pressed herself into him and standing on tiptoes went to kiss him, but Tim moved his head back.

She gave him a puzzled look. 'Tim?'

'I'm sorry, Angela,' he said sincerely. 'I really am. And

I wouldn't hurt you for the world, but I have to tell you I'm in love with someone else.'

Fury screwed up her pretty face. 'You've been seeing someone behind my back?'

'No, I haven't, Angela,' said Tim. 'I would never do that.'

'If you haven't been two-timing me then how on earth can you be in love with—' She stopped, and her expression went from furious to white-hot rage 'It's that bloody Carmichael woman, isn't it?'

Tim didn't deny it.

'How could you?' she asked as tears gathered along her lower eyelids.

'I'm sorry,' he repeated.

'Well, it's a pity you didn't think to mention you were in love with another bloody woman when I invited you home to meet my parents.'

'I would have,' said Tim. 'But I've only just realised it myself.'

A fat tear rolled down her cheek, but she dashed it away and tore open the door.

'Goodbye, Angela,' Tim said quietly. 'I wish you all the best, I really do.' And he stepped over the threshold and strode off down the street towards the main road.

'You do know, don't you, Tim,' she called after him, 'she'll never give you a well-ordered home or the family that I could?'

And she was right, of course, but then Tim didn't care, because if Fliss loved him nothing else would matter.

Chapter twenty-two

FLISS GLANCED AT the clock above the heavy oak entrance doors of Thames Magistrates' Court for the third time in as many minutes.

'I'm sure it won't be too much longer,' said Prue, who was sitting beside her on the hard wooden bench in the waiting room.

They weren't alone: H Division had clearly had a busy weekend. Along with a couple of spivs in pin-striped suits, smoking on the bench opposite there was a woman with a black eye and an unshaven chap with a front tooth missing, plus a handful of spotty-faced, nervous-looking youths lolling about in the corner.

The door leading into the court opened and an elderly police officer holding a clipboard stepped out and looked around at the assembled offenders. 'Miss Carmichael?'

Fliss stood up and straightened her skirt. As she was going to be appearing before a member of the hierarchical establishment, she had felt it prudent to leave her trousers in the wardrobe and had donned instead her dark mulberry suit, a plain white blouse and her least flamboyant hat.

She turned to her sister. 'Do I look all right?'

'You'll do.' Hugging her, Prue kissed her on the cheek. 'I'll see you out here afterwards.' And she headed for the door to the public gallery on the other side of the black-and-white-tiled atrium, her heels echoing around the space as she went.

'As long as I don't get sent down for hard labour in Dartmoor,' Fliss called after her.

'This way, miss,' said the court officer.

Fliss followed him through the door into the court itself.

The court had been built a quarter of a century before out of the same solid red brick as Arbour Square police station, which adjoined it. However, unlike the waiting area outside with its high arched ceilings and marble floors, the court decor mimicked a well-to-do townhouse or country residence, with leather-upholstered chairs and oak panelling.

After making her way along the narrow space between the dock and the observers' gallery, Fliss reached the steps. Grasping the wrought-iron handle, she made her way up.

'Good luck, miss,' said the officer. 'You'll need it cos Sir Randolph Ewing is on the bench today.'

Fliss frowned. 'Is he harsh, then?'

The officer laughed. 'We don't call him "send-'em-down Ewing" for nothing. I tell you, he would've convicted the midwife who slapped him at birth for grievous bodily 'arm 'ad he been able. He's just gone out for a slash, but you'll see for yourself when he comes back in.'

313

With this piece of information rattling around in her head, Fliss stepped up to the railing surrounding the dock and placed her hands lightly on it. She glanced across to the public gallery. Along with the usual collection of spectators with nothing better to do than listen to the proceedings, in the back row sat Nellie, Doris and Maureen, with baby Pattie on her knee. Prue mouthed 'good luck' across to Fliss, then slipped into an empty chair next to them.

Turning towards the other side of the court, Fliss spotted War Reserve Constable Davidson with a purple, green and yellow streak across his forehead. Idly, her eyes moved over the handful of policemen and court officials sitting at the long desk until her gaze fell on the man sitting at the end: Detective Inspector Tim Wallace.

Dressed as always in his dark suit, spotless white shirt with a neat tie-knot anchored at his throat, he was nothing short of temptation on legs. For there was no denying the fact that, annoying and opinionated through he was, he was also tempting. Very tempting.

Their eyes locked and Fliss's heart thumped uncomfortably in her chest a couple of time before thundering off at breakneck speed. Staring across at him, the urge to leap down from the dock, dash across the courtroom and throw herself in his arms rose up in Fliss so forcibly that her fingers curled on the iron railings just in case, in a rash moment, she gave in to the impulse.

'All rise,' said the court officer in front of the long oak bench.

314

'Thank you, Sergeant,' said a man's voice, in an accent that would make a BBC announcer sound like a barrow boy.

Tearing her eyes from Tim, Fliss turned to the man she should have been focused on: the Thames Court's magistrate. Complete with black robes and horsehair wig, Sir Randolph Ewing JP lumbered along behind the light-oak bench to take his seat beneath the gilded lion, unicorn and quartered shield of the Crown fixed to the wall.

With heavy reddened jowls, a bulbous nose and a look of barely concealed belligerence to the world in general and to those standing before him in the courtroom in particular, he reminded Fliss of her deceased Great-uncle Josiah d'Apremont. Josiah was notable for very few things in his long life, other than a general intolerance of anyone walking upright on two legs, rather he doted on the assortment of feral cats that ran wild around his rambling country pile in Northampton. Her mother always described him as eccentric, whereas Fliss thought the phrase 'barking mad' was much more accurate.

'Thank you, Mr Pugh,' said Sir Randolph, settling himself into his throne-like chair.

Pushing his spectacles back up to the bridge of his nose, the magistrate's clerk consulted the very large ledger open on the table in front of him.

'Miss Felicity Hermione Evadne Carmichael, you are charged with assaulting a police officer and causing a breach of the peace,' he said. 'How do you plead?'

Fliss pulled herself up to her full height. 'Not guilty.'

On hearing her voice, the magistrate raised his hedgerow-like eyebrows. 'Miss Carmichael!'

'Yes, Your Worship,' Fliss replied, seeing Tim shift forward out of the corner of her eye.

'What does your father do?' he asked.

'He's the rector of St Winifred's Church in Stepney,' she replied, as an image of her mother's outraged face swam into her mind.

The magistrate's scraggly eyebrows rose even further. 'Is he indeed? Well, in all my twenty-seven years on the bench I don't believe I've ever had a clergyman's daughter stand before me in the dock.' He studied her for a moment or two longer then his attention shifted to the clerk. 'I suppose we ought to hear the evidence, Mr Pugh.'

'Calling War Reserve Constable Davidson to the stand,' called the clerk.

Davidson sprang to his feet and with his flat cap tucked under his arm, he marched across the courtroom and into the raised witness box as if he were parading before the King.

The usher swore him and a couple of women in the public gallery nudged each other and looked expectantly, hoping, no doubt, to hear some scandal about a local clergyman's daughter that they could repeat on the street corner.

Davidson cleared his throat. 'On Thursday the first of May, I was proceeding in a southerly direction along Watney Street when …'

The war reserve officer ran through the events of the

previous Thursday; although to be honest, you'd be forgiven for thinking he was describing the Siege of Troy rather than a scuffle outside a grocer's shop.

Feeling the weight of Tim's eyes on her, Fliss stole a quick look at him to find him gazing intently at her, which caused a very pleasant sensation to curl in her stomach.

'And after Miss Carmichael struck me with the banner she was brandishing—'

'I wasn't brandishing it,' Fliss burst out, tearing her eyes from Tim. 'I was holding it.'

'Be quiet, Miss Carmichael,' barked the magistrate.

'And so I arrested her, Your Worship,' concluded Davidson.

'Nearly pulling my arm out of its socket in the process,' added Fliss. 'We were protesting peacefully until Constable Davidson turned up and started throwing his weight about.'

'You bloody bully,' shouted Nellie..

'Yeah, manhandling innocent women,' added Doris, shaking her bony fist at the officer in the witness box.

'Silence!' barked Sir Randolph, casting a ferocious glare towards the public gallery. 'Miss Carmichael.'

Fliss straightened up.

'You've heard what the constable has said. Have you anything to say for yourself before I pass judgment?'

'Judgment?' said Fliss. 'What about the other witnesses?'

Sir Randolph turned to Davidson, who was still standing in the witness box. 'Are there any, Constable?'

317

'There were a couple of other women from this Housewives' League whatnot milling about, but I doubt they saw anything,' he replied, without glancing at Fliss.

'Well then—'

'Excuse me, Your Worship,' said Tim, rising to his feet and stepping out into the space in the middle of the courtroom.

A scowl settled on Sir Randolph's heavy features. 'Inspector Wallace?'

'With your permission,' Tim's cool gaze shifted from the bench to the witness box, 'I think perhaps, Constable Davidson, that it may have slipped your mind that Mrs Tucker was standing beside Miss Carmichael when the incident occurred.'

A deep-red flush coloured the constable's throat and cheeks.

'I believe she was,' he forced out between ridged lips.

'And is she in court?' asked Sir Randolph.

Maureen jumped up. 'I am, Your Lordship, sir.'

'Very well,' said the magistrate.

Settling her daughter on her hip, Maureen made her way down into the main area of the court and stepped into the witness box that Davidson had just vacated.

'In your own words, Mrs Tucker,' said the magistrate wearily.

Blinking rapidly, Maureen took a deep breath. 'Well, see, Your Honour, sir, it was like this ...'

Maureen recounted the happenings outside Banfield & Son the Thursday before, except now they resembled a Sunday school tea party rather than a legendary battle in antiquity.

'We was just making our point about shopkeepers hiking up their prices; that was until that roz—' Maureen checked herself and pointed at Davidson, who was now sitting among the other police officers in court. 'That policeman started dragging Miss Carmichael away. She slipped and the banner she was carrying 'it the constable on the nut.'

'Thank you, Mrs … Mrs …' The magistrate dismissed her with a wave and Maureen stepped down from the witness box.

Sir Randolph turned his attention back to Fliss.

'Have you anything to say for yourself, Miss Carmichael?'

'Just that as citizens of this country it is our right under common law—'

'Do not lecture me about the law of this land in my courtroom, Miss Carmichael,' he interrupted. 'It seems clear to me that you did in fact strike Constable Davidson with your placard. That much is evident by the livid bruise on his forehead. Whether this blow was intentional or accidental is neither here nor there because you cannot go around assaulting officers of the law. I therefore find you guilty of assaulting Constable Davidson and occasioning a breach of the peace. Has the defendant any priors, Mr Pugh?'

'No, Your Worship,' replied the clerk.

'Very well.' The magistrate fixed Fliss with a steely

stare. 'Miss Carmichael, as this is your first offence, I fine you ten pounds with a month to pay and you will be bound over for a year, meaning should you appear in court and be found guilty of a similar wrongdoing within that time this offence will be taken into account. Do you understand?'

'Yes, Your Worship,' Fliss replied, feeling like a ten-year-old standing in the headmaster's office.

She turned to step down.

'And Miss Carmichael ...'

She looked around.

'You're obviously a well-brought-up young lady from a respectable family, pretty too,' Sir Randolph said, giving her what she imagined was a paternal smile. 'So might I suggest that instead marching about the streets making a nuisance of yourself and attacking policemen, you find yourself a nice young man and settle down? Dismissed.'

Fliss stared wordlessly at the aged dispenser of the law then she stomped from the dock. As she reached the bottom step, she glanced across at Tim again only to see, damn and blast him, the same barely concealed amusement on his too handsome face as he had had in the charge room.

Having signed the paperwork and been given the top sheet, Fliss made her way out into the foyer. Prue was already there and waddled over.

'Are you all right, Fliss?' she asked, slipping her arm through her sister's.

Fliss nodded. 'Although the fine means I'll have about

thruppence left in my post office savings account.'

'Well, at least you didn't get hard labour in Dartmoor,' Prue replied.

Fliss forced a smile.

'There she is,' shouted Nellie, as she and the other women rushed towards her.

'Well done,' said Doris, patting her on the shoulder. 'Standing up to that miserable old bugger.'

'Much good it did 'er,' said Maureen, tucking her baby back in her pram. 'Ten blooming quid.'

The women's attention shifted to something behind Fliss.

'Got to get back, luv. Me old man'll be shouting for his dinner,' said Nellie.

'Me too,' said Maureen, kicking off the pram brakes. 'Baby needs feeding.'

'Yeah, we'll see you later, Fliss,' added Doris.

The three women shot off.

Fliss gave her sister a puzzled look. 'What was all—'

'Miss Carmichael,' said a deep voice behind her.

She turned and found Tim standing there.

If he'd looked enticing sitting across a courtroom, looking down at her from under the brim of his fedora he looked positively sinful.

'In-inspector Wallace,' she said, as her heart fluttered. 'I didn't expect to see you in court.'

'But we're glad you were there,' cut in Prue, 'to remind that officer that there are two sides to the story.'

'My pleasure, Mrs Quinn,' he replied.

'Yes, thank you, Inspector,' said Fliss, 'for stepping in like that so the magistrate heard both sides of the story.'

'Just doing my job,' he replied, his eyes dark as they looked into hers.

As the activity around her stilled, Fliss stared wordlessly up at him.

His gaze changed in a way she couldn't identify then he raised his hat.

'Nice to see you again, Mrs Quinn,' he said, giving Prue a quick smile before his gaze returned to Fliss. 'As our paths seem to have a way of crossing, Miss Carmichael, I'm sure I'll be seeing you soon.'

Replacing his hat and after giving her one last unreadable look, he turned and headed for the exit, Fliss's eyes following him every step of the way.

Once he had disappeared from sight, Fliss turned back to Prue.

'What?' she said, seeing the grin on her sister's face.

'He fancies you,' Prue replied.

'Don't be daft,' said Fliss, ignoring the glow spreading through her.

'He does,' insisted Prue. 'And you fancy him, too.'

'Now you're being ridiculous.' Fliss forced a light laugh. 'And even if I did, it wouldn't matter because he's already got a girlfriend.'

'Looking like that I'm sure he has,' Prue replied. 'But I'd bet a pound to a penny, her days are numbered.'

Chapter twenty-three

THE SLIGHTLY NERVOUS fair-haired secretary knocked lightly on the door then, without waiting for a reply, grasped the handle and opened it.

The round-faced man sitting behind the desk looked up from the pile of paperwork in front of him and his scraggly eyebrows pulled together. 'I thought, Mabel, I made it clear I didn't want to be disturb—'

'Detective Inspector Wallace to see you,' she cut in as Tim strode past her into the office.

It was just after eleven thirty on Wednesday 14 May, the week after he'd been in court for Fliss's hearing.

Having arrived at his office in Wapping nick just after eight, it had taken him a full two hours to deal with the dozens of reports from the previous night's six-hour bombing raid.

It was mainly looting, but a couple of bodies had been found that looked as though they might have died elsewhere and been dumped in the rubble after the raid – a method that was fast becoming the disposal means of choice for local villains. Having prioritised and allocated each case to a CID officer, he'd jumped on the train at Wapping to Whitechapel, followed by a ten-minute tram ride up Cambridge Heath Road to Hackney Town Hall. The grand mid-Victorian building sat like a fat toad on a lily pad opposite the one-time workhouse that was now the Bethnal Green Infirmary at the top end of the old Cambridge Road just before it changed into Mare Street.

Although like Stepney Town Hall in Cable Street the lower floors of the council headquarters had been largely given over to the ARP and council welfare departments, the upper two floors had been taken over by the Ministry of Food, and it was from these offices that North East London's regional food distribution was handled.

Blinking rapidly behind his wire-framed spectacles, Mr Pollock, the fleshy middle-aged man responsible for food distribution at London Dock rose to his feet.

'I'm sorry to just call on you like this, Mr Pollock,' said Tim, 'but if I could have a few words about an ongoing police investigation.'

'Well, actually, Inspector,' he replied, 'it's not all that convenient at the moment, but if you'd like to—'

'Under the Emergency Powers Act,' cut in Tim, regarding the man behind the desk icily.

Pollock's jowls quivered ever so slightly then, after a moment, he waved his secretary out. She left, closing the door behind her.

Stretching his arm from his sleeve, Pollock looked at his wristwatch.

'I've the area food coordinator arriving in a short while,' he said, 'so I can only spare you a few moments. Now, how can I help you?'

324

'Firstly, I'm sure you're aware that food looted from London Dock warehouses during bombing raids is now readily available in grocery and butcher's shops all over East London and as far away as Romford Market in Essex,' said Tim.

Disapproval furrowed Pollock's forehead. 'Yes, I know, it's quite shocking, but I hear the police are arresting black-market racketeers and recovering looted goods each day.'

'We are,' said Tim. 'But what we recover is only a fraction of what has been stolen. Most of it seems to evaporate into thin air.'

'Sold under the counter, no doubt,' said Pollock.

'A small proportion, maybe,' said Tim, 'but I'd say the only way a criminal gang could dispose of the three tons of tinned fruit, meat and fish that disappeared from the Ceylon and Thailand wharf a week ago is by passing it off as legitimately signed off for sale by the Ministry of Food. And the only way they could do that, Mr Pollock,' he continued, looking hard at the inspector, 'is if they were able somehow to obtain the correct Ministry of Food paperwork.'

Under the stark illumination of the fluorescent strip light, small beads of sweat glistened on the food inspector's receding brow.

'I suppose they could if they managed to forge it, but all our certificates have a specific watermark so it wouldn't be easy. Still, there might be someone out there who could do it, Inspector.' He gave Tim an ingenuous wide-eyed smile and heaved a heavy sigh. 'Where there's a will there's a way, as they say.'

'I imaging money has more to do with it than will,' Tim replied. 'Turn-a-blind-eye, manipulate-the-figures or amend-the-paperwork sort of money, don't you think, Mr Pollock?'

The inspector's fleshy cheeks trembled again and beneath his pencil moustache his mouth pulled into a tight line. 'As you seem to be implying that someone in this office is in league with these black-market criminals, I hope you have some evidence to back up your accusations, Inspector.'

The corner of Tim's mouth lifted slightly. 'Not yet, Mr Pollock, but I will have.'

Pollock's shoulders relaxed a little. 'Well, be assured, Inspector, I'm as keen to put an end to this theft and racketeering as you are, so if I hear anything or notice something amiss I'll contact you straight away.'

Tim smiled artlessly at the chief food inspector then rose to his feet.

'Thank you for your time, Mr Pollock,' he said. He took a couple of steps towards the door then paused and turned back.

'Oh, just one other thing, Mr Pollock,' he said.

The inspector looked up from the dockets and invoices in front of him.

'Do you know Harry Gunn?'

'Gunn. Gunn,' he repeated, as he considered the question. 'I can't say I do.'

'I just thought I'd ask as you're frequently in London Dock,' said Tim.

A smug expression slipped across Pollock's chubby face. 'My job is to deal with the directors of the import companies and the managers in the Government suppliers in London Dock, not the dockers and navvies on the quayside. Now,' said Pollock, looking at his watch again, 'if that's all, Inspector, I have a mountain of paperwork to—'

'Sorry, what is the time?' cut in Tim, 'my watch seems to have stopped.'

'A quarter to one,' Pollock replied testily.

Tim's well-drawn eyebrows rose in surprise. 'It can't be?'

'Here, see for yourself.' Pollock thrust out his arm and Tim looked at the watch on his hairless, pink wrist.

'So it is,' he replied. 'I'll leave you to it then and thank you. Our little chat has been illuminating.'

Tim was mulling over his conversation with the food inspector as he made his way back down the echoing staircase, but as he turned the corner he was surprised to see none other than Fliss Carmichael engaged in an animated discussion with the young woman behind the reception desk, a queue of men and women waiting behind her.

As the May weather had suddenly turned very much warmer, today she was wearing a flowery dress with a sky-blue cardigan and heeled sandals.

Pausing at the bottom of the stairs, Tim allowed himself the pleasure of watching the woman he unexpectedly found himself in love with as she debated with the receptionist for a moment or two, then he made his way across.

'Miss Carmichael,' he said, stopping behind her.

She turned and looked up.

A spark of something flashed in her eyes, which made his chest swell.

'DI Wallace,' she replied. 'What are you doing here?'

'I could ask you the same thing,' Tim replied. 'I'm just following up some inquiries; what about you?'

'I'm trying,' she glanced at the stony-faced receptionist, 'to have a word with Mr Pollock.'

'And as I've already told you, Miss Carmichael,' snapped the red-haired receptionist, 'Mr Pollock is unavailable.'

'And you don't know when he'll be free,' said Fliss.

'No, I don't,' replied the other women. 'Now, if you don't mind.'

She looked pointedly at the line of people.

Frowning, Fliss opened her mouth to speak.

'I tell you what,' said Tim before she could say a word, 'there's a British Restaurant across the road, so why don't I take you for a cuppa?'

'All right,' she said after a second or two. 'But on one condition.'

He smiled. 'And what's that?'

'I can have a bacon butty,' she replied. 'I missed breakfast this morning and I'm starving.'

Tim laughed. 'One bacon butty coming up.'

They made their way past the red fire extinguishers and sand-filled bucket out into Cambridge Heath Road.

As it was lunchtime the street was filled with shoppers and tradesmen going about their business. That is, as far as it was possible to go about your business after another night of heavy bombing: all branches of the ARP were still out in force along with the council workers. The faint whiff of sewage on the spring breeze suggested that a main drain close by had been ruptured, and the gutters resembled a dirty, fast-flowing stream caused by a broken water pipe that a team from the Water Board were desperately trying to fix further down the road.

After stopping at the kerb for a moment as a fire engine filled with exhausted-looking firefighters trundled past, Tim and Fliss walked between the metal studs marking the crossing then up the gravel path towards the Bethnal Green Museum.

Holding the door open for her, Tim followed Fliss into the cavernous space beneath the high-vaulted ceilings, the low hum of voices echoing around the space.

The ground-floor area was filled with factory workers sitting around long trestle tables at one end while women with small children tended to congregate at the other.

'You find us a table and I'll be back in a jiff,' said Tim.

He crossed to the serving area and gave their order into the woman behind the counter.

As he waited, Tim's eyes returned to Fliss, who had found an empty table over on the far side and was sitting, head bowed over her notebook. A lock of hair had escaped from the red ribbon around her head and nestled on her cheek.

'There you are, ducks,' said a matronly woman in an off-white overall as she plonked a loaded tray in front of him. 'One and nine.'

Tim handed over a florin.

'And you were lucky,' she said, handing him a thruppenny bit. 'That was the last of the bacon.' Her gaze flickered across to where Fliss was sitting. 'Your young lady?'

Tim smiled and picked up the tray. 'Not yet.'

He strolled back to Fliss.

'There we are, madam,' he said, as she looked up from her work. 'A cup of Rosie Lee and a bacon sandwich.'

'What is this place?' she asked, as Tim placed the tray on the table and took the seat opposite.

'The Bethnal Green Museum,' Tim replied. 'It was built seventy or so years ago to take the overspill from the Great Exhibition. They're all packed away in the two upstairs galleries, but if you look up you can still spot the odd thing or two through the balustrades.'

Fliss raised her gaze and Tim took the opportunity to appreciate the sweep of her long eyelashes.

'Did you come here as a child?' she asked, taking a tentative sip of her tea.

Old images of him and Arthur with their noses pressed up against the museum's glass cases loomed into Tim's mind.

'Yes,' said Tim. 'My mother brought me and my brother most Sunday afternoons when we were kids.'

She gave him a thoughtful look. 'Didn't Harry Gunn say something about your mother when we met him in the dock that—'

'Who's this Pollock chap and why were you trying to see him?' Tim asked, annoyed with himself for mentioning his mother. It wasn't that he didn't want to tell Fliss about his chaotic family life and how Arthur had died before he was old enough to have long trousers. He did. In fact, there was no one on earth he wanted to share the troubles of his early life with more than Fliss. But not here in the middle of a busy government feeding centre.

'Mr Pollock is the Ministry of Food's chief inspector for East London,' she said, picking up her sandwich. 'Because I'm following a story.'

'About rationing?' asked Tim, blowing the steam off his cup.

With a mouthful of bacon butty, she shook her head. Finally, she said, 'About how food seems to arrive at the docks and then disappears into thin air.'

'Dockers are notorious for smuggling stuff through the dock gates.' Tim forced a light laugh. 'If I had a pound for every one of 'em who'd been through Wapping nick's charge room I'd be a rich man.'

Fliss frowned. 'I'm not just talking about a couple of tins of peaches walking through the dock gates in someone's pocket. I'm talking about a systematic scam that takes food from the warehouses on an industrial scale and sells it on. And I'm gathering evidence to prove it.'

'What sort of evidence?' asked Tim.

She studied him for a long moment.

'I suppose I can tell you.' She leaned towards him and spoke in a hushed voice. 'Firstly, I've lost count of the number of women I've spoken to who say that although there might be nothing much on the shelves and only offal and scrag end in the butchers' windows, if you know where to shop and have the money you can get anything from a side of best beef to freshly ground coffee.'

Tim took a mouthful of tea. 'That's hardly evidence, and as I just said dockers are—'

'"Notorious for smuggling stuff through the dock gates." I heard you,' cut in Fliss in the same low tone. 'I recently interviewed a Mrs Wiggins, whose husband was the general manager at Logan and McKay's – he was supposedly killed in the Devonshire Arms pub when it was bombed back in February.'

'Like hundreds of others that night, I suspect,' replied Tim, who had his own suspicions about the death of Mr Wiggins.

Fliss took another bite from her sandwich.

'Except,' she said, through a mouthful of bread and bacon, 'Mrs Wiggins was baffled as to why her husband was in Limehouse when he was supposed to be visiting his mother in Stratford. And he was teetotal. Took the pledge on a Methodist youth camp when he was sixteen.'

Despite unease prickling between his shoulder blades, Tim maintained his genial expression.

'And,' Fliss continued, looking across her cup at him, 'six hundredweight of tinned fruit was taken from the warehouse the night he died, so how do you think the thieves managed to offload a haul like that without someone noticing?'

Although he had a good idea how Harry and his gang had sold on such a quantity, hence his visit to Pollock, he shrugged.

Fliss gave him a pained look. 'I thought you were supposed to be a detective. It's obvious, isn't it?'

Tim maintained his baffled expression.

'To sell that amount of food without raising any suspicion, someone must be giving them the government paperwork,' she concluded.

'I suppose that might be the case, but I need hard evidence before I can start kicking down doors and arresting people. Have you got any?'

She pressed her lips together. 'Not yet. People aren't keen to talk. But once I've discovered who the leader of the gang is, you and your boys can arrest the whole lot of them. I'll have such a scoop that I wouldn't be surprised if the nationals pick it up.' She gave him the brightest of smiles. 'And who knows? I might end up working on the *Herald* or some other daily off the back of it.' She frowned. 'All I've got to do is find someone who isn't too scared to tell me who the big man is behind the robberies and I'll be home and dry.'

Tim smiled and took a sip of his tea, praying silently that no one ever whispered Harry Gunn's name to her.

'There you are, miss,' said the elderly court clerk behind the arched meshed window as he handed her the receipt.

'Thank you,' said Fliss, watching her hard-earned ten pounds disappear into the drawer beneath the counter.

It was just after two p.m. on Friday and she was once again in Thames Magistrates' Court, but thankfully this time she wasn't waiting to stand in front of the magistrate as she had almost two weeks before.

Having queued for fifteen minutes behind a couple of spivs, a labourer with a lovely pair of black eyes and an old woman dressed in rags smelling like a brewery, she'd finally reached the front.

'And perhaps next time you'll think twice about creating a ruckus in the street and biffing a member of the constabulary,' the clerk added.

'I certainly will,' Fliss replied, answering his censorious look with a cool one. 'As soon as shopkeepers and stallholders stop racketeering.'

'Well then, miss,' he replied, looking over the top of his half-rimmed spectacles at her, 'I'll no doubt be seeing you again.'

Giving him a tight smile, Fliss tucked the receipt in her purse and stepped away from the window.

Hooking her satchel over her shoulder, she started to wend her way through the people milling about in the foyer waiting for the afternoon's proceedings to start. As you'd expect, there was a huddle of uniformed and plain-clothed police officers lounging over by one of the court doors, smoking and chatting as they waited to be called in. Although she tried not to, her eyes drifted across just in case DI Wallace was among them.

He wasn't and ignoring the twinge of disappointment, Fliss continued on towards the main exit and she soon found herself standing outside on the pavement in Aylward Street. Turning towards New Road, she started to walk back to the *Chronicle*, but she'd only taken a couple of steps when she heard her name being called.

Turning, she saw Sister Martha carrying a loaded basket and waving at her from the other side of the street. As always, the elderly nun was dressed in her light-grey, mid-calf-length habit with her matching wimple held in place by a white band.

'Hello, Fliss,' said St Winifred's lay sister as she reached her. 'Are you off somewhere nice?'

'I'm afraid not, just the office,' Fliss replied. 'What about you?'

'I'm visiting Marie Lampton,' said Sister Martha. 'She just had twins, so I'm taking her a few baby bits that I found in the Bring and Take that might do her a turn. Mind if I walk with you?'

'Of course not,' laughed Fliss. 'In fact, I'd be glad of the company. But let me carry that basket.'

The nun's slender shoulders relaxed.

'That would be a blessing, my dear,' she said, her thin lips lifted in a soft smile. 'I'm not as young as I used to be, and this basket seems to be getting heavier with every step.'

Fliss hooked the basket over her arm and they turned in the direction of Commercial Road.

For the last few nights, having grown tired of flying the same old route to London, the Luftwaffe had decided to visit the seaside. Sadly, ports like Harwich, Ipswich, Grimsby and Yarmouth had borne the brunt of the enemy's nightly attacks. That said, after suffering a full week of incessant bombing from dawn to dusk the previous week, the ARP clear-up teams were still very much in evidence. Although the glass had been swept up and rubble removed from the carriageway, teams of worker were now engaged in fixing large wooden beams to the sides of houses to prop them up.

'I saw your piece in the *Chronicle* about St George's and St Dunstan's District Nursing Association,' said the lay sister as they fell into step. 'I'm glad you focused on the nurses rather than the Association board, as so often happens.'

'Well, they are the women doing the work, not doctors and businessmen on the board,' said Fliss.

'I quite agree,' said Sister Martha, as they side-stepped a whirl of dog dirt. 'Although I imagine you'll have quite a lot to write about after your valiant stand in Watney Street.'

'Valiant! Some would call it disgraceful,' said Fliss, as her mother's sour expression loomed into her mind.

Sister Martha's almost invisible eyebrows pulled together. 'Well, lots of people grumble about the high prices and those lining their own pockets at others' expense, but you actually did something about it and I call that admirable.'

Squaring her shoulders, Fliss stood a little bit taller.

'Although I suppose it cost you dear,' added the nun, as they reached the end of the street and turned into Commercial Road.

'Best part of my savings,' Fliss replied. 'Still, it might have been worse if Inspector Wallace hadn't stepped in.'

Sister Martha's eyebrows rose. 'That wouldn't be Timothy Wallace, would it?'

'Yes,' said Fliss. 'Do you know him?'

'I do,' said the nun. 'In fact, I've known him since he was in short trousers, but the last I heard of him he was a detective sergeant in Hampstead.'

'Well, he's gone up the ranks again because he's a detective inspector at Wapping now,' said Fliss, her heart doing a little tap dance as she said his name.

'I'm not surprised,' said Sister Martha, as a horse-drawn milk float rattled past on its way back to the dairy. 'Even as a boy I knew Tim would make something of himself despite the rough start he had in life.'

'I heard that his mother is in an institution?' said Fliss.

'Yes, Warley way, out in Essex, I believe,' the nun replied.

'Do you know why?'

'I'm afraid I don't,' the nun replied. 'When I returned from a month-long visit with my sister in Scotland about fifteen or sixteen years ago another family had moved into the Wallaces' flat in Peabody Buildings. Father Aiden had taken Tim under his wing, and he was staying at St Mungo's Rectory. Why do you ask?'

'Oh, no reason,' she replied airily.

Sister Martha's soft grey eyes studied Fliss more closely, so pushing aside the image of Tim looking down at her from beneath the brim of his hat, she grinned. 'Just my journalistic instincts for a good story, I suppose.'

Amusement flickered briefly in the nun's eyes then she too smiled.

'I'm afraid this is where we must part company, my dear,' she said, as they stopped on the corner of Philpot Street.

'So it is.' Fliss handed the nun her basket. 'Well, it's been lovely chatting to you.'

'Likewise,' Sister Martha replied. 'See you on Sunday.'

Fliss turned and continued along the road.

'Oh and, Fliss …' called Sister Martha. Fliss stopped and looked around. 'Please give my regards to Tim when you next see him.'

Fliss nodded and walked on. Although her mind told her time and time again that she shouldn't give a jot if she never saw Tim Wallace again, her heart just called her liar.

'And both twins have been given a clean bill of health, Mrs Wilcox?' said Fliss, looking across at the slender young blonde-haired woman sitting on the armchair opposite her.

'Oh, yes,' said Evie Wilcox, looking at her with the tired eyes of a new mother. 'Sister Sullivan from the clinic at Monroe House said considering 'ow they arrived in the world, Paula and Peter were as bouncing a pair of babies as she'd ever seen.'

It was just after three in the afternoon and Fliss was sitting in Evie's minute living room in her third-floor flat in Trinity House. The triangular block of dwellings was situated on the corner of Hannibal and Redmans Roads opposite the pile of rubble that had been the Victorian church of Christchurch and the Bricklayer's Arms public house, respectively.

Like many tenement blocks in the area, the flats had been built in the last century by philanthropic organisations such as the Peabody, Guinness and Rothschild Trust, to provide better housing for the skilled workers and tradesmen. However, with eight dwellings on each of the four landings sharing one toilet at the far end and only one washhouse for all thirty-two apartments, the tenements were now some of the most dilapidated buildings in the area.

'I'm very glad to hear it,' said Fliss, closing her notebook and slotting her pencil back into the space in the spine. 'Well, I think I've got everything. And thank you for letting me interview you.'

Tucking her pad into her satchel on the floor, she grabbed the handle and stood up.

That's all right, luv,' said the new mother, rising to her feet. 'Are you sure you don't want a little cuddle?'

Fliss glanced at the pine-wood drawer with the two sleeping babies lying top to tail in it and then back to their mother.

339

She forced a smile. 'I wouldn't want to wake them.'

Hooking her satchel over her shoulder she crossed the spotless lounge to the front door with Evie half a step behind.

She opened the door and stepped out onto the narrow landing then turned. 'Thank you again and many congratulation, Mrs Wilcox.'

There was a small cry and Evie rolled her eyes. 'No rest for the wicked, eh, Miss Carmichael?'

Fliss smiled and leaving her interviewee to attend to her babies, she turned towards the stairs. But as she placed her hand on the narrow, wrought-iron banister to make her way down a door on the landing below opened.

'Are you sure, Mrs Conway? After all, this is the fourth time in as many weeks,' said the dark-brown voice that haunted Fliss's dreams, echoing up the stairwell. 'Next time it might be more than just a black eye.'

'I know you mean well, Inspector,' a woman's voice replied, 'but you know 'ow it is with my Mackie. He ain't a bad bloke and if I hadn't nagged him about the 'ousekeeping he wouldn't have gone off on one, like he did.'

'But, Mrs—'

'And thank you for dropping by.'

A door closed with a click. There was a pause then the sound of footsteps drifted up.

Adjusting her satchel, Fliss hurried down and reached the ground floor as Tim was about to walk through the archway to the street.

'Inspector Wallace,' she called.

He turned and beneath the brim of his fedora his weary expression brightened.

'Miss Carmichael,' he said, as he waited for her to reach him. 'I don't know, first the Docks, then the Ministry of Food and now Trinity Buildings; I'm beginning to wonder if you're following me.'

Raising an eyebrow, Fliss gave him a cool look. 'Don't flatter yourself, Inspector. I've got better things to do than dog your footsteps.'

Tim laughed and it rolled through Fliss like a sizzling wave.

'I happened to be interviewing someone in one of the third-floor flats, if you must know,' she continued, over the sound of her blood drumming in her ears.

'Are you going back to the office?' he asked. 'Because if you are I'll walk with you as I'm on my way to Hessle Street.'

'Actually, I am,' said Fliss, falling into step beside him. 'I need to write up this article. It's about a woman who was buried under a fallen building and gave birth to twins before the rescue and first-aid crews could get to her.'

Tim looked amazed. 'Were they all right?'

'Thankfully, yes,' said Fliss, as they crossed into Jamaica Street. 'Why were you visiting Trinity Buildings?'

'Just following up on a report,' Tim replied, a touch of sadness in his tone.

'Of a woman being assaulted by her husband?' asked Fliss. He gave her a sharp look. 'Voices echo.'

He sighed. 'Yes. An all too common occurrence on a Friday and Saturday night, I'm afraid.'

'Forgive me for asking, Inspector,' said Fliss as they stepped around a pile of roof tiles on the pavement that had been dislodged in the previous night's air raid, 'but I thought the police didn't get involved in disputes between husbands and wives.'

Tim's mouth pulled into a hard line. 'That might be so in other nicks but not at Wapping. As far as I'm concerned, some chap taking his fist to his wife after a couple of beers is the same as if he'd punched someone in a bar fight, and I make sure they are reported as such.' He sighed again. 'Unfortunately, as the wives have to sign the charge sheet as witnesses, nine times out of ten they withdraw the complaint before it gets to court.'

'Is that why you were talking to the wife?' she asked, as an ambulance and an ARP van passed them.

Tim nodded. 'Mackie Conway is a brute and I've lost count of the number of times he's been thrown in the cells for fighting. And when he's got a drink inside him his favourite pastime is using his wife Ida as a punchbag. I was trying to talk her into giving evidence against him, but she won't hear of it.' He gave a mirthless laugh. 'Even has the idea it's her fault.'

'Which it isn't,' said Fliss.

'No, it's not!' Tim replied emphatically. 'And it's for that reason whenever a report like Mrs Conway's comes across my desk I either follow up myself or get one of the DIs to because …'

'Because of what happened to you,' said Fliss softly. Tim gave her another sharp look. 'People talk.'

He acknowledged the statement with a nod and lapsed into silence for a minute or so, but as they reached the Essex Arms at the corner of Commercial Road, he cleared his throat.

'I was fifteen at the time and just getting ready to sit my school certificate. My mum had scrubbed floors during the day and took in piecework sewing shirt collars at night to get me to Raines Grammar School. She was doing the same for my brother Arthur, who was nine, and so to try to take some of the financial burden off her I'd got myself an evening job at Padbury & Son Printers in Whitechapel High Street. I was out that night when my father got home from the pub.' He paused and a hard-bitten expression spread across his chiselled features. 'My father was a drunk. Even as a small boy I remember him staggering home in a rage and hitting my mum. The neighbours were always calling the police, who always left without doing anything,' he continued, as they reached the chemist on the corner of Philpot Street.

'Anyway, on Friday the sixteenth of July 1926 I got home at about a quarter to twelve, to find two constables from Arbour Square police station standing outside our flat having just received yet another call from the neighbours. I imagine they thought they were coming to a routine domestic argument, but instead, when I let them in, we found my mum and brother unconscious and my father slumped in the corner in a drunken stupor. He was charged with two counts of grievous bodily harm, but by the time his case came up in the Old Bailey a month later it had been amended to manslaughter as Arthur died a week after the assault without ever regaining consciousness. My father was given fifteen years and died in Wakefield Prison eight years ago. I didn't go to the funeral.'

'And your mum?' asked Fliss, her heart aching at the raw wound evident in Tim's voice.

'She spent three months in the London Hospital,' he replied. 'But although she regained consciousness it was clear her facilities had been affected so they transferred her to Warley Mental Asylum in Brentwood.' Despite the pain around his eyes, Tim's lips lifted in a small smile. 'She is the special someone I go to see every week.'

Fliss stopped walking and turned to face him. For all the conflict and animosity between them, Fliss knew that it would have broken her heart to see her mother in such a pitiful situation so she could only imagine the pain Tim went through each time he visited his mum.

'I'm so sorry; if I'd know it was going to be so painful for you then I—'

'No, it's all right, Fliss,' he cut in. 'I don't mind talking about what happened, especially to you. In fact, I almost told you when we were in the British Restaurant, but I let the moment slip by and well ...' Their gaze locked for a moment then he smiled that smile of his and Fliss's insides turned to jelly.

Thankfully, just before she became a quivering wreck

at his feet, Tim glanced up briefly. 'I think this is where we part company, Miss Carmichael.'

Fliss looked around and realised they were outside the garment wholesalers on the corner of New Road.

'Oh, yes,' she said, although truthfully she could have been anywhere on the planet, for all she knew.

'Well, good luck with the article, and I hope to see you again.'

'Well, you obviously will because I am actually following you,' she replied. 'But not for any reason other than I don't want to miss out on a good story.'

A smile tugged at Tim's well-shaped mouth and his eyes twinkled for a moment. 'And I was wrong about you, Miss Carmichael,' he said, his gaze capturing hers. 'You may have been born into a well-to-do middle-class family, but you really do understand and care deeply about ordinary working people.'

He touched the brim of his hat and went on his way.

Standing on the pavement, Fliss watched him cross to the other side of the road and disappear out of sight. With the story he'd just told her racing around in her head, she stared after him. She had been wrong about him, too. He wasn't an instrument of the state, an establishment lackey or an oppressor of the proletariat, he wasn't even a self-assured senior police officer any more, he was a man. A man who'd suffered unimaginable loss and yet who had, through strength of character and courage, risen out of the tragedy to be the most honourable and honest man she'd ever known.

Also, although she didn't quite know how or when it had happened, the truth was that somewhere along the way over the past three months she now realised she'd actually fallen in love with Detective Inspector Timothy Charles Wallace.

Chapter twenty-four

'RIGHT,' **SAID HARRY,** scanning the assortment of Gunn family menfolk gathered around him, 'let me go through it one more time.'

'Do we have to, Harry?' said Ben, as a bomb landed somewhere near and the light above them danced on its flex.

It was just before eleven at night and the air raid had been going since just after eight thirty. Harry's crew had started drifting in about an hour later and now were all here, including his father, Joe, who was sitting to his right on a wheelback chair.

They were at the back of the Bull's Head's cellar, clustered around a couple of wobbly beer-stained tables with glasses in their enormous paws. As it was Thursday night with payday tomorrow, most of the regular were a bit light in their pocket, so when Tubby Bell had rung for last orders half an hour ago people had started drifting home, leaving only the Gunn family beneath the cellar's blackened beams. Actually, that wasn't strictly true because Harry needed another van to complete his plan so he'd pulled Tommy Lavender in on the job.

'Yes, we bloody well do,' growled Joe Gunn, glaring at Ben. 'Because we're not just having away a couple of boxes of fags or tins of peaches, but a warehouse full of meat worth a fortune on the black market, so listen up.'

Looking suitably shame-faced, his youngest son buried his nose in his pint.

From beneath his shaggy eyebrows Harry's father gave him a small nod as an explosion nearby reverberated through the cellar.

Putting their hands over their glasses to prevent dislodged plaster from above ending up in their pints, the men leaned forward.

'*The Countess of Fife* is due to arrive in the first week in June, either Tuesday the third or Wednesday the fourth,' continued Harry. 'And I've bunged Popeye Roger ten bob to give us the call at the gate to unload her. This will give me a chance to have a shufti inside to see the lie of the land, as it were. We'll meet back 'ere that night when I'll set out the final details. I had a word with Rita, who works in the office—'

'Oi, oi,' laughed Frankie. 'A word? Is that wot they're calling it now, Harry?'

There were a couple of sniggers and wolf whistles and Harry grinned.

'All right, settle down,' he laughed. 'Anyhow, the upshot is Pollock's booked in for the Friday to check it over and issue his certificates, so we have Thursday night to get it away. 'I've got punters lined up from West Ham to Southend, and all stops in-between. We've our two

Leylands and Tommy's Morris van, and as soon as each one is loaded, they can push off. But we ain't got freezer lorries like the Ministry of Food, so there can't be any balls-ups. We have to get it out of that warehouse and on the road in two hours – any longer in a metal truck and carcasses will start to pong, and as I don't want to ditch three hundred quid's worth of rancid meat in Barking Creak you'd better keep sharp or you and me will be having words.'

In the half-light of the cellar, the men nodded.

Joe took a mouthful of his drink. 'Wot about the guard?'

'Sorted,' said Harry.

'And Pollock?'

Harry grinned again. 'When I'm done wiv him 'e'll be falling over 'imself to do us favours.'

Tommy cleared his throat. 'You know, Harry, Wallace is still mooching around asking questions.'

'Anyone blabbing?'

Tommy shook his head. 'I've not heard nuffink.'

'Good,' said Harry. 'But get the whisper around I'll be dealing personally, like, wiv anyone who does.'

'But Wallace is like a dog wiv a bone when he gets a sniff of something,' continued Tommy. 'It was 'im who nabbed half of Black Reggie's gang red-handed in the Blackwall Steamer company warehouse.'

'And 'e took down the Moses twins and their protection racket in Spitalfields,' added Sammy. 'Their crew are banged up in Holloway on a ten-year stretch now.'

'Wot about this copper then, Harry?' asked Ben, blinking rapidly as he looked across at him. 'I can't get sent down. Not with Doreen about to drop our sprog any day and—'

'For Gawd's sake. No one's sodding well going away nowhere for nuffink.' Another bomb shook the room and Harry looked skywards. 'Don't you worry about DI Wallace none,' he said, as his mouth lifted into a malicious smile. 'Even coppers can turn up dead in a pile of rubble.'

With the wail of the air raid siren filling his ears and after another long Wednesday interviewing witnesses and sifting through robbery reports, Tim stepped out of Wapping nick into the inky darkness of the blackout and turned left towards Tower Bridge and Leman Street section house.

The tall warehouses on either side of Wapping High Street loomed over him as he walked along the now deserted warehouse.

Two ARP wardens from the Tilbury shelter were ushering the last few people down the steps by the time he reached them fifteen minutes later. They gave him a friendly wave as he turned into Goodman's Alley, which was a shortcut to his destination. However, after he'd walked just a few yards Tim became aware of footsteps behind him.

It could just be someone taking the same cut-through to Leman Street, but then again a copper who didn't keep his wits about him when he suspected he was being followed was likely to end up a dead copper.

Maintaining his leisurely pace, Tim walked on, but on reaching the dog-leg corner to the right in the dank passageway he dashed forward a few yards and slipped into a factory doorway, holding his breath as the sound of footsteps grew closer.

As the nearby clock of All Hallows by the Tower began to chime, a shadowy figure hurried past the doorway and Tim pounced.

Grabbing the man in a chokehold, Tim shoved him forward into the rough brickwork of the wall opposite, anchoring him there with the weight of his body.

"Old up, Inspector Wallace, sir,' shouted Tim's stalker. 'It's me – Tommy. Tommy Lavender.'

Somewhere to the south of them, probably in the vicinity of New Cross or Catford, the first wave of bombs found their targets and Tommy's sharp profile was illuminated in the red glow.

Letting him go, Tim turned him around. 'All right, chum. What's your game?'

'I've g-g-got some information?' Tommy replied, dusting down his light-weight jacket. 'About a hit on the Imperial and Britannia's warehouse.'

Tim's brow drew together. 'When?'

'Next week.'

Another rumble ran through the air as more munitions crashed to earth, this time to the west of them, somewhere around North Woolwich.

'Who's organised it?' asked Tim.

Tommy chewed his lower lip and didn't answer.

The clang of a brass bell cut through the air as a fire engine tore down the road towards them.

'It's Harry Gunn, isn't it?' said Tim, once the vehicle had passed.

Tommy nodded. 'And it's big. I 'eard 'im and his old man discussing it in the Bull a few days ago.'

'Is Pollock, the food inspector, involved?' Tim asked.

Again, Tommy nodded.

'E's been writing up dodgy Ministry certificates for knocked-off gear for Harry at a couple of quid a piece, but now Harry's got 'im on the hook for something that's worth more than a pound or two back-handers,' he said, confirming what Tim already suspected.

'What about you?' he asked, as grit showered down on them from a burning armament.

'No, not me,' Tommy replied. 'I ain't got nuffink to do wiv it. Honest, Inspector Wallace.'

Tim studied him for a moment then spoke again. 'You've been a lot of things, Lavender, but never a grass before, so how do I know Harry hasn't sent you to set me up?'

'Straight up, Inspector Wallace, I ain't.' Although you could barely see a hand in front of your face, Tommy looked around nervously. 'If Harry knew I was even talking to you I could—'

'End up as dead as a dodo on a bombsite with your head stoved in like that poor chap Wiggins from the Logan and McKay?' interrupted Tim.

At the mention of the deceased warehouse manager,

fear flashed across Tommy's weasel-like face in the red and yellow glow lighting the skies above them.

'I … I … wa-want you to kn-know, Inspector Wallace, I 'ad no 'and in that,' Tommy stammered.

'What about the old nightwatchman, Wilf Farmer?' asked Tim.

'I wasn't there; on my muver's life, I wasn't,' Tommy replied.

Tim's mouth pulled into a hard line as he studied Stepney's notorious chancer.

'Honest, Inspector Wallace, sir,' continued Tommy when Tim remained silent. 'I admit I might be a bit light-fingered from time to time, but I ain't no murderer.'

Tim scrutinised Tommy Lavender's face for a long moment then the scream of a bomb hurtling to the ground what could only have been a few streets away filled the air. Particles of burning cordite sparked into minute stars as they were blown skywards in the explosion.

'Thanks for the information,' said Tim, hot air stinging his face.

'If I 'ear anything else I'll be in touch.' Tommy turned in the direction of the Tilbury shelter but Tim grabbed his arm.

'And when you do, Lavender, I'd advise you not to sneak up behind me,' said Tim. 'Because next time I might not be so gentle.'

*

'You all right, Gov?'

Tim looked up at Alex sitting on the desk opposite his. 'Course. Why'd you ask?'

'Because you've been staring at those notes for half an hour,' his sergeant replied.

It was just after five in the afternoon and they were in the CID office on the second floor of Wapping police station.

Like the rest of the station, the room was in dire need of redecoration and had been for the past ten years, as the grey-tinged walls and colourless lino testified. Of the four desks in the room, Tim's was the only one that had all four legs the same length.

They weren't alone as a couple of uniformed officers were giving a report to Ted Spencer, a DCS who'd been drafted in from Bethnal Green nick to cover one of Tim's colleagues who had been injured by falling masonry the week before.

'I'm just mulling over a few things about the case,' Tim replied. 'Why don't you pop up to the canteen and get us both a cuppa?'

'Right you are,' Alex replied, scraping his chair back as he stood up.

Tim watched his lanky sergeant cross to the door for a moment then turned his attention back to the pile of witness statements that he and Alex had gathered over the past weeks.

Well, that's to say his eyes returned to the sheets of paper, but his mind raced back to the problem that had been clawing at his guts since his interview with Pollock and his encounter with Tommy Lavender: Fliss.

To give her credit, she had come to the same conclusion as he had that the recent large-scale thefts from the warehouses couldn't be written off as opportunist looting – it was clearly the work of an organised gang. What she hadn't yet figured out, thankfully, was that the leader of this criminal enterprise was Harry Gunn. But if or, more probably given her sharp wits, *when* she did …

The image of Fliss's body, broken and lifeless, lying on a pile of rubble loomed into Tim's mind and fear tore at his chest. He stared blindly at the words on the paper for a moment then jumped to his feet, almost upending his chair as he grabbed his jacket from the back.

Shoving his arms through the sleeves as he marched across the room, he only just avoided crashing into Alex, who was coming back into the office carrying two mugs of tea.

His sergeant gave him a perplexed look. 'Gov?'

'Sorry, Alex,' Tim said, without breaking his stride, 'there's something I have to do.'

Fifteen minutes later, Tim reached the Crown and Dolphin public house on the corner of Commercial Road just as St George's Church nearby struck six o'clock. Shoving the door open, he stepped inside. The Dolphin had the same mahogany bar, board floors, dartboard and decrepit tables and chairs as dozens of other public houses dotted around the area. However, it had one thing that made it unique: the skull of the notorious

Highway murderer John Williams. The skull had been unearthed by the gas company when laying pipes along the street outside at the turn of the century and now grinned down at the Dolphin's customers from pride of place above the bar. However, Tim wasn't interested in a murder from the last century; he was here to prevent the possibility of another, which threatened to rob him of his sanity.

Tim spotted the man he was after sitting on a bar stool and clutching his end-of-the-working-day pint.

Weaving his way between ARP personnel having a swift half before reporting for their night duties and grubby labourers washing the dust from their throats, Tim made his way over.

'Evening,' he said, hopping onto a stool alongside the other man.

The editor of the *East London Chronicle* looked around.

'Inspector Wallace, fancy seeing you here,' Sid Longman said. 'Although I doubt it's by chance.'

Tim smiled.

Reggie, the Dolphin's barman, waddled over.

'What you having?' Tim asked the man next to him.

Longman swallowed the rest of his drink and handed the empty glass across the bar. 'Same again.'

'And I'll have a lemonade,' said Tim, handing over half a crown.

'Of course, I forgot you're the only copper on H Division who doesn't drink,' said the *Chronicle*'s editor. 'Understandable, I suppose, after—' Catching sight of

Tim's implacable expression, Longman cleared his throat. 'Anyways, what can I do you for, Inspector?'

Reggie returned with their drinks.

'Well,' said Tim, pocketing his change and picking up his glass, 'it's about a story one of your reporters is following.'

Chapter twenty-five

'AFTERNOON,' CHIRPED Fliss, as she strolled into the *Chronicle*'s office.

'Ah ha,' said Norman, looking up from his typewriter. 'The wanderer returns.'

'I've been out gathering information for a story,' said Fliss, crossing to her desk. 'It's what journalists do.'

'And how goes the revolution, my dear girl?' asked George through the tortoise-shell cigarette holder clenched between his teeth. 'I hear theatre and arts critics are to be the first against the wall.'

Fliss gave him a sweet smile. 'Don't worry, George, I'll make sure the workers' council know you're totally harmless because no one reads any of your reviews.'

The *Chronicle*'s arts and theatre critic clasped his hands dramatically to his chest. 'M'lady has no mercy.'

'Or time,' said Fliss, dumping her notebook on her desk. 'So if you don't mind.'

George glanced at the clock, which had just ticked over to five o'clock. 'Time for us adjourn to the other office, Master Ogdon, for a couple of stiff ones, me thinks, and leave the *Chronicle*'s very own Madame Liberty to wave her red flag.'

Rising from his chair and grasping his walking cane, silver-headed George Templeton made for the door. Norman stood up and followed him out.

As the door clicked shut, Betty came out from the tea-room. 'Thank goodness. Honestly, Fliss, they've both been going on like a couple of old women over a backyard wall all afternoon. The kettle's just boiled if you want a cuppa.'

'Perhaps in a while,' said Fliss. 'I want to type up my notes first.'

Tucking her skirt beneath her, Fliss sat down at her desk and removed the dust cover from her typewriter.

Rereading her notes, she sucked her teeth. Having interviewed Wilf Farmer's daughter Lily and Mr Wiggins' widow, plus what she'd gleaned from talking to shopkeepers, dockers at the dock gates and housewives on street corners, she almost had enough. Almost! If only she could find someone brave enough to give her the name of whoever was running the show, then she would be home and dry. Of course, she'd have to inform the police before going to print, but the minute the gang was behind bars she could run the story as an exclusive, perhaps even attracting the attention of one of the dailies.

She was certain DI Wallace had a pretty good idea who was behind the slick operation, but also knew she'd have more luck getting blood out of a stone than prising the name out of him. Infuriating man!

The memory of the expression in his eyes as they stood together at the corner of the street a few weeks before materialised in Fliss's mind. A smile lifted the corner of her lips. Perhaps she should take a leaf out of Mata Hari's books.

Images of her and DCI Wallace entwined together replaced the previous ones and a fizz of excitement rolled through her.

She tried to push her thoughts aside but instead she found herself wondering if he had a hairy chest and then imagining running her fingers over it. She'd felt his arms around her briefly before, but to feel them pressed onto the bare skin of her back and of – my goodness – his strong hands …

Fliss wriggled on her seat and sighed. The stark ring of the telephone brought her back to the here and now.

Betty picked up the receiver and Fliss got back to work, retrieving two sheets of foolscap from her desk drawer and feeding them into the roller of her typewriter with a navy carbon paper sandwiched in-between. However, she'd only just pushed the return leaver on her second line of typing when the door opened and Mr Longman walked in.

'Ah, Fliss, good, you're still here,' he said, looking nervously across at her. 'Can I have a quick word?'

'Of course,' she replied.

She stood up and made her way across to his office.

'Close the door, please,' he said.

'Goodness, this sound serious,' laughed Fliss. 'Am I getting the sack?'

'No, no,' said Mr Longman. 'In fact, I'd get rid of Gert and Daisy out there before you, Fliss; you're our best reporter.'

'Thank you,' said Fliss. 'Are you giving me a pay rise, then?'

Longman forced a smile. 'I want to talk to you about this story you're chasing about the docks.'

'What, you mean the one about the gang breaking into warehouses and stealing tons of food?' said Fliss.

'That's the one,' said Longman.

'Well, it's obviously a well-planned operation,' said Fliss. 'I mean, with the blackout and the police stretched to their limits because of the air raids, any thief worth their salt could steal a couple of boxes of tinned fruit, but it's a different matter to take tons of foods.'

'You're probably right, Fliss, but—'

'To do that you have to be able to pass off what you've stolen as legitimate supplies,' Fliss cut in. 'So the thieves would need someone inside the Ministry of Food office. My money's on Mr Pollock at their office in Cambridge Heath Road. According to one of the typists in the Ministry of Food offices he has trouble working a desk pencil sharpener, so I doubt he's the brains behind the operation.' Her brows drew together. 'If I could only find someone brave enough to tell me, but whoever it is leading this gang is clearly dangerous because everyone is too scared to talk.'

'Which is why I want you to drop the story, Miss Carmichael,' Longman said.

Fliss looked at him incredulously. 'Drop the—'

'It's too risky,' cut in her boss.

'But—'

'I'm sorry, no story is worth getting yourself killed for,' interrupted her boss. 'And I certainly don't want to have to face your grieving parents if you're found dead in a pile of rubble like Wiggins.'

'But I'm so near to—' Fliss's brows pulled together into an angry line. 'Who told you about Wiggins?'

Her boss looked taken aback. 'What?'

'How do you know about the dead manager from Logan and McKay?' Fliss repeated.

Panic flashed across her boss's face. 'Er ... well, y–you must have told me.'

'I know for a fact I never did, so how do you know?' Fliss asked again.

He held her hard stare for a moment then let out a long breath. 'Look, Fliss, the police are—'

'The police!' Fliss stared at him for a moment then her eyes narrowed. 'Has this got anything to do with DI Wallace, by any chance?'

Her boss's startled expression gave her the answer.

Fury burst in Fliss's chest.

Balling her fists at her side, she stared blindly at the man on the other side of the desk for a long moment then, without a word, stood and strode out of the office.

Crossing to her desk, she picked up her notepad and shoved it in her handbag as Mr Longman came out of his office.

'Where are you going?' he asked as Fliss hooked the strap over her shoulder.

Fliss gave him a tight smile. 'Wapping police station.'

Chapter twenty-six

'Is **THAT THE LAST** of them, Father?' asked Tim, as ten-year-old Micky Shannon headed through the boxing club's open doors.

'That it is,' Father Aiden replied.

'I'm pretty sure Rory Wheeler will be fighting fit when he gets into the ring with the Repton lad at the end of the month,' said Tim, looping up one of the club's skipping ropes.

It was just after seven, and feeling a great deal happier about Fliss after his chat with Sid Longman the day before, he'd left Alex to finish off and file the last few reports and walked out through Wapping nick just after four thirty. After a quick bite to eat in Kate's Café on the Highway, he'd made his way to St Mungo's Boys' Boxing Club to help set up for the evening.

'Mainly thanks to you, Tim,' the priest replied, as he secured the punchbag to the wall with a stout leather strap. 'He was a right tearaway when he got here, but all your work has paid dividends – and not just in the ring.'

'Well, better to get the lad on the straight and narrow now than have me arresting him five years down the line,' Tim replied.

Bending down, the old priest went to pick up one of the leather medicine balls and winced.

'Shoulder playing up?' asked Tim, putting the tied rope into the metal storage box at his feet.

Father Aiden nodded. 'I overdid it shifting some chairs in the church hall last week.' Putting his hoary left hand on his right shoulder, the old man rotated the joint slowly. 'That'll teach me to forget I'm sixty-three not thirty-six.'

Tim laughed. 'I can finish up here, so why don't you push off and have a hot bath to ease it?'

Father Aiden pulled a face. ''Tis but a twinge.'

He reached for the heavy leather ball again and gasped.

'Go on, Father. Before you make it worse.' Tim held out his hand.

Father Aiden's ferocious eyebrows pulled together. He chewed his lips for a moment, then, shoving his hand into his loose-fitting training trousers, he pulled out a bunch of keys.

Tim took them. 'I'll drop them back at the vestry later.'

'Thank you,' conceded the older man. 'Although I'm after wondering how much of a soak I'll be getting in the regulation six inches of water.'

Tim grinned. 'Well, perhaps if you add a couple of shots of Jameson it might do the trick.'

The old priest's craggy face lifted into a smile, and he picked up his kitbag and shuffled towards the door.

'I'll see you next week,' said Tim.

Father Aiden raised his hand in acknowledgement, then disappeared through the door.

Alone in the gym, Tim slid the metal box with the skipping ropes under the skirts of the central ring then turned his attention to the floor mats. Stacking them neatly by the wall and picking up a pair of stray gloves by the dumbbell rack, he wedged them alongside the rest in the store cupboard and locked it.

Satisfied that everything was as it should be, Tim picked up his kitbag and headed for the showers at the back of the gym. Strolling into the white-tiled room, he dropped his bag on one of the changing benches then went across to the row of gun-metal-grey lockers fixed to the right-hand wall. Opening one, Tim retrieved his clean underwear, casual slacks and shirt and hung them on a hook above the bench. Then he took off his soft boots, sweaty singlet and boxer's shorts, opened his knapsack and grabbed his towel and soap holder. Flipping the towel over his shoulder, he padded naked across the cold floor to the row of showers. Placing his wash kit on the top of the four-foot-high wall obscuring the bathers from anyone walking into the changing room, Tim turned the red dial and water spurted out of the saucer-like fitting over his head.

It was cold, of course, as thanks to the country-wide coal shortages luxuries such as lighting the boiler were banned. However, after an hour of dodging about in a ring, Tim wasn't worried.

He let the water run over him for a moment, then picked up his soap holder and took out the slither of soap. Stepping out of the stream, he rubbed the soap vigorously over his face and torso, lathering it under his arms and through the hair on his chest, before working his way down.

Satisfied he'd completed his task, he was about to return the tiny tablet of soap to the plastic holder when an image of Fliss gazing down at her inky fingers floated into his mind and a smile lifted the corner of his lips.

Closing his eyes, Tim tilted his head back and let the water wash over him. His mind ran through all the infuriating things about Felicity Carmichael and how he wouldn't rest until she was his wife.

Of course, it wouldn't be easy, but then faint heart never won fair lady, as they say, or in Fliss's case not so much fair as stunningly beautiful, exceptionally intelligent and brave to the point of recklessness.

With very pleasant images of Fliss playing over in his mind, Tim let the icy stream wash over him.

'DI Wallace!'

Tim's eyes snapped open. 'Miss Carmichael?'

'Yes, and I want a word with you,' she shouted back.

Stepping out from under the water, Tim grabbed his towel.

'I'm in the shower,' he called back, wrapping it around his waist.

'Well, come out!' she yelled back.

'I've got no clothes on,' Tim replied.

'Then you'd better find some, Inspector,' Fliss bellowed. 'Because I've already been to the police station and the section house looking for you, so if you're not out here by the time I count to ten I'm coming in.'

Tim stood motionless for a moment.

'One!' she shouted.

Running the towel over himself, Tim dashed across the tiles to where his clothes were hanging.

'Two!'

Hopping on one leg, Tim managed to get his pants on by the time she'd got to five and his trousers by nine. He did a couple of fly-buttons to secure them on his hips before grabbing his shirt, and after a bit of trouble poking his still-wet arms through the sleeves and deciding not to attempt to get his sock and shoes on, Tim marched out of the changing room as Fliss shouted ten.

She was wearing a pale-green summer's dress fastened with small heart-shaped button at the front. In contrast to her feminine attire, Fliss was standing just in front of the boxing ring with her fists dug into her hips, her feet planted squarely on the lino floor and a look of utter fury on her face. Had she donned a pair of boxing gloves, she wouldn't have looked more like she was ready for a fight.

However, as he emerged, hastily fastening his trousers, an emotion he couldn't quite interpret flashed briefly across her face before the scowl returned.

Tim stopped a few feet from her and smiled.

'So, Miss Carmichael, what is so urgent that you have to threaten to march in on me while I'm taking a shower?' he asked.

'You told Mr Longman to kill my story about the gang behind the recent series of warehouse robberies, didn't you?' she shouted.

Tim fastened a couple of shirt buttons. 'Yes, I did.'

Fliss's expression went from angry to enraged. 'You have no right to trample on press freedom.'

'Perhaps not,' he said.

'Then why the hell did you do it?' she shouted, throwing up her arms in exasperation.

Abandoning his shirt buttons, Tim's mouth pulled into a hard line. 'I would have thought that was obvious, even to you. Because it's bloody dangerous.'

Fliss gave a mirthless laugh. 'You make it sound like I'm skulking around the docks in the dead of night.'

'I wouldn't put that past you,' he replied.

She rolled her eyes. 'All I've done is ask a few questions.'

'A few questions that could end up with you beaten to a pulp like Wilf Farmer or lying dead on a pile of rubble with your head bashed in,' Tim replied, his heart tearing a little at the thought. 'I think you're forgetting, Miss Carmichael, that this "story" you're chasing isn't to discover who made the scones for the vicarage tea party,' he continued as two splashes of red coloured Fliss's cheeks, 'but who is stealing several tons of goods—'

'I bloody well know that,' she yelled, her hands balled into tight fists. 'And I'm not your simpering girlfriend who believes men should tell us what we should do and think.'

'No, you're not. You're the most stubborn, bone-headed, opinionated woman I've ever met,' Tim bawled back.

She raised an eyebrow. 'Am I now?'

'Yes, you are,' he snapped.

'Well, for your information, Timothy Wallace, you are the most stubborn, bone-headed, opinionated man I've ever meet.'

'Well, that makes us quits then, doesn't it, Felicity Carmichael?'

'Yes, it jolly well does,' she snapped.

'And Angela isn't my girlfriend.'

Fliss eyes flew open. 'Isn't she?'

'No, not any more,' he replied. 'We parted company a few weeks back.'

Her gaze flickered briefly over his open shirt and that unfathomable emotion flitted across her face. 'Oh.'

The urge to cross the space between them and take her in his arms swept over him again, but Tim held it in check.

They stared at each other for a long moment, then Tim sighed.

'Look, Fliss,' he said, raking his fingers through his hair, 'I'm sorry but—'

She sprang forward and threw herself into his arms.

It took Tim's brain a second or two to realise what was happening, but as her lips pressed hungrily onto his, his arms wound around her and every part of him came alive.

As the myriad pleasurable sensations subsided and awareness returned to her brain, Fliss opened her eyes and found herself lying on a pile of gym mats and staring at the metal girders of St Mungo's main hall.

Somewhat obstructing the view of this everyday Victorian engineering was Tim's left ear and bare left shoulder, as he was slumped on her with his head resting on her equally bare shoulder, his lips lightly pressed against her neck.

As soon as DI Wallace walked out of the changing room, Fliss realised that she should have counted to twenty because he'd only just managed to get his trousers on and his arms in his shirt. However, his half-dressed appearance answered a number of questions Fliss had found herself pondering over the past few weeks. Firstly, as she suspected, his stomach was clearly defined and washboard flat, while the rest of his upper body was muscular. He also did have a hairy chest, which spread evenly across his pectoral muscles before tracking down in an orderly fashion to his navel.

As furious as she had been, watching him coming towards her with his shirt billowing behind him, desire had pulsed though her so forcibly Fliss had actually felt a little faint.

And that smile, too.

Reminding herself that she'd been marching back and forth across Stepney searching for him for almost three hours, Fliss had somehow resisted the urge to dash towards him and run her hands slowly over his torso, but as he started to apologise, a very different emotion replaced her anger.

She actually had her arms around his neck before her brain had caught up with her actions, but when he took her in his arms and kissed her back, desire burst through her, and she was lost.

She couldn't describe what followed in detail if her life depended on it, but what she could recall was his strong hands on her thighs and her fingers threading through his chest hair and her dress fluttering to the floor as her fingers unbuttoned his trousers.

He still had his shirt on, but his trousers and pants were tangled with her brassière and knickers on the floor by their feet.

The truth was she was lying naked on a pile of floor mats in a boxing gym, but with Tim's weight now pressing on her, his tousled hair against her cheek and his breath lightly on her throat, Fliss didn't care, because she loved him.

And she did. Not just because she'd been to some undiscovered paradise twice in the past half an hour, but because … well, just because. Even she, with the whole English language at her disposal, couldn't find the words to explain why she loved him, but she just did.

Twisting her head slightly, she studied the way his evening bristles were visible above his skin. Gazing at the point where they gave way to smooth skin for a moment, Fliss was just about to press her lips to it when he raised his head and leaned it onto his elbow, looked languorously down at her and smiled.

The frenzied waves that had only just subsided rolled through Fliss again.

She smiled back and they stared at either other for what could have been a second, a minute or even an hour, then he lowered his head.

Fliss's eyelids fluttered down as she opened her mouth to receive his lips …

Just as one of the two outside doors at the other end of the corridor creaked open. Fliss and Tim's eyes blinked open and their heads snapped towards the door on the other side of the central boxing ring.

'Inspector Wallace!' shouted a man's voice from the corridor.

'Who's that?' whispered Fliss.

'My sergeant, Alex,' Tim replied in the same hushed tone.

'What does he want?'

Tim frowned. 'How do I know?'

'Are you still here, Inspector?'

Tim sprang up and grabbed his clothes.

Scrambling across the brown lino gym floor to gather up her underwear and dress, Fliss gave him a hard look.

'I'm just about to have a shower, Alex!' Tim shouted back. 'Why don't you meet me back at the station?'

'I would, but …'

Panic flashed across Tim's face as he looked at Fliss.

Fliss, who was all but naked and with her heart hammering in her chest, froze for a moment but as door from the corridor into the hall squeaked open, she dropped to her hands and knees and practically threw herself under the skirt of the boxing ring.

Swivelling around on her knees, she looked back at Tim, who, satisfied she couldn't be seen and clutching his clothes, bolted for the changing room just as footsteps sounded in the room.

In the darkness, Fliss hastily dressed as best she could as Tim's sergeant walked around the ring towards the changing room. When he stopped, Fliss peeked under the leather curtain at his black shoes facing towards the changing room.

As silently as she could, and trying not to imagine the spiders or the mice droppings around her, Fliss crawled towards the other side of the ring. Lifting up the flap, she rolled out again. Peeking over the edge of the canvas-ring floor she saw Tim emerge from the changing room in his trousers, shirt open and carrying his shoes.

With the sergeant's attention on Tim, and clutching her shoes and satchel to her chest, Fliss tiptoed across the gym.

'Sorry to disturb you, Guv,' said Alex as Fliss reached the door.

She turned and Tim's eyes flickered onto her briefly before returning to his subordinate.

'That's all right,' he said, smiling as he sat on a bench to put on his socks.

'I would have waited,' Alex continued, as Fliss inched one of the doors open and slipped through the space, 'but I knew you'd want to hear straight away. We've had word.' Fliss strained to hear through the gap between the doors. 'The gang are planning to strike the Imperial and Britannia next Thursday.'

'Perfect,' she heard Tim reply. 'And when they do, we'll be waiting for them.'

Smiling, Fliss placed her shoes on the floor, stepped into them and then silently left the building.

Chapter twenty-seven

'HAVE YOU SEEN your sister, Felicity?' asked her mother, looming over her as she sat in a garden deckchair.

Fliss raised her eyes from her book. 'She's having a lie-down.'

'A lie-down!' said Marjorie. 'It's eleven o'clock in the morning.'

'And Prue is six months' pregnant,' Fliss replied, re-crossing her legs and straightening the folds of her skirt.

It was Saturday and she was sitting at the far end of the garden under one of the three apple trees.

In contrast to her mother, who was wearing a russet-coloured dress and jacket plus the obligatory string of pearls, Fliss had dragged her six-panel aubergine-coloured skirt out of the wardrobe and teamed it up with a short-sleeved cream blouse with mother-of-pearl buttons.

She had positioned her deckchair in the only area of lawn that had escaped the shovels and pitchforks of St Winifred's Dig for Victory club. However, although the hollyhocks, delphiniums and phlox in the herbaceous borders had disappeared, there was a pleasing quality to the rows of cabbages and carrot fronds swaying in the breeze and the small orange flowers on the tall runner beans.

'Apparently the baby kept moving so she had an uncomfortable night,' Fliss explained.

'Well, I can sympathise with that, at least,' her mother replied. 'Being in the family way is like having a roller coaster inside you. You were the worst, of course. Twisting and turning; I hardly had a wink of sleep for months, after which I had fifteen hours of pure agony until you deigned to make an appearance.' Her mother's deep-set grey eyes fixed on Fliss through her spectacles. 'I should have known then the heavy cross I would have to bear.'

Fliss gave her mother a sweet smile by way of reply.

A peal of childish laughter drifted over the vegetable beds and they both looked around.

Ingrid and her two children had just come out of the back door with Father Danny. He was laughing and holding a football, while the children danced around.

Marjorie studied the small party as it made its way out of the rectory's side gate.

'Well, I've got things to do, even if our curate hasn't,' she said, pulling on her dove-grey summer gloves. 'Oh, and remind your sister that she's manning the jam and cake stall at this afternoon's church fair.'

With that, Marjorie marched past the lines of vegetables and back into the house.

Alone in the garden, Fliss turned her attention back to her book, but after reading the same paragraph three times she gave up and closed it. The sunlight dappling through the leaves as they swayed in the warm summer air, however, did nothing to calm the turmoil that was raging through Fliss.

Because, as well as being the day of St Winifred's annual summer fair, it was also the day after she'd stormed into St Mungo's Boys' Boxing Club.

Letting her head rest back on the horizontal wooden bar, she gazed up at the half-formed apples on the branches for a moment then closed her eyes.

Immediately her mind conjured up images of Tim's eyes, lips and body, along with the excitement of his hands on her skin, his mouth hungrily pressed onto hers and the exquisite moment of bliss before they both dissolved, breathless and sated, into a tangled mass of clothes and limbs. She'd gone to give him a piece of her mind and well … Let's just say now Fliss knew what she'd been missing with Giles, she felt quite sorry for Gwen.

'Miss Carmichael.'

Instantly recognising the deep voice, her eyes sprang open.

Tim was standing just where her mother had stood not five minutes before. He was dressed in the suit he'd been wearing when she'd fallen into his arms on the day of her interview, which now seemed like a lifetime ago. In addition, he was freshly shaved and his dark-brown hair had been recently trimmed.

With the man she'd been thinking about constantly just a few feet away, her emotions and senses went into complete turmoil. Her eyes wanted just to take in the very sight of him while her lips needed to kiss every inch of him.

'I rather think we've moved past the formalities, don't you?'

Amusement flickered in his eyes. 'You're right.' Tim shifted his weight from one leg to the other and back again. 'Look, Fliss, I know we haven't known each other very long—'

'Four months,' said Fliss.

'Yes, four months,' agreed Tim. The corner of his lips curled slightly. 'And, well, we didn't get off to the best of starts ...'

'You mean with me being a raging revolutionary and you being a lackey of the state?' said Fliss.

'I was thinking more of my trying to keep the King's peace and arrest criminals and you starting a riot and ending up in front of the magistrate,' Tim replied.

Fliss suppressed a smile.

'And of course, we're from completely different backgrounds, but even so ...' Taking off his hat, Tim pulled up the sharp crease on his right trouser leg and got down on one knee.

Fliss's heart did a fandango as she gazed lovingly down at him.

He took her hand.

'Felicity. Fliss ...' He cleared his throat. 'Will you marry me?'

With the sunlight through the branches dappling his handsome face, Fliss studied him.

'I think you're supposed to say something,' he said, looking up at her.

The word 'yes' bubbled up, but as it reached her lips Fliss's brows drew together.

'Why?'

He looked puzzled. 'Why what?'

'Why, if we're so different, are you asking me to marry you?'

'Well, Fliss,' he said, 'after yesterday evening in the boxing club, I feel it's the honourable thing to do.'

'Honourable!'

Tim squared his shoulders. 'Yes, it is. I took advantage … seduced you, and … and therefore, I should—'

'Make an honest woman of me?' Fliss cut in, glaring at him.

'No … I mean yes, but …' He raked his fingers through his hair. 'Look, Fliss—'

Uncrossing her legs Fliss jumped up, her book thumping Tim in the chest.

'Unlike your simpering girlfriend, who—'

'I told you, Angela and I parted company a few weeks ago,' Tim cut in. 'Because—'

'Even so, I'm not some delicate Victorian virgin,' she said, looming over him as he knelt on the grass.

'Er, I know, but if you let me—'

'Tell me, Tim,' continued Fliss, her heart thumping in her chest, 'as you're clearly no virgin either, do you propose to every woman you have a fling with?'

Tim's mouth pulled into a tight line and he rose to his

feet.

'I've never proposed to anyone before. And a fling?' Standing just a foot or so away and several inches taller, his eyes hardened as they gazed down at her. 'Is that what you think we had yesterday, Fliss?' he said, in a low voice that vibrated through her bones. 'A fling?'

'What would you call it, then?' Fliss snapped. 'A tumble? Hanky-panky? A bit of the other? Whatever you call it, Tim, it's hardly a good reason to walk down the aisle, because in my book the one and only reason two people should get married is because they love each other so much they want to spend the rest of their lives together.'

'I agree, Fliss. Which is why—'

'So no, Tim,' Fliss cut in, red mist framing her peripheral vision. 'I won't marry you to salve your conscious or some outdated idea of chivalry, not now and not ever. And don't ever ask me again.'

With her head pounding and her heart in tatters, Fliss span on her heels and marched toward the house, tears of fury gathering in her eyes. After half a dozen steps, she turned.

'And just to put the record straight, DI Wallace,' she shouted across the top of the sprouting potatoes plants, 'I seduced you.'

With her eyes closed, Prue ran her hands over her swollen stomach as she listened to the twittering of the birds nesting in the laburnum outside her bedroom window. Well, it was Fliss's bedroom really these days, but as they had done for most of their lives, she and her older sister were sharing, except at night when they decamped to St Winifred's air raid shelter.

Moving back into the rectory hadn't been quite as bad as she thought it might be, largely due to having Fliss here. Firstly, because just as when Mavis Dunmore had bullied Prue at school and her older sister had socked her in the nose, when their mother started on about Jack, Fliss steamed in on Prue's behalf. However, perhaps selfishly, having Fliss here also meant that their mother had someone else she could be outraged at.

Prue was just wondering what Mrs Lavender might magic up for lunch when the bedroom door burst open.

Prue opened her eyes.

'Fliss,' she said, as her red-faced sister stomped into the room. 'What on earth has happened?'

'DI Blooming Wallace, that's what?' Fliss replied, going to the dressing table and pulling a folded handkerchief out of the top drawer.

'What about him?' asked Prue.

'Oh, you mean other than him being the most infuriating, unreasonable, pig-headed man in the country? Probably the world,' Fliss replied, marching across to the wardrobe.

'What, are you in trouble again?'

Dabbing her eyes, Fliss shook her head.

'Well, what?'

'He proposed,' sniffed Fliss.

Prue sat up and stared at her sister. 'He did what!'

'Asked me to marry him,' Fliss replied. 'Down on one knee, no less, under the apple trees.'

'I didn't know you had been seeing each other,' said Prue.

'We haven't,' said Fliss, trooping back to the dressing table. 'I mean, we do see each other now and again because of my work,' she added, waving her handkerchief airily in front of her.

'And when you get yourself arrested,' said Prue.

Fliss raised an eyebrow. 'I've been arrested once, Prue, and in a very good cause, I might say.'

Prue was puzzled. 'I don't understand. If you've only met each other in passing, why on earth would he ask you to be his wife?'

Breaking eye contact with her, Fliss stamped back to the wardrobe.

'Because …' She straightened her completely flat collar in the long mirror on the central door then turned to face her sister. Chewing her lip for a moment, she finally spoke again.

'Because last night we … well, we … All right we ended up … you know, having a bit of the other, as they say around here.'

Prue stared at her sister in disbelief.

'And it wouldn't have happened if he hadn't …' Prue listened as Fliss went through the events of the previous day, which culminated with her and Inspector Wallace rolling about on the floor of St Mungo's Boys' Boxing Club floor. 'I didn't mean it to happen,' her sister concluded.

'He seduced you!'

'No, he didn't. In fact,' Fliss gave her a sheepish look, 'you could say that it was the other way around. When he came out of the changing room with his shirt open … well,' she shrugged, 'I just rushed at him. Honestly, it's never happened before, not even when I was with Giles. I don't know what came over me.'

'I do,' said Prue, unable to suppress a smile. 'And it's number one on the list of deadly sins.'

'And now he thinks he's honour-bound to make an honest woman of me,' said Fliss.

'Did he say that?'

'Well, no, actually I did,' said Fliss. 'But that's not the point. I don't want to marry Tim because he feels obliged to but because he loves—'

'So you do want to marry him, Fliss?' cut in Prue.

Fliss forced an unconvincingly hearty laugh. 'Marry him! Are you mad? I wouldn't marry Tim if—' She stopped and her face crumpled.

'Oh, Prue,' she said, throwing herself on the bed opposite. 'I almost said yes because – and don't ask me how – I'm in love with Tim. Last night was … well, let's just say a very different experience, and I know that's because I love him. I had hoped, given his … er, enthusiasm last night, that he loved me, too, but when he came out with all the rubbish about the honourable thing, I …' Putting her elbows on her knees, Fliss buried her face in her hands.

Prue crossed to her sister's bed and sat beside her, putting her arm around her shoulder.

'Come on, Fliss,' she said, squeezing her gently. 'You don't know that Tim doesn't feel the same way as you.'

Fliss looked up. 'Then why didn't he say it?'

Prue opened her mouth to speak but Fliss put up her hand.

'I'm sorry, Prue, I've got a splitting headache; would you mind getting me a cold flannel? I think I'm going to have to lie down for a bit.'

Prue kissed her sister on the forehead then went over to the square Edwardian hand basin fixed to the wall in the corner. Taking Fliss's flannel from the supporting bracket beneath, she ran the cold tap for a moment then, wringing it out, went back to her sister's bed. Fliss had already kicked off her shoes and was lying on the candlewick counterpane with her head on the pillow.

'Thank you,' she said, taking the flannel and arranging it on her forehead, then closing her eyes. 'And if I never see Tim bloody Wallace again this side of Eternity it will be too soon.'

'And then, Mum, she had the blooming nerve to tell me that she wouldn't marry me just to salve my conscience or some outdated idea of chivalry,' said Tim.

Nancy Wallace smiled lovingly at him from her wheelchair, but, as always since that fateful night, said not a word.

They were sitting under a flowering cherry tree in the grounds of Warley Hospital on a balmy Monday afternoon two days after his fruitless visit to St Winifred's Rectory.

He hadn't planned to visit today; in fact, by rights he should still be at work, but having been awake since three that morning reliving moment by moment, word by word, the scene with Fliss in the garden, he was in no fit state for anything, let alone unravelling evidence. He'd watched the light from the east crest the factories and offices opposite the section house with his mind veering wildly between desolation and anger. And blaming himself for coming over as a complete arse.

By the time he'd dragged himself into work, he looked like he'd climbed off the coroner's slab at the hospital. Not that anyone noticed; after a solid week of night-time raids, everyone in East London looked as if they'd been exhumed from their graves.

After reading the same report twice and biting off the head of a newly recruited war reservist for using a 214b form to report looting instead of a 214a, he'd told Alex he had something to do for a few hours but would be back late afternoon.

He'd nearly missed the stop because he'd fallen asleep in the train, but thankfully managed to jump out before the carriage he was travelling in reached the end of the platform.

The fifteen-minute walk from the station in the sunshine had restored him a little, so by the time he arrived just before one, half an hour ago, he was at least in command of his temper if not his aching heart.

After a bit of searching, he had found a wicker wheelchair that must have come out of the Ark. Tim had lifted his mother gently into it and then pushed her across the lawn to a secluded part of the garden.

Since then, he'd told his mother everything about Fliss, from finding her blind drunk on a gravestone right through to her shouting at him on Saturday afternoon, in no uncertain terms, that she never wanted to see him again.

'I tell you this for nothing, Mum,' Tim continued. 'Fliss Carmichael is the most infuriating, unreasonable, pig-headed woman in the whole of country. Probably the world.'

Pressing his lips together, he stared across the Essex countryside at the barrage balloons, shining pink in the afternoon sunlight, as they bobbed over the factories along the Thames Estuary.

'She has a ruddy opinion on everything and won't budge an inch if she thinks she has the right of it. Plus, by her own admission, she's a terrible cook.' He gave a hard laugh. 'Honestly, what man in his right mind would want to marry her?'

A squadron of spitfires from Dunmow Airfield streaked across the sky in a V formation and Tim watched as they headed towards the Garden of England, to defend Kent.

'But I do, Mum,' he said, emotion tightening his throat. 'The truth is I love her. More than I ever thought possible.'

Tim looked down at his mother, huddled in the old wheelchair, the paisley shawl he'd bought her for her last birthday draped loosely around her shoulders. Her white candyfloss-like hair made her look ten years older than her forty-seven years. After fifteen years of immobility, her legs and arms were only a few stages above skin and bone, and her once-rosy cheeks were now caved-in hollows.

Tim returned to his contemplation of the bright-blue sky for a moment then, as desolation swept over him, he bent forward, rested his elbows on his knees and buried his face in his hands.

Logic told him after his ham-fisted attempt at a proposal he'd lost Fliss for ever and he should get over her. Unfortunately, his heart refused to accept this. Instead, it conjured up various scenarios in which he might have the opportunity to make good his blundering ways.

Of course, he knew that instead of stupidly couching his offer of marriage to Fliss as his honourable obligation because of what happened had in the boxing gym, he should have just come straight out and told her the plain truth: that he loved her and wanted to spend the rest of his life with her.

Behind the blackness of his closed eyes and with the bleakness of a life without Fliss stretching before him, desolation swept over him.

Chapter twenty-eight

THE ANCIENT CHINAMAN with a droopy boot-lace moustache who was standing behind the counter measuring rice into half-pound bags acknowledged Harry as he walked into the Far Eastern grocers in Three Colt's Lane in the heart of East London's China Town.

Like all the shops in Limehouse, the atmosphere was heavy with the smell of tobacco mixed with some imported herbs which the Chinese seemed to start smoking in their cradles.

Passing the tea chests of what looked like dried garden weeds and dirty pebbles, Harry continued through the narrow, dimly lit shop. He pushed aside the bead curtains and trotted down the dozen steps to the basement.

If the atmosphere in the shop above was foggy, it was positively a pea-souper in Chin Loo's illegal gambling joint, and with more than a whiff of opium mixed in.

Like many basements in the area, it had a bare beaten-earth floor on which half a dozen baize card tables were set out, each with men huddled around them. In addition, at the far end was a long table with a roulette wheel at one end and a dozen or more men sitting around it.

Dotted among the male customers were a handful of slender Chinese girls in silky, high-necked dresses.

Taking a long drag on his roll-up, Harry peered through the miasma and ran his gaze over the customers until he spotted the gambler he was seeking.

The girl at the player's shoulder looked around as Harry approached. Her dark, almond-shaped eyes gave him the once-over before resuming her scrutiny of the game.

Picking up his cards, the man in front of Harry spread them in his chubby fingers.

'You'll never win with a pair of fours, Cyril,' Harry said.

Cyril Pollock, the Ministry of Food's chief inspector for East London, looked up sharply. 'Harry.'

'And is this Mrs Pollock?' he asked, indicating the girl.

Giving them both a cool look, she slinked away.

'Chuck 'em in and I'll buy you a drink.' Harry nodded towards the two barrels with a plank resting across them that served as the establishment's bar.

Throwing his hand towards the dealer, Cyril rose clumsily from his chair and followed Harry.

'You've dragged me away just when my luck was about to change,' Cyril said, as Harry ordered two bottles of pale ale.

'Yeah, for the worse,' Harry replied. 'How much are you into Chin Loo for?'

'A few pounds,' Cyril replied guardedly.

'Thirty-four quid and fifteen shillings, to be precise,' Harry replied. 'Not to mention the three quid you owe

Fat Tony for that three-legged 'orse you had your money on last week. But rest easy, me old mate, because I've paid them off.'

Pollock took a swig from his bottle and his face lit up. 'You have? You're a real pal—'

'So now, Cyril, you owe me,' cut in Harry, his eyes flint-hard as his merry expression disappeared.

'O-of course,' stammered Cyril. 'Just say the word and you can have all the food certificates you need.'

Putting a beefy arm around his shoulder, Harry pulled the rotund food inspector into a crushing hug. 'This time I'm after a slightly bigger favour.'

'So, comrades,' said Gordon Potter, cutting across Fliss's jumbled thoughts. 'It is proposed that the contingent from the Stepney branch attending the meeting at the Ministry of Supply on the twentieth of June will comprise of Mrs Weinstein, Mr Riley and Miss Carmichael. All those in favour?'

Everyone around the table raised their hands.

'Passed unanimously, comrade secretary,' concluded Potter, who was sitting in his usual place at the top of the table.

It was just before eight and as usual on the first Thursday of the month Fliss and the other committee members were sitting around the table in the Old Globe's upstairs room.

'Well,' said Gordon, casting his eyes over the assembled company, 'unless there's any other business ...'

Someone raised a hand to ask something, but Fliss's mind had already returned to Tim.

She could rationalise what had happened at the boxing club as purely physical: two adults who in an unguarded moment were overcome by their needs.

That might well have been the case for him but for her now, having tasted his lips, felt his hands on her skin and had the deepest fulfilment in his arms, every part of her ached to have the same again and for the rest of her life.

Staring blindly at the table wood grain a surge of longing rose up in Fliss, but a hand waved in front of her face quickly dispelled the memory of Tim's lips pressed on hers.

Fliss blinked and looked around.

'Welcome back,' said Harry, grinning down at her.

Fliss looked puzzled.

'You were miles away,' he explained.

'Sorry,' she replied, gathering herself. 'It's just work, that's all.'

'You've not been sacked, have you? Because if you have,' Harry punched his right fist into the palm of his left hand, 'I might have to have a word with your boss.'

Despite her heavy heart, Fliss laughed. 'No nothing like that. In fact, Mr Longman told me I was his best reporter. Too good, it seems, as he wants me to stop digging into who's behind all the recent warehouse thefts and large-scale looting in the dock.' The scene in her boss's office the week before loomed in Fliss's mind, and despite her heart aching for him, fury at Tim's interference ignited again. 'Well, not him, exactly, but blooming DI Wallace—'

'Wallace?' Harry gave her a sharp look. 'What's he—'

The sound of the air raid siren on top of Bancroft Library nearby cut between them.

'I'd better get to the shelter,' said Fliss, raising her voice to be heard over the incessant drone. 'I'll tell you about it another time.'

Gathering her meeting notes together, Fliss slipped them into her satchel and hooked it over her shoulder.

'I tell you what, it's a bit of a trot from here so let me give you a lift,' Harry suggested.

Fliss glanced at the clock. 'All right, my sister will worry if I'm not there when the bombing starts.'

'Follow me.'

Shouldering his way through, Harry guided Fliss down the stairs to the main doors and towards the grey Bedford truck with a tarpaulin body parked outside.

The beams from the searchlights along the river were already criss-crossing the blackness as Harry opened the door. 'Your carriage awaits, m'lady.'

Putting her foot on the ridged plate and grasping the window support, Fliss climbed aboard and Harry jumped in a few moments later. Taking a cigarette from the packet in his pocket, he lit one then shoved the keys in the ignition and the van juddered into life.

'So what's the class-traitor Wallace done now that's

got you so riled?' he asked as they pulled away from the kerb to join the stream of traffic.

'He leaned on my boss to make me drop the story about the docks, and just when I'm this close to finding out who the ringleader is.' Raising her hand, Fliss pressed her index finger against her thumb.

'I would have thought he would want to know who was behind the looting in the docks,' said Harry, as they stopped to let an ARP van out from a side street.

'Oh, I'd bet a pound to a penny he knows already,' Fliss replied. 'He just doesn't want me to find out. Says it too dangerous.'

'Well, what can you expect from an establishment lackey with an oppressive attitude to women?' said Harry, rolling his eyes.

Fliss frowned.

Despite being absolutely furious with Tim, she thought Harry's description of him was a little unfair. She took issue with Tim for interfering in her job, but knowing he was concerned for her safety warmed her heart.

'I bet he wouldn't try to stop a male reporter following a story,' added Harry.

'I bet he wouldn't,' snapped Fliss, as her smouldering anger flared again. 'But don't worry, I'll have the last laugh.'

''Ow's that, then?' he asked, as they pulled up outside St Winifred's Church.

Fliss gave him an uncertain look. 'I shouldn't say.'

Knocking the central lever out of gear, Harry yanked

on the handbrake. Half turning towards her, he slid his hand along the bench seat and leaned over her until his nose was only a few inches from hers.

'Come on, Fliss,' he said, clenching his cigarette between his teeth and breathing smoke over her. 'I'm as keen as anyone to get these exploiters of the proletariat for their own gain.'

Fliss coughed. 'Well, I don't—'

'And if you can't trust a comrade in arms, who can you trust?' He raised a sandy eyebrow.

Fliss studied him for another moment or two.

'The police have had a tip-off that the Imperial and Britannia warehouse is going to be hit. Inspector Wallace will be waiting and so will I – at Wapping police station, ready to report the story,' said Fliss, over the rattle of the idling engine. 'But that's strictly between you and me, Harry. Do you understand?'

He frowned. 'Course. I'll keep shtum, on me muver's life.'

Grasping the handle, Fliss opened the door. 'Thank you again for the lift.'

'Any time,' he replied, the glow from his cigarette lighting his face with a red glow. 'And good luck with your story.'

Chapter twenty-nine

WITH THE HOODED headlights of Wapping nick's ancient police van highlighting the glistening cobbles after the early summer shower, Tim braced himself as the vehicle shuddered to a halt halfway down King David Lane.

The blackout had started an hour ago at just before eleven p.m. and they were parked, as Tim had instructed, in the shadow of the Jacobson warehouse, a short walk from the entrance to Wapping Basin, beyond which lay the Imperial and Britannia's refrigerated warehouse where, according to Tommy Lavender, Harry and his gang would be striking that night.

Squeezing the lever, Sergeant Morrison, who was driving the ancient bone-rattler, yanked up the brake.

Mosher – or Mo – Morrison was one of the old-time coppers who'd probably joined the force while Tim was still running wearing a bum-rag.

Turning off the engine, he turned to Tim. 'Over to you, Guv.'

Tim twisted around in his seat and looked into the body of the old van.

'So, before we get out,' he said, looking at the dozen uniformed officers squashed on the benches on either side of the van's gloomy interior, 'are you all clear about where you're to position yourselves and what to do once the operation starts?'

There were nods and murmurs of, 'Yes, Guv.'

Tim cast his eyes over the squad he'd pulled together for the operation and chewed his bottom lip.

These days Wapping police station was trying to cope with double the crime with half the manpower. Just two and a half years ago if he were about to confront and arrest a bunch of criminals robbing a warehouse red-handed, Tim would have been able to draft in dozens of seasoned H Division officer. Tonight, however, the squad he was leading had only four regulars in their number, including Tim himself. The rest were either special constable or war reserves.

Pushing aside his underlying unease at the possible readiness of the untried recruits, Tim carried on. 'Remember the gang are planning to move in as soon as the enemy aircraft release their bombs, so it's vital that you stay out of sight until you get the signal.'

There was another rumble of agreement plus a deal of scraping and stamping of feet on the van's bare metal flooring.

'And quiet,' barked Tim. 'There're six, possibly seven, members of this gang and if we're to have a hope in hell's chance of rounding them all up in one fell swoop then we have to surprise them, so if any of you so much as fart

I'll be writing in your pocketbook, d'you understand?'

There were a couple of sniggers and another round of head-nodding.

'Good,' said Tim. 'Let's go.'

Sergeant Morrison opened his door and got out. Tim did the same on his side and Alex, who was sitting between them on the front-bench seat, climbed down after him and the two of them walked around to the back of the van.

Morrison had already opened the rear doors by the time they got there, and officers were clambering down. Saluting Tim, they lined up and, keeping in the shadows of the building, made their way towards the river. Reaching the corner with the Highway, Tim raised his hand and the column came to a halt. Peering around the corner, he glanced up and down the cobbled street. Satisfied that other than a couple of vans parked way off by Glamis Street the road was clear, he signalled forward. The first two officers broke ranks and, as if on an ordinary beat patrol, ambled along the Highway. Walking at the regulation three miles an hour, they carried on until they reached the brick fortress-like structure that marked the entrance to Shadwell Basin, then they disappeared.

Tim signalled the next pair forward.

Twenty minutes later, after the last pair of constables had departed to their allotted hiding places, Tim turned to the uniformed sergeant behind him. 'Can you keep the gatekeeper company, Mo, so he doesn't get too chatty when the Gunn crew turns up?'

Touching the peak of his helmet, Sergeant Morrison marched off.

Taking his muted torch from his pocket, Tim pointed it at the pavement between his and Alex's size tens.

'Have you got your gun?' Tim asked.

Alex opened his jacket to reveal the Webley revolver stowed in his underarm holster. 'I hope I don't have to use it.'

'So do I,' Tim replied. 'But Harry Gunn and his crew have killed once, so I doubt they would think twice about murdering one of us. Keep an eye on them, Alex.' He glanced towards the high brick walls surrounding the dock. 'They're good blokes but a bit wet behind the ears as far as police work is concerned, and I don't want to have to pitch up on someone's doorsteps tomorrow and break the news to their missus that they're a widow.'

Alex nodded and after an ARP Heavy Rescue lorry rattled by, Tim's sergeant stepped out and headed for the dock gates.

Tim leaned against the rough brick of the warehouse for a moment then the scream of the air raid siren on top of one of the store houses in Tobacco Wharf echoed between the high walls along the Highway.

Beams of white light streaked the sky as the searchlights along both sides of the riverbank scoured the inky blackness for the first wave of enemy aircraft fast approaching from the south and east. Checking his own Colt revolver was still secure in its holster, Tim left the warehouse's shadows and strode across the cobbles.

The sound of the Joe Loss Orchestra drifted from the wireless in the corner of the rectory's small parlour, but mellow though it undoubtedly was it did nothing to soothe Fliss's throbbing head.

She had hoped to type up her notes for the feature she was doing about how, with prices so high, many women were choosing to go without meals themselves in order to feed their children. However, after she lost her train of thought for the third time and the ribbon got jammed in the spool, she gave up. The only small silver lining to what was otherwise a completely wasted evening was that her mother had been out at a meeting so Fliss was spared another lecture about, well, take your pick, because according to Marjorie Fliss's sins were many and growing by the day.

Although the Luftwaffe had yet to make an appearance, her mother was now tucked up in her truckle bed alongside her husband in the rectory's cellar, while the rest of the household had all gone over to St Winifred's shelter for the night. Fliss should have gone too but wasn't in the mood for company, although she had promised Prue that she would join them if the air raid sounded.

Her unsettled mood and lack of concentration weren't helped by the fact that she'd spent the last week, while bombs dropped all around St Winifred's shelter, wide awake and staring up at her sister's bunk bed. It hadn't been the explosions rocking the earth and the accompanying screams that had woken her in the small hours, but the fact that her mind couldn't rest. And who was to blame for the bags under her eyes and the band of steel around her forehead? None other than the most infuriating man in the country – probably the world – DI Wallace.

And for goodness' sake, why did he have to blooming well propose? Yes, yes she'd heard him burbling on about all that outdated 'honourable thing to do' stuff, but if he hadn't asked her to be his wife she wouldn't now, damn and blast him, be wondering if she should have heeded her yearning heart and said yes.

And she would have – and forgiven him, too, for his insufferable interference in her job – if he'd only said that he loved her. But why would he when he so obviously didn't. So instead she was replaying in her mind, moment by moment, word for word and gesture by gesture, the scene in the rectory garden.

Feeling her temples start to pulse, Fliss rested her head back, closed her eyes and attempted yet again to calm her raging emotions. Breathing deeply, she focused on shifting her mind off DI Wallace and on to, well, anything else.

The midnight pips sounded and the plummy BBC announcer began reading the last news bulletin of the day. He started with the army's continued successes in North Africa before moving on to the navy's relentless hunting of U-boats in the Mediterranean. The newsreader had just moved onto a light-hearted report about children in a Norfolk town taking part in a scrap metal collecting competition, when Fliss heard shouting coming from the kitchen.

As Father Danny was atop St Winifred's bell tower on fire watch, Fliss rose to her feet and headed off to investigate.

'When he finds out you've snitched on 'im to the rozzers …' Fliss heard the rectory's housekeeper yell as she approached.

'Well, he won't, I tell you, Ma,' a man's voice replied, 'because 'im and the rest of his family'll be banged up in the nick.'

Fliss marched in to find Mrs Lavender, gnarled fists dug into broad hips and her face screwed up like a shrivelled walnut, standing over a wiry chap with blond hair and sharp features, who was lounging in one of the kitchen chairs.

They looked up as Fliss walked in.

'It's midnight, Mrs Lavender,' Fliss said.

'I know, Miss Fliss, but I was waiting for something to arrive,' she replied.

'What?' asked Fliss.

'Me,' said the young man. 'I'm Tommy. I said I'd fetch 'er 'ome.'

'So what's all the shouting about?' said Fliss, looking from mother to son and back again.

''im.' Mrs Lavender slapped Tommy across the back of his head. 'This bloody idiot son of mine and the biggest gang of villains from Aldgate Pump to the Bow Bridge.' Mrs Lavender smacked him around the head with the back of her hand again. 'He's gone and informed on them to that blooming copper who was here in the garden with you a few days ago.'

401

'You mean DI Wallace?' asked Fliss.

'Yeah, that's the geezer,' said Tommy. 'And as I said, Mum, Wallace and the boys in blue will be waiting for them when they arrive at the Imperial and Britannia's tonight so by this time tomorrow Harry Gunn and his bloody family will be banged—'

'Hang on,' said Fliss, unease prickling between her shoulder blades. 'Harry Gunn?'

Tommy nodded.

'Are you talking about a big chap with reddish hair who works in London Dock and is the convener for the Transport and General Workers' Union?' asked Fliss.

'Yeah, that's the fella,' Mrs Lavender replied.

Fliss looked confused. 'But he's a member of the local Labour Party.'

''E may well be,' said Tommy. 'But there ain't a crate, a barrel or a sack that disappears through the dock gates that Harry and his bloody family don't take a cut of.'

'And now you've ratted on him to the cops.' Mrs Lavender pursed her lips. 'Blokes have ended up in the mortuary for less.'

Tommy rolled his eyes 'Are you mutton Jeff, Ma? I told you. Wallace and his lads will be ready to pounce the moment they show up.' He chuckled. 'I'd like to be there just to see the look of surprise on his ugly mug when they do.'

An image of Tim lying cold and lifeless on a mortuary slab loomed into Fliss's mind and an icy chill ran through her.

Turning, she dashed out of the kitchen, snatching her coat from the rack as she raced across the tiled hall floor. With her heart thundering in her chest, she yanked open the front door and tore off towards Shadwell Basin, just as the air raid siren on top of Redcoat School at the bottom of the street began to scream.

Chapter thirty

With the metallic smell of blood wafting around him, Tim blew on his hands and rubbed them together to warm them.

When he'd last looked at his watch ten minutes ago it had been a quarter past twelve, and although it was a balmy June evening outside, in the Imperial & Britannia it was as cold as a January morning.

However, the slight discomfort of spending hours in a refrigerated warehouse would be worth it when he caught Harry Gunn and his family of crooks red-handed.

The Countess of Fife must have been crammed to the gunnels, because there were dozens of pigs, cows and sheep carcasses strung up by their hind legs all around him. A veritable fortune in meat. No wonder Harry was interested. And no doubt all his black-market chums in Essex and at the other end of the Blackwall Tunnel in Rotherhithe, Bermondsey and North Kent, too, would be rubbing their hands in glee.

Tim was standing in number-one section of the warehouse, behind a row of headless, hollowed-out pigs that were hanging from hooks fixed to the ceiling. Other members of his squad were stationed in other sections and concealed near the exit to catch any of the gang who tried to make a run for it.

Somewhere close by a bomb struck the earth, shaking the concrete beneath his feet and setting the headless corpses of the countless livestock around him bouncing on their chains. In the dark of the warehouse, Tim gave a rueful smile.

As no air raid siren had sounded all night Tim had hoped that they might escape a visit from the Luftwaffe. However, with bright flashes of yellow and red streaking off exploding armaments under the cracks beneath the warehouse doors and through the shuttered windows, it was clear the Gunn gang wasn't the only danger facing Tim and his team tonight.

He looked at his watch again and drew in a long breath. Almost half past midnight!

Whatever else Harry was, he wasn't stupid. You didn't steal tons of meat which would go off in a day or two without having lined up dozens of black-marketeers ready to take it off your hands. But Harry and his crew were cutting it fine to get this lot loaded and on the road before the blackout ended.

The ack-ack guns on Tower Green rattled out another round and Tim rubbed his hands together again, schooling himself to be patient.

There was a faint creak, and a beam of light from outside streaked across the floor as the small door within the main gates opened and closed.

Taking his gun from its holster Tim held his breath as footsteps tiptoed along the passageway between the rows of carcasses until a shadowy figure drew level, then Tim sprang out.

Swinging his left arm around the figure's shoulder, he was just about to jam the barrel of his gun into their back when the scent of perfume filled his nose and a stray lock of hair feathered across his cheek.

Releasing his captive, and with white fury rising in his chest, Tim turned her around.

'For God's sake, Fliss,' he hissed, retuning his gun to its holster. 'What the hell are you doing here?'

'Looking for you,' she replied in the same hushed tone, as another bomb shook the building.

'And what was so important that you've run through an air raid?' he snapped, struggling to keep a grip on his anger. 'And how did you get past the main gate—'

'Harry Gunn knows you're here!' she shouted.

Tim stared at her for a second then he erupted. 'Bloody Lavender, when I get hold of him, I'll—'

'It wasn't Tommy,' she cut in. 'It was me.'

'You!'

Another blast boomed through the air and the orange-red flare illuminated the interior of the warehouse. Seething, Tim gazed at her.

'You in there, Guv?'

'What is it, Alex?' Tim asked, without taking his eyes from Fliss.

'Lavender's fed us a kipper,' his sergeant shouted back. 'It's not the Imperial and Britannia the Gunns are hitting but the Iberian Wine and Spirit warehouse in St

406

Katherine's. Their nightwatchman's just phoned the nick.'

Tearing his eyes from Fliss, Tim turned. 'Get the boys back in the van and go.'

'What about you, Guv—'

'Just go!' bellowed Tim.

His sergeant ran off.

Tim turned back to Fliss and his mouth pulled into a hard line.

Even if Alex and the team got to St Katherine's Dock, it would be bloody pointless as the chances were that the Gunn family would have already been in and cleared it out.

Months of investigation and hours of meticulous planning to put an end to the criminal activity of Harry Gunn and his gang all flushed straight down the khazi, and for what? Because she, Miss Felicity bloody Carmichael, wanted to get a good story for the front page.

A flare of red-hot burning light, which perfectly matched Tim's raging fury, lit the warehouse interior again.

'Tim, I'm so sorry—'

Tim raised his hand palm outwards and she closed her mouth.

Even though his temples were throbbing, he gazed down at Fliss's upturned face.

He did love her, but just at that moment he wanted to roar at her rather than take her in his arms.

Spinning on his heels, Tim strode towards the warehouse gates. 'I'll take you home.'

Slamming the small door open, he stepped out into the black of the night.

He took a couple of strides then stopped, waiting for Fliss to catch him up, but as he stared blindly at the burning skyline, he heard a different set of footsteps.

He spun around.

An explosion towards the Tower half a mile away lit up London Dock and Harry Gunn standing fifty feet away.

In the red glow of the burning buildings around them, Harry grinned. 'DI Wallace. Fancy meeting you here.'

Tim froze for a moment then forced a casual expression onto his face.

'Shouldn't you be at the Iberian Wine and Spirit warehouse with the rest of your crew?' he asked, praying that Fliss wouldn't step through the door.

'See now, Inspector, when that posh bit of skirt you've been sniffing around for weeks let slip that you were on to my little game, I tell you straight I wasn't 'appy. Not one bit.'

'I bet you weren't,' said Tim.

'But then I 'ad a bit of good fortune. A little birdie whispered in my lughole that the Brick Lane Mob were going to screw the Iberian on the very same night as me and my lot were planning to do this place.'

Harry looked up at the tall warehouse. With his attention elsewhere, Tim stole a glance at the door he'd just come out of.

Thank goodness!

Knowing Fliss, his overriding fear was that once she got wind of what was going on she'd come storming out. Thankfully, bone-headed though she was, even she seemed to have the good sense to realise that giving Harry Gunn an earbashing wasn't the most sensible thing to do just at the moment.

'What a coincidence,' said Tim, as Harry's attention returned to him.

'Wasn't it?' said Harry. 'So now, while your rozzers are throwing Russian Boris and his ugly bunch in the back of a police 'urry-up wagon, my lot are parked up on other side of the dock gates waiting for my signal.'

'Well, that's all very interesting, Harry.' Reaching beneath his jacket, Tim pulled out his revolver and pointed the barrel at the other man. 'It's a pity you won't be making it.'

Harry grinned and his eyes flickered onto something over Tim's right shoulder, but Tim resisted the temptation to look around.

He tightened his grip on the revolver. 'Harry Gunn, you're under arrest for—'

Pain exploded in Tim's head.

The gun slipped from his hand, and he stumbled forward.

Feeling blackness swirling around him, Tim tried to remain upright but instead sank to his knees.

'Credit where credit's due, for a copper you're pretty sharp,' he heard Harry's voice echo around him. 'But you ain't as sharp as me, Timmy Boy.'

Shaking his head, Tim tried to rise to his feet but then another blow just above his right ear sent stars exploding in his vision before everything went black.

As the man behind Tim landed the second blow across his skull, tucked in the shadow beside the open warehouse door, Fliss clamped her hand over her mouth to stifle a scream.

Unsurprisingly, Tim collapsed immediately and now lay unmoving on the stone of the dockside, with Harry and his companion, who looked like a younger version of him, standing over him.

'Is he dead?'

Harry shook his head. 'Not yet, Ben.'

'Should I whack 'im again?' He raised the spanner he was holding menacingly.

Again, Harry shook his head, then, bending down, he hooked his hands under Tim's limp arms. 'Grab his legs.'

Ben did as he was told and the two men hoisted Tim up from the floor. Dangling him between them, they carried him to the edge of the dock, swung him once, then let him go. There was a pause followed by a splash.

Fear burst through Fliss but she stifled the overwhelming urge to rush out. Getting herself thrown into the dock after Tim would help neither of them.

'The tide's on the turn,' said Harry. 'By the time they find him washed up on Canvey Island mudflats he'll be full of water.' He slapped the younger man lightly on the upper arm. 'Now come on, we ain't got all night.'

They marched off, their studded working books crunching over the Portland stone blocks of the dockside as they went.

Gingerly poking her head around the edge of the door, Fliss watched until they had disappeared into the darkness then she dashed to the edge of the quay.

Fearing the worst, Fliss looked down.

Tim was floating with his head was just above the inky-black water of the Thames.

Panic rising with every second, Fliss looked around and spotted a set of steps worn with age and covered with vegetation just a little further down the quayside. Dashing to the top and steadying herself with a hand on the rough stone wall of the dock, she made her way down. She slipped once, landing on her right hip, and took the skin off her knuckles, but ignoring the pain she continued down until she reached the water's edge.

Hooking her left arm through the loops of one of the ropes dangling down into the water from the massive iron moorings of the dock, and hoping her fourth-year freestyle swimming certificate would finally prove its worth, Fliss slipped into the water.

She caught her breath as the icy water engulfed her up to her chest, but clenching her teeth and getting what purchase she could on the stone foundations, hand over hand on the rope, Fliss floated her way towards Tim.

Thankfully, the drone of the enemy aircraft above was fading as they were returning to their bases in Picardy

411

and Normandy, but even so, the destruction continued as collapsing buildings on the other side of the docks threw great sections of masonry and metal into the water.

Judging she was within touching distance of Tim, Fliss stretched out her hand but just before her fingertips reached the left lapel of his jacket a section of wall from the warehouse at the end of the docks plunged into the river, pushing a wave along the length of the enclosed basin. The empty barges tied up together at the far jetty let out a hollow boom as they jostled together. The ships still at anchor pitched and rolled as the water passed under their hulls. Tim rode on the crest of it for a moment, then sank beneath the oily surface.

Fliss lunged and, stretching every sinew in her arm, grabbed his hair. Her fingers stiff with the cold and the current dragging Tim's inert body down, she gritted her teeth and summoned every ounce of strength. Finally she managed to pull him clear of the water and towards her.

Holding him close and keeping his head well above the surface, the two of them bobbed up and down a couple of times until the upheaval had calmed, and Fliss was able to slip her arm under Tim's right shoulder. Then, grasping the rope hanging down from the dock, she floated them, inch by inch, back to the steps.

Feeling the firm stone beneath her feet, Fliss moved them up the steps one at a time, backwards, until only Tim's legs were still submerged. Her shoulders screaming with pain and each breath tearing at her lungs, Fliss paused.

In the illumination from the burning docks, she shifted around to look at Tim. His eyes were still closed but his breathing was regular, which was some comfort. She ran her fingers gently over the massive lump on the back of his head, then turned it slightly to inspect where the second blow had landed. Whatever had struck him had created an open wound. It has stopped bleeding but that wasn't the worry. With East London's sewage system suffering the same damage as the houses it served, goodness only knew what germs were already flowing around in Tim's blood stream.

Running her free hand over his face as she gazed down at Tim, tears pinched the corners of Fliss's eyes.

What if …?

She blinked the tears away.

Somewhere to the south of her a low hum reverberated through the air, heralding the imminent arrival of another wave of enemy bombers, and as the first explosion sent shockwaves into the night sky, she heard the roar of lorry engines heading along the quayside.

The vehicles stopped just above her head, so gripping Tim tighter she shifted them along the step towards of the dock's stone wall and into the shadows.

She heard the engines switch off, doors open, and what she guessed were tailgates banging down.

'Right, get on with it,' Harry's voice said.

A number of hobnail boots crunched across the flagstones towards the warehouse, she assumed, but other footsteps sounded overhead.

'Well?' said Harry.

413

"E's gone,' came the reply.

'Good riddance,' said Harry. 'Now we ain't got all night, so let's get cracking.'

A bomb fell somewhere close by and another cordite-laden blast pulsed through the air.

Holding Tim a little tighter, Fliss pressed her cold lips on to his cold forehead and did something she hadn't really done properly for a long time: she prayed.

As she'd been doing for what seemed like an eternity, Fliss covered as much of Tim's body as she could with her own as the vacuum created by an explosion near by tugged at her hair. Clamping her jaw tight, she listened as heavy boots marched back and forth on the quayside above her and she prayed once more that they would just get back in their vans and drive off with their illicit haul.

As the disturbed air settled, Fliss looked down at Tim, who still lay inert in her arms, and the tear in her heart got a little deeper. In the flickering glow of the blazing buildings surrounding her, she ran her stiff fingers gently over his cheek. Dipping her head, she pressed her lips onto his forehead and letting them rest there, closed her eyes.

'Is there much more?' shouted Harry, from somewhere above her.

'The Bedford's nearly full,' a voice replied.

'Well then, get the rest in and go, Frankie,' said Harry. 'Unless you fancy meeting the Essex rozzers on the Romford Road when the sun comes up? Now get lugging.'

A couple of men laughed and then footsteps faded as those overhead headed back into the warehouse.

'Where am I?'

Fliss looked down at Tim through her tears to find him looking back up at her with vacant eyes.

'Oh, Tim. Thank God, thank God.' Fliss sobbed quietly, hugging him tightly.

'I've got to find Fliss!' he shouted, trying to free himself from his embrace. 'She's in danger. Let me—'

'Shussssh,' she hissed, glancing up at the edge of the dock.

Ignoring her and with panic writ large across his face, Tim continued to struggle. Fliss threw her leg across his body and anchored him to the steps. Gripping his face between her hands and with their noses just a couple of inches apart, Fliss locked her gaze with his.

'Tim! It's me,' she whispered as loudly as she dared.

He stared up at her for a long moment then the vacant look vanished from his eyes.

'Thank God,' he laughed.

Fliss glanced anxiously back up at the dock edge. 'We have to be quiet because—'

Tim's face contorted with pain and his eyes rolled up into his head.

'For God's sake, Tim. Wake up!' Fliss hissed.

For what seemed like an eternity he didn't respond, then his eyes opened. 'Fliss?'

'I'm here,' she said, hugging him to her.

In the red glow from the burning warehouse, he frowned slightly. 'I was angry with you.'

'It doesn't matter,' she replied, running her hand over the damp hair plastered across his forehead.

An arc of light from Tower Green's ack-ack guns traced across the sky, illuminating half a dozen bobbing barrage balloons.

Pain screwed up Tim's face as his eyes started to disappear upwards again.

Fliss shook him. 'Stay with me, Tim.'

He blinked and mercifully the light returned to his eyes.

A bomb crashed to earth somewhere to the west of them, sending another pulse of air across the water and setting the barges rumbling again. Although the outgoing tide meant they were now lying clear of the water, the after-wave washed up the steps and soaked them to the skin anew.

As the river's dirty water receded, Tim grasped Fliss's upper arms with both hands. 'I love you, Fliss.'

His eyes clouded again, and his head flopped.

With tears flowing down her face, Fliss smacked his cheek. 'For the love of God, Tim—'

She heard boots crunching towards the rounded edge of the dock above and held Tim tightly to her, freezing with fear.

'Right, Harry, that's about the lot,' said a male voice. 'I wonder why Tommy Lavender didn't show.'

'I don't know, Ben,' Harry's gruff voice replied. 'Who d'you think tipped off Wallace? But don't you worry none; I'll be dealing with that rat la—'

Tim's head rolled against Fliss's shoulder, and he let out a long moan.

'D'you hear that?' asked Harry.

'Hear what?'

'Sounded like someone groaning,' Harry replied.

'Probably a rat or something,' Ben replied.

A pair of heavy boots stomped a few steps.

Fliss looked up as the steel toecaps of two boots appeared over the edge of the quay. With her heart hammering in her chest, she held her breath.

Tim shifted in her arms, grimacing, and under her hand she felt a low rumble start in his chest. She put her hand over his mouth and his eyes flickered as he tried to twist his head free. She let go and as his lips parted Fliss pressed hers onto them. Tim's mouth opened under hers immediately and as her kiss deepened, he quietened.

'Come on, Harry,' said Ben. 'We've got punters waiting.'

There was a pause and then the sound of boots walking away. Two doors opened and closed, then an engine started up. It idled for a moment then the vehicle roared away.

Lifting her head, Fliss looked up to see the first streaks of light towards the Royal Docks to the east.

A row of explosions flared in a neat sequence some way in the distance, then the drone of the enemy plane

417

changed, indicating that having emptied the bomb bays they were heading home.

Tim lay peacefully for a moment then started gagging. Grabbing him, Fliss rolled him on his side and he vomited. Taking her wet handkerchief from her cardigan sleeve, she wiped his mouth.

'And I love you, Tim,' she whispered.

Ripping off her jacket, Fliss draped it over Tim's shoulders then ran up the steps to the dock. She scanned the vast open space of London Dock.

'Inspector Wallace!'

She turned and saw Tim's sergeant at the far side with a couple of constables.

'Over here! Quick!' she screamed. 'And fetch an ambulance!'

Chapter thirty-one

'THANK YOU, NURSE,' said Tim to the very young-looking nurse in the pinstriped lavender uniform who had just set a cup of tea and a Rich Tea biscuit on his bedside locker.

'Sure, 'tis my pleasure, Inspector,' she replied. 'And it's grand to see you've perked up a bit.'

She was being polite: he'd caught sight of himself in the mirror that morning while the barber was shaving him, and even after three days he was still a mess. Well, the bit he could see was, as most of his head was swathed in bandages.

'Awake, don't you mean?' Tim replied.

She glanced down at the watch pinned to her apron bib. 'It's almost visiting time, so your young lady should be in soon.'

'My young lady?' said Tim.

'Indeed,' said the nurse. 'She's been here every day. Sat by your bed she did all day the first day and wouldn't move. To be sure, Sister would turf the Devil himself from hell, but your young lady wouldn't budge.'

Tim smiled.

'Is she your fiancée?' asked the nurse, straightening

the blue counterpane and starched sheet covering Tim.

'Not yet,' said Tim, smiling again at the thought.

'Anyhow, I best be about my business,' said the nurse, 'before I have Sister after me.'

She left and Tim picked up his cup and saucer. The tea was, as ever, stewed and lukewarm, so he swallowed it down in two gulps, but as he returned the crockery to the bedside locker a hand bell sounded outside his white metal and glass cubical followed by a number of footsteps and low chatter.

With his eyes glued to the open door the nurse had just disappeared through and his heart hammering in his chest, Tim waited. Then Fliss walked through the door and Tim let out the breath he didn't know he'd been holding.

She was wearing the same skirt and blouse she'd been wearing when he'd made a complete balls-up of proposing to her. Her lovely auburn hair was gathered back on both sides of her face and held in place with tortoiseshell combs. The rest was loose and sat in gentle waves on her shoulders. To be honest, it was worth almost dying just to see her standing there.

'Hello, Fliss,' he said.

'Hello, Tim,' she replied, standing at the end of his bed holding a basket. 'How are you feeling?'

'Like I've been hit over the head with a brick,' he replied. 'How are you?'

'I've got a streaming cold and a ruined pair of shoes, but other than that I'm none the worse for spending two hours in the Thames,' she replied. 'Actually, it was a spanner Ben Gunn hit you with. I found it on the quayside and gave it to your sergeant as evidence.'

The corner of Tim's mouth lifted slightly. 'Have you ever thought of volunteering for the Women's Auxiliary police force?'

Amusement flickered in her eyes. 'And be bossed around by you? Not likely.'

They gazed at each other for a moment then Fliss left her post at the end of the bed and sat in the chair at his bedside. She placed her basket on her knee.

'I know people usually bring flowers, but I thought I'd bring you something to help you recover.' She pulled out two oranges and placed them on his bedside locker next to the empty teacup.

Dragging his eyes from the woman he loved, Tim glanced at the fruit that was as rare as hen's teeth then returned his whole attention back at Fliss.

He raised an eyebrow. 'Tommy Lavender?'

'He felt bad about what happened.' Fliss rummaged around in the basket again as Tim studied her profile. 'And I've also got some fruitcake. And don't worry. Prue made it.'

Tim laughed. 'Thank you.'

'Do you know that Harry Gunn and he's whole crew have been arrested,' said Fliss.

'Yes, Alex popped in first thing this morning and told me,' Tim replied. 'Caught red-handed on the Romford Road by Essex Police thanks to your information about where they were heading.' He raised his eyebrow again. 'I bet you got a good story from your swim in the docks.'

'I certainly did,' said Fliss, with more than a hint of pride in her tone. 'Mr Longman is putting out a *Chronicle* Special this Friday, with my name right there under the headlines as the reporter. He thinks the *Sketch* or the *Mirror* will run it too.'

'Congratulations,' said Tim. 'It's well deserved.'

'Thank you.' She inclined her head and a wisp of hair escaped its moorings and curled onto her forehead. 'And Alex thinks you'll get a commissioner's commendation. And probably promotion to Station Inspector, as apparently Wapping hasn't got one.'

'Actually, Fliss,' he said softly, 'if anyone should get a commendation for anything it should be you because if you hadn't climbed down and pulled me out of the water I'd be dead.'

She gave him an uncertain glance from beneath her long lashes. 'Do you remember what happened?'

'Bits,' he replied. 'I remember us in the warehouse then coming face to face with Harry, but after that it's a blank. I remember feeling wet and with something hard in my back. Then I opened my eyes and found you were holding me. It's a bit sketchy after that. The next thing I knew I woke up here about six o'clock last night.'

'Do you remember saying anything?' she asked, her lovely brown eyes looking into his.

He shook his head and wished he hadn't, as a dart of pain cut across his right temple. 'What did I say?'

'You were just rambling,' she replied, lowering her eyes.

Tim reached across and took Fliss's hand, and her gaze returned to his face.

'I have no idea what I said while lying drenched to the skin and semi-conscious on the steps in London Dock, but I do know exactly what I should have said in the rectory garden.' Holding her hand firmly, Tim locked his gaze with hers. 'I love you, Fliss.'

She blinked. 'Do you?'

'Yes, I do,' he said. 'Although I only realised it a few weeks ago, I know now that I've loved you since the moment I found you blind drunk on that gravestone. Not only that, but I want to spend the rest of my life with you. I'm not in a position to get down on one knee at the moment but, Felicity, Fliss, would you—'

Fliss held her hand up. 'I told you never to propose to me again.'

Tim looked at her in dismay. 'But, Fliss—'

'No.'

Letting go of her hand, Tim slumped back against the pillows and with the pain in his heart outdoing that in his head, he closed his eyes.

He felt the mattress dip and opened his eyes to see Fliss perched on the bed, smiling down at him.

'You might as well get used to the fact, Tim, that I'm a woman of my word.' She ran her gaze slowly over his face for a moment then reaching down she pressed her lips onto his.

Heedless of his protesting shoulder and neck muscles, Tim's arms wound around her immediately and held her to him, returning her kiss with every fibre of his body and soul.

Too soon her mouth left his. She sat back and smiled.

'I love you, too.' Fliss took his hand and looked deeply into his eyes. 'So as you're not allowed to propose to me, Timothy Charles Wallace, will you marry me?'

Happiness burst through him, and he laughed. 'I most certainly will, on one condition.'

She laughed. 'All right, as long as it isn't that I learn how to cook.'

He shook his head then drew her back into his arms again. 'That when you get as furious with me as you did at the boxing club, you make sure you tell me about it in the exact same way.'

'It's not much further, sweetheart,' said Tim, smiling down at her from beneath the brim of his fedora as they reached the row of farmworker's cottages.

'Don't worry,' she replied, smiling and squeezing his arm. 'It's a lovely day and what better way to spend it than walking in the June sunshine up a country lane with my fiancé.'

It was Tuesday afternoon and four days since he'd been pronounced fit the previous Friday after spending a full week in hospital. Although the stitches from the gash had been removed, his hair was only just sprouting on the patch they'd shaved surrounding it. It was not too much of a problem when he had his hat on, but he would have to keep his head at a slight angle to hide it for the wedding photos in four days' time.

Fliss had collected him from hospital and taken him back to the section house so he could make himself respectable before they went to the rectory.

Leaving Fliss to tell her sister and the rest of the rectory's residents their good news, Tim had formally asked Fliss's father for permission to marry his eldest daughter. After which, hand in hand, he and Fliss had told her parents their plans to marry.

Her father was delighted. Her mother was less than enthused but brightened slightly when Fliss informed her that Tim had been promoted to be the senior officer at Wapping police station.

Today, she was dressed in a summery cotton dress with a mulberry and emerald print and matching green cardigan, plus her low-heeled court shoes because he'd warned her it was a bit of a walk from the railway station.

Although the pungent earthy smell of the countryside was a bit much for a city boy like himself, with the warm sunshine on his face and Fliss on his arm sporting his newly bought engagement ring, there were worse ways to spend a June afternoon.

However, as they reached the solid-looking stone gateposts of Warley Hospital, the niggle of worry in Tim's chest started again.

Coming to a halt, he turned to face her.

'We're here.' He frowned.

Fliss gave him a worried look. 'Is your head hurting, Tim?'

'No, thankfully the headaches seem to have gone,' he replied. 'It's just … well … I'm not exactly taking you for an afternoon out in Buckingham Palace, Fliss.'

'I know, you've said, but it doesn't matter.' Fliss squeezed his arm again. 'If this is where I have to come to visit your mum, then that's absolutely fine by me.'

Standing on her tiptoes, Fliss kissed him lightly on the lips, but as she turned to go through the gates Tim caught her to him. Capturing her in his embrace, he lowered his lips onto hers, her mouth opened under his and her arms wound themselves around his neck.

Feeling his need for her rising, Tim savoured the feeling of her body against his for a moment longer then, reminding himself why they were there, he released her.

They exchanged fond looks then Tim put his hand to one of the metal gates and pushed it open.

He guided Fliss along the all-too-familiar gravel pathway until they reached the shoddily painted main door. Walking beside her up the worn steps, Tim pushed open one of the doors.

Briefly acknowledging the receptionist sitting behind the desk with a curt nod, Tim led Fliss through the half-glazed door and into the main corridor. With the pungent odour of the institution wafting around them and passing the sad, lost souls shuffling, rocking and muttering who were dotted along the walls, they finally reached a scuffed set of doors at the end of the depressing hospital corridor.

Stopping, Tim looked down at Fliss holding his arm.

She smiled and reached forward to press the bell.

After a moment or two the door creaked back and a solid-looking woman with mousy hair in an oversized grubby overall stood in the doorway.

'Good afternoon, Mrs Baxter,' said Tim, causing a look of panic to flash across the ward orderly's fleshy features.

She opened the door a little wider. Tim let Fliss walk through first then followed her into his mother's ward.

Fliss's hand hooked back on his arm as they walked past the unoccupied ward sister's office and after retching from the smell of the sluice, they walked through to the garden.

Stopping on the step outside the French windows, Tim looked around, spotting his mother in a wheelchair over by the small patch of heather in what was left of the flower border. He glanced down at Fliss, who gave him a loving smile and squeezed his arm reassuringly.

Placing his large hand over Fliss's small one, he led her across and stopped in front of his mother.

She was in a dress he'd bought for her some while back, and her hair, although in need of a wash, had at least been combed today. Her shawl was draped around her shoulders against any sudden chill.

They stood there for a moment, then Tim bent forward and took his mother's hand. Her head turned, but as always her eyes as they rested on him were unfocused.

'Hello, Mum,' he said, forcing a smile. 'This is Fliss. Do you remember I spoke to you about her last time I came? Well, I have some very good news. We're getting married this Saturday at St Winifred's Church.'

His mother's vacant smile didn't waver and letting go of her hand, Tim straightened up.

Fliss stepped forward.

'Hello, Mrs Wallace,' she said, smiling at the woman looking blankly back at her. 'I'm so pleased to meet you.'

Bending forward, she rested her hands lightly on his mother's shoulders and gave the woman crumpled in the wheelchair a kiss on her right cheek.

'Would you like us to tell you what we are planning for the wedding …?'

'So, you see, Mrs Wallace, although it's been a bit of a rush, we're more or less set for Saturday,' said Fliss, perching on one of the metal garden chairs Tim had fetched for them.

It was now some forty minutes since they'd arrived and Tim had watched as the woman he would love until his dying day told his mother, who stared blankly back, about her parents, her brother Rob and sister Prue, before explaining that because there was no time to call the banns, they'd had to get a special licence from the bishop, and how her mother wanted to have a catered function in a hotel but that they'd said they'd rather a small wedding lunch at the rectory.

'I'm afraid I can't tell you what my wedding dress looks like because I haven't got one yet,' she laughed. 'But my mother and Prue are taking the tube to South Kensington tomorrow so fingers crossed I'll have something better to wear than my old party dress on Saturday.'

'I know whatever Fliss walks down aisle wearing she will look absolutely beautiful,' said Tim, 'because she always does.'

He and Fliss exchanged devoted looks and then Tim noticed his mother's eyes had closed.

'I think Mum's tired,' he said.

Fliss nodded.

'I'm trying to get her a place in St Joseph's Convent in Mare Street,' Tim said, as they studied his mother lying crumpled in the wheelchair. 'But sometimes I wonder if I will ever get her out of this dreadful place.'

Fliss took both his hands and shook them.

'Yes, we will,' she said, looking him square in the eye. 'Because we will move heaven and earth until we do.'

As he gazed down at her, Tim wondered what on earth he'd done that the universe should favour him with the love of such a beautiful, intelligent and fearless woman as Fliss Carmichael.

Chapter thirty-two

WITH HER HEAD resting in the dip of Tim's shoulder and her fingers threaded through the hair on his bare chest, Fliss listened to the steady beating of her husband's heart.

They were lying in a rather grand brass bed in the honeymoon suite in the Rose and Crown Hotel on the Wivenhoe Road, just on the east side of the River Colne which gave the ancient city of Colchester its name. As the sun had crept under the heavy blackout curtain while they slept, bathing the room in soft mellow light, Fliss guessed it was probably somewhere close to eight o'clock on Sunday morning.

Tim lay beside her without a stitch of clothing, his left arm around her, his eyes closed and the hint of a smile lifting the corners of his lips. She was in the same state of undress, as her frilly nightie hadn't even made it out of the suitcase. In fact, when they got to the hotel other than a few essentials, the clothes they'd brought with them were yet to be unpacked.

Because since they were shown to their hotel room late yesterday afternoon, they hadn't left it.

They'd all but torn each other's clothes off as soon as

the door was closed and spent their first few hours as man and wife rolling about the bed stark naked. They'd paused only when room service brought their dinner before returning to their very satisfying exploration of each other's bodies.

Resisting the urge to stretch up and press her lips on his, Fliss let her gaze run over him, studying every detail from his broad chest with is dark covering of hair down to his flat stomach then to the sheet that was draped over his hips and the tops of his thighs.

Remembering what joys lay beneath the flimsy covering, Fliss's gaze lingered there for a long moment before returning to his face.

Raising her hand slightly, she looked at the slender band of gold on her finger that Tim had placed there almost twenty-four hours before.

Although she'd hinted that Fliss wasn't really entitled to wear white, her mother had offered her daughter her own wedding dress to wear for her big day. However, as she didn't want to look like a character from *The Great Gatsby*, and after searching through every rail in Derry & Toms' bridal department, Fliss had settled on a cream shot-silk dress with a square neckline, button-fastener fitted sleeves and a small train. In keeping with her elegant dress, she'd forgone a veil and opted instead for a headband of waxed orange blossoms.

Thankfully, Rob's company was still waiting to embark at Southampton, so he had been able to secure a weekend pass. Dressed in his captain's uniform, he'd had more than a few admiring glances from the young ladies of the parish, including, a little surprisingly, Hester Kratz. Back at the rectory after the ceremony, he and Tim had spent a great deal of time laughing and joking with each other.

Her mother, of course, had rounded up some distant relatives from the Home Counties to fill the first few pews on the bride's side of St Winifred's, plus some old school friend of hers from Cheltenham Ladies' College, called Davina, who Fliss had never heard of but who her mother told anyone within earshot was married to a baron.

Instead of being packed with distant unknown relatives, the pews on the groom's side of the church had been filled with uniformed police officers and CID colleagues of Tim's from Wapping. The rest of those who witnessed their wedding were members of the congregation and a few of Fliss's friends from the Stepney Housewives' Defence League.

Father Danny had taken the service, so when she walked down the aisle on her father's arm to join Tim in his best suit and with a look of total love on his impossibly handsome face, Fliss thought she'd burst with happiness.

'Good morning, Mrs Wallace.'

Fliss turned to find Tim gazing at her with a look on his face that had her insides humming in anticipation.

'I still don't think your mother's very happy about us moving into the rectory,' said Tim, smiling down at her.

'Neither am I,' said Fliss. 'I was hoping not to have to look across the table at her each morning.'

'Well, fingers crossed there'll be something sitting in my tray when I get back from our honeymoon informing me that I've been allocated married quarters.'

'Let's hope,' Fliss replied, imagining them making love in Rob's room opposite her parents' bedroom and her mother complaining about the noise over breakfast.

Fliss gave him a sideways look from beneath her lashes.

'It's a shame we've only got three days for our honeymoon,' she said, trailing her index finger down the line of hair on his stomach.

Drawing her into his embrace, Tim rolled over her in one swift movement and his mouth closed on hers. Fliss's arms wound around his neck and enjoying the sensation of his chest hair against her breasts, she gave herself over to the pleasure of Tim's kiss. After a long moment, he lifted his head and smiled down at her.

He repositioned a stray tendril of hair with his index finger. 'I love you.'

She gave him a languid smile. 'I know.'

He rolled off her and stood up, allowing Fliss to appreciate her new husband's perfections from a different angle.

Reaching out, Tim took hold of the sheet and pulled it off. His gaze ran slowly over Fliss, sending coils of excitement and anticipation pulsing through her.

'You know, Fliss,' he said, as his admiring gaze returned to her face, 'as beautiful as you looked walking down the aisle towards me, I have to admit, I very much prefer what you're wearing now.'

Amusement tugged at Fliss's lips. 'Same here,' she said, her eyes running slowly over Tim's hard, muscular and aroused body.

Breathlessly, she waited then after several heartbeats, Tim got back on the bed. Gathering her into his arms he covered her body with his and recaptured her lips in a deep and passionate kiss.

Winding her legs around him, Fliss closed her eyes and gave herself up to a lifetime of love as a policeman's wife. Who would have thought it?

But she wasn't selling out to the establishment or the bourgeoisie, because the socialist theorists were completely wrong.

Marriage wasn't an institution imposed on workers as part of the capitalist system; it was a blissful coming together of two people who loved each other so much that eternity was much too short a time for them to express it fully. And thank goodness she'd waited until she met Tim to discover that truth.

Acknowledgements

I would like to mention a few books, authors and people to whom I am particularly indebted.

As always, in order to set my characters' thoughts and worldviews authentically in the harsh reality of the spitfire summer of 1940, I returned to *Wartime Britain 1939–1945* (Gardiner), *The East End at War* (Taylor & Lloyd), *The Blitz* (Gardiner), *Living Through the Blitz* (Harrison),*The Blitz* (Madden), *The Wartime Scrapbook* (Opie)and *London's East End Survivors*(Bissell).

To ensure I set Fliss in the correct political time and thinking of the early 1940s, I found Barbara Castle's biography, *Politics & Power* (Martineau) and *Waiting for the Workers: A History of the Independent Labour Party* (Thwaites) particularly helpful.

For Tim's wartime police world I delved into *The Metropolitan Police at War* (Howgrave-Graham), *The Secret History of the Blitz* (Levine), *An Underworld at War* (Thomas) and *Dark City: Murder, Vice and Mayhem in Wartime London* (Read).

Finally, to steer me through the wartime workings on London Docks and a docker's working day I am grateful to have found *London's Royal Docks in the 1950s* (Smith) and *Dockers' Stories from the Second World War* (Bradford).

I would also like to thank a few more people. Firstly, my very own Hero-at-Home, Kelvin, for his unwavering support, and my three daughters, Janet, Fiona and Amy, who listen patiently as I explain the endless twists and turns of the plot.

I'd like to thank my agent Kate Burke, from Blake Freidman Literary Agents, for her steadfast support and encouragement. A big thanks goes to Sarah De Souza for her detailed and insightful edits and to Alison Tulett. I'd like to extend that thanks to the wonderful team at Atlantic Books for all their support.